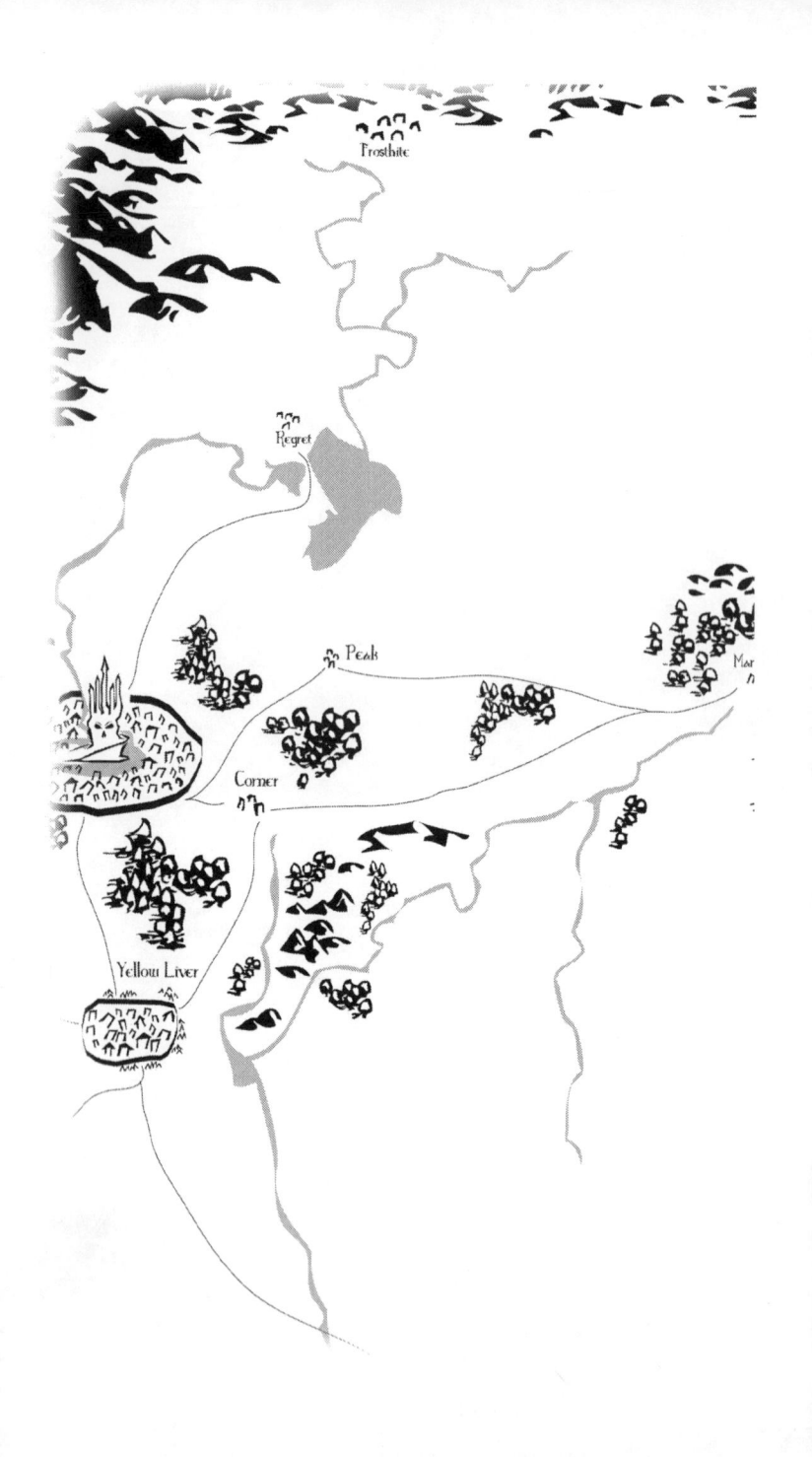
Frostbite
Regret
Peak
Mar
Corner
Yellow Liver

The Spikelands

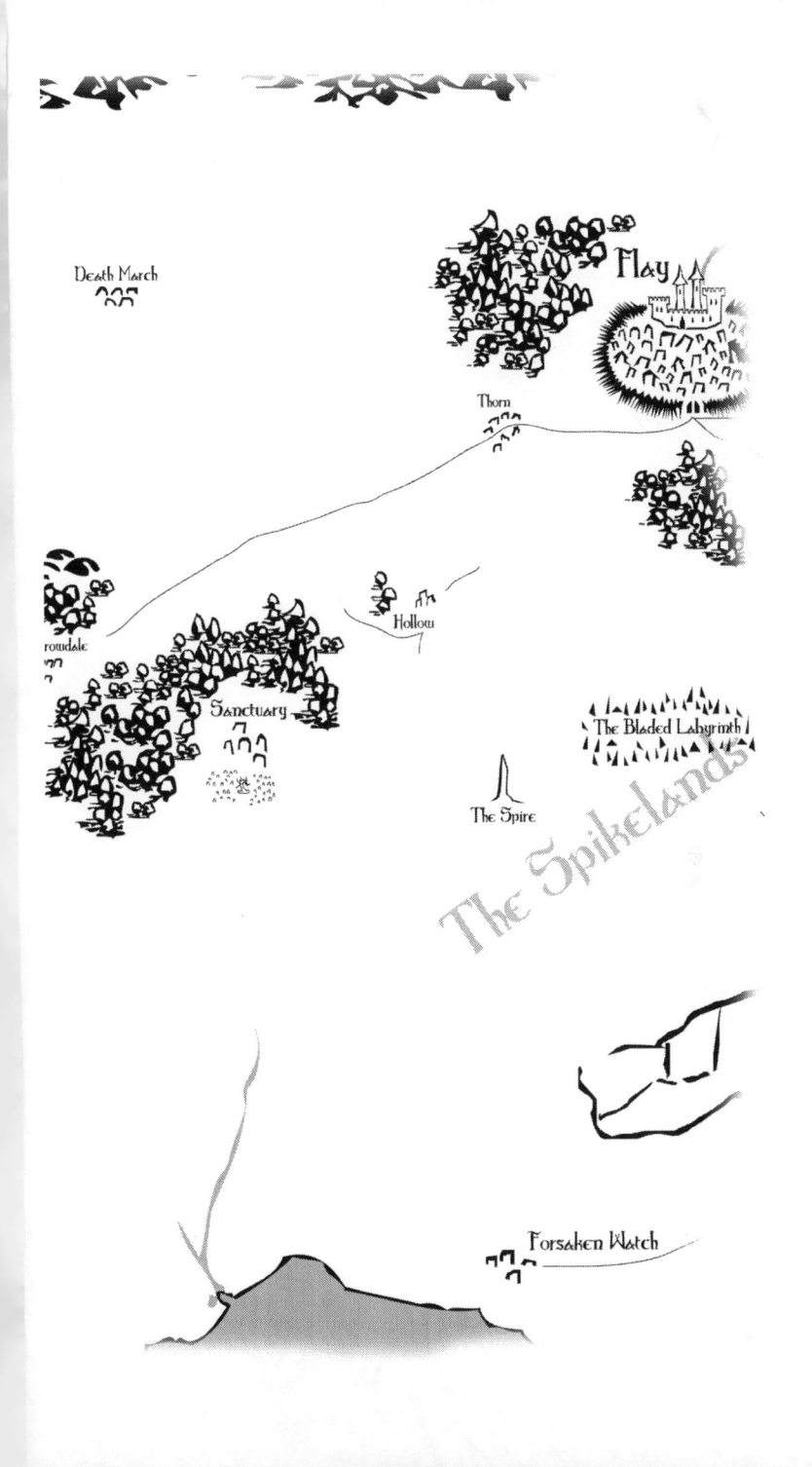

- Death March
- Flay
- Thorn
- Hollow
- rowdale
- Sanctuary
- The Bladed Labyrinth
- The Spire
- Forsaken Watch

The Saga Of Ukumog

Wracked
Desecrated

DESECRATED

By Louis Puster III

Sean,

The AndoCon 2016 dealers room would not have been the same without you. Wait... you missed most of it! Ooops!

Best,
Louis Puster III

This is a work of fiction. All the characters and events portrayed in this book are either products of the author's imagination or are used fictitiously.

DESECRATED

Copyright © 2012 by Louis Puster III

All rights reserved, including the right to reproduce this book, or portions thereof, in any form.

Edited by Morgan A. McLaughlin McFarland
Cover Art by Chandler Kennedy
Maps by Louis Puster III

First Edition
ISBN 1460901150
ISBN 978-1460901151

For Colin, Chris, and Kate

Prologue

There was silence between us as we picked ourselves up off the stone floor of the Ghoul's lair. That same silence lingered as we sloshed our way through the dark tunnels. Fear lingered in the blackness of the tunnels, emanating from somewhere beyond my dark sight. The wounds that both Brin and Avar harbored made our journey through the cramped passageways difficult, but we found our way out the same way we came. It was the silence that bothered me.

When we arrived at entrance hole we had climbed through, I could see the distrust in Brin's face that I had only felt lingering on the way there.

"You ok?" I asked with as much compassion as I could manifest.

"I'm fine. Let's just get out of here."

She climbed out first, and then I helped lift Avar out through the hole. For a moment I stared into the dark passage we had come from, and in my head the battle with the Ghoul flashed through my mind. There was a sickly sweet feeling in my gut when my mind turned to touching the blade. The moments I remembered focused on the blade slashing at his flesh filling my mouth with a sugary flavor, and a strange hunger washed over me.

Desecrated

"You coming or not?" Brin shouted impatiently from above.

I abandoned my dark thoughts and climbed out of the hole. The surface that greeted us was not much different than the swirling chaos we had left behind. I suppose it was naive to think that the death of the city's secret master would instantly change it. We hid from the violent storm raging in the streets while we made our plans.

"Once we get out of the city, we are heading to Flay," Brin said, coldly.

"What? I thought you wanted to go after the wizard in Skullspill." Avar gripped the wound on his side and grimaced.

"Change of plans. Before the Ghoul died he said that the King knew about my father's death."

"The King? You are kidding me. Well, that should be a fun attempt at an audience." Avar tried to push through the pain with humor.

Brin ignored the sarcasm and continued making her case. "I figure we will go north to Marrowdale and then head east to Flay from there. Might be rough, though, if there is an army or armies on the road between here and there. If the Rotting One's force has retreated, that is probably the same route they will take."

"We could just go east and maybe get to Sanctuary that way."

"No. Your old man would not be happy to see us." I could not tell if her disdain was directed at Avar's father or if she was just upset at me.

"Brin, you killed an uzkin' Doomed. I think he would offer to marry you," he chuckled which was quickly interrupted by a painful wince.

Prologue

With a hint of frustration she looked away from Avar and out into the riot in the streets just on the other side of the wall.

"You did kill him, didn't you?"

"Something like that happened," she said, shooting me a venomous look.

Avar looked at both of us confused. "Sheesh. You get knocked out during one fight and you miss out on everything."

"No kidding," she said with an unspoken hatred.

I didn't say a word.

Chapter 1

The earth beneath our feet crackled and crunched as the fifteen of us climbed away from the sacked city of Yellow Liver. It was Brin, Avar, myself, and a small host of refugees with nowhere left to go in the city they used to call home. Somehow, they saw the determination to escape in our eyes and just started following us. It had been just a couple of them at first, but quickly it avalanched into our current number. Brin was not happy about being in such a large group. I heard her occasionally muttering to herself about thinning our number before the creatures of the wilds did it for us. This threat I did not think she would act upon, however the dark mood that had followed her out of city made it hard to tell. Brin's mood wasn't the only thing that seemed to be following us.

Apart from muttering and travel, there wasn't much conversation during the first day. The moment the sun dropped below the horizon that changed, and so did my senses.

"So, are you one of the Tainted?" One of the refugees asked me.

"Something like that." I dismissed the conversation, because I felt the hairs on my body stand up. Something was out there in the darkness. Something was hunting us.

"I have never met one of you before," she said, ignoring my attempt to end the conversation.

Chapter 1

"Neither have I."

Confused by that remark, she disengaged from our conversation and went to talk to Avar instead.

The air smelled a little sharp, as if there were some of the bite of winter in it. I scanned the rocks, trees, and tall grass which surrounded us. A few times thought I saw movement, but it was only the wind.

"There is something following us, Brin," I whispered to her.

"I know. It's been there almost all day. It's one of the reasons I took us completely off the road. Don't want to get caught by both an army and some ghoul that followed us out."

"What are we gunna do?"

"We?" There was no secret smile in her face for me anymore. "I am gunna sit back and watch you kill it," and she walked away from me.

You deserve this ya know. She has a right to feel betrayed.

How? How have I betrayed her? Even I am not sure what happened back there.

From the beginning you knew that she didn't trust easily. It will take much more than a winning smile to return that.

From my place in the middle of the group, I watched her long dark hair bounce as she traversed the terrain. When she turned her face to the side I saw something I hadn't before, the face of a frightened little girl. The conflict in my own soul was deafening. I could not imagine what it was like to have a past. Years of real memories and experiences shaping who you were, adding layers of heavy armor to the scared child deep inside. I had no such armor.

The first time we made camp, the discussion of where we were heading began. One of the refugees started it with a simple question: "Where exactly are we heading?"

Desecrated

"We," Brin's emphasis was not subtle as she pointed to her, Avar, and myself, "are going to Flay." There was some murmuring in our small crowd. "If you don't like it, you don't have to follow us."

"If we follow this way, won't it take us to Marrowdale?"

"Yes."

"But Marrowdale was razed by the Baron's army some months ago," explained the refugee.

"Really?" Avar's concern denoted more than just worry about some unknown citizens.

The refugee answered Avar's concern, "Yeah, the Sacred Skull marched in and took some of the people prisoner and killed the rest, then burned the town to the ground. I heard one of the guards talking about it one day. They said that something had escaped from there, or something."

Spoken concern about running into that 'something' that had escaped caused the volume of the conversation to go up. Refugees started fighting with each other about what to do. Some on the side of risking things on their own, others saying that they had a better chance with Brin than anywhere else. Once someone called her a madwoman, and then she stood up, and set Ukumog free with its usual clink!

"Listen. You don't have to follow us. You can go your own merry way. Or hell, when we get close to Skullspill you can go there for all I care. Here you only have one choice: Do what I say or get the uzk out of my sight."

Silence. Everyone was staring at the runes on Ukumog that glowed with a dim menacing light, a light that grew slightly brighter as Brin's temper flared. There was no more talk of anyone leaving the group. If anything, her display of strength caused them

Chapter 1

to cling to her more. Hushed whispers about how the Lords had sent them a savior from the chaos and death of Yellow Liver were heard more than once by my prying ears. I did not bother to correct them.

Miles of uneasy landscape passed under our feet. The ragtag group quietly following our leader. Our company silently trusted that she would take us somewhere safe, but Avar and I knew that our destination was anything but. The dry clay and rocks beneath us became slowly wetter as we moved north. The tattered mossy edge of foliage met us like the threshold into a new world. As we went up one particularly tall hill, I looked behind us. Our persistent unseen pursuer was still nowhere to be found, but the view of the world from there was not something I expected.

It had been days since we left Yellow Liver, but several small columns of smoke could still be seen against the twilight on the horizon from where we had come. Looking west, I could see the dusty green darkness that was the Forest of Shadows. I wondered if the Shadow waited in his bone covered hut for our return. Somehow I felt as if he were watching us. Glowing trails of torchlights could be seen on roads below us. Travelers, armies, refugees, it didn't matter; from up there they all looked like fireflies slowly drifting down the winding trails. A few beads of rain landed on my head and Brin stopped us all from gazing at the horizon. Pulling my hood over my head, I turned to follow her and my vision shifted itself in ways that humans' cannot. On the shadowy horizon I saw perched on a cliff which seemed risen out of the ground like a listing gravestone, a tall and ominous castle.

Even with my advanced sight, I could make out few details of its silhouette against the deep purple sky. Still, the tall towers looked like barbed spikes rising into the heavens. Below the spires I could only make out the multitude of roofs that resided beneath. The large city had the cliff with the forbidding majesty of the castle

Desecrated

directly in its center and around it a very high and similarly spiked wall. It was when I noticed the violent waterfall that came rushing out from between the castle and the cliff it sat upon, only to see the water disappear behind the cityline below. Somehow I suddenly knew the name of the distant city: Skullspill.

Off the hill we went and soon, I could scarcely see the tips of the towers.

"Wrack, right?"

"Yeah."

"I'm Samuel. Just wanted to thank you and your friends for letting me tag along. Don't think I would have made it out of there."

"It was a bit rough."

"Listen, I know that the war between the Lords is really not–"

"The who?" I interrupted.

"The Lords." When I didn't respond he continued. "The Baron and The King."

"You mean the Doomed?"

"Uh." He looked around with fear in his eyes. "No one calls them that. Without them we would all be doomed."

My raised eyebrow in his direction was hidden under my hood, yet somehow I think he felt it.

"So, what I was saying was this: If I can do anything to serve your master for saving me, I would be happy to."

"I don't have a master."

"Ha ha! Right. No, I am serious. I have always been loyal to the Baron, and since you saved my butt–"

Chapter 1

"Seriously." I interjected again, "I am not one of the Doomed's minions. I have no secret agenda of an ancient hidden undead lord in my deeds. Besides, the 'lord' of Yellow Liver is dead."

"What?"

"The Ghoul. He is dead."

There was a moment of silent shock before he fell to his knees and started babbling to the sky asking forgiveness for minor ways in which he had failed his Lord and master. Whichever one that was, though his comments made me think it was The Baron. From this dramatic reaction, it was obvious that he at least knew about The Ghoul. In some small way it made me ponder if he knew about the tribute in blood the citizens of Yellow Liver were forced to pay. A twinge of anger rose in me and that rage wanted to feed Samuel to whatever thing had followed us out of Yellow Liver. Eager to get away from Samuel, I moved over near Avar. "Tell me more about the Doomed." I whispered.

Avar looked around to see if anyone was listening. "That is a difficult conversation at the moment. Too many prying ears." Silence fell between us, but then he whispered, "What did you want to know?"

I smiled. I knew that Avar's pure excitement about history would prevent him from being as tight lipped as Brin. He also had no reason to mistrust me, as he hadn't seen the dark power rise out of me in the Ghoul's chamber. "Why would anyone worship them, as these people seem to?"

"Well, when you aren't given much choice it makes things easy. All their lives they have thought that the 'Lords of the Land' were gods made flesh. When you are an ancient powerful creature

Desecrated

it is easy to convince people of whatever you want to. The Doomed have established themselves as kings and deities. Has been that way for generations."

"Generations? Just how long have they been here?"

"Thousands of years, Wrack. Thousands. There is no real calendar that reaches back to the Cursing, but people who have studied history think it reaches back about three or more thousand years."

"Someone like your father?"

"Yeah, he is one of them. How long they have been around isn't really the problem, though. It is that they are quite literally immortal. Some of them even seem human, but most of them are in some twisted form."

Flexing my cold dead hands I said, "Most things seem twisted to me. You are going to have to explain that a little more."

Avar sighed. "Well, you know how you appear dead to us? Most of them also appear dead. One of them is even a skeleton dripping with viscous blood."

"What? And people think that these monsters are their saviors?"

There was a tiny hint of cynicism in his laugh. "When everyone you know believes something, it makes it easy to believe it too. Life is hard enough, most people are not willing to open their eyes to the truth."

Everyone I knew said that these 'Doomed' were a blight upon the world. Did Avar's wise words apply to me as well? Was I also part of the blight he wished to purge?

"Master is different. Master knows about the world, he has just forgotten," came the voice of Murks into my head.

Chapter 1

"I am not sure I want to remember, Murks. The Ghoul talked to me like he knew who I was. I didn't like that. Whatever dark secrets are in me, I don't think I want to know them." My gaze moved uncontrollably to Brin's lush mane of dark hair.

"Wrack?" Avar's voice broke me out of the internal conversation with my hidden passenger. "Did you hear that last part?"

"Um. I guess not."

"I was just saying that not everything that seems scary is twisted in a dark way. The ancient people used to draw the deities as dragons of various colors. They were often seen in a–"

"Great circle with each dragon holding the previous one's tail in its mouth?" I interjected.

Avar's face betrayed that I had stolen his thunder, but it quickly changed from that to a question mark. "Yeah. How did you know that?"

"I think I have seen it in a dream."

"Says the guy who never sleeps. Funny."

"Yeah. I guess you must have told me about I before," I lied. "So each of the Dragons is a different one of the ancient gods?"

"Yep. No one has really worshiped them in hundreds, if not thousands, of years though. Well, save one." His gaze drifted up to the moon which hung low on the horizon.

"This has something to do with the moon doesn't it? I can't help but notice you have a bit of a connection to it."

Avar seemed genuinely happy I asked. "Yeah. Her name is Ssli'Garion. She is the lady of the moon. In the ancient days, it was she that guarded the world against corruption and fed the people inspiration in all its forms. Art, poetry, and many prophecies. It was believed that when a person died, they would meet her in the silver forest up there," he nodded at the silvery orb in the sky.

Desecrated

"Protect from corruption? She kinda messed that up, didn't she? I mean look at this place." I pointed at the blackened trees, dry red earth, and stiff yellow grasses.

"Well, she couldn't step down here and stop what happened. She did have people who tried to stop the Cursing. Honestly though, my father is much more the expert about things that happened surrounding that. It says something, though, that her inspiration is still heard through the voices of bards. Or it was anyway." He frowned in Brin's direction.

Brin, her father, this Silver Lady that was Avar's godly patron, the Doomed: they all were connected. The Shadow had said something, too, about my connection to them. Seemed impossible to think that I was somehow tied to this great drama that had been playing out for thousands of years. Still, the mysterious moments alone with The Ghoul in his pit seemed to do nothing but support this idea. "And that sword…"

Avar shook his head a little. "I dunno. Brin says it was her father's sword. It's hard to imagine him with such a brutal weapon. The stories always paint him as a kind man and a hero. 'The man with a laugh and a song that could warm any heart that was not Doomed.' That is how my father talks about him anyway."

Both Avar and I slipped into our own thoughts. My eyes kept drifting to Ukumog's glowing markings dimly pulsing there in the moonlight. The horrible magic that lay hidden inside it frightened me. If I hadn't known about Brin's dark mood before she possessed the blade, I might have supposed that it was passing its anger onto her as it had passed it onto me. Perhaps that is the secret of the Bard. A charming man, prophet, and good father until the blade would take him over, wherein he would be transformed into a titan of dark power. If this were true, Brin's normal disposition

Chapter 1

would make it hard for us to see if the sword were about to take over. Fear of prying ears prevented me from mentioning these thoughts to Avar. Perhaps a different time.

The sky grew darker and Brin eventually decided to make camp. Many of the refugees were asleep almost instantly. As usual, I found myself unable to slumber. Avar followed the refugees to sleep, which left Brin and I alone. From across the camp, I kept catching her staring at me. It could not have been clearer that she still was having issue with the events of days ago, but I wasn't sure what I should do. I did not want to cause the conflict to get worse by batting the bees nest, especially while she had Ukumog ready to work its particular bit of magic. I thought it best to let her come to me when she was ready.

My gaze shifted to another woman in the camp. She lay silently awake, her vacant eyes filled with flickering reflections of the camp fire. Her name was Sally; I had caught that a few days before. When I first saw her, something seemed familiar. Not familiar in the way that things from my dreams seemed familiar. This was something much more recent. She caught me staring at her and quickly her eyes shot back to the tiny fire. A few moments later she looked back and saw me still looking at her.

"You'z name be Wrack, yeah?" She asked with the same nervousness that I had seen in Avar when he wanted to change the subject.

"That is what they call me."

"I'z Sally." An awkward pause inserted itself into the conversation. "Fanks for lettin' uz come alung wif yas." She smiled a bit. It revealed that she was a pretty woman some time ago. The rough life in Yellow Liver and the events that led to its messy end had taken a toll on her. Her pretty smile had somehow survived. "Whun ull dat mess stardid, I'z funk I'z wuz a gonna."

Desecrated

"It was pretty rough. What about your family?"

"I'z dinnae hav one. Dem ull ded."

I nodded.

"I'z fink I'z seen you befur. You evur drink at da Hedlez Murmaid?"

Suddenly it became clear. I saw her the night that I met Brin and Avar. "Yeah. I drank there once. I even stayed in one of the rooms upstairs."

A look of frightening recognition flashed across her face.

"You ok?" I asked, hoping to find out the source of her concern.

"Oh, it's nuffin. I'z guess I'z just finkin' abowt dem peoples in Yellow Liva. Awl gettin' eated and fings."

With a heavy sigh I replied, "Yeah. It was pretty horrible."

"I bets you see lots of 'orrible fings, yeah?"

"What happened back there is about the most horrible thing I can remember."

We both sat in silence, watching the fire dance as it consumed the life from the glowing sticks at its core. Sitting there, watching those glowing tongues lick the wood over and over caused a hunger to grow inside me. I closed my eyes and let the hunger take me somewhere else.

"Are you listening to me?"

"Doubtless I am, my lord Baron." I responded, but it wasn't me. It was the voice of The Ghoul.

Opening my eyes, I saw that I was in a large stone throne room. Red marble pillars trimmed with golden rings held the heavy ceiling far above my head. Thirty or so feet from where I knelt there

Chapter 1

was a set of wide steps. After three such steps was a dais so large one might call it a stage. A few guards stood at either side of the stage and in the center was a copper throne so aged and corroded it no longer held the color of copper. The jade green surface looked rotten. Seated on the throne was an animated skeleton, gory blood still clinging to its bones. The red and black finery it wore was soaked in the blood and in its hand was a silver scepter with a large purple gem atop it.

"I gave you the town of Yellow Liver to test you and you have proved yourself useless as a lord. What do the humans produce? What do they do? Other than serve as your personal feeding ground. Hrm?"

Anger grew inside me, but I dare not speak. The power of The Baron was too great. Looking down in shame, I prepared myself for the onslaught of disappointed scolding to wash over me.

"I don't even know what to do with you," he continued. "It really is a horrible shame." The sound of boney fingertips tapping filled the hall as The Baron sat back on his throne and pondered.

Hoping for a reprieve, I started to lift my head. My eyes shifted around the room, and I saw the crowd amassed in the shadows of the room. At least a hundred people were present to witness my humiliation. Teeth grinding like millstones, my hunger and rage grew. In the corner of the room there was a collection of weapons and armor on glorious display. Among them was a suit of plate decorated in the finest carvings. The scenes upon the armor shown skeletal remains all bound together with worming tentacles. Distinctly different than The Ghoul's thoughts, there was a painful alert that shot through my mind at the brief look at that armor. Now both The Ghoul and I were fueled with anger.

Desecrated

"I know what I shall do." His harsh voice brought fear to us both and tempered our anger a bit. "Nothing. I realize now that no amount of lessons or punishments will change what you are, Ghoul. Return to your pit, devour your humans. I care not what happens to you. Look at you. You are nothing but filth. At one time you may have served me well, but now–you are nothing but a liability." Even without the flesh of his face to produce a disdainful sneer, I felt one anyway.

"But. Master…master, doubtless there is still some way for me to serve you!" We fell to our knees, begging for The Baron's acceptance. Even the endless hunger within us was lesser to our desire to have the favor of our master.

"No. Your use to me has come to an end. Get out of my sight," the Baron commanded.

Tears blurred my vision of the stone floor beneath my huddled body. Closing my eyes I felt a single tear leave my face and I heard it kiss the floor beneath me.

"I told you get out of my sight! And don't come back until the job is done."

The smell of the woods surrounded me. Opening my eyes I saw gigantic trees with branches that could reach the heavens. Green life teemed around us and the air was fresh. Hidden in the woods with me was the commander from my previous dreams, still wearing that macabre armor of bones and tentacles. His voice told me that it was this man who was also the skeletal 'Baron' from the previous vision. "Commander, they are but harmless children and old men," said one of the soldiers hidden with us in the woods.

"It matters not. The King bids us destroy this place, and so we shall. Do you question the King's order?" He began drawing his sword.

Chapter 1

"No commander. I merely question the tactics. We can slaughter them all with just a few men. Why bring the entire squad?"

"Because, Sergeant, in that tower is one of the most powerful men alive, a Wizard who could burn this entire forest to ashes with a wink of his eye. This is why we needed the help of ancient enemies to get here, and now we will not fail."

The Sergeant saluted the Commander and then went off to the other men. Once he was gone, the Commander turned to me and smiled a twisted smile. "Today, Palig, we will either change the world forever or die trying."

"I have no doubt it will be the former, m'lord," I said with The Ghoul's voice. The gurgling whine, which usually came with it, was gone, however. This confirmed my thought: *This must be a memory from before the Cursing.*

The soldiers began to creep their way towards the open glade where the ancient colossal tower stood proudly. We moved to take up the rear and the Commander turned to me. "No Palig, I need you to remain here and end any that try to escape, or for you to report back should we fail. You are far quicker than my men. Besides, you enjoy the hunt more when they are already afraid." Again I saw the sickening smile and the violent glimmer in his eye.

My mind screamed, *KILL HIM NOW*! But this body would not comply. I felt myself smile at him. "Good luck m'lord. Send some blood to the Silver Forest for me."

"I will, old friend. See you soon," the Commander smiled and patted me on the shoulder before heading off with his men.

The soldiers engaged the children and weaponless adults in the clearing. More unarmed peasants came fearfully rushing out of the tower at the sight of the squad. Inside I cringed in terror as I saw the parade of metal grind through the helpless children. I could do nothing to save them, again. This vision was far worse, however,

Desecrated

for part of me was delighted to watch all their innocent souls be sent fearful to the afterlife. At the height of the slaughter, I took a casual look to the other side of the glade and saw a child there. Even from this distance, I could almost taste his fear and horror. Doing my duty, I started quickly slinking through the woods towards the boy's position. Quick glances back to the clearing revealed the Commander's victory and the squad remained at the base of the tower awaiting the Wizard's presence.

The boy remained at the edge of the forest as I stalked him. His entire focus was on the events near the base of the tower. Pride over my skills of stealth forced a sinister smile to my face and I even allowed my speed to slow to make sure he would not take notice of me.

In the clearing, the Wizard arrived through the large doors at the base of the tower. He was followed by some other adults in robes and children who all began to cry out at the sight of the massacre. Iron bands bound the Wizard's hands, but he stood defiantly against the Commander.

Closer and closer I crept towards the boy. I thought of taking a trophy from him once it was over. Perhaps a lock of that strawberry blond hair, or a fragment of the plain robe he was wearing. Maybe even gouge out one of those pretty blue eyes, but those spoil so quickly.

Commotion from the clearing distracted me for a moment and I turned to see what it was. The Commander was shouting at the Wizard. "This should be an entertaining end. So much for the mighty power of the Wizard," Palig chuckled.

The steel sounds of death rang out from the clearing again, and some of the wailing ceased. The Commander was finishing what he had come here to do. My prey, on the other hand, still hid at the edge of the forest cowering in fear. I was close enough to see the

Chapter 1

silent sobs that wracked his body. This was going to be delicious. A small ball of golden light streaked from the fighting in the clearing towards my prey and touched him. "Oh uzk," Palig said under his breath. My pace to catch the boy before he vanished into the woods became faster.

Thirty yards. The boy began to stumble backwards into the woods. Twenty. He was back to his feet and running. Fifteen yards. A great whispering wind rushed through the branches of the trees above me and a low branch blew in front of me. When I pushed through it the boy was gone.

I quickly paced around the last place I saw him looking for some kind of sign of where he went. There was nothing. It was as if he vanished into the wind. "Oh uzk," was the only thing Palig could think to say. Somewhere deep inside, I smiled.

"Fur wot is am wurth, I sorry abowt wot happind in Yellow Liva." Sally's voice brought me out of the dream.

"It wasn't your fault." My voice creaked with weariness.

Her eyes looked down at the fire with guilt. "Sum of it wus. I'z the one who tuld da guard abowt you and Brin stayin' at the Murmaid. Dats why dem came fur you bowf dat night." Remorse prevented her eyes from meeting mine as she spoke, instead she focused on her finger, doodling in the dirt.

The air around me changed from calm to charged. My attention became more focused. The predator in me was awake. "I see. Did they offer you a reward or something?"

Sally's answer could not be formed quickly. The silent seconds of doodling in the dust left me to think the worst of my conversational partner. By the time she opened her mouth to start

Desecrated

speaking, my mind was already telling me I might need to defend myself, so my hand secretly found its way around the handle of a dagger on my belt. "Well, I–"

A great roar rumbled through the camp, shaking the tree branches around us and raising the hairs on my neck. Sally looked around with a terrible fright. Various members of our number started to stir at the sound, except Avar who remained sleeping soundly. Before anyone could get fully to their senses, there was a whooshing sound, and barbed hooks attached to sinuous chains came whipping out of the darkness and lashed into Sally's flesh. I was the only one of group who saw the hooks dig their way into Sally. They found purchase all over her body, and then there was some gruesome tugging as she tried to hold onto the dust at her fingertips. She was able to give me one more panicked look before she was whisked away into the night. Her screams of terror and pain echoed long after her body was gone. Then, with the wet sounds of rending flesh and bone, her screams were silenced. The end of Sally happened so quickly that I had only the time to stand up and draw my dagger. The blade of my weapon was so small, I felt it would be useless against whatever wielded those barbed hooks with such evil precision. My eyes darted over towards Ukumog just as Brin drew it from its ring. *Clink!*

There had been times in our travels together where I thought she might kill someone for disturbing her sleep. The violent stare along with her disheveled hair made it look as if, this time, someone or something would suffer her wrath. Refugees scrambled around the camp, looking for anything they could use as a weapon, most of them grabbing rocks or branches from the ground. Samuel picked up our metal cooking pot. I hoped that he wasn't next to face the fate that met Sally, for I didn't want to lose our cooking pot.

"Not nice master," Murks said into my mind.

Chapter 1

"Did I say I had to be nice?"

"No master, but you did say that things were different. Murks feels sorry for the Samuel man. He is lost and alone," Murks' thoughts came into my head again.

"That makes two of us, Murks."

"Who is Murks?" Brin barked at me, and I realized that I had been speaking out loud.

"Um."

Brin's bare foot repeatedly made visits to Avar's ribs. "Get the uzk up, Shadow Hunter. It's show time."

"MmMph. Huh?"

"There is an uzkin' shadow creature or something out here with us!" She screamed at him without letting him distract her from her vigilant watch for barbed hooks.

"A wha–? Oh my gods!" He scrambled to his feet and clumsily tried to hold some of his bedroll over his mostly naked body.

"I told you that sleeping like that was a liability," Brin's disgust was more than evident.

"Live and learn, Brin. Live and learn." There was a confidence in Avar's voice that I had not heard before. It made me start to wonder what exactly was different about him when he faced horrible creatures and pushy guards. Before my thoughts could wander too far, there was more commotion.

Another blasting roar rolled over our camp making the refugees huddle behind Brin holding their rocks in fear. She stood between Avar and me, him with his mace and shield and me with my daggers. A whooshing sound came like last time and barbed hooks appeared. This time I twisted my sight to see beyond the firelight of the camp and saw the silhouette of a naked, bloated human. There was not a single strand of hair upon its form, but instead it looked

Desecrated

as if more of these twisted hooks were piercing their way through its flesh. While it had the form of a human, the face and movements made me instinctively think of this thing as more beast than man.

Each of us ducked and dodged the flying meathooks with a little help from Brin's swords, which parried at least one of the strands of painful death. As the flickering light moved over the creature that faced us, I saw that it was also marked with savage scars and tattoos that mostly covered its head and arms. The protruding barbs did not seem to do much damage to their host, for as it twisted and turned, they only occasionally gave forth a few drops of viscous blood.

"Wrack? Can you see it?" She quietly asked.

"Yeah. It isn't a pleasant thing."

"Any ideas, Avar?"

He struggled a bit with his answer before replying, "Not really."

"Let's get a better look at this uzker." Following Brin's movements we backed off from the campfire slowly, causing our attacker to be drawn closer to the light.

The plan worked. Closer the thing came to the campfire. I heard gasps from some of the refugees as it became visible to most of us. As the flickering light moved over the tanned bloated skin, I made one quick observation–it was female.

"I am Avar, servant of the Silver Lady! Beast of the Doomed Ones, I cast you out. Begone!" Avar held his mace out and it started to glow faintly. I could feel the hair on my arms stand up.

The creature let loose a howling roar in Avar's direction that was charged with a dark rage. Spittle flew from the deformed mouth of the beast and it took a few mighty steps forward.

"Looks like we will have to do this the uzkin' hard way." Brin's voice was mixed with disappointment and excitement.

Chapter 1

"We are with you, Brin," I interjected before there could be any arguing.

Another roar washed over us. Barbed strands came from a hole in the belly of the creature, which it then cast in our direction with one of its swollen hands. This time Brin parried two of the three strands, but the third caught one of our refugees in the face, tearing open a huge gash before being released from his flesh and knocking him to the ground. The beast drew in the thin chains of the barbs and took another step towards us.

"Whatever this thing is, it isn't from Yellow Liver," said Avar.

"Yeah, well I am about to lose my temper all over it. Ready Ukumog?" As she finished speaking, the sword glowed slightly brighter in response.

Did the sword just actually respond?

"Yes master, it did." Murks answered.

Brin let loose her own howl at the beast and closed the gap between them with a few leaping strides. The creature was caught unready for the onslaught of attacks that Brin brought to bear, but it was able to use the loose strands of chain to block the oncoming assault. After a few quick exchanges between the two of them while we watched, Avar charged in to support Brin. After entering the fray, he bashed the beast with his shield, knocking it off balance. Brin brought her normal sword down to try and sever one of the chains, but to no avail, and the beast instead tangled the chain around the sword and disarmed Brin of it, throwing it in my direction. Brin's free hand found its way to the handle of Ukumog. Avar's mace collided with the chest of the beast and a searing silver light burst forth from the connection. Again the roar rolled over

Desecrated

all of us, and this time the rage was mixed with pain. A huge hand grabbed the top of Avar's shield and pulled on it, trying to disarm him.

Drawing in a deep breath, Brin centered her focus on her enemy. There was a concentration in her that did not seem normal for her demeanor. Ukumog shone mercilessly in the night and left a streak of blue glow as it came crashing down on the arm of the beast. *CRACK!* The top half of the shield was crushed and broken by the powerful grasp of the beast. It screamed, sending shivers down my spine.

The black empty, eyes of the creature focused first on Ukumog, then moved to Brin as it backed away. There was one final roar before the creature fled the camp with amazing speed and stealth. Everyone collected behind Brin again, but remained aware of the darkness around them.

"Uzk that thing was nasty. Still no idea what that was, Avar?" Brin asked, her eyes still focused on the night around us.

Inspecting the broken shield still strapped to his arm, Avar answered, "Never seen anything like it before. If it was a creature from one of the Doomed, it isn't from around here."

"Well what the uzk was it doing following us then? We have pissed off more than just The Ghoul, The Baron, and The King? UZK!" Brin stormed around the camp, her temper making her lose focus about the possible lurking danger. All of the refugees flinched a little at the mention of the Doomed, specifically calling them out by name. None of them were brave enough to say anything, though. Samuel fell to his knees and started praying.

Avar stared at him with disappointment. "They didn't save you. You might want to re-dedicate yourself."

"I will not pray to a heretical God." Samuel responded fearful, yet forcefully.

Chapter 1

A disgusted sound left Avar's lips and he turned away from Samuel.

"If you hadn't fought our lords in the first place, none of this would have happened. We would still have our homes and our families." Samuel's words grew in fervor.

Some of the other refugees seemed to agree with Samuel's sentiment. From where I was, I could see Avar's face and they could not. There was a struggle going on inside his heart. I saw anger and disappointment. Before the fight could resolve into a response from him, Brin gave one instead.

"It doesn't matter. None of that gaak uzkin' matters. We all almost got torn apart by some uzkin' barbed thing and you are fighting over forces that do not give one tiny piece of gaak about you. Shut the uzk up and try not to get us all killed. You keep fighting this way and I will kill you all myself. Got me?"

Fear and silence fell over them. More than one set of eyes darted between Brin's baleful stare and the eager gleam of Ukumog's edge. There was no more talk of that sort that night.

The man whose face was rent open lay crying on the ground. Avar and I went to attend him while Brin separated herself from the camp for a while. His face was opened to the bone on one of his cheeks. "Miracle his eye wasn't torn out." Avar's comment was not entirely comforting. We did all we could to help him, and it seemed that he might recover, though he would need help to stay with us.

After things calmed down and the light of the morning arrived to tear apart the dark night, Brin came and sat with me. "You ok?" I asked after a long uncomfortable silence.

Desecrated

"Yeah. I just hate all the religious talk. My dad used to talk about freedom and goodness in this world overwhelmed with despair and darkness. Sometimes I wish he were still here to tell me the stories again just to let me escape this place. Even just for a little while."

I didn't know what to say, so we just sat together in silence and watched the sun come up. When the sky was finally lit she said to me, "Screw the roads. We are going deep into the wild. Nothing will be able to find us between here and Marrowdale, though that wounded one will slow us down."

"If it helps, I will carry him. He doesn't look too heavy."

"Deal."

"You're right master. Things are different. You never would have offered to carry someone before. Murks is happy." He spoke in my head. Knowing I was making a change for the better, I couldn't help but smile. Brin even smiled back a little. As horrible as the few hours before had been, I cherished that moment.

After breakfast was cooked in the undamaged cooking pot, Avar walked up to Brin and I, "Either of you seen Samuel? His stuff is gone."

"Idiot probably thinks that he is safer on his own. I hope he gets uzkin' eaten by that thing." Brin said hoisting up her belongings and starting to walk deeper into the woods.

For him to have snuck off in the night without me knowing I must have slept, but I hadn't noticed. After the shock of that realization faded, I had the distinct feeling that this would come back to bite us.

There was no complaining or arguing from any of the refugees for the next few days as we struggled through the knotted dead brush to reach Marrowdale. My journey was hampered by

Chapter 1

the wounded man, David, whose strength faded over the journey. At first he was just using me for support and direction, as we had bandaged over his eye. After a few days though, I was carrying him in my arms. David was not a small man, and the ease with which I was able to carry him was surprising to me. Once I started carrying him, he spent the time mostly sleeping. When he was awake, conversation was awkward. When I wasn't struggling to keep up with Brin's pace, I often wondered what I would say to a man forced to carry me through the woods. "So, what did you do back in Yellow Liver?"

"Huh? Oh. I–I was a street merchant. My cart was mostly crap," he struggled out a laugh, "but the best days where when I had fresh fish."

"Why were those the best days?"

"It was the water. The water that was near the city was bad. So good fish was hard to get."

"So the days you had fish were profitable?"

He chuckled a bit, "I guess. The best thing about it was watching people's face light up when they knew they were going to get a decent meal. Made me feel good."

David's comments made me glad to be carrying him. He was a man who found joy in delivering hope to those who had little. It made me happy that we didn't abandon him. His fellow refugees did not seem to be cut from the same cloth. Every night I would try and tend to his wound the best way I knew how, but it didn't seem to be getting any better. In fact, it seemed to be getting worse. From our journey through the Forest of Shadows, I knew that Brin had some skill with healing wounds, so, about three or four days after we had faced the beast, I approached Brin with the intent of asking her for help. My face must have betrayed my desire before I could even speak it, for as I walked up to her she spoke.

Desecrated

"Things not going so well for what's his name, eh?"

"Um. Not sure, really. The wound seems to have gotten darker, even blackish in some spots, and the pus is not looking the same."

The curve of her mouth made me believe that she was about to say that we leave him behind. I mentally prepared myself to defend David's life with my words. "Lemme come take a look at it," she said, catching me off guard.

"Uh oh. I must be in bad shape if you brought the boss lady." David struggled to laugh.

Ignoring his comment, Brin pulled back the binding and studied the wound a bit. "I need some stuff. Be back in a bit." And with that she rushed off into the night.

In the silence waiting for her to return, I did what I spent most of my time doing. I watched. I watched the people of the camp in their conversations. I watched some of them trying to sleep. I even watched a few of them look over at David and me with concern. Not one of them was brave enough to ask if he was ok. It was then that it occurred to me that ever since the attack, the refugees have given David a wide berth, like the death they smelled on him was contagious. Those looks had been cast in my direction before, and not in one of my crazy visions either.

I remember seeing eyes with that look in them staring at me from every opening on the streets of Yellow Liver when that ghoul attacked me and stabbed me with the black talon. Eyes keen to watch, but no spirit strong enough to stand up and do something about what was happening. Loathsome lurkers who selfishly guarded their own pathetic lives when even one of their own lay stricken with a debilitating wound. There were no guards or ghouls here for them to fear, yet somehow the hold of the Doomed still

Chapter 1

lay claim to their courage. My jaw clenched and deep inside me I was happy that my last memory of Yellow Liver was that it lay in smoking ruins.

"Now this is the master I remember. Full of darkness and hatred." Murks' voice entered my head.

My thoughts connected my current emotional state to the same experience as when I held Ukumog. My eyebrow twitched and my guts became knotted. "Yeah. Well. Maybe things aren't as different as I thought."

"Master is always different. Every time."

"Every time? What do you mean, every time?"

"Jeez. Talk to yourself much?" Brin had returned, her arms full of various plants and mosses. She knelt down next to David and started sorting out her collection of woodland goods.

"Yeah. I suppose I am."

Tight-lipped as ever, Brin just continued working on David and changed the subject. "Can you bring me some of the water from over there."

I followed her direction to get some of the water from Avar, who offered one small complaint about how the water was for cooking, but gave it to me anyway. Brin cleaned David's wound and mixed some of the herbs, breaking some of them and squeezing out their oils. The idea to ask her where she learned about the plants and such arose, but I thought better of it. Generally those questions were answered with a reference to her father, and I did not want to open that topic. Not at the moment.

"There. Keep the bandages tight. I made some more of the poultice for you to apply when you change them tomorrow when we stop. If it starts to ooze through, make sure you tell me." She wiped her hands together and began to stand, but before she could get away David grabbed one of her wrists gently.

Desecrated

"Thank you. For everything." He lowered to a whisper, "I know who you are, and I know what you did back there. Thank you for that too."

The muscles in Brin's jaw flexed. She looked like she was both angry and suddenly trying to fight back tears. With a flick of her arm, she pulled away from David's weak grip. "Just take care of that wound."

Her prickly attitude washed over him and left him unfazed. As she gathered her gear and stood up I heard him humming something and quietly a tune left his lips, "...we know their names..." Her pace stopped as the tune fell to her ears, but it only slowed her for a heartbeat before she charged forward at her usual gait back to her bedroll. "I'm right, aren't I?"

"Excuse me?"

"Brin. She is the Bard's daughter, isn't she?"

Not knowing what to say and what to keep secret, I remained silent.

He nodded at me. "I heard him once. When I was a kid, my mother took me to see him perform. I remember because it was so crazy. We had to get there through some awkward series of back alleys and went into the basement of a butcher shop. There he was, surrounded by people and hanging meat. Somehow appropriate for Yellow Liver. Some of the tunes still rattle around up here from time to time, but the thing I remembered most was that sword."

At the mention of it, my attention was fully his. "What sword?"

He subtly pointed at Brin. "The wicked one." All the talking was causing him pain, but it didn't stop him. "I remember, because it seemed so strange. He had it hidden of course, but it was just tucked under a rag off to one side, and I could see the handle. When I saw it on her hip, I knew she had to be his daughter. The

Chapter 1

day before the King's army attacked there was a rumor that she was outside the gates singing to the crowd. When I heard about it, I didn't believe them."

"Hush now, David. You have to rest."

"Wrack?"

"Yeah?"

"Thanks for not leaving me behind."

"Thank me when you get better and we are out of this mess."

He just smiled and went to sleep. Before long I was left alone with the snores of the camp.

Desecrated

Chapter 2

After many days of quiet travel, we started to climb a rather sizable hill, pushing through grasping underbrush and low hanging dead branches to reach whatever lay on the other side. David was now well enough that he only needed me for support, so the two of us were slower than the rest of the group. Brin's pace seemed hurried, which usually meant that we were close to our destination. The group of refugees, still afraid more of the world than our leader, stayed tight to Brin's rear, leaving David and I far behind.

"Mind if I ask you a question?" David asked with a bit of a strange tone.

Hesitantly I replied, "Sure."

"Who is it that you talk when you are alone? I can't always sleep through the whole night, and I know you don't really ever sleep. I hear you sometimes having conversations with no one."

"Myself mostly."

David gave a little laugh, "I've been around people that talk to themselves. You are talking to someone else. Who is it?"

He was asking about Murks. *How many times have I sat talking with him while he mended my robes?* Too many to count I would wager. I hadn't even told Avar or Brin about Murks. My

Desecrated

worry was that Avar would finally see me as a shadow creature, and I would lose the only two friends I had in the world. Still, I knew that if I lied to David he would know.

"You don't have to tell me if you don't want to," he filled my silence.

Murks stirred in my robes slightly. No doubt he sensed my discomfort. "No, it's fine. I mean, it's complicated."

His brow furrowed. "Complicated? That's not the answer I was expecting." There was disappointed curiosity in his voice.

Uncomfortable silence lingered. As close as David and I had gotten since the attack, I felt guilty not opening up to him. The feeling reminded me of the time right after Brin, Avar, and I had escaped from Yellow Liver the first time, and how I held back the information about the ghoul attacking me with the black talon.

"Master, if you tell the nice man about me there will be no taking it back," Murks said in my mind. As much as my heart wanted to share this secret that I had kept from my only friends in the world, my lips remained firmly shut.

The chill of the coming winter had started to take its hold. My joints felt stiffened by the cold and my flesh hardened. In the quiet of that afternoon, I could even sometimes hear my flesh creaking like a suit of old leather armor. I needed warmth. Carrying David must have held off my unnatural hunger for the warmth of life. There in the silence it made itself known. My eyes tracked the movements of the refugees ahead of us. The chill in the air also stung them. Sharpened by the cold, my senses knew that they too had been put under alert. Something dangerous was among us, and for once I knew it wasn't Ukumog.

Hours went by as the crisp earth crackled and crunched under our boots. The cold turned my feet to numb marble and my hands to icy fire. I wanted to take the heat of something, to

Chapter 2

claim it as my own and find fleeting respite in the gentle relief that warmth would bring. "I haven't been awake very long," I blurted out. "I woke up in a grave near Yellow Liver maybe two or three months ago. Time is hard for me to track, really. It all seems to blend together."

"Woke up in a grave?" David's curiosity was piqued again. "My understanding is that the Doomed created your kind out of living people."

"I dunno. Whatever happened to me before that shallow hole I crawled out of is a mystery to me. I sometimes get flashes, though. Hard for me to tell if they are memories or dreams."

"Maybe they are a little of both?" David replied after quiet moment. "I sometimes have dreams that are part memory and part something else."

"Possible. Honestly, I can't remember the difference between a memory and a dream. One happens while you are awake, the other when you are asleep. Both seem as flawed as whatever visions are haunting me." A few steps were made in silence, but then I continued. "Take Avar for example. He wants so badly to be the man his father wanted him to be. He dreams of one day being a hero that can free the people from the Curse. Why is it that he seems happy about the destruction of Yellow Liver, while Brin and I seem unhappy at best?"

David chuckled, "Perspective, my dear Wrack. Perspective. Eight people can see the same event and come away with eight different stories. If you were to ask everyone with us about the night we were attacked, or even about that fool Samuel, everyone's story would be different. People see the world through the lens of their own experiences, prejudices, and beliefs. That's why Avar will always think that the Doomed are his enemy, and Samuel his saviors. It is all about perspective."

Desecrated

A smile came to my face, "You are a wise man, David. Perhaps the wisest man I know." Then with a chuckle I said, "But I don't know very many people."

Together in that moment we laughed as friends. The hunger inside me was forgotten, at least for the time being. Another hour or two passed with David and I chatting about nothing, and just as we crested the large hill Brin came up to us. "We are here. The ruins of Marrowdale."

All around me the refugees were frightened. They muttered about how the Baron had called in his armies to bring fire down on the people who lived in Marrowdale. "What happened here?" I asked David quietly.

"Truth be told, only those who were here know, but most of them are either imprisoned or dead. As the story goes, the Baron grew displeased with a small group of folk who lived here. They had apparently found the ancient secret he kept hidden somewhere in this little town. To put those who found his secret in their place, he killed everyone except their families and burned the village to the ground. The families of those rebels were taken back to Skullspill and are probably rotting in a prison there still."

"How long ago did this happen?" I asked.

David sighed, "Not this past fall, but the one before. Horrible thing, but there was only about a hundred or so people living here."

"What secret could be so important that he would kill all these people, yet he didn't have it guarded?"

"I don't know. The friend who told me the news said that it was the Tomb of the Betrayer, but I think that is just a story."

"Tomb of the Betrayer?" I asked, confused.

Chapter 2

David chuckled, "I keep forgetting that you don't remember anything. The Tomb of the Betrayer is a legendary magical prison where the Doomed locked up one of their own kind. Would have to be powerful magic to seal away one of the self-proclaimed gods of our world."

His answer hadn't helped. While I understood the words he spoke, I had no idea what he was talking about. Avar had once mentioned that one of the Doomed had turned against the others, but there had never been mention that they imprisoned the traitor. "So is that prison here?"

"According to my friend it is, but how to open it or where it is exactly, well, your guess is good as mine." David leaned heavily on me. The travel of the day had worn on him, and he was gathering strength for the descent into the ruined town.

From up on the hill, all I could see was the outline of where buildings and their individual rooms had once been. They just remained as thick black lines drawn into the flat space that was the old town. A road, slightly overgrown by dark vines, ran through the center of the small collection of foundations and then off to both the east and west. The trees and plants had all given up their leaves and that added to the dead feel of the place.

As we descended the hill towards the town, Avar said something to Brin and headed off in a different direction. I wanted to ask him where he was going, but I thought better of shouting after him. Traveling with David down the hill was more difficult than I thought. Several times he lost his footing and I had to hold him up, all the while hoping I never lost mine. This slow, careful travel made me very aware of the small clouds of ashy dust we were kicking up. When we got to the bottom, everyone except for Brin huddled together near the corner of what used to be a building.

Desecrated

They reeked of fear and the acrid stench of it awoke my hunger again. Gritting my teeth, I helped find a place for David to rest and wandered away from the group.

"What is happening to me, Murks? Why am I feeling this way?" There was acertain desperation in my voice.

The hemodan did not respond.

Trying to hide the fact that I was taking to myself, I put my head down and whispered into my robe forcefully, "Tell me what is happening to me."

"Master does not want to know."

"Yes. Master does want to know. Master needs to find a way to stop this."

"Humans have to eat. Master does too."

"Ok. So what do I need to eat Murks? What is it that I am hungry for?"

The little figure in my robe became overwhelmed with sadness. His emotions flooded into me and my eyes became blurry with the welling of tears. "Master–Master feeds on life," the sound of his tiny voice trailed off as if he were about to cry.

"Doesn't everything feed on life? Everything eats something else." My whispers had become louder.

"Master doesn't understand. Master feeds on life. Not flesh or blood, but life."

Frustrated, I wanted to pull the little hemodan out of his secret little pocket and yell at him. I wanted him to explain exactly what he meant by 'life'. I wanted him to tell me why I was this way. However, Brin distracted me from my anger.

"You ok?" Brin's voice almost made me jump out of my skin.

"Yeah. I am–"

Chapter 2

"NOT fine. Wrack, I just caught you uzkin' talking to yourself. What in the sundered gate is going on?" With arms crossed, she waited for an answer.

The light made her dark hair glow in the sunset. Even from this distance, I could taste the warmth of her skin. The fight inside me had to come to an end, so I made my mind surrender to my heart. "I was talking to my friend Murks." Surprise shot through the little hemodan's mind.

With the same suspicion that a parent treats the lies of a child she simply responded, "Murks?"

"Yes. Murks."

Green eyes attacked me through slitted lids. "Fine. If you don't want to tell me, that's just great. Just know this–I hate it when people I care about keep secrets from me. Get me? If you want to keep trotting around with Avar and me, you better start telling me the truth."

"I am telling you the truth."

"About some uzkin' ghost that you have been talking to?" She turned to the empty air on one side of her, "Hello, Flabbity Jab! I'm Brin! How are you? Yeah? I agree, it sucks that you don't uzkin' exist," then she turned back to me and shot me a venomous look.

A tiny rustling started in my robes from near my chest. Knowing that Murks was about to appear, I put the end of my sleeve down near the ground and he climbed out. Shock and terror flooded Brin's face, and the two of them stared at each other for a long time. Brin's brow furrowed and she bent over to get a closer look at the dark clumpy lump of blood and dirt that made up Murks' tiny body. "Holy gaak. You have a uzkin' hemodan!" She quietly exclaimed.

"It seems that way, yeah."

"Seems that way? When the uzk were you going to tell me?" She exclaimed, trying to control her voice.

Desecrated

"Just never seemed like the right time."

"Wait, I have seen you before."

Fear hit me from the little hemodan before me, and he took a step away from the excited woman with the evil sword. "You saw him before?" I tried to interrupt.

Changing her focus to me, she seemed more excited than angry. "Yeah! He was there in the lair of the Ghoul with us. I saw him drinking the blood of the Ghoul or something."

"That was my blood actually. It was in a black talon. The Ghoul was using it for some kind of magical thing."

"Wait, how do you know he got your blood?"

Sighing I responded, "I told you about that ghoul that attacked me when we left Yellow Liver. Well, he stabbed me with that Talon and it drained some of my blood."

Confusion made her face crinkle. "What the uzk would he want with your blood?"

I shook my head. "I have no idea."

Turning her focus back to Murks, "This is really amazing, Wrack. I can't believe you hid him from me."

"After how you treated that last hemodan we ran into..."

Brin chuckled, "Yeah, that. I suppose you have a point." She reached out a hand to the little reddish brown figure. "Hi, I'm Brin."

Murks hesitated and looked over at me. I nodded to him and he shook her index finger with his bloody mitt. "Me am Murks. Murks serves the Master."

"Fine by me, as long as your master is Wrack and not one of the Doomed," she said smiling. Then turning back to me she continued, "Might want to keep this from everyone else. At least for now. Avar might not be so understanding."

Chapter 2

"To be honest, I thought you would have a problem with it."

She laughed, "Nah. One of my father's friends had a hemodan. He used to tell me that magic would make more sense when I got older. It still freaks me out sometimes, but I am glad I have had some exposure to it. Unlike the rest of the world. Since all they know are the horrors that the Doomed craft into reality..."

Murks was happy to be out of the closed space in my robes. He wandered around and explored his immediate surroundings, being careful to never stray too far from me. Brin and I sat there watching him take everything in. It was the first time since the fight with The Ghoul that I had felt the contentment that her presence had brought previously.

"So, where did Avar go?"

My sudden question brought her out of whatever she was thinking about. "Uh. Oh yeah. He went off to a cache that the Shadow Hunters keep things in. Apparently they communicate through leaving notes under rocks or something. He said something about supplies being there too."

"Good. We could use some of that," I said to fill the conversation. I didn't really have to eat, so I hadn't been paying attention to the food supply. Something that I was mostly grateful for, though at times, I was envious of the joy that my companions seem to get from the flavor of certain foods. To me, most food was just what I imagine the color grey would taste like.

Now that things seemed better between us, I wanted to talk to Brin about what happened the night we killed The Ghoul. My mind raced with all the things I wanted her to know. How Ukumog had made me feel when I touched it. How it had flown through the air into my grasp. Who I had become while under its power. I wanted her to know that I was as scared and confused about that

Desecrated

night as she was. It was hard to find a way to bring it all up. A few times I opened my mouth to say something and ended up faking a yawn or just closing it again. Her attention was ever focused on Murks running around our feet as we sat on the ruined walls of a large building or looking up to check on the refugees.

"Brin, I–"

"Whoa, did you notice that before?" She pointed at something behind us.

Defeated by her interruption, I turned to look as Murks ran into the ruins behind us to also see what she was pointing at. There in the burnt ruins stood part of a wall. Unsure how I had not seen it, my curiosity grew and I started to walk towards it. Black vines had grown up and around the standing empty rectangle that seemed only slightly larger than a person, but there it stood alone in the ruins. The three of us walked over to it and discovered that it was the standing frame of what looked like the back door of whatever building used to be where we stood. No thoughts past through my head before I started tearing at the vines to see how this one frame stood while the rest of the town lay in complete ruin. Under the vine lay warm colored wood, with the brass of the hinges still clinging to one side. It looked dirty, but untouched by the flames that had consumed the rest of its body.

"That's odd," I said under my breath.

"What?"

"Look at this. This door frame is completely untouched by damage or fire. It is almost like it was built after the building around it was destroyed."

With her normal disbelief, Brin said, "Why would anyone build a doorframe after the building was destroyed?"

Chapter 2

"I don't know. And look here, the hinges are still here." My fingers rubbed the nails and explored the grime that had lived on them since the destruction of the door that they once held. "But the nails which held the door were burned. How would a doorframe survive a fire and remain standing after the walls around it were nothing but ruin?"

"It must be magic, Master."

I nodded at Murks, who was at my feet also investigating the strange frame. Something caught my eye at the apex of the frame, the very place where there would be a keystone should it have been an arch. The unknown thing shined as the light of the sun, low on the horizon, came across it. Pulling away the vines around it, I saw what had called out to me. It was a hook.

From behind me Brin asked, "What is it?"

"A hook." My response almost seemed more like a question. The tarnish steel of the hook was attached to the frame via an icon that depicted the disturbing smile of a man. The smile was so wide and large that if it were on a real person would probably cause extreme pain, yet there was a look of malice in the metallic eyes that gleamed there in the diminishing light. "Why would anyone put a hook just over the door?"

"Maybe they hung a chime over the door to alert them of customers?" Brin brainstormed.

"No, the hinges open the other way."

"Decorations for different holidays?"

"It seems too ornate for that. And the point of the hook even looks slightly barbed."

Desecrated

Brin dug her boot into the dirt and tried to come up with a solid explanation. Without thinking, I reached my hand forward to touch the metal of the hook. My finger drew slowly closer to its thirsty point, and just before I would have let it pierce my flesh my mind took me somewhere else.

The expansive sky hung over my head. The world around me was peaceful and alive. Green forests with a backdrop of breathing mountains capped with snow. Both the view and the chill in the air took my breath away. Before me stood one figure who somehow was only a silhouette in this bright daylight. The outline of this form would change in tiny flashes before me.

First, it appeared as the outline of a tall and slender woman, with rivers of flowing hair that caressed the edges of her body. Quickly it shifted to that of a man, slightly shorter than the woman before him, but dressed in a doublet and cape. His hair fell around his shoulders and as the wind toyed with it, I noticed that he wore an earring shaped like a teardrop from his left lobe. The sword that hung from his belt was thin and had a basket hilt, yet it remained silently in his scabbard.

The form changed again, but this time I recognized the outline of the man I had seen many times in my visions. His armored body was nearly completely covered, save for his head. His hair was slicked back, and curled as it reached his neck. A soldier's sword hung at his waist, long and heavy. While the other forms had looked directly at me, he turned to one side and I saw the pointed beard that haunted my dreams. It was him. It was the commander who killed the old man at the tower. It was The Baron.

Chapter 2

Suddenly the form changed again. From the dark outline before me, all I could tell was that this man wore the clothes of a farmer. His hair was long, yet tied away from his face on the back of his head. In his hand was a common rake that he leaned upon. While I could not make any more details about this man, I was overcome with a sense of sorrow and dread. Somehow I wronged this man, and yet the dark stranger that was me was proud of what I had done.

The world flashed before me again and I saw the empty doorframe. I stood in the same place that Brin and I had discovered it, yet the ruins of buildings and even the dark and cursed ground was not there. Instead the world was still showed signs of green, even through the fallen leaves and chill in the air. This was not like the world I knew, a place full of disease, filth, and grey death. Instead of the wood frame I had seen before, there was an iron rectangle that stood before me. At the point of the keystone was the same exact symbol, along with the hook that was its companion in my waking life.

Again I was faced with the figures, each of them appearing in turn. First this time was the farmer. A light past quickly over him and I saw briefly his calm and gentle face, but his shadow did not match that which I saw. In his shadow I saw the image of a huge hulking monstrosity, a creature with many arms and clawed hands that undulated in anticipation of violence.

Then I saw The Baron again, his dark gaze and weathered face still holding the ambitious disdain I had come to know. Impatiently he stood, as if he waited for me to act. The thin neck of his shadow was the first thing I noticed about it. There was no doubt that the shadow of this terrible man was a skeleton wearing this same armor and holding a scepter.

Desecrated

Within the dream, my mind pained me as it gave me a vision of the scepter itself, away from this beautiful landscape and shadowy people. It was half as long as a sword and gleamed of silver. Intricate designs were finely etched into the surface of it, making rings which led from base to tip, and at the top were sharp spines that grasp a large amethyst shaped like two pyramids attached at the base of one another. Another flash of pain and I was returned to the shadow before me.

This time it was the young man dressed in a fine doublet. Trimmed with fine green silk, the doublet and cape were indeed masterfully made. Upon his sword belt, cape clasp, and even a ring he wore was the symbol of a raven with wings spread as if it were about to land upon its prey. His blonde hair blew in the wind, joyfully exposing his handsome face. The earring was a red stone caged in gold and dangling from his left lobe. His shadow seemed oddly the same, yet there was something ominous about the way the shadow itself stood. I could not put my finger on exactly what it was that bothered me.

The beautiful woman came last. Her raven hair seemed like strands of the very night sky, dark with shimmering spots of light that danced away from the sun. Her clothing was sheer enough to allow me sight of everything that made her a woman, yet she did not seem cold or embarrassed to be so vulnerable there in the open. Around her head was a circlet made of pure white metal with a single amber stone pressed into its center. There was something dancing behind her eyes, something that told me that she was not human. Her shadow seemed as though she were wearing a dress woven from thousands of spiderwebs. Even her head and hair lay mostly contained in the tangling webs. It seemed as though she were half trapped inside a cocoon. She looked as if she were about to speak, and then was gone.

Chapter 2

Replacing her, I saw the frame again, this time covered in wood, and the framework of a building was erected around it. Between me and it was a small crowd of soldiers holding prisoner the finely dressed young man. His clothing had been torn away, and he remained shirtless in the cold. The marks upon him told me that he had been beaten and tortured. His strength barely gave him the ability to stand, and so he leaned heavily upon his captors.

Among the soldiers was their commander, their Baron. The red rotting of his flesh already taken hold, so that half his face had been replaced by an empty bleeding skull. Still his gravelly voice boomed out, "This day I commit you to your resting place, Rimmul. May you rot in this maze." He motioned towards a soldier, and a person dressed in shabby clothes came forward. He lifted his arm towards the hook and as his sleeve fell back, I saw the bandages covering the many wounds in his flesh. As soon as the hook tasted the delicious life within his blood, the frame flashed with light and in its wake a dark hallway appeared beyond. "You know what to do with him." He barked at the soldiers carrying him. They nodded and went into the passageway.

The scepter in The Baron's hand pulsed with a deep blue light and the Baron carefully admired the gemstone atop it. With a sickening grin he spoke to it. "Aw. Do you want out, my love? Now that your precious traitor is dead you can spend eternity in there, with your accursed spiders." Sinister hatred lived in the laughter that rose from him first and then from the rest of his men that joined him in spiteful celebration.

A flash, and now I was standing inside a tavern at night. There only a small amount of light coming from the dying fire within the hearth, but the low light was not a problem for me. I could see clearly, even in the darkness. The common room of the tavern where I found myself was empty and beyond the bar, lurking in

Desecrated

the back of the room like a hidden scorpion, I saw the door. Above it was the hook, just as it had been in all the other visions. Before I could go investigate, a young woman came sneaking down the stairs from above. She opened the front door to let three young men in as well, but did so very stealthily. Each of them slinked into the room, only opening the door wide enough for each of them to pass.

"I think I found the way in to the Maze," she whispered to the largest of them. "Not sure exactly how it works, but it fits the story he told us."

"Really? Where is it?" asked the skinny fellow that came in behind the large one.

As they crossed the room, they looked directly at me but did not seem to notice me. It was as if I were simply a ghost haunting the room. The rugged young man that had come through the door last remained quietly in the back and watched for onlookers.

The four of them wandered to the back door and she pointed out the hook. "There. I don't know why I never noticed it there before."

"Well, what do we do with it?" The large one asked her quietly.

She shrugged, "Not sure. How did the thing go again?"

Quietly rifling through his pockets, the skinny one produced a scrap of paper and read aloud,

Chapter 2

"Inside a warlord's open wound
princely guests find themselves bound
keeper's blood knows the way in
hidden beneath a sadistic grin

halls twisted like the makers mind
made with powers of the forbidden kind
beware those who would enter this maze
high will be the price he pays

the master of these hidden halls
knows every creature therein that crawls
nothing hidden from his eyes
thus a journey here is most unwise

twisting, turning, falling down
souls buried in the ground
thoughts of entry you should not entertain
else in the depths you may remain"

They all looked at each other in silence, trying to figure out some elusive riddle, that is until the curious young girl spoke up, "Well, it looks like the hook has some dried blood on it. I am gunna try something," and she rose her hand as to prick her finger upon it.

The stern rugged one stepped forward. "Bad idea. I am not sure you should do that."

"What could happen? It probably isn't going to work anyway," the big one replied.

The rugged man sighed, "Fine. Do whatever you want."

Desecrated

"Ok. Here it goes," she said and stood on the tip of her toes to reach the hook.

I could hear her take air in sharply as the metal of the hook drew a lusty drink from her flesh, but nothing seemed to happen. "Well? What happened?" The skinny one excitedly asked.

Disappointed the girl responded, "I don't think anything happened. Ugh. What do we do now?"

From behind them all the rugged one asked, "Did you try opening the door?"

The big one stared at him for a moment before grasping the handle and turning it gently. "It's stuck," he complained.

"No, silly, it is just locked," the young girl said, and she turned the handle on the bolt holding the door shut.

The bolt clicked open, and the big one gave a look to the rest of them that seemed ask, "Are you ready?" After getting silent confirmations from his companions, he pushed the door open. Instead of the snow dusted woods behind the building that they were expecting, they found the same dark hallway that I had seen The Baron send his men into. All four of the brave youngsters went through the door, but before they could close the door behind them, I heard the big one say, "Boy, your dad is going to be pissed."

With this friendly jab and the closing of the door, they were gone. The world faded to black around me, and yet I saw a glow in the air before me. The unearthly beauty of the raven haired women appeared softly in the light. Her slightest smile sent a tickle up my spine. Her lips did not move, yet I heard her say, "Find me." With this final request, I found myself in the dream no more.

Chapter 2

"Wrack?" Brin's voice was filled with concern. I felt her hand on my shoulder, shaking me gently. My eyes opened to meet the soft emerald of her gaze. "You ok?"

"Yeah," I replied weakly. "I am fine."

She withdrew from me, with even the quickest of glances I could see her frustration. "Where do you go when you are like that? It's like you are in an uzkin' trance or something. It is very, very strange. I worry that your mind is being attacked from outside. Perhaps even from the Doomed that made you, whichever one it is."

"I see things, Brin. Things that were or are. Maybe they are just meaningless dreams, I don't know."

"You see things? Like visions? Are you able to interact with them?"

I nodded. "Sometimes. Most of the time they are just flashing images or scenes with people I don't know. I don't know how else to explain them."

Her anger rose, and with it the glowing runes on the Ukumog increased their intensity matching pace with her emotion. "You see? It is secrets like this that I don't like. Let's imagine for a moment that the Doomed can plant images into your mind. What happens if we get into a fight and suddenly your friends look like foes? Hrm? What the uzk do you think happens next?"

"I didn't say anything because I didn't know it was strange. I thought they were just like the dreams that you humans have–"

"You humans? So, now you think you are better than us?!" As her anger piqued, so did the glow of Ukumog. Around me, I felt the air get charged with energy like it had just before Sally had been stolen into the night.

My hands instinctively went up in front of me, empty palms towards her. "Brin. Calm down. I am just figuring all this out. I crawled out of a grave without so much as a name. You and

Desecrated

Avar are my closest friends and I would never do anything to hurt either of you. No one has shown me as much kindness as you two, and I hope that one day I can return the great favor you have done for me."

With arms crossed she silently stared at me, but Ukumog's dimming told me that her temper was fading. "Fine. Then tell me about these visions. In particular the one you just had."

"Well, I remember a seeing flashes of people, one of which I know was the Baron."

"Holy uzk, you see the Doomed in these visions?" She interrupted.

Pretending to be upset, I said, "You want to hear about this or not?"

"Yes. Ok. Right, I'm sorry." She sat on the wall nearby.

"Ok." I joined her on the wall. "To answer your question, I see them in many different times. I think anyway. Sometimes they are who they were before they were cursed, and others after. This vision seemed to center around the doorframe here. I think it has something to do with a place called The Maze, but I am not sure what that means."

"The Maze? Really?" She nearly leapt off the debris. "I wonder if there is anyone still trapped inside. How do you open it, did you see that in the vision?"

"Actually, yes. The hook there. People would prick their finger on it and the way would open into a dark passageway beyond."

She inspected the hook from directly below it.

"Murks not think that a good idea, Brin-lady. The Maze am a dangerous place!" Murks nearly shouted in his tiny little voice from the hem of my robes where he was hiding.

Chapter 2

Brin turned and gave him a little smile. "I might not be the sharpest blade in the rack, little Murks, but I am not stupid. Now Avar on the other hand… Where is that silly bastard? He should be back by now."

"I am sure he is fine. If there is a Shadow Hunter cache nearby, he is probably just trying to carry back more than he should," I said with a chuckle.

Brin too laughed a little and mimicked Avar clumsily trying to carry too much stuff. "Gods, what is with me lately? My moods are all over the place. You must think I'm crazy."

"No Brin. I don't. I think you are taking on more than you wanted with caring for all these people. Which I, for one, am grateful for. But I also think that Ukumog is having an effect on you. Have you noticed that the intensity of its glow changes with your mood?"

A scowl appeared on her face, "When a woman asks you a question like that, you aren't supposed to respond with facts."

"Sorry. My excuse is the same as always. I am less than a year old." I chuckled but she didn't find it funny.

Clink! Ukumog was in her hands and she inspected the surface of the blade. "Does it really change?"

"Yeah, and sometimes it can be a little frightening."

She laughed, "With the stories I have heard about it, Ukumog should be scary."

"I thought it was your father's sword." My statement was nearly a question.

"It was, but he didn't make it. Now, the Shadow Hunters don't believe this, but in Sunder I found a story that said that it was made by the Betrayer out of the blood and bones of a god." The grin on her face told me that this story is the one she would prefer to believe, no matter what may actually be true.

Desecrated

"Interesting. How did your father get it?"

At the mention of her father, her mood became darker, "I don't know the whole story, to be honest. All I know is that he found it. It was after he found Ukumog that he started adventuring. Of course that was before he had even met my mother, so…"

"From all you have told me, he sounds like he was a great man."

Brin's back straightened and her gaze returned to the runes on Ukumog's blade. "I like to believe he was. Some people have told me that he was nothing more than a thief with a magic blade, but I don't believe that."

There was a stone of guilt in my gut for bringing up the subject of her father, but having got her talking about him for the first time I could not help but try to feed my curiosity. "How old were you when he was killed?"

"Almost six. Sometimes I have dreams that make me think I saw it happen, but I know I wasn't there." Her face tensed and she wiped her eyes, preventing the appearance of any tears. "Uzk. Thirty years later and it still tears me up."

Not knowing what to say, I just remained there with her. We watched the refugees all huddled together there in the cold. It made me want to embrace Brin and tell her that everything would be ok. That together we would find who murdered her father, and give him the vengeance that he so deserved. My fear of the hunger for her warmth lurking within me kept me at bay. I just sat there silent and helpless, waiting for the conversation to have some reason to change.

Chapter 2

Sensing my desire, Murks walked in tiny steps over to Brin's boot and hugged it. Surprised, Brin let out a gasp that was nearly half of a laugh and she let the tears escape her eyes. "It ok Brin-lady. Master going to help you make it right. You see," his tiny voice reassured her.

Silently she fought against the sobbing and tears that battled to escape. After many moments of inaction, I could not help but reach out to her. I placed my icy hand upon hers, and gave it a gentle squeeze. Her leaking eyes met mine, and I sat their drinking in the beauty of her darkly framed face. "I don't know what kind of monster I am, Brin. Or what power lies hidden inside me, but while I am here, you are not alone."

Unexpectedly, she lunged forward and embraced me. Her face buried in the folds of my robe, and it quietly accepted her unwanted tears. My arms found their way around her, and I tried to comfort her while I resisted the hunger that battled against my senses. It wanted her warmth, her life, but I could not allow that.

Commotion came from the refugees, and broke the quiet of our time together. Brin abandoned the embrace we shared and quickly brought back her stern and angry demeanor. Murks too scuttled to hide within his secret pocket, while I scanned to see what was going on.

Catching the sight of a familiar tall blonde man, I spoke, "Looks like Avar has returned." The two of us stood and walked over to him and the rest of the group. I gave a single glance to the door of the Maze, standing there exposed in the center of this ruined town. Mentally I said, "We shall see each other again." It being a thing of magic and metal, made no reply, for which I was secretly thankful.

"Brin, we have to get out of here. Something's happened..." Avar was speaking very quickly.

Desecrated

"Whoa, slow down Avar. What happened? Where are the supplies?" Brin asked.

Avar shook his head and became very animated with his arms. "You don't understand. We need to go. Something's happened at Sanctuary. We need to go now."

As if on cue, the sound of many boots thundered upon our position. "Forget about Sanctuary, we might be the ones in trouble here," I said.

Ukumog replied, *Clink!*

Chapter 3

Men coated in The Baron's colors flooded our position. One of the frightened refugees tried to flee in the opposite direction while the rest of them remained huddled like frightened sheep. David could not move on his own so he remained resting upon the ground. Avar's instincts kicked in and he made his mace and shield ready. The shield, while missing the top portion, was still marked with the symbol of the red skull, as he had taken it from a dead guard in Yellow Liver. As the front soldiers came upon us, seeing the symbol distracted them long enough for Avar to strike one of them in the head with his mace. The mace did its horrible work and left the soldier's skull cracked beneath his helm. From behind the front line of the oncoming assault, there came the distinctive *thwap* of a crossbow firing. The sound was followed by a bolt that whooshed by us to steal away the life of the fleeing refugee. As I watched him collapse lifelessly behind us, I felt guilty for never even asking him his name.

Brin's body came to life with battle, her swords and hair began the dance that I had seen many times. Two of the soldiers were dead before they had recovered from the surprise attack from Avar. The other men were not as stunned, and began flanking us on both sides. Before anyone else could do more to tire themselves fighting, we were surrounded and outnumbered by at least three

Desecrated

to one. "Enough!" shouted a voice from the host of soldiers, and instantly The Baron's men paused their engagement. "Lay down your weapons and no one else has to die!"

Avar and Brin hesitated. "What happens when we surrender?" Avar asked after sizing up the fifty or so men that surrounded us.

"You will be placed under arrest and taken back to Skullspill. The magister there will decide what happens to you next. Continue to fight and we will be forced to kill all of you, starting with the unarmed civilians," callously called out the voice of their leader.

"Brin, I can't let them murder these people," Avar whispered to her. "We have to surrender."

Brin's jaw flexed as she ground her teeth. "Uzk!" She howled in frustration. "That's it? All this way, surviving Yellow Liver and we end up arrested?"

Avar threw down his mace, "Look on the bright side. We are finally going to Skullspill."

She ignored his sarcasm and while every other person threw down their weapons, she delayed to show her lack of personal fear of our captors. Only then did she lay down her weapons. As soon as her hand left the handle of Ukumog, the runes vanished.

The person of voice who was barking orders had become known to us as our disarming happened. Even through the visor of his helm, I saw the strange look he gave to Ukumog as Brin laid it upon the ground. "Arrest them," he ordered his men and they came forward with ropes. They tightly bound our hands in front of us, with a large knot between our wrists.

Removing his helmet the commanding officer spoke to all of us, "I am Sergeant Valence. You will not be harmed on your way to Skullspill, so long as you follow my orders without question.

Chapter 3

Any thoughts of escape will be treated with a quick and harsh response." He nodded in the direction of the lifeless man who tried to escape, as one of his men recovered the bolt from the back of the dead man's neck.

Observing the soldiers as they made their arrests, I noticed that a small handful of the men wore a small image of a jawbone as a belt buckle. As I watched the host of our captors, it seemed that those marked that way were higher in station than the others. Indeed, even the Sergeant had one of these same buckles. "Brin, what do the belt buckles mean?"

Still frustrated, she returned a small grunt and a shrug. The soldier who was tying our bonds spoke without looking up from his work. "It means they are part of The Jawbone, one of the elite companies in service to his Holiness, The Baron."

Brin surrendered a snarky laugh, "Don't they have something better to do than to arrest some refugees from Yellow Liver?"

The soldier silently shrugged. From the other side of the group, I heard David's voice. "I can walk, I think."

"You best keep up, or you will be food for the wolves." Said the solider that was tying him up.

David gave a slight laugh, "Well, let's hope it doesn't come to that."

Over the whole camp there wasn't much in the way of commotion or fighting against our captors. The loudest form of dissension came from the venomous glances Brin was giving to the soldiers. A curious look came over the Sergeant and he found himself walking over towards Brin. "What is your name, young woman?" He couldn't have been much older than Brin from the look of him, but his humor rolled off her shell of anger. "I see. Not much of a conversationalist, eh?"

Desecrated

Casually he strode over to the men collecting our weapons from the ground and he reached his hand out to grab Ukumog. Before his hand could connect with the bone handle, he hesitated and looked over at Brin. Rage was rising in her. I imagined that her own inner voice was screaming obscenities at this man who was about to casually toy with the blade she spent years searching for. His hand carefully moved toward the handle. Fingers wrapped slowly around it and gently he lifted the heft of the blade. My muscles flexed, remembering the heavy weight of the flat piece of black steel attached to the leather wrapped bone handle. A dark part of me wished that I were the one holding the blade. Each step he took back towards us seemed like eternity. Everything around us was slow and nearly silent. As the soldiers began tying each of the refugees together in a great chain, all I could hear was the creaking of the knots and the footfalls of the Sergeant.

"So, where did a pretty little thing like you find a nasty piece of work like this?"

"Found it," she responded sharply and then returned to grinding her teeth.

Valence sized her up and then looked back at the blade. "If you keep clenching your jaw like that, your teeth will just grind away. That would be a pity, as I am sure you have a wonderful smile."

She was not amused by his remarks.

"Don't mind if I keep this do you? I am sure that The Baron would love to see it."

"He won't get a chance to see it," she stated coldly.

Valence paused for a moment. "Why won't he? We are taking you to Skullspill, after all."

Chapter 3

"Somewhere between here and there something is going to happen. Something horrible. And when it does, I will have my blade back."

A smile emerged on his face, "Oh, will it now? Lads!" He called out to his men, "Looks like we have a bard in our midst. Next thing you know, she might sing us the song of rebellion." The soldiers gave a scattered laugh. Valence came close to Brin, their faces nearly touching. "Or perhaps, I will just return this thing to my friend Grumth. You remember him. Eh Brin?" Before she could respond, he turned away from her and called out to his men. "Move out! We head for our lord's keep and the heart of our homeland. To Skullspill."

Cheers rose from the gathered soldiers who formed columns on either side of us, and we began our march towards the dark city of The Baron.

Our march only went on for a few hours before the darkness of night fell upon us. During that time, I kept looking for the smallest of opportunity to talk more with Brin about the things I had seen in my visions, but there were too many eavesdropping ears. Instead, I just followed behind her, watching the dark locks of her hair bounce as she led the way on our chain of rope.

Several more hours passed in the darkness of the night. The soldiers were taking us along the roads, which made the travel easier, but it was not easy for the refugees. Many of them began stumbling as we walked, and the threats of our captors could only keep their exhaustion at bay for so long. Before any of the soldiers actually started handing out the death and torture that they were so eager to threaten us with, Sergeant Valence ordered camp to be set. In a short and orderly time, we had found a place just off the road and a camp was created. Stakes were driven into the ground and the great chain of rope that bound us all together was lashed to them. It was so tight to the ground that we could not stand up comfortably, which was exactly what the soldiers had set out to do.

Many times during the camp setup, I found the Sergeant looking over at me with a concentrated stare. More often than not, when he realized that I was looking back he would find some excuse to look away. I remembered how Avar had once told me that the Tainted, as he called me, were somehow imbued with the power of death and thus trapped in a body closer to undeath than life. Finding some time where we were under less scrutiny, I asked Avar, "Tell me more about the tainted."

"Uh, what? Oh. The tainted. Well. No one seems sure about their origins. Some people speculate that they were created by the power of the Doomed. Possibly indirectly. There are soldiers that fight for The King that are undying tainted called revenants." He paused to think, "Hey! You could be one of the revenants! I don't know why I didn't think of that earlier." The happiness that his theory gave him faded as quickly as it had come, "Oh. That is really bad, actually. It means two things. First, you work for The King and as such, you might be compelled to his service. Second, we are being held by The Baron's men, and The King and The Baron hate each other."

"Well, that is comforting," I joked.

Avar kept talking as if he hadn't even heard me, "I suppose the creatures that The Ghoul created in his own image were tainted too. Though if that is the case, it seems to confirm the idea that the tainted are somehow tied to the Doomed. Man, I wish they hadn't taken my book. I need to write all this down."

"Somehow I feel like I should be flattered that you consider me a scholarly project." The dead delivery of my comment made Brin give a sarcastic half laugh.

Chapter 3

"It isn't just that, Wrack. I mean... I haven't ever seen anything like you before. Gaak, I don't even know if you are one of the tainted or if any of this stuff I have been spouting is true. Part of the reason I am stuck with Brin is because I need to experience the world." He gave our captors a wary look. "I just hope I survive to see more of it once we get to Skullspill. The Baron doesn't take kindly to... Well. You know."

Silence fell over us and I struggled against my bonds a bit. The fibers of the rope creaked complaints at my testing its strength. The sound was loud enough that one of the soldiers guarding us gave me a stern look and lowered his weapon at me menacingly. While I knew he wouldn't be able to kill me, I didn't want to make our stay with the soldiers unpleasant for they already scared refugees.

"So, what was it that you were coming to tell us before this all happened, Avar?" When I looked over at him, I found him fast asleep.

"I don't know how he does that so fast. Guess they have to teach them to sleep anywhere," Brin said quietly. "So tell me more about these dreams you keep having."

I smiled. "Well, apart from the Doomed, the one thing I see over and over again is a scepter crowned with a purple stone."

Brin's brow furrowed. "A scepter? Do you see who has it?"

"Yeah." A heavy sigh escaped me. "It is always The Baron who has it."

A shiver ran through her body. "Figures. Of all the Doomed, he is the most ambitious. He is also probably the most arrogant and terrifying. I really have no desire to ever meet him."

"The last time I saw it, he was using it in chorus with that gate we found in Marrowdale. It might be some kind of key or something."

Desecrated

"Have you asked our resident know-it-all about it yet?"

My jaw tightened. "No. I cannot escape the thought that he might just decide that I am some evil creature and try and dispatch me."

She giggled slightly, "I wouldn't worry about that. Avar is pretty convinced that you are important to my quest for revenge." She made a face that was supposed to be Avar. "Golly gosh, Brin. My father says that there are no real coincidences in this world, and the fact that you saved this stranger and he just happened to be this mysterious being. Well, it just has to be part of the untold prophecy," she said in a childish voice mocking Avar. "I just hope his father is right."

Curious about her statement, I interjected, "I thought that the prophesy was told already? How can there be an untold prophecy?"

She rolled her eyes, "Look, I don't know all the details about that gaak. Garrett and the lot of them are convinced that my father was killed before he could finish telling his part of the prophecy, and no other storyteller has been 'blessed' to continue his work." Her sarcasm was thick when she uttered the word blessed. I chuckled a little, and she continued on. "I think the bunch of them are uzkin' daft. Sure, I have seen things I can't explain, but wizards and things can pull magic out of the sky too. I don't understand how it is different when you bring it forth by the will of some stupid moon-dwelling thing."

"So, you don't believe in the same things that Avar does?"

Brin sighed and lay back on the ground. She turned her face to Ukumog's resting place with Sergeant Valence. "I don't know what I believe anymore." Quiet filled the space between us, and before long I was the only one awake.

Chapter 3

There in the camp I sat, alone, lashed to the ground and my fellows. The dark sky above was home to very few stars and a silvery moon that mostly lay hidden behind a misty veil of clouds. In the long reaches of the cold night, all the prisoners twisted and turned, their warmth being stolen by the winter air around us. In her sleep, Brin tried to find some source of warmth to curl around. Only finding my side, she used the fabric of my robes to help protect herself from the cold. What brief contact she actually had with me, made her recoil at my icy touch. Avar was the only one who seemed to sleep soundly, even comfortably, despite the stinging cold of night.

The soldiers did keep a fire burning at their camp, and there were always at least a few of them on watch. A few hours before the late dawn of the winter morning, Sergeant Valence was awake and testing the weight of Ukumog again. Catching my eye, he wandered over towards me. "So what is your story then, friend," he asked while standing with Ukumog gripped in his hand as if he might suddenly need use of its unforgiving edge.

I pondered how to respond. Should I ignore his mocking statement that we were somehow companions? Would any response I gave just provoke an attack upon me or my friends? Why does he care about what I have to say at all? My internal dialogue left him waiting.

"No interest in talking, I see. Can't say as I blame you." He crouched down and placed Ukumog in his lap. He waved off the soldier that had been watching us, leaving only him and me awake near the great chain of prisoners. "I assume you know who she is," he indicated Brin, "and what this frightening thing is." Again he lifted the black blade and pointed it skyward. For a moment he marveled at its form. Even without the glowing blue runes that normally could be seen upon the flat sides of it, the blade

Desecrated

was menacing. Yet I said nothing. "They say that this blade was forged out of pure hatred. Now, I don't believe that emotions can take form like this, per se, but it is an interesting thought. Funny how it glows when she carries it, huh? Perhaps I lack the necessary level of anger. Have you ever been tempted by its horrible beauty?"

I felt like there was something he was trying to tell me. Something he wanted to say but couldn't. Perplexed by the situation I remained silent, as was my way.

"Not your thing then, I take it. War is a nasty thing. Especially when you see it endlessly about you. I'm told that the older you get, the faster that time goes by and how things all just run together. I cannot imagine an eternal life filled with nothing but death. Is that why you ran away? To escape the sinister commands of your masters in Flay?"

"Master, he thinks that you are a revenant from the city of The King who has escaped the bonds of the Doomed. It might be best to let him believe that," the tiny voice of Murks echoed my own thoughts.

I subtlety nodded. "When people talk about eternity, only those who have lived for countless lifetimes can even comprehend the weight that it brings."

Valence smiled, "He speaks at last." His eyes spoke of a great debate wriggling within his mind. "I wish we had more time, friend. But soon we will get to Skullspill, and then you are out of my hands. Know that I am truly sorry for the life we took back in Marrowdale. Our encounter would be different if it were only the other Jawbones and myself." The ground crunched beneath him as he stood and started to walk away. After a few steps he turned and asked, "What is your name, friend?"

"Wrack," I responded without thinking.

Chapter 3

His eyes became slits. "Pleasure to meet you, Wrack." Before he could say anything else, he became distracted with something in the dark woods behind me. His soldierly instincts took over and he threw Ukumog to the ground and drew his own blade. A blade that was long and thin, and the steel of its length was the dark red of a scab over a healing wound. "ALARM!" he shouted. Instantly, his men became whirlwinds of preparation as they collected their armaments.

A wind passed around me as something large flew over my head. The ground crackled with the weight of the man who landed upon it, and the wind that chased him had the smell of death riding along with it. From where I sat, I could only see a dark cloak with long white hair streaming from his head. The cloak was ancient and full of holes, much as my robes looked when I escaped the grave that gave birth to me.

"Ah. Sergeant Valence. Pleasure to meet you and your men again. You must be losing your edge, for me and my men to catch you so off guard." The sinister voice of the white haired man called out loudly. He looked behind him and out of the woods there came soldiers clad in the green and white of The King.

"To arms, men! The Vampire is upon us!" Valence cried out.

The Vampire laughed as if he were cruelly mocking a child that he had just pushed down a flight of stairs. "Surrender now, and I will let at least some of you live," he said brushing back his snowy hair.

Brin awoke and scrambled to sit up. Immediately she started fighting against her bonds trying to get free. Avar and the other refugees awoke thereafter, due to the shaking of the chain of rope that bound us all together. "Oh uzk. The uzking Vampire? We are so dead!" Avar's first words were less than encouraging.

Desecrated

"Shut it, Avar! Everyone, try to get free!" Brin screamed as the battle began around us, and we all struggled at our bonds in vain.

Battle erupted around us. Arrows and bolts were fired back and forth, either side scoring some hits against their opponents. The refugee who was sitting next to Avar received the gift of a crossbow shaft directly in the eye, causing her to fall back instantly like a rag doll. The spray of blood that misted Avar made him hesitate only for a moment, and then added some fervor to his struggle against the rope.

The Vampire had waded directly into the fray and was using both sword and clawed hand to rend The Baron's men asunder, occasionally even tossing maimed bodies this way and that. Valence's dark red blade began to dimly glow with a red aura and he scored a few hits on The Vampire's arm, forcing him to give some ground. As The King's men pushed forward, they completely ignored us. A few only pausing slightly to make sure that there were no armed opponents mixed in with the helpless prisoners. In the few short moments that the battle had gone on, Valence and his men were pushed back, well away from the camp itself, and we all remained subdued behind the back ranks of The King's army. Even from this distance, I saw The Vampire raise the edge of his own blade to the flesh his other arm and carve a long bleeding wound.

Valence, seeing this also cried out, "Close your mouths! To imbibed the blood of this beast means painful death!"

Many of Valence's men heeded his words, but some did not, and were unprepared when The Vampire swung his arm, spraying blood over the men around him. I saw one man catch some in his mouth, and after trying to cough and spit out the foul draught he had been surprised with, black streaks appeared on his face and

Chapter 3

the burning pain that it caused forced him to the ground, where one of The King's men drove his sword directly through his throat exclaiming, "Here filth! Let me help you with that."

Surrounded by death, fear, anger, and the sadistic pleasure of The Vampire, I found an unnatural strength growing in me. My fists clenched, I twisted my wrists and pushed against my bond in an effort to tear free of them. Our force combined, as well as the struggling back and forth of the rope, forced one of the many stakes to pop out of the ground, then another, and another. Things were going well, until a voice cried out on the field. "My Lord! The Blade!"

Instantly, The Vampire turned and looked at his man who was starting to lift Ukumog off of the ground. The runes of the blade had come to life and were shining brightly against the cold night. The Vampire immediately pushed his way out of the fray and leapt to the place where his man held the blade.

"Uzk that," Brin quietly exclaimed, then shouted, "That is my sword, you arrogant blood sucking prick!"

Her shouting had done its work. It distracted the Doomed from the blade for a brief moment. He looked over at Brin and smiled, his fanged mouth betraying his otherwise gauntly handsome appearance. "Do not trouble yourself, little one. I will give you attention soon enough."

Brin's struggle against the ropes became not of desperate attempt to escape, but one of unbridled rage, her eyes wide and screaming for blood, her hair a maelstrom of dark fury, yet no escape from the expertly tied ropes could be found. Her distress made me dig deeper into whatever dark strength lay within me. I pressed against the ropes and felt them creak against my growing power. Icy cold shot through my spine and I felt remorseless hatred fill my heart.

Desecrated

Sheathing his own elegant blade, The Vampire reached for the boney handle of Ukumog. The soldier gladly gave up the blade to his master, and with a sinister grin of victory, the fingers of this ancient Doomed undead wrapped around the macabre handle of the frightening blade. Brin's hatred and frustration filled me, a rage not unlike the one I felt when we faced The Ghoul filled my soul. It was cold and unrelenting. It was merciless and burning. I was lost within a gale of pure malice.

A loud bang rang out over the camp. The Vampire howled in miserable pain as lightening shot from the blade through his body and up into the dark sky. At that very same moment, the bonds that held my right wrist were broken. The Vampire cast Ukumog from his grasp and sent it spinning through the air. Fixated on the stunned Doomed before me, I only felt the rope slacken when Ukumog landed so perfectly in the ground between Brin and I that it sliced the rope that had kept us bound together. Brin did not hesitate when the time came, but instead stood up, and even with her hands bound grabbed the handle of Ukumog and wrenched it free of the cold dirt.

A cry echoed from the back ranks of The King's men, "Hunters!"

More commotion entered the fray, as several more soldiers came rushing into the conflict, all of them wearing silver mantles like the one Avar wore. This addition to the battle caused the seasoned soldiers of both Doomed to become wary, not only of each other, but of the new threat, thus signifying that this new group was no ally to either side. The Vampire grasped his wounded sword hand and grimaced in pain as he shot murderous glances at Brin, who was slowly taking steps toward him, the eager blade in her hand glowing with such intensity that it was hard to look directly at it.

Chapter 3

"That blade does not change who wields it, little one. I have heard the stories of your father's misadventures. I dare say, the apple has not fallen far from the tree. You will both die as fools."

"If my father died a fool, then I would gladly die as one." She coldly responded, but before she could charge at him, a beast shaped like a man lunged from behind our position and collided with The Vampire. The broken chain of rope allowed for the remaining refugees to flee back into the woods where there were more Shadow Hunters motioning for us to run.

"Brin, we have to go," Avar pleaded.

She contemplated charging into the fray. The Vampire had recovered from the shock of grasping the blade and was now completely engaged by the slavering wolfman that he was fighting. She turned and looked at me.

"We should go," I told her.

Without saying another word, we were all running through the dark unknown of the forest, Brin at my side, David running near me, so I could help him up should he stumble in the dark, and Avar running slightly behind us with a small swarm of the surviving refugees with him. The sinister glow of Ukumog told me that it still yearned to taste the life of the Doomed who dared to take the blade as his own.

Desecrated

Chapter 4

The sounds of the battle echoed through the barren trees of the forest, preventing our complete escape from the conflict. Each branch that caught one of the refugees forced a sound of fright from them that just helped their tired and freezing bodies to run even further from the danger that we left behind. The panic that lingered and the darkness of the wood became its own challenge. Our small group started breaking apart, and soldiers from the battle began chasing us through the woods. When I looked behind me, I could no longer see any of the refugees, or even Avar, only soldiers wearing the green diagonal stripe on a field of white; The King's livery.

"Brin!" I called out into the night, hoping that she and Ukumog would come to my rescue. Using my ability to see in the darkness did not aid me. Something was causing the blanket of night to even overpower my dark gifts. Real fear burrowed into my heart. Not fear for my safety, for I had no fear of pain or death. They were my silent companions wherever I found myself. No, it was the lives of those people that were somehow lost in the starless woods.

"Brin! Where are you?" I desperately cried out. Only the shuffling boots of my pursuers could be heard in reply. My strides shortened. I wanted them to capture me. A part of me hoped that through their influence, I would be returned to the people that I cared about. As they came closer, the shadow in my mind played through

Desecrated

the scenes of Brin fighting the soldiers, protecting Avar, David, and the others, but I knew she would not be willing to surrender this time. There would be no bargaining with the menacing edge of Ukumog. The shadow showed me their futile struggle against The Vampire and his men, and as I watched them become overwhelmed, the cold anger I knew so well froze my heart.

Stopping in my tracks, I turned to face my pursuers. Even from the distance between us, I could see fanatical madness in their eyes. I prepared myself against their charge. As the first one came to me, I weaved between the trees and watched as he hacked chunks of wood from the sleeping trunks. Pulling back a branch, I let it snap him in the face and he fell backward just as the second of them came towards me. Again, I dodged his attacks, using the trees as my shield. The giant knot still tied to my left arm became my next weapon, as I blocked his sword and then brought the solid mass of it against the side of his helmet. He stumbled and my first attacker was on me again. This time he was more cautious, even attacking branches of the trees purposefully to prevent me from using them again.

A pain shot through my chest as I felt the force of a crossbow bolt rip through my ribs. Screaming in pain, I saw a small piece of the shaft and its white fletching protruding from the right side of my chest. Instinctively I tried to pull it from my body, but my assailant distracted me with a sword blow to my left arm. Pain and cold flooded my right arm, and I brought my fist down on his sword shattering it with a loud bang that echoed through the trees. While he stepped away, stunned by the surprise of what had just happened, I forcefully removed the bolt from my chest. A spray of black blood exited the wound with the bolt, and I felt Murks scramble through my robes to the location of the wound. Ignoring the tickle of Murks' work, I strode forward and planted the bolt

Chapter 4

upwards through the bottom of the jaw that belonged to the soldier with the broken sword, driving the point of it through the fleshy interior of his mouth to find purchase in his brain. His eyes went wide and a stream of blood poured out through his nose and mouth. When I let go of the bolt, he fell to the ground to rise no more.

The other soldiers did not allow their fanatical desire to follow their master's command overwhelm their critical thinking. Instead they began to try and bait me to attack, hoping to find some weak point on which they could capitalize. Aware of their desires, I also took a defensive posture, secretly hoping that the noise would bring someone to my aid before The Vampire himself arrived to finish me off. Just thinking about his might coming to bear awakened a fear within me that perhaps I could be destroyed. If Avar were right, if I had been created by one of the Doomed, then certainly one of them can unmake me.

The soldier furthest back was attacked from behind by a form with a red glowing sword. "Valence," I whispered. It was enough that the other soldiers engaging me switched targets to the ones that were wielding weapons. As the two forces collided, I did not remain to see who would emerge the victor. Instead, I fled deeper into the darkness of sleeping trees.

Not far had I gone, before I encountered something else. The hairs on my neck and arms began to stand, much the same way that Ukumog's horrible glimmering countenance or the presence of The Vampire had made me react. Like frightened prey, I collapsed to the ground, and tried to remain silent and still. Be it either of those things, I would rather remain hidden until I knew if it were friend or foe.

Desecrated

"Wrack. Step out from the shadows and speak with me," said a familiar voice. The hairs on my neck told me that the source of this voice was the cause of my unease. "Come now, Wrack. Again, I have no desire to play games."

"Master. Master, Murks thinks that it is the Rotting One."

Murks was right. The voice, this time heard with my ears instead of directly in my mind was the same. The sickly feeling of decay rolled over me as I stepped out of the shadows to face him.

The noble, yet tattered, clothes remained the same as the last time we had met, yet being this close, I could see his one exposed eye. The color of it was a disgusting yellow green, and the edges were caked with tears of pus. "I know of your kind, Doomed. What is it you want with me?"

The Rotting One chuckled slightly, "Of course, right to the heart of it. Yes." A wet cough forced a pause, but then he continued. "All is not as it seems. You may know of us, but know this: Not all of us act with free will. At least not openly."

I scoffed in disbelief, "I don't believe you. It is the people of this world who have no free will. They have been reduced to living in terror." Hate rose within me, and I felt the stinging cold of my dark power rising. The burning force rose in my throat and I had to choke it back.

"The young always see the power of the old as chains which hinder them. What is different about you and your friends, Wrack, is that you have the power to change it. There are those of us bound into this," he motioned to himself, "horror, that yearn for freedom as well. The girl you are with. Is she truly the daughter of the last Bard?"

Stunned by what I thought he was saying, I hesitated to respond. Finally something in me changed, and I knew somehow that this cursed man needed my help. "Yes. Yes she is."

Chapter 4

A rotten smile erupted on his hideous face. "Good. Remember yourself, Wrack. Only after that will you be able to help her fulfill her duty. Both to herself and to the world."

"And how exactly do I do that?"

The knowing smile on his face returned no answers. "You will find your friends in that direction. I will harry those after you."

"Aren't they your men?"

His form became translucent, and within moments he was nothing but a green cloud of filth that crept along the crispy ground. Not waiting for an answer, I turned and ran in the direction that he had instructed. I suddenly felt like a pawn being played in a game where I had not been informed of the rules.

It wasn't long before I found the group of them. Most of the refugees, Brin, Avar and some of the hunters had rejoined. They looked as if they had been in a fight. All of the refugees that had previously been unarmed were now carrying makeshift clubs in their still bound hands.

When they noticed my approach, one of the hunters called out, "Who goes?"

I saw Brin squint, and she must have seen me in the shine of the light of Ukumog because before I could respond to the hunter she called out, "Wrack!" and began closing the distance between us. "Are you wounded? I heard you cry out, but couldn't find you."

Her concern was touching, and the soft look in her eyes made the cold pain of my dark power fade. "I am fine. Ran into some of the King's men back there, and I think that Valence is there too. I saw his sword."

"The creepy red glowing one?" Avar inquired.

I nodded.

Desecrated

"Right, we should keep moving then. If they are still fighting each other, the dark woods will make it easier to escape," one of the hunters said while trying to catch his breath. Without saying another word, the group began moving like a pack of wolves through the forest.

"Where are you taking us?" Brin asked the hunters who were leading the way.

A girl with long silky hair and cat-like eyes replied, "To Sanctuary."

This was all the answer that Brin needed, but I had no idea what Sanctuary was. Yet I trusted that Brin would protest if it was somewhere she did not wish to go. As the clash of the battle behind us grew distant, more hunters joined us from the dark woods and the pace of our flight was finally slowed. Two of the refugees succumbed to the complaints of their weakened bodies. Before I could come to their aid, our newfound allies stepped forward to lift them off the ground. "We have to keep moving," explained a large bearded man between heavy breaths. "Whichever side is victorious back there will no doubt come after us."

"Was that Ferrin back there?" Avar asked the bearded man.

"How do you think we found you in the first place, Avar? You little git, I thought we lost you back there when we got separated." He stepped forward and embraced Avar like I imagined a brother might.

"Good to see you as well, Bridain. I got the note about Sanctuary being under attack, but I didn't have time to head in that direction before we ran into trouble. It tends to follow Brin around."

Brin ignored his comment.

"Excuse me, but what is Sanctuary?" I asked sheepishly.

Chapter 4

Bridain gave me a quick glance, and then looked harder a second time. "Blimey, Avar. You didn't mention anything about traveling with one of the tainted."

One of the other hunters interjected, "Perhaps we should dispatch it right now."

Avar stepped between them and me, "No, no. This is Wrack. He is ok. He helped us kill The Ghoul back in Yellow Liver."

"What? The Ghoul is dead? No wonder the Doomed have all been woken from their lethargic slumber. You lot kicked over the hornet's nest," Bridain seemed so proud of Avar, I thought for a moment that perhaps they actually were brothers.

The silky haired woman smoothly chided, "How exactly did you kill one of the Doomed?"

"With this," Brin forcefully raised Ukumog to show them.

All of the hunters stopped and starred at the hungry blade. Fighting off the shock, Bridain spoke, "Oh my gods. You have the blade. For the love of the Silver Lady, after all that time. You actually found it?"

"No thanks to you lot. In fact," she turned to the cat-eyed woman, "Varif, you said I would never find it. If I remember correctly you uzkin' said it was destroyed when my father was killed. So uzk you."

Varif just glared at Brin with no possible return comment, because she was not the type of woman to ever admit she had been wrong.

"I suppose you all read the message, Bridain." Avar interjected, and when his comment was only returned with blank looks he continued, "The one that said that Sanctuary was under attack?"

Varif looked over at Bridain, then cast a dispassionate look back at Avar. "It is still under attack, Avar."

Desecrated

"What Varif means is that it is constantly under attack." Bridain had more to say, but would not say it. With the looks I was getting from the host of hunters, the fact that they had a possible servant of the Doomed in their midst was obviously the reason they were not forthcoming with any secrets.

"Cut the gaak Bridain," Brin barked in her usual way. "Tell us what the uzk is going on."

Bridain stared at her for a moment, but didn't answer. In silent frustration, he turned back to the journey ahead of us, still trying to put distance between us and the battle which now was distant enough to only occasionally bring a shout or scream to my enhanced senses.

The tension, while we marched through the woods, was thick. I knew that all the hunters were just waiting for the command to kill me. Each step seemed like an eternity. My mind played through the declaration of attack and the actions that followed. No matter the scenarios that I imagined, none had a good outcome. The least horrible of them was if I just let them end me without a struggle, mostly because I hoped it would be quick so that it would not put Avar and Brin at odds with them. The dark part of me did want this situation to turn nasty, and I had to fight it to prevent a verbal outburst while they silently fought over what to do with me.

The early lights of dawn burned the sky when a rustling came from the foliage near us. Quickly, I looked over to see a man in tattered clothing pushing through the unforgiving brush towards us. "Brin, someone is coming," I directed her to what I saw.

Her stance changed to be more ready for an assault then, as the man came into better view, her posture slackened. Avar cried out, "Ferrin!" and broke from the group to meet the gruff little man. The entire company came to a halt at Ferrin's arrival. He grunted

Chapter 4

hellos to everyone as he approached, even allowing Avar to give him a small hug, though his face while hidden from Avar showed that he was not very happy about it.

"Wot lads! We'z gave them the wot for, eh?" he exclaimed with celebration.

Bridain pushed through towards him, "You sure you weren't followed?"

"Nah. The only nasty fing ol' Ferrin smelt on the way back to ya is with ya." His beady eyes fell directly on me. "Wot you lads doin' marchin' wit dis fing?" Slowly he took steps toward me, each of them giving me the impression that he might pounce on me at any moment.

"Easy Ferrin. That tainted is a friend of Avar's," Bridain said with a mixture of truth and sarcasm.

Avar again found his way to Ferrin's side. The small beastly Ferrin had a face nearly covered in scraggly dark hair that made Avar's tall boyish form and this dark furry short one look like opposites in nearly every respect. "Wrack is ok, Ferrin. He helped us kill the Ghoul back in Yellow Liver."

Shocked, Ferrin's head snapped from me to Avar. "Wot? You actually wants me to believe dat you killed one of the Doomed?" He laughed a dark and harsh laugh. "Next you be tellin' us dat you got the beautiful Brin *singin'* at night."

Blush flooded Avar's already chapped face. "No, really. We killed it."

Ferrin paused for a second, then started to laugh again. "Bridain, you put da lad up to dis nonsense?"

Unable to remain silent any longer, Brin stormed over to Ferrin, "Quit laughing, you mongrel. We did kill him and here is the proof." With that she nearly planted the dimly glowing Ukumog in his face. "Still think it's funny?"

Desecrated

"Whoa. And you saw dat fing die, did ja?" Ferrin asked Avar.

Avar's eyes danced a bit before he answered, "Well. I, uh. Well. I was wounded and wasn't awake for the end of it all. But I saw the nearly exploded corpse of the thing."

"The Ghoul almost killed him, is what he means. What, you don't believe me? Uzk you, Ferrin. And uzk you too, Verif, just for good measure." Brin stormed back over to me and with a *Clink!* Ukumog was back dangling from her belt.

Ferrin lifted a dirty hand to his thick matted hair and scratched at it. Something about it seemed like a dog trying to get at his fleas. "So, you kilt it den Brin. You. Wif dat nasty bit of steel."

"Yeah. Yeah I did. But I couldn't have done it without both Avar and Wrack," she lied and shot me a look after it was done. It was a lie that had to be told; I had no desire to hold onto the glory of those harrowing moments in The Ghoul's lair. Nor did I think telling the truth about how I had been the one to wield Ukumog, and how something terrible awoke within me in brief time I was attached to the blade, was a good idea. She knew that if the hunters were told the truth, they were even more likely to cry for my blood.

Caution changed Ferrin's face, and he slowly stepped towards me. He sniffed the air as he came closer and stopped before he entered a distance where I might be able to do him harm. "Smells like dust and dirt, dis one does. Nufing like dem tainted dat work for da King. Wot's yor story den, eh? Come down wif a nasty case o' death?" The dark laugh rumbled through him again.

"Something like that," I calmly responded. "I don't like this touch of dark magic that haunts me anymore than you, believe me."

Chapter 4

"Dats the trouble, mate. I don't believe ya. Tainted ain't to be trusted. One second it's ull, 'Oh woe is me,' and the next ders a knife in yer eye. I'll be watchin' you, mate. Make no mistake." With his face and body he made a tiny lunge at me to emphasize his statement. The fact that I didn't flinch upset him, I think, because he walked away grumbling to himself.

"Ok then. Well. If Wrack is coming with us then you are going to have to vouch for him, Avar and Brin. Garrett isn't going to like us bringing a tainted into Sanctuary. If it is even possible," Bridain's voice had the tone of defeat.

Worried I whispered to Avar, "What does that mean?"

"Sanctuary has protections. He might be right though. You might not be able to get in. If you can't, well. They might just kill you on principle."

"Right," I sighed. "Best to hope that I can then."

The dawn came and we continued to march through the woods, and the travel continued through the next day as well. At one point it seemed that we drew close to Marrowdale again, but with the landmarks that I saw, I could not be certain. In the silent company of the hunters, I took up the task of counting the people traveling with us. There was Brin, Avar and me. Of the refugees, David and only four other refugees remained of what I believe was originally fifteen. Having suffered only the loss of three before the skirmish between the Baron's men and The Vampire, it seemed that things were worse than I had remembered. Perhaps many of them had either gotten lost or died in the woods while I was separated from them. The hunters numbered seven in total. Bridain, their bearded jovial leader. Verif, the silky haired woman with catlike eyes. And Ferrin, the short bestial man. The others had not volunteered their names, or even been willing to speak in more

Desecrated

than whispers while I was around. This made our total company to be numbered at fifteen. The group was the same size as what we had with us when our flight from Yellow Liver had begun, but now our path was completely different.

"I hate that we are going away from our goal," Brin vented privately to me early in the day. "We are going in completely in the wrong direction from either finding the supposed secrets in Flay, or hunting down that uzkin' wizard in Skullspill."

"Once we deal with this emergency for Avar, we can get back to it. I doubt the sovereign of Flay is going anywhere. And the wizard, well, he might just vanish again if he hears us coming," I said calmly. "Avar needs to be here. He just hasn't really been himself since that fight with the ghouls where that fellow Matthew died. Maybe reconnecting with his father, no matter how strained their relationship, will help him."

Brin clenched her jaw in frustration, "Yeah, you are probably right. I just hate getting side tracked. Really felt like I was finally getting somewhere."

I just smiled at her because I knew continuing to talk about it would just keep the anxious fire in her alive. When we stopped for an afternoon meal, Brin continued to quietly fume about her situation. One of the hunters came over to us and handed a small portion of the stew the hunters had made for everyone to Avar.

He gave her a boyish smile and said, "Thanks Tarissa."

Once her hand was free, she brushed her shoulder length blonde hair over her ear and smiled in return. "You're welcome Avar." Her brown eyes soon fell on me, and her young, innocent face turned to stone instantly. "Do you want some?" She asked me coldly.

"No. I will be ok. Make sure that the refugees have enough."

Chapter 4

Brin reached out without saying a word and took one of the steaming bowls from Tarissa. She looked at Brin with a brief moment of disdain and then continued about the camp.

Curious, I couldn't help but ask, "So, do you know all these people very well, Avar?"

Between slurps of his stew and with a mouth half full of food he replied, "Yeah. Grew up with most of them. They aren't so bad. Well. Varif and Tarissa are kinda exceptions. Varif is a sorcerer of sorts, and Tarissa enjoys sneaking around and stabbing the enemies of the hunters a little too much, I think."

"Apart from Bridain and Ferrin, they all seem so young."

Avar chuckled. "Yeah, the hunters don't exactly get much of a childhood. We start learning about the Doomed and how to fight them as soon as we can hold a sword. Some of us are just better at it than others." He frowned a bit. "I have always been better at the scholar part than the fighting part." Then shrugging he continued, "But, we all have our goddess given talents. I mean, Ferrin over there is not just a hunter. He is a guardian. One of the blessed children of the Silver Lady."

Confused I asked, "What is different about the guardians?"

"Did you see that wolf thing that was fighting The Vampire?" He didn't wait for a response. "That was Ferrin. The Silver Lady blesses the guardians with powers that allow them to transcend the fragility of human life. There just isn't that many left."

I could not believe what I was hearing, "Are you saying he is some sort of werewolf?"

Desecrated

"Well, yes, actually. But it isn't just that. The silver light of the moon actually flows through their veins, and as such the power of the Doomed is not as strong over them. Ferrin was one of my teachers growing up. He can be more than a little gruff at times. Sorry about what happened earlier."

"I kinda expected it. It surprises me that they actually let me live. So, about these guardians. If they can fight the Doomed toe to toe like that, why don't they all just swarm them and take them down?"

Avar let loose a heavy sigh, "Everyone asks that question. In fact it was my first question about them too. Ferrin really only ever said that they tried once, and it didn't go so well. On top of that, since the power of the gods has been kinda sealed off from most of the world, there haven't been any new guardians for a long time. I also don't think that they can just shrug off the power of the Doomed. They can just take more punishment from their dark magics than we normal folk can. That's all."

What a world I found myself in. Ancient undead lords of such dark power that they can seal off the very gods. Wizards and their little blood created servants. Swords that gleam with such malice that their thirst for blood is almost palpable. Now, I find that there are men who are imbued with such power of their forgotten gods that they can transform themselves into furious killing machines. I began to wonder if the monster inside me was the magnitude of horror I thought it to be. After all, if those who wish to heal the world are monsters too, how bad could I really be?

"Time to get moving!" Bridain bellowed before I could get lost any further in my thoughts, and before long we were back on the trail.

Chapter 4

Just before dusk we found our way to a clearing in the woods. It was flat and had hints of green amidst the usual pale yellow grass. The very air here calmed my restless spirit. I knew we had come to the place they called Sanctuary. Try as I might, however, I could see no buildings or people, just an open field of dying grass trying to choke out the few blades who dared to be alive.

Avar stopped and with glowing smile asked me, "Do you see it, Wrack?"

"I see a field, but I feel the calm in the air."

He slapped his hand on my shoulder and chuckled. "Breathe in the calm air and feel the life around you. Here in this place, you will find Sanctuary."

My eyes slowly closed and I felt a peace enter my mind. Something buried deep inside my forgotten life churned in the depths of my thoughts. For a moment I felt the rush of a losing battle around me. I heard the screams of my loved ones being killed. I knew the piercing stare of The Baron that haunted my dreams. As I breathed out, I let the calm wash over me and push those visions of conflict back into the depths of my memory. The smell of food and the buzz of happy people rose from the silent field to greet me and when I opened my eyes I was surrounded by many faces and a town of five buildings.

Bridain's face held confusion and worry. Ferrin's was full of contempt, as was Verif's. An older man with a bushy upturned mustache pushed through the crowd to see me. His blue eyes glimmered with so much determination and life; I knew he had to be Garrett, commander of the Shadow Hunters and father of Avar.

Desecrated

There was only a tiny moment of silence before the stern man confirmed his identity by living up to everything Avar had spoke about him, "What's this? You bring a one of the Tainted into our midst, Avar? Have you completely lost your mind?"

"Father–"

"Commander," Garrett interrupted.

Avar's tone changed to that of controlled anger, "Commander Garrett, this tainted is Wrack. He has helped Brin and me not only find the blade of her father, but also helped us kill The Ghoul!"

"You did what? You killed The Ghoul?"

"Yes, Commander. The Ghoul is destroyed, Yellow Liver is free."

"Foolish boy. You have woken the ancient evils from their stalemate by creating a vacuum of power, and we are not ready to take advantage of the situation. We are beset by an unknown attacker, and have been forced into a defensive position, yet you bring it upon yourself to dispatch one of the Doomed and ignore the messages sent out for all of us to return. Well done, apprentice. I hope your quest for personal glory is not the end of all of us." When he stopped, Avar looked like a puppy that had just been beaten by his favorite toy. "As for you," Garrett now addressed Brin, "I expected the flagrant disregard for our mission from you. I am sure that your father is smiling down on you from the silver forest because of your accomplishments. But, I would ask that you co-ordinate with us in the future should you just decide to go off and kill one of the enemy. The purpose of having one of us with you was that we could aid each other, not just us helping you with your mad quest for revenge. As to–"

Chapter 4

"Take your head out of your own ass for a second Garrett," Brin interrupted him. "Two things: We killed The Ghoul because he was starting to unleash his flesh eating minions on the people of the city AND because the Rotting One had marched an army on the city itself. In the chaos we did the best thing we could do. You haven't seen your son in almost two years, and this is how you treat him? And yet you have the gall to talk about how my father is smiling down on me? Uzk you, Garrett."

"Brin, it's ok." Avar meekly interjected.

"No Avar. It's not ok. Fathers shouldn't treat their children this way."

Garrett could remain quiet no longer, with a controlled booming voice he responded, "Enough. I don't have time for these petty arguments. Brin, as per the promise I gave you years ago, you are always welcome here. That thing that travels with you, however." His angry gaze fell on me and he pondered. I saw dark wheels turning in his head and I just waited for the order to cast me out or to have me killed. "It can stay, for the moment. Odd that the defenses didn't just destroy it. Because of this curious behavior and the strange manner that it has found its way to us, I cannot help but think that perhaps the Silver Lady wishes it to be so."

Of all the things I had imagined as his coming words, these were not in any way what I expected. Completely stunned, I could not even form a measure of gratitude before he continued on.

"Now. In celebration of Brin's deeds, we will have a dinner tonight where we will also fill you in on the matter which plagues us currently. Until then." With a formal nod, Garrett turned and strode off.

"That went better than expected," I said to no one in particular.

Desecrated

"You could have left out the insult, Brin. Father just doesn't have the family thing. He only has one thing on his mind. Duty," Avar said sadly.

Brin nodded, "He was just pissing me off, as usual. Anyway, dinner and then maybe we can find out what is going on around here. Ok, Avar?"

"Dinner sounds wonderful."

Bridain showed us to the bathhouse where we could wash up and get ready. The warm and clean water in the tubs were two things I had not yet experienced with bathing. To be surrounded in such soothing warmth, it filled me with a comfort that even seemed to make the fear and desire fade from my mind. I wanted to remain in its embrace forever. I could even sense little Murks, doing his best to mend the new tears in my robes while I bathed, and there was even comfort in that connection. When the water began to cool and I opened my eyes, before me I saw the glowing malice of Ukumog as it leaned against the wall. There was a tiny splash beside me, and when I looked over, the naked form of Brin was sliding into the tub next to mine.

"Eyes front," she yelled at me.

Awkwardly turning away I muttered, "Sorry. I didn't know it was you."

"I thought you were asleep. Since I hadn't seen that before, I figured you wouldn't want me to wake you. I just got tired of waiting." We sat there in the splashing quiet of the bathhouse, enjoying this comforting moment devoid of barbed beasts, vampires, and soldiers wearing the red skull of The Baron. We both silently stared at Ukumog and the door, knowing that we would have to return, if only to sate the terrifying hunger within the blade.

Chapter 5

A bell rang through the little town when it was time for dinner. As I made my way from the hot dressing rooms of the bathhouse to the giant mess hall, I marveled at the fine clothes and armor all trimmed in silver that the hunters wore. Even Avar was wearing a silver sash and finer clothes than I had remembered seeing on him.

"Why is everyone dressed up?" I asked him.

"Oh! Tonight isn't just to celebrate Brin killing The Ghoul, it is also one of the many feasts of the moon that all worshippers of the Silver Lady are supposed to have. I do them in private since Brin gets pissy when she sees me do them."

"Of course I do. All this ritual gaak is stupid. Uzkin' zealots," Brin muttered.

Before we could find a place to sit, one of the hunters came up to Brin, "Miss Brin, Commander Garrett has requested that you sit with him at his table."

She sighed deeply, "He what? Well, I am not going up there unless Wrack and Avar can sit with me."

Surprised by her response, the young hunter awkwardly responded, "Um. Let me check with the commander," and he scurried off to do so.

"Why does he make such a fuss over you?"

Desecrated

Annoyed by the whole situation, Brin refused to even comment. Luckily for my sake, Avar was envious enough of his father's attention that he offered an answer. "Because of who she is. He knows that the last Bard was Brin's father. Heck, I bet father even knew him. The Bards were blessed people of the Silver Lady, touched with divine inspiration, and the mouthpieces of the prophecy. There are people in this hall that think that Brin might be the next Bard."

"Uzk that," Brin muttered. "I am not going to be sitting around singing songs for pennies and then run off to die on some fool's quest." I saw the muscles in her jaw flex as she ground her teeth together. I knew we had tread too roughly on the subject of her father.

Over at the table with Commander Garrett, the hunter speaking to him gestured at the three of us. Garrett's face did not hide how upset he was very well. Even from across the room, I could hear him shouting at the poor hunter who had delivered the message. In short time though, the hunter came back to us, "The commander would be pleased to have all three of you at his table for this evening's feast." Then he escorted us to the table at the far end of the room where the commander was sitting. All the people at the table stood, including Garret himself, as Brin approached.

Searching the crowd, I saw countless unknown faces staring at us. Their delight to have Brin among them was obvious, as was their disgust at my presence. As we drew closer to the table, I saw a face in the crowd that was familiar. He was young, but very well built, with blonde hair, somehow older than he was in the fragments of my memory. My curiosity urged me to go speak to this familiar face and discover just how knew him, but Avar pulled

Chapter 5

me back to walk with us when I tried to step in that direction. "Whatever you are trying to do, this is not the time for it," he whispered.

"Good evening, Bria–" Garrett began before Brin stopped him.

"Brin. Just Brin."

"Fair enough. Welcome, Brin, to the commander's table. Please, sit here next to me. Avar, you and this Wrack thing can sit over at that end."

"No. Where they sit is where I sit, Garrett. I don't give an uzk about your formalities. These are my companions, my friends, and I will sit with them."

His eyes became slits. "Very well, then. Let us make space for our new companions. Bridain, please move down."

Bridain, and several other obviously high-ranking hunters, shifted their seating to allow for us to sit down. I was nearly forced to sit between Avar and Brin, as Garrett wished to have her at his side and the hunter that would have been next to me should Avar been between insisted that Avar sit next to him. From across the table, the other hunters eyed me with nothing but suspicion and had their own conversations, some of them about me, as if I was not even in the room.

As everyone was ready to eat, Garrett excused himself and stood up at his seat. With a booming voice that filled the hall he called out, "To our patron, Ssli'Garion, the Silver Lady. Princess of inspiration and hope, guardian of innocence and peace, mistress of all art and beauty, and keeper of the long dead. We come this night to pay you tribute. Without the subtle light of the moon we would be lost to darkness. Even now, heroes rise to your cause and the howl of your ancient warriors bring fear to those who tried to cast you out. As we gather this holy night, the night of the fullest

Desecrated

moon, we give to you thanks. Thanks for bringing inspiration to your daughter, Brin, and guiding her to destroy one of the most foul Doomed. The legacy of her father shines brightly in her eyes, and we thank you for this beacon of hope. Bless us that your hunters will have the strength to overcome the trials ahead of us, and in doing so free the hearts and minds of this world from the shroud of fear and ignorance. Amen."

A chorus of "Amen" rang through the hall, spoken by everyone save for Brin and myself. Dinner progressed painfully from there, as I felt nearly alone in this giant hall of people.

The clattering dance of the forks, knives, and spoons in the room began to drown out the small talk around me that was not intended for my participation. I watched how people used their utensils in very different ways, some holding their fork in their right hand with the prongs down, and others using it more like a sharp shovel. Scattered through the people I could see, there were those who constantly used both hands, and never took a second to switch which hand the fork was in, and others who would slice their food and then switch to eat. After observing this activity for some time, I chuckled to myself.

"It is amazing the things you pay attention to when no person is willing to engage with you."

"What was that?" Brin asked politely.

"Nothing." A pause hung on the end of my reply but Brin went back to eating and trying to ignore the idle praise of the hunters on the other side of the table. I wanted to interject and tell them that their praise was falling on deaf ears, but again I saw that familiar face within the crowd.

He was tall and broad shouldered with short dirty blonde hair and an oblong yet roundish face. *Where had I seen him before?* Then it struck me. He was the tall boy I had seen in the vision about

Chapter 5

the magical prison at Marrowdale. "Brin. Brin, I think I recognize that fellow. Over there," I said, keeping my voice and indication as subtle as possible as not to raise undue suspicion from our hosts. Brin, however was not as subtle as she tried to follow my indicating eye gestures.

"Who? The short, skinny one?"

"No, the tall, large one. The blonde."

"Ok yeah, I think I know the one. Where did you see him?"

"In the vision I had in Marrowdale. I think he was one of the kids that opened it."

Finally noticing our whispering, Garrett spoke loudly at both of us, "Is there a problem, Brin?"

"Nope. Everything is fine. This food is amazing." She scooped up an oversized spoonful of potatoes and shoved them in her mouth. "MmmmMmmm."

Garrett looked a little annoyed by this obvious derailing of his question. He might have even taken her animated expression of the food's deliciousness as some form of insult. If he did, he could not come up with a response that he felt was worth sharing. Instead he stood up and tapped his fork against the side of his cup. The clanging echoed through the hall and quickly the clattering dance of forks and knives came to an end. "Brothers! This night we have come together to celebrate our patron, but not only that. We have come to celebrate a great victory for our side in this war that has raged for three thousand years. One of the Doomed has been sent back to the writhing pit of shadows that spawned it. Here, with us tonight are the heroes that vanquished it: Avar my son and Brin the Bard's Daughter."

The room exploded with cheering applause. The hunters pumped their fists over their heads in chaotic triumph over one of their ancient foes. Avar stood up and waved to the people cheering

Desecrated

him. With a look that said she was about to do something stupid, Brin also rose from her chair to meet the adulation. Twice she started to say something, but the banging, cheering, whistling noise of her audience drowned out any attempt for her to communicate. A smile appeared on her face, and to those of us at the table with her, it seemed that she blushed slightly.

Eventually the roar died down, but as it did I heard a second roar of a different crowd fill my mind. As Brin began to speak, I drifted away from the hall full of hunters on that night, and found myself on strangely familiar shores.

When the fog in my mind cleared, I found myself sitting in the same hall. Instead of the hunters who surrounded me with hateful stares, I was greeted with heroic smiles. I stood behind the same table at the end of the hall, and next to me was the largest man I could ever imagine. His wavy blonde hair shone like gold in the dim light of the meeting hall, and his handsome face was framed on the bottom by a square and solid jaw. Massive shoulders held up silver-plated mail, which was covered in very similar runes to Avar's armor. The rest of his giant form was also clad in silver-plated mail, with intricate and beautiful designs flowing through it. Just looking at him, I suddenly knew what the word hero had always meant.

"Brothers. We gather here tonight to celebrate our patron, Ssli'Garion, the Silver Lady!" He bellowed loud enough that even those men who stood outside on the porch of the hall could hear his words clearly. "Soon this terrible war will come to its end. Soon the greed of Ravenshroud will be satisfied, and while we could not topple their mighty empire, we should be proud that we,

Chapter 5

The Brotherhood, have stood as the mountain as the ocean tried to push us aside. How many lives have been saved because we would not yield? And yet we remain. Some among you have asked me, 'Lucien, why must we give Ravenshroud the treaty that they desire?' My answer is simple, because it is the will of our Lady that these wars come to an end. There is too much blood in the Silver Forest, brothers. We must do what we can to stop the flow of it."

When Lucien paused, there was a rising cheer from the crowd and it was then that I realized that the entire hall was filled with men and women standing shoulder to shoulder. There seemed no room for tables, or chairs, and I could see the crowd spilling out all the entrances to this room and as far as I could see. Hundreds of soldiers, all wearing the silver shoulder guards of the Shadow Hunters, yet these were not the Shadow Hunters. My mind shuffled through everything I knew trying to discover when I was, who these men were. Not from within, but from without I received my answer.

"Twenty days from now, we will travel to the ancient temple of the gods and there we shall work the magic to weave our fates together. All nations will be bound together in a magical pledge to the gods; never shall we know the misery of this war again!" Lucien's booming voice had given me enough. This night was in celebration for the ritual that was to come. The ritual that was to bring all men together, but instead it brought the Cursing upon them.

A heavy hand fell upon my shoulder. Looking up, I saw that Lucien was looking at me fondly as the celebratory waves of hope washed over us from the crowd. My heart sunk. They did not know that they were standing upon the precipice of their doom, and

Desecrated

that the future held thousands of years of stark misery. There was something else in my hesitation, however. Some dark secret I was keeping from Lucien and it ate at me.

Passively, I waited for the crowd to steal Lucien's attention, and then I slipped through the proud faces and friendly pats on my back out into the night air. As I had suspected, we were in the place I knew as Sanctuary and the world was a very different place. The me in the vision paid no mind to the lush world that lay spread before him in the silvery night, but I enjoyed the fresh clean air that we both breathed. I found myself retreating away from the joyous sounds from the mess hall, and made my way down a road that did not exist in the Sanctuary I knew. We went past buildings that likewise had vanished from my time, and I saw that this place was much more of a little town than the five buildings that remained standing in my version of it. Meandering through the town, I even saw the walls of the town that had men patrolling their tops.

Eventually I came to a small shrine, filled with sweet smelling flowers all open and drinking in the rays of the moon. I stood with only the flowers and the moon as my companions in the open-aired holy place for quite some time. My eyes traced over the silver inlaid designs on the four pillars that helped create a sense of space, but were not attached to wall or roof. Regret plagued me. A regret for something as yet undone. A lie of omission. My thoughts were interrupted by the sound of quiet footfalls on the stone path behind me. "I am fine, Marec. You don't have to come check on me. I'm fine."

"You just said you were fine twice. That tells me something is bothering you," Marec said from behind me. When I turned, I was met by a tall man with dark strong features. Hints of grey

Chapter 5

glimmered in his hair and his soldierly face wore at least one day's worth of dark stubble. "Since we freed you from them, I haven't left you alone. Why would I start now?"

The flowers danced gently in a breeze that flowed through the shrine. I let the wind pass deeply through me and then, after it calmed me a bit, I let it escape into the breeze that had brought it to me. "I am starting to have second thoughts, Marec. I am not sure that grandfather would have approved."

"The old man would have told you to do what you thought was best. You know that." Marec searched for the right words. "He has been dead a long time. It is your decision now. There hasn't been a day I have known you where I questioned your ability to make the right choices. Why now would you second guess yourself?"

Ashamed of something he did not know, I turned away from him. "Things are different now, Marec. Se'Naat changed me. I am not the same man I was before."

"If I know anything about you, it is this: You are the most stubborn, headstrong, brilliant man I have ever known. I knew your grandfather for a long time, and you aren't so different from him."

I smiled at Marec. I knew he would protect me from even myself if he could. There was a comfort in knowing that, but inside me there was also a hate. A hate that I could not control. A hate that I wanted to let loose. The hate was the secret I kept from them. They couldn't know how deep or intense this hate was. If they knew, it would change everything.

I moved to speak, but before any words could escape, an alarm sounded from the walls. The sound of the alarm bells was echoed by another, and another, until the sound of the bells seemed to come from every direction. Floating subtly, amidst the alarm, the sound of clinking chains were woven in. Somewhere a prisoner struggled futilely against his metal bonds. As the volume of the

Desecrated

chains grew, the sound of the alarm and my time in the shrine with Marec faded. Darkness consumed me, and left me only with the sounds of the prisoner. My prisoner.

Hot metal was crashing against a forging hammer. With each blow, the sound of the chains could be heard. This black steel formed rings that locked together to hold my unseen prisoner. Then suddenly, blood pooled at the base of a white marble altar, wrapped in these black chains. Steam rose from the blood as it made its journey across the stone floor, making a circle around the altar. When it touched the chains a great hissing was released and the metal cooled instantly. The prisoner struggled in his bonds again, and I heard her laugh.

The streams of blood became red flowing hair, writhing like snakes. The hair stretched and grew until it was impossibly huge in the darkness. A little laugh came from the moving center. The laugh was soft and sinister, muffled by the dark red curtain of snake-like hair. I searched for a face in the maddening maze of hair that entangled me. The laugh mocked my struggle and no matter which way I went, it seemed like the source of the hair was nearly within reach. Suddenly the strands closed around me, sealing me away from the outside world in a constricting cocoon of red. The air was pushed out of my lungs. Try as I might, no air could provide even the smallest scream for help.

Doors opened before me and I stepped upwards through them to the outside. The top of my robes hung down over the rope holding them to my body at my waist, leaving my torso completely naked in the moonlight. Exhaustion wracked my body, and I threw the still glowing forge hammer into the dirt at my feet. My pale arms were covered in a thick blanket of blood from my fingertips to my elbows. My unknown betrayal complete, an unearthly rage welled up inside me. A roar was loosed from my mouth, and the

Chapter 5

blades of grass in that empty field were instantly changed from lush green to dead yellow as it screamed by. Even with this venting, my anger was overflowing. The very earth at my feet became scorched with my hatred. I found no comfort in the motherly embrace of moonlight. I found no solace in the clean night air. In the misty distance of my mind, I heard the red woman giggle softly. As I stood alone in the night seething with hatred, ghostly alarms rang. The ringing grew and grew, until they were so very close. I felt Brin touch my arm and her concerned voice called out to me, "Wrack, are you ok?"

Opening my clouded eyes, I found myself still in the mess hall. The alarm bell was ringing outside and all of the hunters were hurrying to respond. Brin and I stood in the back of the hall, a calm eye in the storm around us, and she asked me again. "Wrack? Can you hear me? Are you ok?"

Shaking off the confusing world of the vision, I mostly came to my senses. "Yes. I am ok. I just had another vision. This one was more intense than the last few have been. I'm not sure what is happening."

"Well, I am not as much of an expert as Avar or his father, but I would say that maybe you have been awake long enough that you are starting to remember more." Now that she knew I was ok, she began her own preparation for whatever surprise the alarm brought with it. Ukumog's glow was slowly pulsing in and out of a medium intensity from Brin's belt. A fight was coming. We all could feel it.

Desecrated

Brin suddenly looked at me with uneasy shock and slowly raised her hand to point at my face. Pressing my fingertips to my cheeks, I felt them wet with tears that were stinging my eyes. Bleary eyed, I looked around the hall. For some reason, I still found it hard to leave the last vision behind me. "Brin?" Uncertainty filled my voice, "I–I think I have been here before," I said weakly.

Her eyebrow arched in disbelief, "What does that mean? You think you have been to Sanctuary before? That is impossible Wrack. Not only would the Hunters spike you on sight, no one here recognizes you."

"I know it seems impossible, but I just saw something. Something from a time before now. This place was a walled town, there were hundreds of soldiers here."

With a furrowed brow and downturned mouth, she looked at me with disbelief. "We can talk to Garrett about this gaak later. Whatever that alarm is for comes first."

I nodded, completely uncertain about what was going on in my head while the alarm bells kept ringing outside. I was more than a little distracted.

Chapter 6

With our feet pounding against the stone floor of the mess hall, Brin and I rushed outside to discover the cause for the alarm. Our world went from chaotic panic to hushed stillness nearly instantly, for all the hunters in our view were silently creeping around the areas between buildings. The scene was odd, each of them with their weapons at the ready and knees bent moving with as much fluidity as their armor would allow. All of them were searching for something unseen. Flashes of hand signals became the only quick movements among them, for they were all dead silent. Not knowing how I could help, I lingered on the porch of the mess hall and waited. Distracted as I was, my mind drifted back to the visions I had just seen. I tried to hold tightly onto the details that were already fleeing my memory. My eyes darted around the stone buildings of Sanctuary in my current time looking for similarities. I tried to connect the two time periods together, hoping that somehow it would force the memories to stay.

Murks became restless in my robes and crawled across my chest to peek through the hem that rode up my torso. While my hidden little friend searched for the cause of alarm, I examined the buildings near me. The mess hall in particular was nearly right out of my vision. There was obvious wear and repair that changed the surface details of it, but in shape and character it remained the same. Even the ground in front of it seemed familiar, and the other structures that stood had similar elements of time-worn maintenance and hints of familiarity. Turning my attention away from the center of town, I searched the horizon for any sign of the stone wall that surrounded the town in my memories. My eyes could only discover uneven terrain covered in vegetation that struggled to grasp the tiniest hint of life.

A whisper from unknown lips invaded my ears, "Did you hear that?"

"I think it came from over here." Came another unknown voice's reply.

Turning my attention back to the hunters around me, I saw flurries of hand signals that fell uselessly on my senses. There was something there, something strange on the air. Deeply, I took in the scent that seemed obfuscated amidst the smell of armor and dead grass. It was a putrid smell, harsh and bitter. My mind tried to explain it, and the only thing I could come up with was sweat gone sour. The complex pattern of smells only weaved this sour stench in with perhaps every eight or so threads, making it vanish just long enough for me to think it was gone before it would return. Each time it came back, it was slightly stronger. The source of it was drawing nearer.

"Murks smells it too, Master." His thoughts merged with mine. "Murks thinks it is a lizard thing."

Concentrating hard on not speaking, I was able to return my thoughts in kind, "A lizard thing, Murks?"

"Yes, Master. A lizard thing. A man thing. A man lizard thing."

Slightly confused by his comment, I tried to imagine what manner of creature he was describing. I thought of the tiny colorful lizards which I caught glances of in the wasteland between Yellow

Chapter 6

Liver and the Forest of Shadows, nimble quick bodies with long tails. Then I imagined a man, with the colorful skin of those lizards and a tail as long as his torso. His face nearly the same, but with a wider lipless mouth, and a tongue that sometimes searched the air for something unknowable to anyone but himself. No matter how my mind changed this funny creature, it could never make it something horrible. Certainly nothing worth the heightened state of alert we were all in. I couldn't have been more wrong.

A whispered commotion began in the center of the little town. Hunters slinked to the source of it from every direction. When I quietly walked up, I had trouble seeing what was happening because of all the people gathered around. A break appeared in the crowd and I saw the source of the concern: a tiny pinhole of white light floating slightly above waist height. Not only was it odd to see light with no apparent source floating there, but the intensity of it was nearly blinding.

The air around all of us became charged with fear and excitement. Everyone who could see the light stayed glued to it. Those who couldn't see through the crowd began quietly searching for other ones like it.

The light twinkled and moved ever so slightly up and down. Dread suddenly filled my mind; something unseen was here among us, and it wasn't here to make friends. Within my robes, Murks could sense my anxiety and clutched himself to both my robes and the flesh of my chest. I felt the sting of his little claws digging into me, but I paid it little mind. The light grew slightly larger, and twinkled fiercely as it did so. "Get ready," I mumbled to myself.

Desecrated

The hunter next to me whispered back, "What?" But before I could repeat myself the light surged in power. The hot center of it becoming the size of a large fist. As the light poured over us, blinding nearly all the on looking eyes, it revealed the thing that held it.

Standing with the source of searing light in its left claw was a human-shaped lizard thing. Unlike the one I had seen in my imagination, this one was covered in black and red plates of scaly armor and spines. The face of the thing was somewhere between a snout and a beak and was trimmed with razor sharp malice of a mouth. While it was not wearing much in the way of clothing, it did have a harness that crossed its chest, and it wore a few belts, all of which were used to hold pouches or weapons. Both the hunters and this thing remained inactive for a moment. Fear rolled over some of the hunters present which was shattered by someone screaming, "Darakka!" By the next heartbeat the fight had begun.

With no weapon or real desire to come face to beak with this darakka, I pushed my way out of the fray. Hunters of all sizes and shapes could not wait to get into the battle, and if it were not for the fact that the darakka was at least a foot taller than every hunter present, it would have disappeared completely into the swirling mass of armored bodies. The usual sounds of battle flowed outwards from the center, and from the fragments of words I could catch, it seemed that the darakka was giving all of them a good fight. I believed myself useless in the combat. I just wandered back away and tried to assess more of my surroundings.

The very first thing that I noticed was that the alarm bell was still ringing from far off. Between clashes of steel, draconic roars, and bloody screams, I tried to ask one of the Hunters that was away from the cloud of combat, "Why is the alarm still ringing?"

Chapter 6

A look of shock crossed his face for a second, as if he didn't believe me, then he muttered, "Oh uzk," and ran off toward the alarm, leaving me back in the town beside the fray, feeling as useless as usual. A low rumble rolled over me from the battle with the darakka; followed abruptly by the shortened scream of someone else.

"The battle goes badly, Master," but Murks only told me what I already knew. Frantically, I began looking for some kind of weapon. My daggers had been lost to Sergeant Valence and the Baron's men, but they were weapons I had found along the way. I just needed something to defend myself with. Searching the ground I found stones, a few bits of wood, and dirt. The roars from the battle made it seem that these would all be rather ineffective choices. A painful yowl from the crowd, however, caused me to reflexively pick up a piece of wood and turn around in case the creature was bearing down on me.

As the crowd fought, they tore up what little grass was there on the dirt road between buildings, and a great cloud of dust began to form around them. Their battle companions pulled maimed and wounded hunters from the surging crowd. "You there!" I felt shouted at me.

"Yes?"

"Come over here and help me!" It was the blonde hunter whose round face had been in my vision about the maze. Mixed with both the desire to help and with curiosity, I ran over to him.

"Help me with the wounded," he more ordered than asked as he shoved some scraps of torn cloth into my hands. Without hesitating, I got to work binding the wounds of those that would live.

Desecrated

The wounds on these hunters were a combination of claw, beak, and blade. Glancing over my shoulder each time I heard the crowd open to pass through more wounded, I kept trying to find out how our side was fairing. I also couldn't help but wonder where Avar, Brin, and David were. Once the battle started, I completely lost track of them all, and I had the usual wary feeling that came over me when Brin wielded Ukumog.

"You aren't binding the wounds tightly enough," the young hunter said to me without looking up.

Trying to pull the cloth tighter, but aware that my full strength might do more damage than good, I asked, "Like this?"

"That's better. We just need to stop the bleeding. Hard to really take care of them with all this fighting going on." He looked into the crowd just as another wounded was coming out. This time the hunter being carried was dead, his throat torn open and a slice that had released his guts from inside the mail shirt that had not done its job. "Uzk. Too many wounded. From the sound of the alarm, there are more coming. This is bad."

An urge rose in me to connect with him. Letting it have control, I quickly blurted out, "I'm Wr–"

"Wrack. I know who you are," he never looked up from his work, but instead fell silent for a moment. His silence held my attention as I thought he might continue. Just as I looked downward to continue my work he spoke, "I'm Gordon, but everyone calls me Gordo."

"Good to meet you Gordo," I returned to working on the many wounded hunters before me in silence. Part of me wanted to ask about Marrowdale and the Maze, but I decided against it. Seeing him up close now, I could tell he was different. Darker, in a way. The time between when he and his friends opened that door

Chapter 6

and now had not been kind to him, and if I pushed him it might quickly turn this man who could become an ally into an enemy, so, I bit my tongue and went back to my work.

The crowd kicked up more dust and dirt, some of it was accidentally sprayed in our direction, occasionally showering Gordo, the wounded, and me with sprinkles of dirt. Brushing the dirt from the hunter whom I was bandaging, there was a sudden chill in my skin. My lungs stung, like I had just breathed in cold air, and I looked up into the battle beside me. The crowd had parted this time to avoid the lumbering attack of the darakka. Its large blade came crashing into the dirt not one body length from me, sending dirt in every direction. Gordo quickly grasped his weapon, and I scurried away on my back. Again I felt the chill and this time saw the dark blade of Ukumog came whirling past the side of the darakka. Attached to the handle was a struggling Brin. The fearful strength with which she usually wielded Ukumog was eerily not present in her eyes. She was breathing heavy and looked as if she had just climbed a mountain before the battle.

"Look out!" Gordo screamed at me and moved to intercept the attack from our reptilian enemy. The clatter of their swords had an unusually low sounds to their collision as he parried the mighty strike. Gordo's blade had a deep red tint to the steel, much like the sword I saw Sergeant Valence wield. Again and again the two of them locked metal on metal. The rest of the crowd tried to get in blows where they could, but it seemed that most of their weapons were not powerful enough to pierce the thick draconic hide of the darakka.

While the beast was distracted, Brin hit it solidly from behind, and Ukumog cracked its way through the creature's armor and found purchase in the soft flesh below. Unlike usual, the blade remained silent at this discovery of blood. The runes remained tiny

Desecrated

etchings devoid of their customary blueish glow. After screaming in pain, the darakka turned its attention fully to Brin. Raising the heavy serrated edge of its blade over its scaly head, it then brought the blade down so fast and hard that when Brin parried it, she had to do so with both hands. The sheer power of the attack knocked her backwards. Gordo began muttering, "Patron lady, know my heart and fill me with the inspiration to do amazing deeds that will inspire others."

The darakka continued his assault on the prone Brin, her hands now spread on the blade using the flat of it as a shield. While Ukumog was undamaged by the series of bone crushing attacks, Brin was not so fortunate. Her arms nearly buckled under each attack, and I could see her strength beginning to fail her. Fear flooded me, and as I was helpless to do anything on my own. I screamed at Gordo, "Strike now!" And he did so.

Gordo's blade deftly sought the hole that Ukumog had made in the creature's armor on its lower back. The blade seemed to move in slow motion as it slid directly into the crack and Gordo forced the razor sharp tip through the soft tissue found inside. The scream that issued forth from the failing darakka was an aural potpourri of human and lizard, agony and fear. This unsettling sound did not stop the determined Gordo; he twisted the blade, making more of the armored flesh pop and crack and unleashing a river of black blood. The other hunters soon leapt to action and began pummeling the wracked monster with their weapons until finally the thing lay silent in a black pool.

Pushing through the crowd, I found my way to Brin and helped her get to her feet. As I made my way there, Murks dropped out of the bottom of my robes and snuck through the boots of the

Chapter 6

crowd to sip on a small amount of the darakka's blood. I, too, would have been unaware of his tiny presence if I were not linked with his mind, so none of the hunters even realized he was among them.

Brin was completely exhausted, so I slowly began moving her to the porch of the mess hall. As we stumbled away from the corpse of the thing Bridain called out, "Get the stone! Quickly now! Cover it and do not let any of its light escape." One of the hunters threw the stone into a small canvas sack and tied the neck shut. Shortly after the light was gone, the alarm stopped ringing in the distance. "Damned gleamstone," cursed Bridain as he and Garrett walked off with the satchel.

Before long Avar found us. "Good fighting there, Brin," he said sheepishly and joined us on the porch. The three of us sat enjoying the quiet after the battle. A quiet that would not last.

About an hour passed with little activity. I helped Gordo shuffle off the wounded to the town's infirmary while Brin and Avar rested on the porch. The other hunters in the camp went about the town looking for more enemies, and looking to repair and fortify the buildings in case of another attack. Before I could start helping Gordo patch up the wounded, or even just start up a conversation with him, a messenger came looking for me.

"Wrack. Commander Garrett would like to meet with you in his meeting hall."

Confused by this summons I said, "Are Brin and Avar coming too?"

"Yes, you were the last one I found. If you would like, I can show you the way."

"Go ahead," Gordo jumped in, "I can take care of this lot."

"Thanks Gordo. Come on then. Let's not keep the Commander waiting," I said turning to the messenger.

Desecrated

Following the messenger out into the street, I could not help but look over to where I knew Brin had been resting. The Commander bore no love for me, of this I was positive, and I wanted to make sure that I wasn't foolishly walking off to be killed. Neither Brin nor Avar could be found in the main thoroughfare of the town, nor did I see them on the way to the Commander's house.

The messenger took me around behind the building to the back entrance. As we passed behind the house, I noticed that behind some of the buildings lay an expansive graveyard. The small makeshift tombstones closest to me were all different in size and forms, but as my eyes drifted deeper in, the rows started to become all worn stones that may have been resting in that field for hundreds of years.

The yard looked to be well maintained, and in the center of all the graves there rose a sculpture of a leafless tree with the moon in its branches. The smooth white stone made the tree almost seem to glow in the silvery light of the moon. The statue stood upon an ancient stone disc that was riddled with runic markings, some of which looked the same as the runes that were etched in the armor that the hunters bore. Abating my curious desire to explore this ancient graveyard, I followed the messenger towards the back room of Commander Garrett's house. From outside I could hear a passionate discussion in raised voices.

"No. Avar, you don't understand. We are not entirely sure who this enemy is. Somehow she has control of the darakka and through them she has control of the freth. These are not enemies to be taken lightly. We need–" Commander Garrett's fire-fueled rant was cut off by Bridain coughing loudly as I entered the room. All eyes silently fell on my messenger escort and me. Having delivered me, and saluting to the Commander, the messenger turned and left

Chapter 6

me standing just inside the doorway. The room was so quiet that I could hear the shifting of every chair and even the slight sound of the candles burning.

"Right. Have a seat Wrack. We were just bringing Brin and Avar up to speed on the attacks here," Commander Garrett motioned towards one of the many empty seats crammed into this small room.

Gently pushing my way through the small crowd assembled in the room, I found my way to Brin. She smiled and pulled at my sleeve until I was planted in the seat next to her. "Why was I called in here?" I whispered to Brin.

She smiled and patted me on the hand. "Because I told them to invite you. We are a team, Wrack, and I won't let these stuck-up pricks forget that."

My smile was cut short by the booming voice of Commander Garrett, "Now that we are all here." He cleared his throat with a look of disdain on his face. "We are dealing with an unknown enemy. She has been staging scouting attempts at our borders, sending in patrols to breach our defenses, even attacking our people as they come or go. Some of her minions carry notes from her, directed by name to me, notes that we only can collect if we kill the creature baring it. No matter the sharp politeness of her messages, they all have one thing in common: the threat of violence."

One of the other hunters raised his hand and only spoke after the Commander nodded at him. "Sir, are we facing one of the Doomed here?"

"We don't think so, Corporal. While she calls herself The Mistress in each of her notes, we have no record of that being a moniker of one of the Doomed. The only Doomed who might have a name we don't recognize is the Betrayer, whose original name was removed from all record by the others after the Betrayer turned on the rest of them. Being as this woman has control of ancient creatures who are mentioned as servants of the divine, we think it is very unlikely that she is aligned with the Doomed."

"No disrespect sir, but wouldn't it be very bad for us if one of the Doomed somehow managed to control the very servants of the ancient gods?"

"Indeed, it would. We have to remember that the Doomed are not just some power-hungry wizard out to control the universe. They already wield enough power to cut the influence of the gods off from the rest of the world and set themselves up as their own pantheon of deities." Garrett paused for a moment to see if the Corporal had any more questions, then he continued. "We do not have enough information at this time to determine exactly what the goal of the enemy is. There is a small group of our men in the Spikelands trying to hunt down the source of their current assaults. The fact that they now have fragments of the gleamstone is troubling." He motioned over to Bridain who then brought over the sack. Commander Garrett reached into the sack and pulled out a stone that shone with a dark mirror like surface. "The gleamstone is a piece of the sacred silver forest brought back by an ancient thief who told his lover that he would steal the moon for her. It might look like just a polished stone to the unknowing eye, but in the moonlight it shines as brightly as the full moon on a cloudy night. It also has the unfortunate ability to see through the illusionary barriers that we have over this place. It seems that this Mistress is breaking it into smaller pieces and handing it out."

Chapter 6

A dozen whispered conversations filled the room and Commander Garrett's eyes flitted back and forth across the many groups discussing what he had just said. Between the three of us, Avar was the only one whispering, and all he said was, "Well uzk. We need to get that stone away from her."

Raising his hands to regain control of the room, Commander Garrett boomed out, "Calm down everyone. Our order has been around since before the Cursing and we shall be around a long time after. Now, Bridain and I have been discussing–"

A young hunter sweating from a long sprint burst through the door. "Commander, there is another patrol on the outskirts. They look like freth."

"Uzk," muttered Garrett. "Bridain, gather everyone together. Let's push out and meet the enemy while they don't expect it."

"Yes, commander," Bridain nodded at Verif and Ferrin, and the three of them left quickly.

Before anyone else could depart, Garrett looked over at Brin. "Are you with us Brin?"

"Yeah, Garrett. I'm with you."

Within ten minutes every able-bodied hunter was in the center of town and as a group we made our way to the edge of the illusion keeping us safe from the outside. On our way there I saw a watchtower built into the branches of a tree, and hanging in the tower was a large bell. Undoubtedly this was one of the alarm bells that alerted us to the presence of the darakka before, but now it lay silent.

While I could not see the barrier that separated the hidden town of Sanctuary from the outside, I could certainly feel a place where the air was not as fresh. Before we could breach that barrier, Commander Garrett gathered all the hunters together. "This night we have faced an ancient race, both powerful and divine, and in our Lady's name we have driven back the invasion of the unknown enemy. Out there is a force of freth, the ancient servants of the gods. They are not simple humans, but creatures filled with the fervor of divine tyranny. In the old days, they were granted to those who served Ulintarni, the patron of tyrants and dictators. They are not invulnerable, but the fight will be hard. Stand by your brothers and we shall prevail, for they too are cut off from their lord and must be diminished in their power. They will offer you no mercy, so give them none in return. Fight well, my brothers." As he spoke the final words, he raised his sword into the air where it shone in the fleeting moonlight. In response to his call, all the hunters raised their weapons in similar salute.

Beyond the sea of raised swords and the hidden barrier I could see a moving force in the rapidly fading moonlight, dark figures that looked human from where I stood. Yet, when my vision twisted beyond that of normal sight, their difference became clear. Their skin was a dark red and had a faint glow as if they were filled with liquid fire. Even with my unnatural ability to see over distance and through darkness, I saw no color in their eyes, just shiny black orbs framed with that same dim glow. There was something ominous and familiar about them. A dizzying circus of memories danced in my head, all of them involving violence or treachery. At the head of this group of dark warriors was another of the darakka. It was tall and wore a skirt made of long red fibers bound into tassels at their base by a hem of silver skull beads. This fight was going to be difficult.

"Dem freth is 'ere Commanda," Ferrin growled. "Old Ferrin can smells 'em." Garrett gave him a nod, and with that Ferrin and one other hunter split away from the crowd and ran off to the right of us into the trees.

Chapter 6

"Right, then. Here we go men," Garrett turned and faced the direction of the oncoming force. The hunters formed themselves into a cloud of organized chaos. There were not the strict lines that the freth had in their ranks, yet their scattered stance left me thinking that there was some reason to it all. As a group, we all walked towards the enemy, our pace quick until we reached the border of the protection.

The darakka leader held up a fist the moment we came into view and his company of freth ceased their march instantly. Garrett made the same motion shortly after we all cleared the border. A hand caught my arm and when I looked back it was Gordo. "We are supposed to stay back and help the wounded, Wrack." His order was not unexpected, especially since I did not have a weapon. The thought of staying behind while Avar and Brin fought for their lives was not something that made me comfortable, however.

Sensing my hesitation Brin spoke up, "It is ok, Wrack. If I need you, I will call out." Her words were followed by the secret smile that always seemed to only show for me.

"Don't get yourselves killed out there," I tried to muster as much humor in my voice as I could. The truth was that this conflict scared me. Even The Ghoul seemed like nothing in comparison to the sinister force that lay before us.

"We will survive," Avar added. "I hope."

Our goodbyes said with unspoken words, I joined Gordo at the rear of the force of hunters.

"Don't worry Wrack. Our boys will be ok," Gordo tried to comfort me. His effort showed that he was getting past the fact that I was some horrible undead thing.

"Thanks Gordo, but just hours ago the whole force of hunters faced off with just one darakka and it was a rough battle. Now there is one of them and a whole bunch of these freth things."

Desecrated

Gordo smiled knowingly and clapped his large hand down on my shoulder. "Preparations have been made, my friend. Don't you worry."

But worry I did. The two groups stood faced off with each other, silently waiting for the other to make a hostile move. Eventually the darakka leader rumbled out some words. He was too far and his voice too deep for me to understand what he had said from that distance. "Did you understand that?" I asked Gordo.

He shook his head, "All I heard was RoroROorORorooroORororoar." Then he chuckled a bit.

Gordo's sense of humor about this dire situation was actually putting me a little on edge. It was making it difficult to concentrate my hearing towards the battle. Focusing my mind and trying to push out any external distractions, I finally could make out the conversation happening far away from me.

"If this were true," Garrett boomed, "your Mistress would not send a force of creatures to our door, but an emissary. Or come herself. Frankly, darakka, we don't believe you."

The darakka hissed with anger, "Human, you do not realize the mistake you are making. It is your choice to live or die, and you choose death."

"We have stood at the crossroads of life and death many times and we are still here. Do what you have come here for. I am done talking to you." With that, Garrett stepped back into the ranks and raised his sword. Other swords joined his in the air and they all seemed to glisten in the moonlight.

There came no mocking laughter from the enemy. No scoffing remark either, just the simple command to charge. Reacting to the aggression of the freth army, the hunters braced themselves for the attack. When the clash came, the freth were broken like a waterfall crashing onto a rock below. The Hunters stayed tightly

Chapter 6

together, fighting shoulder to shoulder with men in the middle using silver tipped spears through the front ranks, spears, which I had somehow not even noticed anyone carrying until they were piercing the glowing flesh of the freth.

Shocked, I reflexively asked Gordo, "What? Where did those spears come from?"

With a knowing smile he replied, "Keep watching. We have more tricks up our sleeve."

The darakka leader tried to use his size and might to break the front line of the now round formation of hunters. When he charged, forward a salvo of silver streaks shot through the air from the nearby trees. When I blinked and looked at him again, there were five arrows protruding from the armored hide of his torso. Confused by the surprise attack, he halted his charge and backed away from the fray. The freth continued their failing assault, but now that the surprise of the hidden archers was broken, volleys of arrows were fired towards the enemy at will, many of their shafts finding deadly purchase in their targets.

The freth seemed so overwhelmed with their lust for blood they did not notice their leader giving ground, but he had not made a call for a retreat either. More and more of the freth fell on the hunters, and the pressure of their numbers began to push the tide of the battle. From where Gordo and I stood on the other side of the barrier, I could see Ukumog as it rose and fell on the other side of our allies. There were screams of pain erupting from the tight hedgehog of silver wearing warriors, yet they did not break or run.

"Shouldn't we do something?"

Gordo looked sternly at the battle. "Not yet. We are here to pick up the pieces, Wrack. If we run out there, then there is no safety net. Besides, we have one more thing that will come into play. Let's wait until at least that happens."

Desecrated

My silent question about the remaining card to be played was answered before I could even form the words to ask. A feral roar rolled over the field and from the bushes near the darakka, a shape both wolf and man leapt from the shadows. Before the growl could vanish, the wolf man was clinging fiercely to the back of the darakka. The darakka howled in miserable pain as the wolf man buried its snout into the flesh of the darakka's neck. Rivers of black blood flowed unabated down the darakka's body. The reptilian warrior flailed in vain trying to grasp the hide of the wolf man.

Sensing their leader's peril, some of the freth broke off their attack to aid the darakka. This not only gave the archers more targets to pick off safely as they made their way towards their leader, but it also split the force pushing on the hunters. Before they could reach their leader to defend it, the wolf man had torn out the darakka's throat and broken its neck. Deftly the wolf man leapt off the falling corpse of the draconic leader and landed on all fours. It growled with such fury that it gave these ancient servants of tyranny pause. With blinding speed, the wolf man returned suddenly to his slaughter, tearing through the flesh of the freth and causing a chaotic fountain of glowing blood to emerge where both he and the freth had stood.

"Holy gaak!"

Gordo laughed, "Yeah, guardians are a tough bunch when they get rolling. Much more effective in packs though."

I blinked at him with disbelief, but Murks silently agreed with him. Then I couldn't help but wonder what my little hemodan knew about these wolf men guardians. A cry loosed by one of the freth interrupted my thoughts, and I saw those freth who were not engaged in the battle beginning to run. The hidden archers fired at those trying to run away, and their arrows landed with lethal

Chapter 6

precision. The hedgehog of hunters on the ground began pushing outward, and rolling over their foes. It wasn't long before not a single freth was left alive.

"You dinnae even leave any fur Ferrin to chase!" exclaimed the wolf man before he loped off into the shadows.

Gordo and I moved forward to help the wounded and try and patch up those who needed our help. There were surprisingly few wounds that looked mortal and not a single person of our number was slain. Considering how poorly the hunters did against that first darakka, I was surprised.

The look on my face must have betrayed my shock because Gordo proudly spoke, "See Wrack, when we are ready for them, it's a whole different story."

"Yeah, I just wish we could be prepared for everything all the time," muttered Bridain as he passed by.

Remembering the spears, I searched the area for them, and could find not a single person carrying one. It was as if I had imagined that they were there at all. "What happened to the spears?" I openly asked.

Both Bridain and Gordo laughed. "Every army has their secrets," Bridain smiled and walked off to meet Garrett.

This secret made me feel exactly like the outsider they wanted me to be.

After we all got safely back to Sanctuary the day had finally broken. In the light of the sun's rays the little battered town gave up some of the secrets hidden in the shadows of the night. The stalagmites of ancient buildings poked through the yellow brush here and there, and some of the rolling horizon became forgotten fortifications abandoned ages ago. I could picture in my mind what I knew the place once looked like. I had been here before. Somehow

Desecrated

I had just forgotten that, like everything else prior to my escape from my mossy womb by that waterfall. Even that event started to seem both as if it had just happened, but also happened in another lifetime. As Brin would say, my perception of time was all uzk'd up.

Patrols went back to their duties. People went off to rest. Garrett and Bridain took Brin and Avar to go plan, and I found myself tending to the wounded with Gordo. I found surprising amounts of joy in helping these men and women that I didn't know. Something about doing my small part to help their bodies heal was very satisfying. The only troubling part was helping the ones that seemed unlikely to make it. There was no joy in their struggle, and most of the time I couldn't tell if my actions were really helping or hurting.

One of the wounded in particular was a young boy who had suffered greatly during the first battle. John's wounds were seeping brown fluid, and Gordo seemed to think he would not make it. While I was bandaging and checking the others, I could not help but look over at young John. I really wanted to help him. After several hours of work, Gordo started gathering up his things. "I think I am going to try and get a few hours of sleep. If you need anything or something happens, come get me."

I nodded at him, still sneaking looks over at John.

"You going to be ok here?"

Nodding again, "Yes. I will come get you if anything changes."

His eyes searched my face for a moment and then he was gone. I was left alone in the barracks with the eighteen wounded. As the hours went by, I attended them when it seemed that something might be wrong or if they simply asked. Being in Yellow River among the people outside the walls, I had seen suffering, but this was more present suffering. More visceral. The people of Yellow

Chapter 6

River lived in the protracted suffering of neglect, very different from the immediate and possibly unexpected shortness of physical pain. My curiosity was again engaged in their pain. I could not feel the long suffering of their wounds, for mine would heal too quickly, nor did I fear the bitter sting of death, for I was trapped in my tattered form. While I wondered what their fear tasted like, I envied them. They could escape the misery of this world. Their struggle could come to an end. My struggle was endless and timeless. I understood, for perhaps the first time, their fear of me. I was nothing like them. Once upon a time, had I been? There was no one to answer that question.

John's wounds worsened over the course of the day. I could taste his life fading away. "Master," came the tiny voice of Murks in my head, "you should leave. Murks is afraid of what would happen if he fades away while you are here alone."

"Afraid, Murks? Why afraid?"

His little body stirred with anxiety, "Because, Master. If you feed that part of you, will you become something else? Murks knows that you are happy. Murks likes this. Murks does not want Master to become like he was before."

Taking in what Murks was saying took me some time. I stared at my hands as I flexed them. Open and shut. Fist and palm. Tight and relaxed. I felt the cold life flowing through me; it wanted to be sustained, but my heart wanted something else, something that the cold pain of my dark power could not give me. Life.

"Let's try a little magic then, shall we, Murks?"

The little hemodan was silent, contemplating what I was thinking. "Yes Master. Murks will help you." With that, he climbed out of his little pocket in my robes and hid just inside the hem until I was closer to John.

Desecrated

As I approached, he climbed out and down my arm to the unconscious solider laying helplessly before us. Letting my instincts take over, I bit my thumb hard enough to draw blood. For a moment, my mind flashed back to the time in that warehouse where I created Murks without thinking about it. These warnings did not stop me, however, as I peeled back some of John's bindings and dripped my thick black blood into his wounds. Feeling slightly weaker, even just at the loss of those few drops, seemed unusual. How many times had I lost more drops fighting thorny bushes in our travels? Murks rebound the wound that I had uncovered, and after checking to make sure everything was in order, leapt back onto my sleeve and returned into the folds of my robe.

"There, Master. It's done. He will survive."

Dizzy, I found my seat near the entrance of the bunkhouse. "What did we just do, Murks? I mean, I didn't say any words or anything."

"Master's blood will do the work he wanted. The soldier will survive. You will see, Master."

I would just have to have faith. Faith that I had not brought ill upon the suffering boy, but instead healed his wounds. And faith was in short supply. Before I could wait out whatever I had set in motion a messenger came to the bunkhouse. "Wrack? Commander Garrett wants everyone to come to the mess hall."

"Who will watch the wounded?" I asked, not really wanting to leave my handiwork unattended.

The messenger shrugged. "I am sure they can be without you for a little while." Before I could respond, he departed and left me with little choice but to follow.

The main street was filled with men and women walking to the mess hall, and by the looks of the porch, inside it was standing room only. Working my way through the crowd a bit, I was able to

Chapter 6

push through enough people to see the hunters assembled and even see Garrett at the back of the hall. I arrived just as he was calling things to order.

"Settle down. Settle down. First of all I want to congratulate all of you fine men and women for the bravery and devotion that you showed last night against the darakka and his freth army. Well fought by all of you. Every single one of you played a pivotal role in that battle and you should be proud to stand with heroes at your sides. Well, except perhaps Ferrin," he paused masterfully as the crowd laughed. "In all seriousness, without the watchful eye of our Lady, we would be lost. Lost to a world that has no room for innocence or beauty. A world that I certainly would not want to live in. So, on behalf of myself, the other commanders of the Shadow Hunters, and even the Silver Lady herself, I thank you for your service." Choked up for a moment, Garrett cleared his throat. The paused was filled with an overwhelming sense of support, so much so that one person in the crowd began clapping. This caused an avalanche of hands to clap together and cheering to begin. Only with my enhanced sight could the tears welling up in Garrett's eyes be seen. It made me wonder if Avar really knew his father at all, or if his envy over his father's duty clouded his view.

"Settle down!" Bridain bellowed over the crowd, which quickly became quiet.

Garrett nodded at Bridain in thanks and then continued, "The enemy we fought last night is not new. It is an ancient enemy of all people who wish to be free. The soldiers of Ulintarni, the lost god of tyranny, now have fallen under the command of someone else, someone who calls herself The Mistress. Over the past several months, we have received a few notes from this person and last

Desecrated

night was no change to this pattern. When the body of the darakka commander was searched, or rather what was left of it," he shot a glance over at Ferrin.

Ferrin shrugged and loudly responded, "Wut?!"

Garrett ignored the interruption and did not hide the humor in his face but quickly composed himself and continued, "She again had a message for us. Until now, it hasn't seemed as though the threats of The Mistress were real. Bridain and I thought that perhaps she was some bandit lord trying to use the fear of the Doomed and the might of the darakka to usurp control over this part of the land. After last night's display, we can no longer ignore her threats. To this end, let me read to you the message that she has sent us.

'Commander Garrett,

Surrender now and your men will be spared in the world that is to come. Curses cannot last forever - and you lack the means to undo that which was done. These freth were but a scouting party. When my army arrives, we will accept your surrender.

The Mistress'

There was silence in the hall as everyone took in the words from the message. "This is a threat we can no longer ignore. We do not know who this Mistress is, nor do we know what she ultimately wants. Brothers and sisters, make no mistake, we are officially at war."

Chapter 6

The crowd came to life with whispered commentary. After a few moments, Bridain raised his hands and bade the noise to cease. "As the commander has said, we know precious little about this enemy. We know that she controls an impressive ancient force and that she has access to a gleamstone. One of these things we can undo by stealing the stone. The other, well, we will have to determine how exactly she has control of these forces and try and find a way to cut her off. From what Verif and Tarissa have told me, the food that the freth were carrying tells us that they came here by way of the Spikelands, which means that we are going to have to send out scouting parties to try and find the gleamstone and any other information about the force against us."

A hand shot up in the front of the crowd and Brin's voice suddenly could be heard, "I will take a group to the Spikelands, Bridain. No offense, but I can track better than most of your hunters and no one will suspect me or Wrack as being from Sanctuary. We might be able to get where you lot cannot."

Garrett and Bridain locked eyes and then nodded to one another. "Very well, Brin. You and Wrack will go out into the Spikelands in search of information and the gleamstone. We will send groups of other scouts as well, not only to gather information, but also to scatter the focus of the enemy in hopes that an opportunity will present itself. Unit leaders should meet with Garrett and me in the war room."

"If there is nothing else," Garrett picked up at the end of Bridain's sentence, "then the meeting is adjourned. May the Silver Lady bring you the inspiration we all need on this, the first day of our new trial." There was a banging on the table where they both stood and then the crowd began flowing out of the mess hall. Brin made her way through the crowd to find me near the front of the building.

Desecrated

"Well. As soon as you are ready, we can go."

"Is Avar not coming with us?" I was not pleased at the idea of breaking up our little team.

Brin sighed. "I don't think so, Wrack. It might just be you and me this time. Avar's got hunter stuff going on."

All my humor left me. "I suppose I am ready now. It is not like I have any gear to carry or food to get ready."

"Uzk. Food. Avar does all the cooking." I could see the wheels in her mind turning. "Give me a second to talk to Garrett. Meet me out front when you are ready?"

"Sure," I said to her back as she walked away. Shaking my head at her determination not to cook, I slowly walked out front.

The other hunters were running about, like their anthill had been kicked over. Leaning against the railing on the porch of the mess hall, I watched them hurry and scurry. The busyness of it all was relaxing.

"Are you and Brin going out there alone?" David's voice brought me out of my trance.

My eyes found his face full of worry. "We will be ok, David. Brin is very tough, and I can't really die. Even if we don't find the gleamstone, we will be ok."

He stood in silence for a while, watching me watch the people. With stammered urgency he finally blurted out, "I want to come with you."

There was an earnest need in him to repay us for saving his life. I could see it in his eyes. "David. You are still recovering and the hunters need people here."

"Yeah, but the hunters didn't save me. You did. I owe you this much, Wrack. Let me repay you."

Chapter 6

The dark part of me awoke. I had leverage over this wretched soul. Better to save this debt for a bigger task later. "I appreciate that you want to help us, I do. I tell you what. When the time comes that I really need your help, I will ask. In the meantime, why don't you stay here and help Gordo with the wounded while I am gone."

A joy that only a sense of purpose could bring dawned on David's face. "Ok, Wrack. I'll do it. Truth be told I am a little relieved. I didn't want to end up holding you and Brin back."

"It's ok, David. We each have our part to play. Yours just hasn't come quite yet. Be patient." I couldn't tell who was speaking to David. Was it me, or the monster that lived inside me?

David smiled and went off to talk to Gordo. I saw them from across the street as they conversed, David motioning towards me. With a confirming wave I gave my approval, and Gordo waved back. The two men walked into the infirmary where all the injured hunters lay recovering.

"Alright," Brin had returned, and was still in an obvious rush. "Avar is coming with us. We will pick you up some weapons or something while we wait for him."

"Ok. Anything else I can do?"

She chewed on the nail of her thumb nervously. "I haven't been to the Spikelands in a long time. Uzkin' nasty place. Just be ready," she said and wandered off again.

"Ready for what?" I yelled after her, which she ignored. Deep down, I knew I wasn't ready. How can you prepare for the unknown? Still, like the fool I was, I chased after her, muttering, "This woman is going to be the death of me."

Desecrated

Chapter 7

Before much time had passed, Avar, Brin, and I were leaving Sanctuary. The hunters hugged Avar, waved proudly at Brin, and cast hateful stares at me. In the fringes of the crowd there were hidden smiles being quietly worn for us, however. The refugees that we had saved from the fallout of Yellow Liver had not forgotten what we had done for them, but their future was still uncertain. They had found a new home among the Hunters, at least for the moment. As we walked through the barrier that protected the small town from the outside world, I wondered what had happened to Samuel. Perhaps it was best that he left us before we ended up with the enemy of his gods. For all I knew, he had been the one to tell Sergeant Valence of our trip to Marrowdale.

"I know it's dark, but let's try and get as far away from Sanctuary as we can before morning," said Brin.

Avar nodded silently. His time with his shadow hunter family had been cut short by Brin's desires, and he knew it. He did not seem happy to be wandering in the wilderness with us again. Even Ukumog's runes had become barely visible in the dark. We were treading off the path of the blade's destiny. For all our sakes I hoped that it would not decide to find other owners to further its agenda of destruction.

Desecrated

With everything that had happened, the three of us were quickly returned to our usual teamwork, Brin leading the way, me using my sight to help navigate from the middle, and Avar bringing up the back and carrying most of the gear. There was comfort in this. More had changed than I knew, however, and more change was on its way.

By dawn we had made it a great distance away from Sanctuary and both Brin and Avar had grown weary. We stopped and made camp, allowing them to get a few hours of rest before we pressed on. The camp we made was on a hill, allowing me to see into the distance, so, while they slept, I took in my surroundings.

The trees and dirt here were really no different than around Sanctuary. Many of the trees were covered in green needles, rather than the mostly barren leafy trees that had been in the area surrounding Yellow Liver. Looking onwards to the southeast, the trees became fewer and fewer, and what lay beyond were mountains of grey sharp rocks. The largest of these rocks rose like a field of spikes for as far as the eye could see. It might take us a day to get to it, but I had a feeling that this was the Spikelands that Garrett spoke of. Of all the places I had been thus far in my travels it seemed like the least friendly, even from such a great distance.

Before the sun was at its peak in the sky, I woke Brin as she had requested. After my companions had eaten, we headed towards our destination. After more hours of silent travel I broke the quiet, "So, what is the plan exactly?"

"Well," Brin answered with a slightly annoyed tone, "we find tracks for the darakka and freth, then we follow the signs back to a camp. Hopefully it will be where we can get more information. Ultimately, we plan to get the gleamstone and take it back to Sanctuary."

Chapter 7

Something seemed off about the plan and I couldn't stop myself from asking, "Isn't that the worst place for it, if it breaks the enchantments on the town?"

"I know. Not like we have much choice though. The safest place for it is right under our noses. We throw it in a hole, someone will find it and then someone else might use it against our buddies."

"Garrett knows what he is doing," Avar chimed in. "He wouldn't ask us to bring it back unless he had a plan."

It was good to see Avar talk well of his father, but there was still something nagging at me about the simplicity of their strategy. I could not help but feel that The Mistress wanted us to gather the gleamstone, and bring it back for her army to attack just at the moment that the defenses were at their weakest. After all, that is what I would do.

As we drew closer to the unforgiving rocky terrain of the Spikelands, the trees began to thin and the ground slowly transitioned from struggling grasses to broken shards of grey stone. About half a day from really being in the Spikelands we had to stop again for Brin and Avar to rest. The ground was hard for me to sit on and I could only imagine how difficult it was for them to sleep on it. True to my thoughts, Brin tossed and turned during most of her rest, and the next day went slower due to her exhaustion.

Mid afternoon we finally found ourselves surrounded by the spiky columns of wind carved stone that gave the Spikelands its name. The temperature there as opposed to the lands just north of us was surprisingly warmer, and the land was much lower as well. Walking on the broken shards of rock that made up the surface of the ground was harder than I anticipated. While Brin and I had difficulty, Avar seemed to be taking most of the journey in stride, even helping to catch me a few times as I slipped on the stones

Desecrated

beneath my feet. This show of dexterity caught my attention, as the Avar that I had come to know was wonderfully nice, but very, very clumsy. Perhaps more of him than just his attitude had changed.

For many days we tried to find a trail for the freth moving through the Spikelands, but were coming up with nothing. The nights lost much of the heat of the daytime. Overall, it was much hotter during the day, and much colder during the night than it had been in Sanctuary, or even in our time in the wilderness. Avar and Brin began sleeping huddled together to warm one another. My body seemed impervious to the change in temperature, but it still remained cold to their touch. The hunger within me wanted to warm itself in the huddle with them, but I knew that its purpose was not my own, so Ukumog and I remained outside in the cold air.

The next day found us traveling in a warm morning. As the sun crested over our heads, I would even say that it became slightly hot. Shifting stones beneath our feet continued to slow our movement, but helped keep us aware of our environment. Brin's nearly constant muttering to herself told both Avar and me that she was having difficulty finding any sign of the freth. Silently Avar and I would exchange the occasional look or shrug because neither of us wanted to risk her rage at simply asking if she were ok. Early in the afternoon I saw a particular stone in the distance jutting out from the rest. It was a spire of a much darker tone than the slate grey that filled the rest of the horizon. The point was lopsided and one side of the slope to said point was jagged.

As we continued to travel, I started using that spire of stone to track how much progress we had made. Each time I looked for it, it was closer than before. Our path seemed to be headed straight in that direction, so I could not help but ask, "Are we heading for that dark spire over there?"

Chapter 7

"Mmm? What spire?" Brin's concentration had been broken, and she was only paying half attention to me.

Indicating with my hand, "That one. Over there. Rising out of the sea of spikes."

Brin lifted her hand to shield her eyes from the bright rays of the sun and scanned the horizon, "I don't see any spire. You think we should head in that direction?"

"Not having much luck?"

"No, and it is uzkin' frustrating. I have tracked in the Spikelands before, and while the stone floor doesn't make it easy, an army should be leaving more signs. If they used the landmark though, there could be signs near it." Her mood seemed to improve.

"Just keep heading in the same direction then. Should take us right to it."

Our pace quickened slightly. Brin was hopeful that the spire I saw would offer some clue that she was missing. As we drew closer to it, I could make out more detail of the stone itself. It was more than simply a color difference that separated it from the grey that surrounded us. The black stone had swirling veins of white and grey spinning throughout it, and the smooth sheen of it said that it had been not worn by the wind, but instead polished by its embrace. By the time I could see these details, Avar and Brin too could see the spire. I was relieved that it was not something from my visions come to haunt my waking life, yet there was some lingering familiarity about it.

When we finally closed in on the spire it was dusk. The cold air was already starting to whip through the stone trunks that made up the spiky forest. The area around the spire was empty, but the smell of cooked food lingered there.

Desecrated

Brin suddenly darted forward, towards the spire itself. "Look. There was a fire here last night." The stones at her feet were scorched and there lay ashen residue that was being toyed with by the wind. "My gut says that there were only three or four people camped here. This doesn't look like the work of the freth."

Confused, Avar walked towards her, "If not the freth, who else? The Spikelands are barely populated and the people who do live here don't camp out in the open."

"Could be one of the other groups sent out from Sanctuary," I added.

"I doubt they could have gotten this far before us." She mused on the markings around the area a bit more, "And if it were a trap, the signs of the camp would be a bit more obvious."

While my two companions looked for more clues, I found myself drawn to the spire itself. Delicate carvings lay upon its surface, swirling designs all sewn together in a never ending maze of circles, the grooves slightly dusty in places and completely filled with dirt in others. Ancient and mighty it was, yet the top of it was severed, much like the ancient tower we found in that clearing in the Forest of Shadows. I felt some connection to this spire, but when I touched it no vision came. My disappointment was so great that I left my hand upon its surface and closed my eyes trying to force myself into the dream-state from where my visions haunted me. Nothing came.

Behind me, Brin and Avar continued to shuffle about with stones clattering under their feet. My fingers found themselves tracing the spirals on the surface of the spire. The feeling that I had been here before was overwhelming. Distracted by my own thoughts, I mindlessly started clearing the dust from the circular trails in the stone's surface.

Chapter 7

"Wrack, what are you doing?" Avar's voice brought me back.

The sun had moved across the sky while I was caught in my trance. I stepped groggily back from the spire and saw that I had nearly cleaned all of the trails of dust from the base of the pillar. "Did you guys find anything?" I tried to change the subject.

"There definitely was a camp here, but it wasn't the freth. Looks more like a camp of people from the north. Maybe even one of the barbarians from north of Flay. No idea what they would be doing down here, though."

"The tribes are under the King's influence, yeah?" Avar asked.

"Last I heard. And this whole area is The Maiden's territory." Brin's response was very matter of fact.

"Wait. There is a Silver Lady, The Mistress, and now The Maiden?" I asked, confused.

Before Avar could respond, Brin answered, "Yeah. Confusing sometimes, I know. If only the Doomed used regular names instead of stupid titles."

I chuckled a little, "Looks like you aren't the only one who knows about the Doomed, Avar."

Mocking my laughter with his own sarcastic version he looked displeased. "You do know that Garrett put me with Brin to learn from her, yeah?"

His sudden turn to serious was unlike his normal jovial nature. My tone turned apologetic, "I know. Sorry, Avar. I was kidding."

"Yeah? Well, I don't appreciate being made to feel insignificant, Wrack. We all learn from each other here, and if you don't like it, then maybe you should go back to Sanctuary and wait for The Mistress to come and attack." The anger in his eyes only lingered for a moment, then it was shattered by a smile. "I am just fooling with you, Wrack." He laughed. "Brin has been all over the world hunting for stuff. She knows a lot more than me, but she doesn't keep a book like mine," he patted the book hanging from his belt, "so she has probably forgotten more than I will ever know."

A slight laugh came from me. "Yeah, I seem to have forgotten stuff too. Like this spire. I know I have seen it before, but I cannot place it."

"Did you have one of your visions?" Brin joined the conversation.

Shaking my head, "Nothing. I know that there is something in there, but I can't tap into it." A shout and clash of arms found my ears from somewhere nearby. "Did you guys hear that?"

Both Avar and Brin turned their heads to listen for whatever had found me. Brin did not respond with words, but instead tore Ukumog from its ring with a *clink!* and began running off after the sound. Avar and I had no choice but to chase after her.

"I really hate it when she does this," Avar muttered as we ran.

We drew closer to the sound through the maze of sharp standing stones as the sun pushed towards the horizon. The clashing of metal and the crashing of stone became mixed with the shouts of men and the hissing of reptile. First we collided with unsuspecting freth and Brin was quick to use the thirsty edge of Ukumog against them. Beyond these soldiers, however, was a group of darakka. From my raised position behind Brin and Avar, I could see three men fighting against the small host of inhuman soldiers. These men, dressed in a mix of leather, furs, and chain, were handily defeating a group of foes that had given the hunters a tough fight.

Chapter 7

Drawing the daggers that I had been given before we left, I charged into the fight. With each swing of those tiny blades, I couldn't help but feel like this style of fighting wasn't really mine. I wanted more reach so I didn't have to get in so close, though, each time I stabbed one of the freth and felt their hot glowing blood spray my cold flesh the hunger in me delighted in taking their heat. Their life. Perhaps being so close when they expired was a good thing. Those delicious moments could help keep the monster inside me at bay. There was fear in my heart, however, fear that feeding the monster too much might wake it up beyond my control, and set it loose upon the woman I had sworn to aid. That was something I did not want.

Much to my surprise, the fight was over very quickly. The skill of these strangers was impressive. As the last blow of his great sword claimed the life of the final darakka, the large fur-wearing man turned a friendly smile to us and spoke, "Velcome to the Spikelands!" His accent was not like any I had heard before and by the look of them, they weren't from any place I had heard of, either.

Avar and I waited to see how Brin reacted. Each heartbeat that went by after the man spoke created more tension. One of the men in the back even started flexing his fingers on the knives in his hands. "You boys certainly know how to cleave a skull or twenty," she finally said to them.

"Da. You as vell. Interesting svord you have." The largest of them was obviously the leader. Behind him the other two men came forward. "I am Nikolai. My brother Piotyr." The two men looked very similar, save that Nikolai's beard was much larger and wilder, no doubt a reflection of the man himself. "And Tikras, our priest."

Desecrated

"May death's gaze not fall upon you this day," Tikras gave a slight bow and pressed his hand to his chest. He had no beard, unlike his two companions, and was the least barbaric looking of all three men. As a group, they looked very out of place in that forest of stone spikes.

"I am Brin, this is Avar, and behind us is Wrack." Both Avar and I waved at the strange men in turn. "So, Nikolai, what are you boys doing out here in the Spikelands?"

Nikolai laughed a bit and looked over at his brother, who was giving Brin murderous looks. "Brin, have you heard of The Mistress?"

Brin nodded slowly. "I have heard the name before."

"Vell," Nikolai paused and subtly checked in with both of his companions. I saw tiny nods in return. "Ve have issue vith her."

"Long way from the northern reaches of the King's lands, aren't you?" Brin asked with a friendly firmness.

"Da. Ve are a long vay from home. In many vays. You seem to have no love for The Mistress either, if I am not mistaken. From the look of your friend, Avar, there, you are Shadow Hunters, da?"

Clink! Ukumog found its way back onto the ring on Brin's belt. "Avar is a shadow hunter, yeah. Wrack and I are just soldiers of fortune helping the hunters out. Have you seen any strange movements of the freth?"

"Freth? Is that vhat these glowing things are?" Suddenly, he whirled his large blade around and brought it down into the still-moving body of a freth near his feet. "Nasty bit of vork, they are."

My eyes fell upon the etching and other decorative work on his great sword. The fluting and design was not like any I remembered seeing, but there was something familiar about the sword. Turning back to Nikolai, he too seemed familiar in some

140

Chapter 7

strange way. Taking second looks at both Piotyr and Tikras gave me the same impression. Had I met these men before? All the places that gave me a similar feeling were ancient, why would these men give me the same feeling? I was filled with curiosity, but my uncertainty kept it in check. The last thing I wanted was to start a conversation with them that I had no answers to.

"The sun, it departs this place. Ve should find a place to camp," Tikras said to Nikolai.

"Perhaps our new friends vould care to share a fire vith us? Eh, Brin?" His warm smile spoke volumes of sincerity, yet, Brin was cautious.

"Ok, Nikolai. Be warned, the tainted that travels with us never sleeps." She indicated me.

All their eyes were on me, and I could feel them looking for weaknesses or signs of treachery. Unfamiliar with this behavior, I just tried to remain as stone faced as I could. Whatever I did, it seemed to work.

"Very good. One of us vill keep vatch as vell. There is a good spot near the spire."

Avar could remain silent no longer. "That was your camp? Excellent. One less thing to worry about."

Brin raised an eyebrow.

"What? At least we don't have to worry about it."

After a quick search by Piotyr, and myself, we gathered anything useful we could find on the corpses, then the six of us headed back through the shale desert to the spire. The mystery of that decorated tall stone haunted me as soon as we came near it.

Desecrated

We made camp near the base of the stone and while Avar and Tikras chatted over the fire, the rest of us looked through the things we had collected. There were a few things scribbled on bits of paper, some shiny rocks, and some bits of food. Nothing that would lead us to where the gleamstone was.

"Uzk. It is going to be very hard to find their uzkin' camp without some kind of clue. Tracking in this gaak is impossible." Brin kicked the ground and sent a handful of flat grey stones skidding away from our camp.

Nikolai tapped me on the arm and whispered, "Your friend has a bit of a temper, no?"

"You might call it that." I reached over and picked up the scribbles, searching for some meaning to them, even if that meaning was just the idle thoughts of our enemy. Avar calling us to eat broke my concentration.

In slurping silence we devoured the simple stew that was given to us. It wasn't until after dinner that Avar let loose his curious questions. "So Tikras, Nikolai mentioned that you are a priest. Which god do you venerate?"

His eyes drifted back and forth from Nikolai to Avar a few times before he answered, "I vorship the god of death. He who valks in the shadow of the Queen."

Both of Avar's eyebrows went up and he tried to play off his surprise, but failed. "Oh! I have never met a priest of Valik before. Not hard to believe, since all religion in this part of the world has been made illegal by the Doomed."

"No one can take avay the faith of the truly faithful. For most others, their faith lay sleeping, under a blanket of fear, just vaiting for the right spark to bring it back to life. And in its flames, the fear vould be consumed." Tikras became very animated

Chapter 7

and passionate while speaking these words. The joy and hope he expressed was not something I would have expected from someone who venerated death.

"Wow. I wish more people had your dedication and passion, Tikras." The smile on Avar's face was full of excitement. "If you have run into the Shadow Hunters, you would know that we all venerate the Silver Lady."

Tikras nodded, "Da. Ve have had dealings vith the Brothe–"

"The Shadow Hunters have crossed our paths before," Nikolai interrupted. "I had a meeting vith their commander, Garrett, about a month ago."

Suddenly Brin became interested in the conversation. "And what did the two of you talk about, if I may ask?"

"Certainly. Ve chatted about The Mistress. A patrol found us here in the Spikelands and vhen ve mentioned her name to them, they became nervous and vanted us to meet vith Commander Garrett. Our conversation vith him did not go so vell."

"What do you mean?" Avar excitedly asked.

Nikolai sighed and stroked his bushy beard a bit. "Vell, he did not seem to believe us about The Mistress. Ve had just returned from our homeland vhere ve vere looking for a veapon to use against her. There have been three times vhere ve have tried to kill her, and nothing vorks."

"Uzkin' red-haired monster," Piotyr muttered under his breath.

The hair on my neck stood up, and my mind snapped back to the vision of red hair that was choking the life from me. *Have I encountered The Mistress before?*

"So you have fought her?" Avar asked, oblivious to Piotyr's comment.

Desecrated

Disappointment filled Nikolai's face. "Da. She is not easy prey."

"I don't think the hunters have seen her, though her minions seem to be trying to pierce the defenses of Sanctuary." Scratching his chin, Avar sheepishly asked, "What does she look like?"

Nikolai gave a belly laugh. "She is tall, but not enough to make her seem inhuman."

"But she is not human, friend," Tikras added.

"Da. She is a foul creature and far from human. Her mane is a mass of vrithing red snakes of hair, each tendril fitted vith a silver serpent's head," Nikolai added.

Piotyr excitedly interjected, "And they float in the air around her.""Da." Nikolai continued, "Her eyes are black and from deep inside them there is a flickering red light. Like a tiny candle in the dark void of the night sky."

A frown appeared on Avar face. "She sounds terrible."

Mocking laughter came from Brin, "Sounds better than a blood drinking ghost king with a vampire for a son and a rotting corpse as his army commander. What did you expect, Avar? Some misunderstood princess that you could turn to the side of good? The old world of princes and princesses is gone for good, and in its place we left with a world full of terrors who feed on our fear and misery."

"Uzk, Brin. No need to be like that. I was just curious." As usual, Avar had been defeated by Brin's cynicism. Without saying another word, he climbed into his bedroll and tried to seal off the oncoming cold night.

Chapter 7

Seeing Avar's preparation, Tikras likewise prepared for sleep. Piotyr and Brin were soon to follow, with Brin waiting until she was sure Avar was asleep before sleeping right next to him, leaving Nikolai and I to watch.

Hours of cold wind and silence flew between us. I spent the hours looking at the designs in the spire, trying to make sense of the carvings, or occasionally looking again at the scraps of paper.

"Strange thing, no?" Nikolai broke into my concentration while I was staring at the stone. "Must have had a purpose at one time, no?

"Certainly didn't end up here by accident." My cold response seemed to kill the conversation.

More awkward quiet passed through the camp. I caught Nikolai looking at me and he tried to play it off as if he wasn't. The first couple of times I ignored it, then I asked myself what Brin would do. My answer was to confront him about it, but perhaps in a less brash way than she would. "Why do you keep staring at me?"

His bushy eyebrows danced a bit while he crafted his next sentence. With a sigh, "I am not going to lie. You look very familiar to me, and I cannot place it. It is that and I am curious about your part vith them," he said, indicating Avar and Brin with his chin. "You are not a shadow hunter, but you also do not seem like a mercenary."

"We are a strange little band, aren't we?" I chuckled a bit. "Honestly, I am sort of duty bound to Brin. She fights things, and I try and help where I can."

"Vhat is it that you are out here looking for?"

"A gleamstone. The Mistress has one and she is using it somehow against the hunters."

With a furrowed brow he asked, "Is that some kind of magic rock?"

Desecrated

"From what I understand it is, yeah." Suddenly I got nervous. Should I have told him that much? In all our travels it seemed like the people that were not trying to kill us were often our friends and at that moment, I did not have Brin's careful suspicion to guide me. I tried to change the subject. "There is something familiar about you too. I noticed it when we first met, but I cannot place it either."

Nikolai laughed, "Perhaps it vas from another life, friend." He took a deep breath of the cold night air. There was something hiding in his thoughts, but I didn't know him well enough to pry. "Time for Piotyr to vake up, I think. Excuse me, friend."

I nodded to him as he stood up and walked over to his sleeping brother. Quickly, my attention returned to the scribbles. One set of doodles caught my eye, a series of v's in a pattern. Turning the paper around in all sorts of angles, I finally stumbled upon holding the paper upside down and in front of my face. My mind placed the now upside down v's on the tips of the stone spikes that made up the maze we were in. The other scribbles next to it seemed like they might be landmarks, or a tracker's journal of some sort.

"Friend," Nikolai and Piotyr had stealthily come to my side. "Ve have something to share vith you."

Piotyr's eyebrow raised at his brother, but Nikolai gave him a tiny nod and he changed his focus to me. "Ve know vhere the stone you are looking for is. The Mistress' army keeps it in their main tent, on the other side of the Bladed Labyrinth." My lack of response prompted him to explain further, "It is a dangerous place vhere the stones are so close together and sharp that it like crawling through a maze of knives."

"Ok, how do we get to it then?"

Chapter 7

Nikolai laughed, "Ve? Ve are telling you, friend, so you can go get it. Ve have no need for this stone. But my brother and I like you, so ve tell you this thing to help you."

"But Nikolai, don't you think that fighting together with the Shadow Hunters would be better than trying to take on The Mistress alone? If you help them, I have no doubt that they will help you."

Nikolai stroked his beard and fell into deep thought. Even in the low light, I could make out the shadows on Piotyr's jaw as he flexed it, grinding his teeth like Brin often did.

"Look. I don't know what has happened between you and the hunters before. And I certainly don't want to tell you how to wage your war against The Mistress, but wouldn't it be easier to have allies than to try and go at it with just the three of you?"

"Da, more swords does make var easier. I tell you vhat, ve vill help get the stone and then ve vill see from there. Attacking her main camp vould be vorth it, even if ve part vays after."

Nikolai's agreement to help us made me somewhat happy. It felt oddly as if I had been reunited with friends for one last push against the enemy.

After we agreed to work together, even if temporarily, Nikolai went to sleep and left me alone with Piotyr. There was not a single word that passed between us in those long hours of the night. Instead, he spent the time polishing his knives and working repairs on his armor. Not once did I catch him looking at me, but I knew that he was always watching.

Morning came, and with it the air began to warm. Nikolai and I explained how they had seen the gleamstone the last time they were in the enemy camp, and how they had agreed to help us retrieve it. There was one thing that he had neglected to mention.

Desecrated

"It has been a veek or so since ve have been there, so the camp may have moved. Vith luck, and the gods on our side, ve vill find them."

Brin's eyebrow was raised. I knew she was annoyed because while left alone, I told them about our mission, but I think she was further upset by the fact that their help might just lead us on a wild goose chase. "So, you aren't completely sure where the stone is?"

"Vell, ve have seen it. Do you have a better place to start looking?"

Brin's temper started to get the better of her. "We were doing just fine until you dragged us back–"

Tikras stood up and put out his empty palms. "Brothers and sister, let us not fight. Valik, sacred is his deathly guise, has brought us together that ve may bring his vrath upon the head of our enemy. Quench this rage in the heartsblood of she who vexes us."

"That is good, Tikras. A little spooky, but good. I agree with him, Brin. If we hurry, we can get there in no time." Avar's trusting nature had returned just in time to bring us together.

Exhaling all her anger over the situation, Brin composed herself as much as she could and nodded in acceptance of the deal. Within no time at all, the six of us were headed off to find the camp where the gleamstone lay hidden.

After about many hours of travel through the stone forest we came upon an open expanse of different stones. They were smaller, redder in their hue, and jutted in every direction creating a confusing puzzle of trails.

Nikolai confirmed what I already knew. "The Bladed Labyrinth."

"It doesn't look so bad." There was an excited, happy tone in Avar's voice.

Chapter 7

Brin laughed.

"The trouble is that each pathvay does not lead you the vay you vish to go. The stones of the labyrinth also shift as you move through, so you cannot alvays go back. There are things that live in there, too, but last time ve found that if you leave them alone they vill do the same." Nikolai's words were not as reassuring as he meant them to be. Still, he nodded to all of us to see if we were ready, and all of us nodded back. The moment we crossed into the labyrinth a chill came over me, and I saw the runes on Ukumog grow brighter. It was hungry, and it smelled the blood of prey.

Our travel through the maze of sharp stones was not easy. Slowly we passed over, under, and around their perilous edges. More than once Piotyr would leave all his equipment behind to shimmy through an area, then we would pass the gear forward, and each take our turns carefully moving through. We could not run or jump, else the rocks around us would shift in the giant piles of thin stony wafers they emerged from. Sometimes we could hear noises echoing through the labyrinth. Neither stones shifting nor the sounds of screeching animals brought any comfort. Whatever called this place home, I certainly did not want to meet it.

Clouds had been gathering in the sky above us all day, and around the time that Avar usually started complaining about stopping for dinner they opened. Rain began falling in great sheets all around us. The random attack of the rain on the stones around us began making them shift unexpectedly, yet we tried to keep moving slowly to prevent more shifting. The storm got worse, and the sky grew even darker. Lightening lit up the sky and the bang of the bolt came right on the heels of the flash. The rain became so intense that I could not see anyone beyond the person directly in front of me, which was Tikras.

Desecrated

We came upon a tiny corridor of stones, with all the blades standing like walls in a hallway. One of these had fallen over and rain was pouring off the side of it. The water was pouring into the shifting stones of the path. The only safe way through was to crawl under the stone, which meant crawling on your belly to get under it. By the time I knew what was happening, Piotyr, Nikolai, and Brin were already on the other side. Avar had passed all his gear through the opening and began shimmying through. Lightning flashed again and I could see the stones of the ground tearing into the exposed flesh of his legs where his pants had become naught but tatters.

Tikras pulled off his armor in the rain and threw his possessions under the stone. "May the guardian of death deliver you to the other side, brother," he said to me with a friendly smile and then began the painful crawl underneath the stone. Moments later I saw his feet vanish into the hole and I was left alone on the other side in the pouring rain.

"Ok Murks, stay in my robe, and I will pass you under the stone," I thought to my hidden companion.

Concern rose in him, and I could feel it as if it were my own emotion. "Murks not want to leave Master. It dangerous here."

"It will be ok Murks. I will be fine," I began disrobing. First I removed the tattered rope that was my belt, the little skulls on the ends jingling silently in the torrent of rain, then my heavy robe, completely soaked with the sky-fall. I had forgotten that my tattered shirt was what Murks had been using to repair my robes while we were on the trail, and I had discarded it weeks ago. There I stood in the storm, naked from the waist up, with tattered pants and boots. Around my neck still hung the enigmatic rusty key that was

Chapter 7

with me when I crawled from the grave that gave birth to me. The frayed bits of leathery straps that were tied around my wrists still remained as well, and had been equally forgotten about.

Folding the robes as well as I could, I tied it with my rope belt. I placed my pouches and daggers inside, and so crafted a tight little package to pass under the stone. There was difficulty when I tried to remember how to tie a knot that would hold the package, but would come undone easily when the time was right. The rain battered down on my skin as I struggled with the rope. As I finally finished the knot, I heard the rocks around me shift. Something was not right. I was not alone on that side of the stone anymore. Quickly, I moved to the fallen blade, and tossed my package under the rock. I shouted through the hole, "I'm coming through!" There was no response from the other side.

The stones shifted behind me again, and I heard one of the blades that made up the hallway behind me sliding. At first it was slow, then it rapidly became like a tree crashing down in the forest with all the thunder that would come with a trunk made of stone. Startled by the noise, I spun around and stood up. The rain was so blinding that I could not see more than a few feet away from me. The water was running into my eyes and making it impossible to concentrate on using my dark sight. Something crashed into the rocks at my feet, and I squinted trying to discover it amidst the sharp wet stones below me. Lightning crashed into the ground nearby, illuminating the entire area. The brief moment of clear sight gave me enough time to see the bloated form of a woman with hooks protruding from her disgusting flesh.

"UZK!" I screamed, and despite the rain I heard the whistle of a chain coming in my direction. Leaping to one side to avoid it I landed on my back, and crashed into hundreds of razor sharp rocks that ripped my flesh to ribbons. From the other side of

Desecrated

the stone, I could see the blue glow of Ukumog and a chill ran up my spine. The cold energy washed over my body and my hands tingled with painful cold. With calculated murder beating through my veins, I grabbed a handful of the sharp stones and sprayed them at my unseen enemy. As the cloud of razors left my hand I sent them as heralds of my hatred, my pain, and my desire to do harm. Streaks of dark purple light trailed after each of the flat stones as they soared to their hungry destinations. Now was the time to run.

I never saw the rocks land, but the howl of pain and frustration from the beast followed me into the hole under the stone. Before I could emerge on the other side, the stone began shifting above me. She was trying to pull it down on me, to crush and sever me beneath the massive blade of rock. Moving as quickly as I could, I tried to get to the other side. My head emerged, but my legs became pinned under the mighty weight of the stone. I screamed in agony and my rage became overwhelming.

My companions on the other side scrambled to try and help. In my legs flesh tore, muscles ripped, bones broke as I twisted myself around so I could face the rocky blade that was pinning me. Avar, Nikolai, and Piotyr pulled on the stone, trying to lift it from me to no avail. My screams echoed in the sky, and I saw lightning jump from cloud to cloud above me. Brin stepped up to the stone, Ukumog held loosely in her right hand, its runes glowing with malicious hunger.

Brin stared at the stone blade crushing me for a moment. Instinctively I reached out and put a hand on her foot in a plea for help. Power shot through me, leaving fire in my veins. Seething anger boiled my mind, and it was all I could do to stay in control of myself. I heard the dark power of Ukumog calling to me, the runes on its sides brightly shimmering in the torrential rain. Brin looked down at me with an empty stare, but her eyes were different.

Chapter 7

Her eyes were glowing with the same blue that danced on the flat of Ukumog. The power was too great for me, so I removed my hand from her foot. As the monster faded from me, I could feel that Murks had also been affected by the silent roar of Ukumog's rage.

Dispassionately, Brin began climbing with little leaps up the side of the stone blade. Each jump she made while climbing caused the stone to press on me harder. With everyone distracted, I saw the package of my robes moving slightly and I felt Murks' frustration in trying to escape so he could help. I wanted to tell him not to show himself, but the power in me was fading as I bled from my legs and back into the innumerable cracks between the stones in the floor beneath me.

"Brin! Brin, what are you doing!?" Avar shouted in concern.

With her free hand she held onto the top edge of the stone blade and pressed her feet against its side, looking like an animal waiting to pounce. "Come get me you ugly bitch!"

Thunder exploded above us, and the rumbling aftershock seemed to last forever. The sound of metal clattering, then grinding, on stone came from above, as Brin dodged the chains that the beast was swinging at her. Below her, Murks burst from the tightly bound package of my things and hurried toward my legs. The other four of our company continued to struggle with moving the stone, albeit they were very distracted by the flying chains and woman with the glowing sword above their heads.

I felt some of the pressure on my broken legs give, as Murks began to dig the stones out from under them. How he was doing that, and how he got under my legs was a mystery to me, but my legs were beginning to become free. Sharp pain followed by intense

Desecrated

heat ran up and down my lower body. My ability to heal quickly had kicked in, and the power within me was knitting my bones and flesh back together as soon as they were not being crushed.

More scraping and clattering came from above. Brin suddenly stopped dodging the chains and for the first time brought up the heft of Ukumog above the lip of the stone and then down on one of the chains as it was being retracted over the stone blade. Over and over she brought down Ukumog on the chains before they could escape back over the edge. At first I was confused about what she was doing, as confused as my other friends who had stopped trying to move the huge rock and just stood dumbfounded watching the dervish above us. Then I realized she was using the flat of Ukumog to drive the chains into the stone before the knot and hook could escape, trapping it in the stone. First one chain became stuck, then another. More chains came over the edge and she continued to escape their danger, and then trap them in the edge of the stone.

A roar of unearthly frustration rolled over us from the beast on the other side, then the chains stopped. Tiny shards of stone began falling from the edge, but only my enhanced vision could make it out in the rain. Another roar bellowed from the beast, this one filled with struggle. Pops and bangs started to come from the stone and Brin let herself drop to our side. "Now she is pissed," she said with a dash of dark humor.

My mind connected to my blood-crafted companion, "Murks, get out of there!"

Immediately, I could feel him scrambling to the surface. "Master should be free if the stone shifts."

Loud creaking escaped the stone and I replied, "Oh, I think it is about to."

Chapter 7

The top of the stone began to move away from us. The sound of metal grinding against stone scraped through the air. The beast was pulling the stone towards her. The stones under me began to shift, and quickly I tried to pull myself free of the trap. Avar and Tikras noticed, and they gently started pulling me free. Piotyr ran over to the stone where my package still lay and snatched it up. Murks had been too late to sneak back into it, so he leapt onto a wet fur hanging from Piotyr's armor and climbed. Looking around at my companions, I didn't think that any of them had noticed the tiny scab colored man who was now climbing up Piotyr's back.

The stone started moving much quicker and with that movement, I was freed. A great splashing of stone and water erupted as the blade fell down into the slivers of slate below. Murks used the distraction to dive back into the package of my gear, while Avar and Tikras pulled me away from the thrown debris.

"Wrack," Brin said calmly, "can you run?"

"Uh." I looked down at my unharmed legs and said with some surprise, "Yeah. I think I can."

"Good." She paused to wrestle with Ukumog's desire to charge forward and fight. For a moment, I thought she would give in to Ukumog's dark thirst for blood, but then "Run!" she exclaimed and turned to run away. Following her lead, we all ran as fast as we could into the dark shifting corridor of sharp stones. Behind us in the dark, the rain pounded on a horror that had been denied her prey. Her howl sent shivers up my spine, and told me that she was not done with us yet, but the sounds of a massive stone being dragged through the shattered flooring told me that we might at least have a head start.

The rain was coming down harder than before and again I could only see the person directly in front of me, which happened to be Piotyr who was still carrying my package. Both he and

Desecrated

I struggled to run in the sharp slippery surface, but run we did. Distance and curtains of falling water muffled the howls of the beast behind us. Brin's cunning trick of driving the chains into the rock had saved us, for the moment. When our pace finally slowed, Piotyr gave me the package and shortly thereafter we stopped so I could change.

"The exit is close," Nikolai assured us. "The camp is not far from there."

"Hopefully they haven't moved," Brin said gasping for air. "I don't relish the idea of coming back through this horrid place so quickly."

"There is a vay around."

"Oh, now you tell us," Brin said with a mocking tone. She opened her left hand to discover that it was sliced to the bone. I tore off a strip from my frayed pants and began binding her hand. There was not even a thought to the small portion of my blood that might have been lingering in the bandages. We needed to close that wound. While I worked, she continued to chide Nikolai, "We could have been killed back there and now you tell us that there is a way around?"

Nikolai shrugged, "Da. I thought that time was of essence."

"Uh. Wrack? What is that on your back?" Avar interrupted from behind me.

"Nothing, I just fell on the rocks and they tore me up a bit." Quickly I went back to unpacking my gear and putting on my robe.

Avar held back the robe as I tried to cover myself. "No really. There is some kind of marking on your back. Hard to see with all the torn flesh though. Are you going to be ok?"

Chapter 7

"Yeah, I will be fine," I pulled the robe out of his hand and finished getting dressed. Before I said I was ready, I checked to make sure I had all my pouches, dagger, and my hemodan safely tucked into their respective places.

In almost no time, we found our way to the exit of the Bladed Labyrinth and found ourselves in a place very similar to the grey spiky horizon on the other side. Just as before, Nikokai led us through the dark rain as if he had been there a thousand times before. Once we were some distance from the labyrinth, we made camp for the night. By morning the rain had cleared. We all wrung out our clothes, and the warm embrace of the following day dried us out rather quickly as we set off to find the camp.

Nikolai and Piotyr working together found the spot where the camp had been, and in the small clearing, there were no tents, just vague signs that a camp had been there.

Brin crouched low to the ground and examined the surface. "From the looks of it, it looks like hundreds of freth were here."

"Hey Wrack, once your back is healed, I want to take a look at the markings on it, ok?"

"Sure Avar." Secretly I wished he would forget about it. Whatever was written back there, I had a feeling it was best forgotten.

"Here we go!" Brin excitedly called out. "This, my friends, is gleamdust." She held up a few fingers covered in a shiny metallic flakes. "They must be breaking the gleamstone into pieces. Nik or Piotyr, have you guys found tracks leading out of here?"

"Nothing vorth following. The stones nearby must have shifted."

Desecrated

My mind turned to the doodles in my pocket. "What if these drawings are a map of some kind?" I pulled the scraps of paper out of my robe. Some of the ink had run from the rain, but the original marks could still be seen.

Avar was confused. "What kind of map is just a bunch of v's and squiggles?"

Ignoring him, I went to the center of the clearing and held up the piece of paper. The material was thin enough that I could make out the shadows of the stones behind the paper when the sun was on the other side. "The peaks of the v's upside down sometimes line up with the spikes."

"Vouldn't you have to look through it at the right time of day?" Tikras asked.

"Yeah. I think these doodles over here say when, and that should be right about now or it is when the sun is on the other end of the sky."

"Vorth a shot," Nikolai beamed with hopeful optimism.

Nothing was matching. I would get one or two of the spikes to line up, but it wasn't working. Brin was looking at the paper over my shoulder, and just as I was about to give up, she put her hands on my hips and moved me about four or so feet to the right. "I think this other squiggle says that you stand here."

"I found a match! If I am right about the rest of it, this means that we go that direction through these stones to get to the next camp."

"Vell done, Vrack!" Nikolai gave me a huge smile. "Let's move on then."

And move on we did. After several hours, we got to another location marked on the scribbles and I was able to use the next scrap of paper to guide us forward. We didn't need the paper for the next direction. The sound of a large camp carried on the wind and led

Chapter 7

us directly to them. As we came up over the dune of stone flakes, we saw the camp in the fading sunlight. There were twenty-five tents in total, all of them white with thin golden stripes and red trim, hung with white banners with red fringe trimming their long triangle shape, emblazoned with the golden face of a woman's head surrounded by a wild cloud of red hair. Five of the tents were larger and more ornate.

Watching the camp for a while from our hidden position, we noticed that there were not enough freth to move all of the tents themselves, let alone be the army that Brin claimed had been at the previous camp. Something was off. "Brin," I whispered, "where are all the freth?"

Her eyes were slits as she concentrated on the camp. "I dunno, Wrack. Something is not right, but we have little choice. We have to get down in there and find the gleamstone. You boys ready?"

Without much hesitation, we all declared our readiness. In the pause before Brin started her charge into the camp, both Avar and Tikras uttered whispered prayers. I hoped that their patrons were listening to their pleas.

It took seconds for Brin and Nikolai to run down the hill. By the time I came into the camp, three freth already lay dead at their feet. Piotyr vanished off to one side of the camp to look for the gleamstone while Avar, Tikras, and I brought up the rear. From every large tent a small group of freth came bursting out, and one darakka came out of one of the tents. Weapons danced with deadly edges all around me, and I let my instincts take over. My body relaxed, and my daggers seemed to move through the air with a will of their own. Even with just these tiny blades, I easily defended myself and the two men beside me from all attacks that I could reach. I could not step away from our circle, however, due

Desecrated

to the limitation on range that I suffered. I let the orchestra of our weapons soothe my mind, and I found myself in the same trance as I had when I was first attacked in Yellow Liver by those two guards. This time was different because I gave in to it. The river of war flowed through my soul. My mind opened and for a moment, I saw how deep the river was.

Chapter 8

The plates in my armor scraped and jingled with every movement I made. With an eerie slowness, they chimed through the air with no other sound reaching my ears. The light around me was grey and hazy at first, like I was deep within a fog so thick that I could not even see most of myself, yet I was moving unhindered by the special uncertainty that a mist this thick should bring. Light flashed, searing away the fog, and instantly bringing the frantic pace of a battle to my mind. On all sides freth and men besieged me. Mud and dirt were flying in every direction as the countless force of humanoid figures tore not only each other, but the world under their feet. The heavy sword in my hand flew with the skill of many battles, and my heart was cold with anger.

"Vhen ve catch this bitch, I am going to make her listen to the list of lives she ended today before I stab both her eyes out and shave her head." Nikolai's voice fought through the clash of the battle to reach me.

"Sounds too good for her." My response was cold and flat.

Nikolai's deep laughter echoed through the fog, and neither of us stopped fighting.

Confusion took hold of my thoughts. Quickly, I glanced around the foggy battlefield and did not see what I expected to. There was someone missing, someone very important to me. The

Desecrated

desire to find them became sharp within me. Frustrated by the helmet I was wearing, I removed it. Stepping back, I allowed my fellows to fill the hole while I regrouped. The cold bit my hands, and I sheathed my sword to breathe warmth into my freezing fists. Taking a moment to inspect my armor, I found torn holes within the mesh. "If we survive this, Marec is going to kill me," I said to myself.

The answer to my lost companion was quickly answered as Lucien's massive hand fell upon my shoulder. "You alright? I have never seen this much ferocity in you before. Fighting alongside the Eisenwyrs has turned you into a fearsome barbarian!" He smiled and laughed.

"We could all learn something from them, Lucien. Not all of us have the advantage of being a brutish giant," I smiled. "I didn't see you there for a second, thought we had lost you."

"Even us giants have to take a step back and rest once in a while." He drank deeply from his water skin.

I looked up and down the field. Thousands of soldiers from The Brotherhood were giving their all to this fight. In my heart, I knew that none of this loss of life would make any difference. "We might stop The Mistress from becoming the ally of Ravenshroud, but it isn't going to stop their campaign. How long can we hold out, Lucien? We have to do something other than fortify in Sanctuary, and hope that they don't mass enough force to destroy us. Have we heard from the Queen of the Shrouded Forest? Surely she will–"

"They aren't going to help us. The ancient denizens of the forest do not care about us. We are but a passing moment in their history. They have never gotten involved in human politics before. Well, apart from the Prince making an appearance at the council twenty years ago. I still believe his presence there was just so that he would have an alibi for General Andoleth's surprise attack on

Chapter 8

the tower. His involvement in that tragedy isn't hidden by that fact, however. Or perhaps he just wanted to witness his own handiwork. All of us there got a gruesome glimpse of that event." A frustrated grunt escaped him. "Makes me want to burn down the entire forest."

At the mention of the tower massacre, my mind spiraled into the dark moment when I watched my entire world get murdered. The despair of that event was still so strong in me, a dark spot in my memory for which no time could heal. Quickly the sorrow became hatred, and that hate became anger, anger became rage, and without another word I placed my helmet back upon my head, and I went off to destroy more of the enemy, an army led by a woman who would be an ally to the man who murdered my family, destroyed my world, corrupted my friends, twisted my own mind, and who would not stop until everyone bowed to his will. The cold air of that misty morning stung my face, but the tears in my eyes were not from that pain, but from something deeper.

A flash of light and swirling mist took me away from the battle. When the blindness receded, I was in the mess hall of Sanctuary. Nikolai, Lucien, Marec, and I were seated at a table with a few other people whose faces I could not place. In solemn quiet we ate our bread and soup, until Nikolai broke the silence.

"My brothers and I vill have to go north and continue the fight." His arms and armor looked exactly the same as I knew him in my waking world. Indeed, there seemed to be no difference in the number of grey hairs that lay peeking out of his bushy beard. Yet, I was different, younger and without the touch of death about me. My mind wanted this to be my reality, a time before my torment. I wanted to remain here.

"How far north will you have to go?" I asked.

Desecrated

"Ve vill take the fight all the vay to the Rise if ve have to. Her actions go beyond just simple alliance to Ravenshroud. She is taking people from their homes and doing strange things to them. I cannot be avay from my people vhile she torments them. Ve pushed her back from here vell, but now it is time to go." As if to emphasize his point, he took a huge bite of his bread.

Lucien spoke before anyone else could, "I think I speak for everyone here when I say we will be sorry to see you and your brothers go. Even your priest fights well, and makes us low-landers think differently about our struggling brothers to the north. May the Silver Lady inspire you to find the success that you richly deserve. You will be missed."

The sounds of a woman quietly laughing came to me. Before I could look for the source of it, my mind was bombarded by a host of images. Twisting strands of red fibers, slithering like snakes. Pain wracked me from somewhere unseen. Rolling rocky terrain surrounded the spire in the Spikelands, but it was whole and unblemished. A giant mountain that rose like the tip of an arrow above its neighbors and piercing the very heavens. Fields of snow, dotted with small villages, their chimneys left smokeless. Pain shot through me again, this time it felt like my arms were on fire. The laughter grew more sinister and the clanging of a blacksmith's hammer began ringing in my ears. The ringing became the clashing of blades, and my eyes opened.

It wasn't the first blow that landed on my flesh that woke me from my dream, nor was it the second. Possibly it was the third or fourth. When I regained my senses, the blade of a freth had cut into the flesh of my arms. Though it struck me with a great deal of

Chapter 8

force, my bones remained intact. My mind only had time to realize that I was wounded, and that somehow I had continued to fight through the dream state. I now found myself escaping the dream, and took in a breath before the levee holding back the mounting pain was shattered. The pain of my unknown wounds ran its course, flooding my brain with agony, but in my half awake mind I turned the pain into something else. There in the laboratory of my skull, my pain became a weapon.

Immediately the cold sting of the dark power that lay dormant in my soul came out of me in waves. I felt the stinging agony leaving my eyes and hands, like heat rising from a nest of hot coals. My movements became smooth and deadly. With every tiny shift of my body I evaded or attacked my opponents. In that moment, I had the grace of a dancer, and the dead heart of a killer. My sudden transformation shocked the freth who found themselves at the other end of my blades. In that brief instant, the part of the circle where I stood changed from the weak spot to a death trap. The freth could not escape fast enough.

My friends all were holding their own, and as I regained more of my senses there was one whispering thought that haunted me. My longing eyes drifted to the dancing edge of Ukumog in the hands of Brin. My teeth ground against their counterparts as I longed to hold the leather wrapped bone of Ukumog's grip, and also to feel the enveloping warmth of Brin's skin. Blood rushed to my face and I felt the hairs on my body rise at the intoxicating thought. I wanted to drink the blood of these freth and their darakka masters. Unable to sate my urge for Brin or Ukumog, I granted myself that desire. While my enemies retreated I licked the blood from one of my daggers. The hot blood was like having fire on my tongue.

Desecrated

Warmth I had not known ever before filled me to overflowing, the tension in my muscles relaxed and I became more focused than I had ever remembered.

A sinister grin appeared on my face and the muscles that held it rejoiced. A forgotten piece of me had returned. The freth facing me gave ground. Their eyes were wide, letting all their delicious fear escaping. Unwilling to let my prey escape, I danced forward with them, then suddenly, I closed the gap and let my blades drink deep of their life. As soon as they had their fill, I moved to the next and the next. Soon I was leaping from enemy to enemy, ending their lives with skill and precision that only a master of death could summon. What disturbed me most was that I found it fun.

None that came forward to fight escaped us. While I killed a great many of the freth, my companions felled their shares as well. Ukumog even came to life while fighting the darakka and it, too, bathed in the deep wells of the dragon-thing's blood. When it was all over, I stood over my victims in pride and horror, and I wasn't the only one.

"My gods, Wrack! What got into you?" Avar asked.

Afraid of the real answer, I just shrugged. Feeling the surge of battle lust fade, I checked my arms for wounds and only found pristine, dead flesh.

"I have never seen you fight like that before. Wow, Wrack. Just – just wow," Avar was speechless.

Brin chuckled, "Yeah, maybe you didn't need me to save your life after all."

I turned to look at her. She seemed to glow with a light that no one else could see. There she was, my beacon, my bonfire, my darkly radiant champion. Feelings of desire, remorse, and hunger pounded in my heart. My breathing became fast and deep and everything became electrified.

Chapter 8

"Wrack? Wrack, what is wrong?" Her concern was touching, but it wasn't enough to pull me away from the emotional frenzy going on within me. "Wrack, you are shaking."

And so I was. My fists were clenched so tightly around my daggers they were vibrating with the chorus of thoughts flowing through me. My eyes shot down to Ukumog, who rested in her hand with runes brightly pulsing. Taking deep breaths, I slowed the chaos in my spirit, and let the pulse of Ukumog match the song in my soul. All became well. "I am fine. Whatever that was just caught me by surprise, that's all," I lied.

"You and us both, buddy." Avar stepped forward and padded me on the shoulder.

Piotyr came rushing up to us. "Quick, follow me."

Follow him we all did, and he led us to a tent that was small, but was decorated as if it were for someone important. Inside there was an anvil that was covered in sparkling dust. The floor of the tent was littered with tiny glimmering fragments of rock, but there was no large gleamstone.

"Oh, uzk," Brin said quietly. "They have broken it up. By the looks of the force they left behind, they are already making their move on Sanctuary. We need to move."

No one argued, no one complained. The six of us quickened our pace and left the camp. At first Brin began leading us back to the Bladed Labyrinth, but then Nikolai spoke up. "Brin, ve can make better time if ve go around. Yes, the trip is longer, but if that thing is still there then we might not make it back. And vith the shifting of the labyrinth... I think I know how The Mistress took her army to Sanctuary. Ve could close the distance, but they may get there ahead of us."

Desecrated

Brin took only a moment to ponder it. "Lead on Nikolai." She wasn't happy about letting go of the leadership of the group, but she needed his help. The look she gave me as she walked past said, "I hope we can still trust these guys."

Days of quick travel passed us by. Rest only came sparingly as we drew closer to our goal. Each tiny hint that we were closing in on Sanctuary, and signs of the army that approached it, charged our group with an energetic desire to press on. Avar in particular seemed to embrace the shorter nights, which was uncharacteristic of the man who used to sleep in as long as possible. Perhaps we were all seeing him grow into the person he was sent on this journey with Brin to become.

The deep wound on Brin's left hand seemed to almost completely fade just a few days after we began our flight to Sanctuary, but I continued to bandage it each time we stopped. We didn't have time to pause and wonder why she had healed so fast, even though I knew the reason.

The sun was reaching the horizon on the day when the terrain changed from unfriendly rock to yellow grass and needly trees. By dark we approached Sanctuary and the battlefield it had become.

Darakka and their freth soldiers were everywhere. We stepped over bodies full of arrows on our way into the town. As we drew closer the bodies of the invaders were sometimes mixed with a few hunters, still wearing their silver mantles. The smell of the blood and death was overwhelming.

Scouting the outside, it seemed that the battle had become concentrated in the center of town and near the great graveyard in the back. Something told me that the latter is where we should go.

"We should see if we can break the siege," offered Avar.

Chapter 8

Shaking my head, "No. What she wants is in the graveyard. Look."

Brin nodded, and we started creeping through the town towards the graveyard. While the battle raged behind us, we came on a small company of freth standing near the center statue. It seemed like an odd place for them to gather, and Brin picked up on it without me having to say a word.

Four of us crept through the graveyard, using the tombstones as cover as we went. The varying nature of the stones made it impossible for us to stay grouped together, so we spread out along the way, with Avar and Tikras staying behind to watch our backs. As we got closer, I paid close attention to the freth standing near the tree sculpture. They seemed completely distracted by the battle happening not far away from them. They were all transfixed with the fight, and seemed like animals invisibly caged while the rest of their pack was loose. "It should be easy to sneak up on them," I whispered to myself.

As if on cue, Brin silently strode forward and brought Ukumog down on the neck of a freth who was standing there. Before his companions could react, his glowing blood was already spilling onto the ground. Ukumog rose to strike again, but met with the blades of the freth. Nikolai, Piotyr, and I forsook our shadows and strode forth into the fray. The remaining three freth were dead within seconds.

The statue had been pushed forward, and underneath its dais lay a staircase riddled with the webbing of thousands of tiny forgotten spiders. The curtains of webbing had already been breached and in the dust on the stairs were many foot prints. I could hear voices inside, but I could not make out who they belonged to. Nikolai signaled to Tikras, and our lookouts scurried across the graveyard to join us. The two of them kept low to the ground as to

Desecrated

not attract the attention of the fighting army in the town. As soon as we were all assembled, Brin nodded to Nikolai, who nodded back, and we descended into the flickering torchlight below.

The stones that made the hallway were blackened with age under blankets of webbing and dust. The working of the stone may at one time been pristine, but time and neglect had certainly had their way with the work that was done many, many years ago. I had flashes of memory of this hallway, the stones pristine and white, gleaming in the torchlight from my memory. This was a sacred place to me, but also a place that filled me with dread. Each step we took made me fearful of the next, and the next. While my companions continued on, I lagged behind quietly for I knew that nothing good lay in the chamber beyond, and I had no urgent desire to meet it.

My friends breached the room and I knew what they saw: a circular room, with four pillars, each one a few feet out from the wall the wall. In the center of the room lay a disc of white stone that rose an inch or so off the floor. In the very center of the disc a sort column rose from it to about knee height. Upon that ornate column, etched with the image of the Silver Forest wherein the Silver Lady resided, there lay an altar, cast of silver and made for both offerings and a place where the Lady could sit should she ever decide to grace her faithful with her very presence. Every surface of the temple would be worked with the flowing designs of the moon and forests. On the walls were once painted tiny people, each of them representing those who the faithful wished to be rejoined with after they were taken from this life, and rewarded with the eternal joy within the silver forest. On the ceiling was an image of the Silver Dragon, in a great circle, holding its own tail in its mouth. The chamber ahead was a place of hope, of joy, and eternal renewal, but no longer.

Chapter 8

The images of lost friends were stripped from the surface of the walls. Every column was covered in the same blanket of webs and dust that could be found on the every other surface. The floor was hidden under ankle deep clouds of dust, stirred by we intruders. And the altar. The altar was concealed under a suit of armor trapped by black chains of iron. The armor lay upon its back, limbs twisted behind it, and wrapped in those dark chains. The ropes of iron snaked around both the body and limbs of the armor, and worked their way around the altar with the pillar beneath, but also were driven into the cracked white stone below by equally dark spikes with rings atop them. The armor, while empty moved, and from it came a low moan and a whimper, the same sound that a broken prisoner forgotten in a dark dungeon and driven mad by isolation would make.

"Ah. We have company after all," a woman's voice echoed down the hall. "You have dispatched my guards, I take it? No sense in calling for help then?"

"Hello, Mistress." Nikolai's greeting was filled with sarcastic poison. His vocal demeanor was a far cry from that of the jovial barbarian that I had come to know.

There was a metallic hiss from within the room followed by laughter, the same woman's laughter that I had been hearing in my visions. I wanted to charge forward into the room to see the source, but my dread kept me at bay.

"Nikolai Eisenwyr," she said. "Wonderful that you and your friends could make it to see this." Her boots clicked and clopped against the stone floor as she paced while talking. "This room contains all I need to become who I am destined to be."

Desecrated

Those horrible black chains rattled, sending shivers of shame down my spine, and the empty armor screamed a muffled scream. As I stepped up behind my friends, I pulled my hood over my head, finding some solace in the shadows they provided. From inside the shadow of my hood, I lifted my eyes to see the room.

It was exactly as I knew it would be, save for the tall woman dressed in red with a black corset over her flowing dress. If not for the floating, writhing nature of her hair, it would have certainly draped upon the ground. Each lock of hair was somewhat matted and at their tip was a silver snake head. The snakes were hissing and looking this way and that, causing her hair to move like a mass of red snakes that had grown from her skull. Her eyes were nothing but black orbs set behind her eyelids and her fingers ended in sharpened nails that seemed more like claws. While her shape might have been one of a human woman, she certainly was nothing of the kind. Deep within my soul a hatred of her resonated, quietly, behind my shame and fear. The puzzle of what I had done, and how I had grown to hate this unearthly woman, taunted me.

I wondered why Brin and Nikolai had not leapt in to attack her, so I continued to search the room. Standing with their backs to the wall around the circle of the room were at least twenty darakka, each standing perfectly still and at attention. Our band could definitely kill a few of them on our own, but not twenty, and certainly not with The Mistress in their midst. Still, I wanted us to attack. From how brightly Ukumog glowed, so did it.

"Once I have tapped into the power that lay within this poor tortured soul, I will have everything. Nikolai. Everything apart from a king, for I will be The Mistress no longer and will claim my rightful place as Queen of this world." Her smile sickened me. "When that time comes, perhaps you will reconsider my offer.

Chapter 8

I would hate to be forced to make one of the Doomed my king, for they no longer have the spark of life that I need. You, on the other hand–"

"Forget it, creature. As long as there is breath vithin my chest I vill fight you. The chains of your enslavement have never reached my heart, and they never shall." He flexed the grip on his sword as he spoke. Nikolai was not one for great speeches, and his restless spirit longed to strike.

"Aww. Such a shame. I will miss your impotent threats, Nikolai." She walked closer to the animated armor, and with clawed fingers caressed the faceplate of the helmet. With mocking pity she said to it, "So long you have suffered. Let us help you."

Unable to remain calm any longer, Brin stepped forward into the room and shouted, "Hey!"

"Oh, Nikolai. Your friend is a feisty one!" Her attention was back on our little group.

Not wishing to be caught by surprise, I moved in behind Brin and readied my blades. The Mistress came around from behind the altar and stood between it and us. Tapping her chin with one of her sharp fingers she asked, "Now, who do we have here?"

The fury growing inside Brin must have driven her forward, for instead of answering the question she charged and attacked The Mistress. Instantly the room erupted with action as the darakka along the walls moved in to protect their master.

We tried to stay near Brin and keep the darakka from attacking her flank, so the five of us held off the swarm of enemies while Brin used Ukumog as a battering ram against the unseen defenses of The Mistress. Again and again the black blade collided with a shield of energy, unseen to the eye save for the moment of collision where a burst of black smoke and flames would ripple out from the impact it suffered.

Desecrated

The sheer number of darakka made this a fight we could not win. At first we held them off with quick strikes and lucky blows, but it wasn't to last. Tikras rebuked them in the name of his god. Piotyr and Nikolai fought shoulder-to-shoulder creating distractions that the other could then take advantage of. Avar fought defensively, and while he landed his share of blows, the enemy pressed him hard. I fought with all the viciousness I could muster, but it wasn't enough. I was being driven back.

Tighter and tighter the circle protecting Brin's back became, until we were all pressed together. In all that fighting we had only felled two or three of them. I tripped on one of the chains while I retreated, then had to scurry backwards away from the darakka. My head collided with the armor upon the altar and its hand reached out to grab my robe. I rolled away from the armor, and Avar filled the hole that I created. There barely enough room for me to stand up as my friends continued to be pressed back. The limited space forced me to pull myself up with the aid of the altar.

The silver surface, while worn and slightly tarnished, was warm to my touch. A shiver ran through me and I was dazed for a moment. When I stood, I found myself directly next to The Mistress, and many of her snakes lunged forward to bite me. Nimbly I evaded them by spinning around and briefly placing my hands on Brin's waist to steady myself as I moved to the other side of her. The briefest of moments passed with my hands there upon her, and her warmth filled me. The smell of her hair intoxicated me and I became dizzy. Pulling my body away from her I felt weakened. The strength of my anger and hatred for The Mistress seemed unimportant. My will to fight had been dulled.

At first I thought it was The Mistress working some magic that had affected me, but then my eyes were lifted to the brilliant blade lifted over Brin's head. It shone with bright blue light, and

Chapter 8

the same dark aura that it had when I held it against The Ghoul. The bitter taste of worry and panic was in the back of my throat, but then the darkness rose within me. It knew something that I did not. My ignorance was quickly remedied as Brin brought down the heavy blade upon The Mistress and in a flash of smoke, flame, and white light her defenses were broken.

The blast from the breach tossed everyone around the room. Ukumog was loosed from Brin's grasp and went tumbling through the air. Time slowed down as the blade turned end over end for ages. Slowly it came down in my direction. I wanted to reach out and catch it. I wanted to know its weight and feel that dark power surging through me. Compelled by the desire of my darker self, I reached out for its bone handle. Before I could claim my prize, my senses came back. It enough for me to gnash my teeth inside my mouth. The pain of the deep bite into my own flesh reflexively curbed my actions. When Ukumog fell, my hand was touching my cheek, the inside of which was bleeding and throbbing with pain. Ukumog's desire for calamity was not stopped by this trick. Instead of landing in my hand, it landed upon the black and twisted chains which held the animated armor to the altar.

There was a *fooshing* sound like fire growing instantly stronger. Heat filled the room and the ball of fire, flesh, and red ropes of hair flew above our heads and streaked out the door. The darakka that remained followed the lead of their master and flowed out the chamber to the surface. We picked ourselves up off the floor and Brin quickly reclaimed Ukumog.

The moaning from the animated armor became even more strained. It started struggling ferociously against the remaining bonds. Uncertain as to what we should do, we backed our way out to the exit. Brin remained standing in the middle of the room with Ukumog viciously glowing in her hand. Everyone stopped when

Desecrated

we noticed that she wasn't coming with us. Instead she was just staring at the armor that was flailing to be free. Its cries became more anguished, as if the pain it suffered before was in its sleep and now it was waking.

"Brin! Brin we are leaving! Brin!" Avar called out to her nervously.

Quickly, I darted forward and placed my hand on her shoulder. Again I was overcome with the warmth from her body and the dark whispers of Ukumog. Shaking off the seduction of power and heat I pulled at her. "Brin. Brin we have to go."

She turned and looked at me, her eyes glowing faintly of the same blue that danced along the flat sides of Ukumog. Her face was as calm and still as an undisturbed pond. She blinked her eyes and the glow began to fade. Pulling her as I backed out, I kept talking to her, "C'mon Brin. We have to go." In her stupor, she couldn't resist my urgings, and eventually the escalating cries of the empty armor chased us to the surface.

On the surface, the army of freth, while not defeated, was retreating. A flaming streak in the sky seemed to be their guide as they hurried to leave. No one had to say anything; we all knew that this war was not over.

Chapter 9

Cleanup of Sanctuary began almost instantly. The first order was to tend the wounded and see to the fallen. Having helped with this before, I began helping those I could. The fact that I could contribute in this manner made me feel good, not like all those times where I sat back helplessly while Avar and Brin fought to protect me. I suppose there was some selfishness in wanting to help others because of my desire to have value.

Avar eventually made his way to the second task. A team, that included him, was formed under the roguish Tarissa to repair and fortify the buildings in case of another attack. Garrett was convinced that The Mistress wasn't finished with her assault. Brin spent her time taking semi-secret meetings with Bridain, Garrett, and Nikolai. She would talk to one of them for a little while and then move to the next. She had this deadly serious look in her eye every time I saw her pass by, and it made me worry.

Once things calmed down a bit, I was able to talk to Gordo for a little while. "So, how have things been since we left?"

He chuckled, "Small talk? Really Wrack? You just don't seem like the type." He took a deep breath and continued, "Things have been rough. The Mistress has been attacking with small forces nearly constantly, trying to poke holes in our defenses. Thankfully

Desecrated

we didn't suffer many other losses, but it has made hunting and other normal tasks difficult. We weren't really prepared for a siege of this sort."

"What about all the people who were wounded beforehand? Any of them survive?" I asked, secretly hoping to hear news about John, the hunter to whom I had given some of my blood.

"Unfortunately, many of them died. Luckily for us, word of the trouble had gotten to some of our sister chapters to the southeast, and they came up to help. I have heard that more hunters from elsewhere might be on their way too. I certainly hope they are. Another attack like last night, and we are all dead. Honestly, they had us dead to rights and then they suddenly retreated. While I have no idea why it happened, I am incredibly thankful."

"What about John, the hunter that was severely injured?"

Gordo gave me an odd look. "John survived. It was really a miracle, considering the severity of his injuries. A few days after you left, he was greatly recovered and shortly after that he was up and about like nothing had happened. Last night he fought bravely in the doorway of the mess hall. He even single handedly held off the entire army trying to push through the main door for a little while." He grew quiet for a moment. I could tell that bad news was on the way. "Right before the retreat, he got distracted for a moment. Bridain told me that he asked everyone if they could hear a pained moaning. The darakka trying to press in took advantage of his distraction and removed poor John's head from his body."

Shocked, I didn't know what to say. All I could muster was a quiet, "Wow. That's horrible."

"I prefer to think that the Lady has a purpose for us all. He fought like a man possessed last night. If he hadn't been there, we might all be dead."

Chapter 9

John's healing was undoubtedly my doing, but the change in his person could hardly be attributed to a few drops of my blood. Still, there was a pride that was born in me. It felt good, not at all like the dark pride I took in watching Ukumog destroy our enemies, or when I gloated over The Ghoul just before I sliced him into bits.

Trying to change the topic after some awkward silence, Gordo said, "David was a huge help after you left. Thank you for sending him my direction."

"Oh yeah? Where is David?" I asked, hoping for good news.

His lips were pressed together. My hopes dropped. "David left Sanctuary after the attacks started in earnest. He volunteered to go find the other groups of hunters and bring them back. He told me he had personal business to the west. Something about Yellow Liver or something."

"Oh," I was confused. David didn't have any family that he spoke of in our time together. Why would he go back to Yellow Liver after everything that happened? Part of it was that I was hurt that he wouldn't have told me about whatever it was that he left behind. Secretly, I hoped it was simply something he forgot and not something sinister.

Gordo and I worked in silence for a while. The number of dead or mortally wounded was very high. This little town of soldiers went from a couple hundred souls to half that number in one night. It felt like no coincidence that such death had come here. After all, when I arrived in Yellow Liver it was a gloomy town with a monster living beneath it, but shortly thereafter an army tried to raze it to the ground. Not only did I appear dead, death seemed to follow my movements. I wanted to blame myself for the events that had happened. Never before had I consciously realized how much guilt I harbored, and I could not remember why. As I

Desecrated

tended to the wounds that could be healed, my mind spun in dark spiraling circles. Instead of the comforting word of Murks or the odd comment of Avar to break me out of it, it was actually Gordo.

"I know these attacks have only been going on for a few months, but I can barely remember what it was like before. So many of my friends I have put into the ground." He laughed, "You wouldn't know this, Wrack, but this place used to be somewhere safe and full of hope." A tear slowly moved down his cheek and he quickly wiped it away. I pretended like I hadn't seen anything.

Well into the day, and after a long silence where Gordo and I kept our head in our work, Brin came in to check on us. "How are you guys doing?"

"As well as can be expected," Gordo responded in a very dour sort of way.

I nodded in agreement.

"Gordo, do you mind if I steal Wrack for a while?"

"Sure. We have taken care of the urgent stuff anyway."

Brin motioned with her head for me to follow and bid farewell to Gordo. It wasn't until we were away from the makeshift hospital that she started talking. "Garrett has requested that we have a little meeting. He wants to talk to us about what happened while we were gone and update us about the fight last night."

"From what Gordo has already told me, it was pretty horrible."

A scream of frustration and pain echoed out from the graveyard, surprising me so much that I immediately was on edge. A few others stopped and looked worried as well, but most continued about their tasks without any noticeable concern.

"And things just seem to be getting worse. Seems wherever we go, we bring death with us," she said somberly.

"Yeah," I agreed.

Chapter 9

Not about to let herself get bogged down in the events of last night, she continued, "So anyway, I think Garrett knows more than he is letting on about this thing under the graveyard, and Avar has some interesting theories."

"Where are the fellows from the Spikelands?"

"In with Garrett. Seems they have more of a relationship than Nikolai let on. Our barbarian friend warned Garrett of The Mistress' interest in Sanctuary and got ignored, apparently."

As we arrived on the steps of Garrett's house I saw Avar seated within. "Sounds like Garrett ignores a lot of what should be important to him."

The first thing I noticed is that there were more people in the room than our last time in here. Bridain and his team were all there, including Ferrin. Avar, Brin, and me along with Nikolai, Piotyr, and Tikras, found ourselves in the back of the room. Other faces of hunters that I had seen around the town but didn't know were also there. The room had enough people in it that it wasn't uncomfortable, but you did have to stand. Bridain and Garrett were talking quietly at the back of the room and after a few more people arrived they ended their conversation.

"Welcome everyone," Garrett called out. "Last night's attack has left us severely handicapped. Since the fighting began, we have lost about forty eight percent of our fighting force. We simply cannot survive more beatings like this. There are reinforcements coming, but they may not get here in time. It has become our job to survive, but not only that. We have to deny our enemy what she wants.

"This brings us to the second topic. Last night she made a move against the graveyard. Under the statue there appears to be a hidden temple, wherein something lays chained to an altar. A decision has to be made about what to do with this thing."

Desecrated

Bridain stepped forward. "It is as yet unclear what she plans to do with the creature. We do know, however, that she plans to increase her power by means of this thing. I have consulted with some of our tacticians and even with a foreign priest to try and find a solution. The best that we can come up with is one of two possibilities. Our first theory is that she plans to set the thing loose with some means of control over it wherein she can punish her enemies and obtain more power. And the second, she plans to somehow absorb the thing's power and increase her own personal control of the world beyond the veil."

Garrett took over, as if they had rehearsed it, "Faced with these two possibilities, we have only one real solution. We have to kill the thing."

The room immediately exploded into a chaotic barrage of questions and comments. Garrett let the wave of commotion roll over him and remained resolute. The only calm faces in the crowd belonged to all the people I already knew. The others began pushing and shouting even louder. In the storm of noise I could make out a general concern for survival. Garrett and Bridain stood at the front and absorbed all the shouting for just a few moments longer. It was strange for me to see the hunters in this light. The last time I was here, they stood as one and followed the orders of their commanders without question. Their suffering had only just begun, and for many of them it was already too much.

Once everyone had a chance to vent their frustration, Commander Garrett raised his hands with open palms toward the assembly and waited for them to calm. "I understand your concerns. Now is the time when we shall all be tested. Our faith and the future of our world is at stake here. Who will stand up to the Doomed if

Chapter 9

we are washed away by this woman's greed? The time for this battle has been chosen for us, not by us, and it is what we do now that matters. Brothers and sisters, find your courage and follow me."

There was a silent moment in the room that was ended by a gesture from Garrett to Varif, who then opened the door. Most of the hunters filed out of the room, quietly whispering encouraging thoughts to one another. For me, there was no comfort. Garrett knew something that he wasn't telling the rest of them. We stood in the back of the room and watched everyone else leave. I knew a special meeting was reserved for us. It was Brin they wanted, but just as before Avar and I remained with her.

Once the room had mostly been emptied it was just Garrett, Bridain, Avar, Brin, Nikolai, Piotyr, Tikras, Verif, Tarissa, and me. As I took stock of who was on the short list, I occasionally met eyes with someone. All of the hunters, apart from Avar, averted their eyes from me the moment they met. The message that they did not really want me there was still loud and clear.

"So, what the uzk is actually going on, Garrett? You have to know more than you told your grunts. We are not going to play your game unless you tell us what is really going on," Brin demanded with her usual charm.

Garrett sighed, "Ever the diplomat, Brin. Your father would be proud."

"My father is dead, you arrogant uzk. I simply want to know what is really going on before you march us all out to get killed."

Bridain puffed out his chest and started gesturing in anger, "Watch what you say, girl. I don't care who your father was-"

"Oh shut the uzk up Bridain. You absolutely care about who my father was. He was your uzkin' prophet, spouting endless amounts of divinely inspired gaak," she said mockingly. Turning

Desecrated

back to Garrett, "If he were here, perhaps he would follow you blindly with hope that all would turn out the way that The Lady intended. I am not my father."

Garrett shifted uncomfortably. "Fine. Everyone sit down." Everyone found a seat, save for Garrett and Bridain who remained on their feet. "The thing in the temple down there is…" A heavy sigh slowly found its way out of his chest. "…one of the Doomed."

A restless stirring filled the room. Even Bridain's face betrayed his level of surprise at Garrett's comment. "What? A Doomed? Here?"

Garrett was as serious as death, "Yes. In the prophecy he is known as The Empty Armor and he has been trapped in the temple for as long as the remaining records show. We don't have anything prior to the schism that happened shortly after the cursing. Well, apart from fragments of the Song of the World from then."

"Song of the World?" I asked confusedly.

Regardless of his frustration with the interruption, and his general disdain for me, Garrett looked directly at me when he replied, "That is what people call the prophecy. It is a song told by many illuminated bards over the ages past. It is the way that the word of the Silver Lady was delivered to her people."

"Thank you." I was grateful for his direct and kind answer to my question.

"How he got in there, we don't specifically know. We think that the old Hunters might have imprisoned him before the fall of the Abomination because they lacked the knowledge of how to destroy him."

I could see the light go on in Avar's eyes. "Wait. So he has been under Sanctuary all this time and you knew about it?"

Chapter 9

"Yes, Avar. The knowledge that we stood vigil over the prison of one of our enemies was a burden passed down from commander to commander. I was as shocked as you all are when I was told. And there is more. The magic that binds him here is connected somehow to the protections of the town. I believe that once he is freed, we will be without them."

"That makes sense. What you all thought was here to protect you from the outside was really just to hide his location from the others," Brin interjected.

Involuntarily Garrett gave a tiny surprised laugh, "You might be right about that Brin. Either way, we don't know how to reseal the prison so we have to deal with it another way."

"Lemme guess," Brin folded her arms, "you need me to kill it?"

"Simply put, yes. We don't know of any other weapon that has killed one of the Doomed before, save for the Betrayer himself. You and your blade is all we have. If you won't help us, we will have to roll the statue back over the temple and just hope that he doesn't escape."

Avar violently stood up. "I hate it when you do that, Dad."

"Avar." Garrett said sternly.

"What?" Avar shouted, "You are always so uzkin' superior until you need someone to do what you want, then you give these impossible ultimatums! How is Brin supposed to react to that? This is just like with Matthew." At the mention of the name, Avar went silent.

My mind went tumbling through my memories trying to find face to put with the name. Something told me that I knew who he was talking about.

"Avar," Garrett's voice was still as calm and authoritative as ever. "Matthew is a completely different issue."

Desecrated

"Is he? Is he? You sent him away, Dad. You sent him away because he just wouldn't fall into line with your perfect idea of what the Hunters should be! He wanted to do something, not sit around in the mess hall and give speeches about how we were changing the world," Avar had become more than just angry. He was flailing his arms around wildly and screaming at Garrett.

Bridain stepped forward to get between them. "Avar–"

Avar pushed Bridain away with much more force than was necessary, driving him hard into a wall. "Back off, Bridain. This is between me and my father."

"Avar, calm down." Garrett was still calm. "What is this about?"

One of Avar's eyebrows twitched with sorrow and rage, "I saw Matthew, Dad. In Yellow Liver."

Garrett crossed his arms and sighed, "Oh, yeah? Did he fill your head with nonsense again?"

Avar bit back the anger welling up inside him. His breathing became heavy, then slowed. "No. He was a guard there. He wanted to protect the people and trying to do so from within the system was the only way he knew how. All because you made him leave the only people he knew behind."

"Hold on there. I didn't make him leave." Garrett's ire was beginning to rise.

Avar laughed sarcastically. "Right. You didn't make him leave. He did that to himself, right, Dad? Never mind that you told him, either you have to submit to my authority as your commander or you will have to part ways with the Shadow Hunters."

Garrett swallowed hard and then said calmly, "It wasn't my fault he could not obey orders."

Chapter 9

I had never seen such anger in Avar's eyes before. He stood there, silently staring at Garrett for what seemed like hours then finally he broke the silence when no one else would, "Matthew is dead, Commander Garrett." He waited for a response and when none came, he continued, "He was standing right next to me one second, and in the next I was sprayed with his blood." Tears started to fill his eyes. There was no way to tell if they were tears of sorrow or rage, but he maintained his angry calm. "Ghouls tore him open, and I couldn't do a thing to save him. He died in my arms, Dad. In his final breath he whispered to me. You know what he said, Dad? He said, 'Good to be with you at the end, little brother. Don't let father ruin your life.' I hadn't seen him in years, only to later wash his blood out of my clothes. He didn't deserve that."

Garrett was speechless and rest of us did not know what to do. By the looks on all their faces, this was not like Avar at all. My memory of Matthew was easy to find once Avar started adding context. No wonder Avar had been so strange and emotional after that ghoul attack. Matthew hadn't just been some guard in Yellow Liver. I regretted my questioning of Avar's behavior and the look on Brin's face told me that she also had regrets.

The silence was too much for him. Avar's face cracked with a forced frown of intense sadness that was quickly followed by uncontrollable sobbing. Everyone in the room waited for Garrett to say or do something, but he remained standing there, with arms crossed, watching his son drown in sadness. Unexpectedly, Brin got up and wrapped her arms around Avar. At first he fought her, pushing her away, but then he gave in and let his tears fall upon her armored shoulder. She held him for a moment and ignored Garrett.

From outside I heard another wail of pain and at that very moment, Ukumog flared. I could almost hear it asking me to take hold of its handle. It begged me to rush down into the temple and

Desecrated

bring the lustful edge down upon the invisible flesh under the armor of the helpless Doomed that was within. It would be so very easy. Two steps over to Brin, where I could easily remove the blade from her belt. By the time they realized what had happened I would be out the door and before they could try and stop me, I would be down in that hole engaged with the beast. The dark hunger filled me again.

Garrett stood up, breaking my concentration. "Well, we need to do something soon, Brin. Let me know what you decide within the hour." With that, he and the rest of the remaining hunters left the building.

Avar was still overwhelmed, not only with the loss of his brother, but the unfeeling father who did not seem to care one bit about his two sons. I pitied the poor man. He traded his sons for the family of duty, but his choice had not led him to happiness. Perhaps joy is not something that he could afford, but it did not seem as if he even cared.

Once Brin was able to calm Avar down, we remained sitting in the commander's room for a little while. My mind was still wrestling with thoughts of Ukumog. Avar eventually broke the silence with more that he needed to let out. "It shouldn't be me, ya know. Traveling with you. It should have been Matthew. He was always the brave one. The one who wanted action. I just loved the stories."

Brin put her hand on his shoulder. "I am glad it is you, Avar. These other hunters wouldn't have the ability to put up with my gaak. Besides, where else am I going to get stupid information about little known history? And you are brave. Don't you remember how you stood up to The Ghoul?"

Chapter 9

Avar laughed, "Truth is, I was scared gaakless. The whole while in those tunnels I was out of my mind. Once we got there though, I just pushed it all aside. I thought to myself, What would Matthew do?"

"And you honored him with your bravery," I said. "None of us chose this life, Avar, least of all me. Perhaps the Silver Lady needed someone with your knowledge to accompany Brin. Someone whose older brother's bravery could inspire him to do great things with that knowledge."

Avar smiled at me, and I knew that he would be alright.

"Ok. Now, about the Doomed down in the temple. I say we uzkin' kill it," Brin said.

We stepped out of Garrett's chamber and immediately saw all the able-bodied hunters preparing for battle in the graveyard. Many of them were patched up from the all the previous fights they had survived over the last few weeks.

A crowd was gathered around the entrance to the temple beneath the statue. Garrett and Bridain were in the middle speaking with several of the hunters who were then walking up and giving orders to others who stood further away. Horrible wails of pain and frustration came up from the temple beneath; the metallic echoes of those cries tore at the fabric of my mind. Brin headed off in the direction of the entrance without much of a care. So, too, the hunters around us seemed unaffected by the terrifying sounds that washed over all of us in waves. Instead, the hunters formed into teams and otherwise prepared themselves for impending violence.

The screams grew louder and more intense as we drew closer to the entrance. Ukumog seemed to be the only other thing as affected by the unearthly sounds as me. The runes on its sides grew in intensity as the screaming did. Focusing on the harsh blue glow of the blade became my primary interest. I followed it with

Desecrated

my mind and my body until we were there, standing over the dusty maw of the entrance. Brin and Garrett spoke, but I could not focus enough on what they were saying to understand it. My soul felt as if there was a great unseen force trying to rip it apart. I could think of nothing but my desire to make the tormented sounds end, yet I felt completely helpless to do anything.

Brin's strides were full of confidence as she walked back over to me, Ukumog swaying from her belt. Looking around, I saw concerned looks in the eyes of the hunters. There they were, preparing to meet one of their sworn enemies, with one piece of unknown in their midst. After all, who was I really?

Trying to fight the bone chilling fear of the screams I engaged the only person around me, "I think your friends don't want me here for this fight, Avar."

He gave me a sad smile and a shrug, and then looked away.

"Have you made any progress on your theory?" I asked.

"What theory?" He half-heartedly responded, distracted by our surroundings.

"Your theory about what or who I am. Or have you given up on that yet."

Now I had his full attention. "Why? Have something new to tell me?"

"I wish that were the case. All I have is more questions."

His brow furrowed a bit. "Well, I do have a couple of ideas. If you fit in with what we know about the tainted. As I have said before, you are somehow linked with one of the Doomed. That being said, I don't really have any ideas as to which one. I mean, I thought it might be The King because his knights are very much like what we know about you so far. Our encounter with the Jawbone and even The Vampire suggested otherwise, though." He paused to look

Chapter 9

up at the night sky. The moon brightly shone through the sparse clouds, making them look like silver outlines of dark lakes in the heavens. "My gods, the sky is beautiful tonight. I feel good."

"It is very pretty. The night sky is one of those things that always looks serene, no matter how much we struggle down here," I mused with him.

His smile was full of charm and warmth, "Don't worry, Wrack. We will figure out who you are." With a comforting pat on my shoulder he walked over to Brin, leaving me to stand alone.

Still trying to fight the haze that entered my head with every howl from below, I began examining the headstones. The ones closest to statue in the center of the yard were so worn that they were only barely distinguishable from weathered rocks laying half buried in a field. Still others had lists of names rather than just one chiseled into their surface. The markings even had different stages of wear, telling me that bodies were added to these graves over time. Realizing this, I looked around at the hundreds of standing stones and wondered how many lives had been lost fighting these timeless tyrants. And now, the inheritors of those lost idealists stood planning their attack on one of these villains. The sheer volume of what was about to happen finally hit me.

Hurrying over to Brin I quickly blurted out, "I don't think this is going to be easy."

"What? Are you talking about me going down there and killing the uzkin' Doomed? He is chained up, Wrack. It is not like he can uzkin' fight back," she dismissed me and walked away in a huff.

Avar shrugged and ran after her while the other hunters continued their disdainful stares.

"This is not going to go well," I said to no one in particular.

Desecrated

"Can Murks help, Master?" asked the tiny voice in my head.

I smiled. He had been so quiet over the last few days, I had nearly forgotten that Murks was with me. "No Murks, not unless you can help us kill the Doomed down in the temple," my thoughts reached out to him.

The silence that came back told me that he had more information, but did not want to give it up.

"Murks. Do you know something that you are not telling me?"

"Master. Murks does not want to say anything that will make Master upset…"

Quickly I was growing frustrated. "What is it, Murks? You can tell me."

His confusion flowed to me through our connection. "Murks has seen a prison like this one before. The chains are part of it. His cries have gotten louder, Master yes? With the one chain broken, he is slowly slipping out. But he is still protected while he is in the chains, Master. As much as you are protected from him while he is in them."

Lost in thought for a brief moment, I tried to figure out where my little hemodan had seen something akin to this place. In my previous life I must have been around one, and knowing only scattered evil feelings from my previous self, I would not be surprised if I had used something like this to trap someone. "Brin will have to break the chains before she can kill it, won't she?"

"Murks thinks so, Master."

"Uzk." I ran over to Brin who was again talking with the assembled leaders of the Hunters. "Brin, can I talk to you for a moment?"

Chapter 9

She turned and looked at me angrily, a faint hint of the blue glow danced in her eyes. "What? What is it, Wrack?"

"I have something to tell you."

"If it involves murdering this uzkin' Doomed, you can say it out here in front of us all." She crossed her arms and wore her stubborn face.

Fabricating my lie to leave Murks out of the story took a second and a sigh, after which I said, "I think I saw something like this prison in one of my visions."

Bridain moved as if he was about to say something but Garrett beat him to it, "You have visions? Visions of what?"

Avar jumped in to my defense. "About a lot of things, Father."

Garrett grunted in disapproval of the F-word.

Undaunted, Avar turned back to me. "What did you see?"

"The images were all mixed up but one thing was clear, you will not be able to kill it until the chains are all broken and it is freed," I lied.

"Really? We have to let it out?" Avar asked in earnest.

I nodded.

Bridain laughed, "Of course he would say that. He is one of them! We should have killed him back in the forest. Where is Verif? Verif! Tie this thing up!"

The short, silky-haired Verif came over to me with a strange fine rope in hand. Looking to Brin, I found her face to already be empty of compassion or care. The hooks of Ukumog's lust had already robbed her of her feelings. Just as before, I surrendered to the hunter's judgment.

Avar however protested. "What? You can't tie him up! Hasn't he proven himself enough?"

Desecrated

From over their collective shoulders, I could see Nikolai nodding subtly at me with distress in his face, denoting that Avar was not the only one who objected to how I was being treated.

"It is ok, Avar. Bridain is just doing what he thinks is best," I tried to calm him.

He silenced his complaining and with acceptance he said, "After. After this is over." He clenched his jaw and exhaled through his nose. His senses collected, he turned back to Bridain, "Fine. What do we do next?"

Verif took me away from the leaders discussing their tactics. "I know you have a hemodan," she whispered to me. "One day you will have to show me that trick." The smile she gave me was accompanied with a slight lifting of her eyebrow.

To say I was surprised by this flirtation would be an understatement. I gave her an incredulous look and bit my tongue in case this was some kind of test or trap. While trying to examine her face for any hint of deception, she wiggled an eyebrow at me again and then quickly turned away.

"Murks thinks she likes you, Master."

Maybe he was right, but I certainly wasn't going to give them any more reason to want me dead. Verif left me kneeling with my hands and feet tied, then those binds tied to one another. If I fell over, I didn't think I could get back to my knees without help. It was a good thing that I barely noticed the cold, for I wasn't able to move for quite some time. It wasn't until the wind started to pick up that I even really noticed that it was more than chilly out there among the graves.

From where I was bound, I could see the entrance to the temple and the crowd of hunters that crept ever closer to it. It was unclear to me what they were waiting for until I took note of how they acted when the moon peeked out from behind the clouds above.

Chapter 9

"I think they are waiting for a sign from their patron to move, Murks. What do you think?"

"Master might be right. But, Murks thinks that Brin seems ready to go, Master."

My eyes immediately switched to watching her from across the yard. Normally when getting ready to fight, her body could not contain all of her energy. She sometimes even paced or tapped her foot to release it. This time though, she was eerily still. The night in the labyrinth where that barbed monster almost killed us came to mind. The dispassionate look on her face that I saw that night filled my thoughts. As if to confirm my fear, the glowing light of Ukumog screamed from her hip. I knew the dark thoughts that were its weapons; I could only hope that Brin was stronger than I and had some way to stave off the terrible thirst within the blade.

The bandage was missing from her hand. "She must have realized that her wound was healed. I wonder when she noticed it."

"Master should be careful. Magic is powerful, but magic that uses blood? That is very very powerful."

"Did I use magic to heal her, Murks? As I recall, it was an accident that I bandaged her with cloth soaked in rain and my blood."

"You can lie to your friends, Master. You can even lie to yourself. But you cannot lie to Murks."

Had I done that on purpose? More importantly, would Brin start showing amazing feats of strength or stupid bravery like the boy John had? The last thing I wanted was to hurt Brin. The idea that I had somehow infected her with my torment worried me.

Cold winds blew through the graveyard, and the clouds above began to sprinkle their burden on us. Snow, grey and ash-looking fluttered down on us in the moonlight. The first few flakes that drifted past my face tickled me. There was a simple joy in this

Desecrated

quiet moment, and my mind drifted briefly to a time long ago when I had known snow as a child. The memories were so fragmented that they only left me with a feeling of happiness, something I hadn't truly known in my current life. This fleeting feeling did something to me however; it gave me a tiny seed of hope.

As the snow filled the air with silence, the Hunters decided that it was time to enter the temple. The leaders went in first, along with Brin and Avar. Our barbarian friends remained on the surface, waving more groups in and standing guard with those who remained on in the graveyard. Somehow I could feel every step that Brin took towards the Doomed in that temple chamber. Every inch that she grew closer to him sent a different cold down my spine, the cold darkness of the power that lay hidden within me.

I struggled against myself. Breaking my bonds would be bad enough, but doing it with powers that even my own friends were not aware of would cause suspicion that I could not bear. For the sake of everything they had done for me, I had to remain Verif's prisoner.

Even though I was outside and above, I could feel the clash of Ukumog against the chains within. The crash of each broken link echoed up from the temple, and the power of those sounds seemed to ignore the falling blanket of snow. The calm of the snow conflicted with the struggle that was hidden in the temple and in me. From nowhere I had the urge to go inside and stand beside my friends as they fought the Doomed. Mindlessly, I struggled against my bonds.

Another clash thundered out from the stairway. My desire grew even stronger making my fight with the rope more violent. Verif looked over her shoulder to check on me. Her observation only made my struggle pause for the briefest of moments. Having been discovered, my rage against the rope became even more violent. I

Chapter 9

fell over onto my side, and pulled hard against the rope to try and break it. Snow from the ground was kicked into my face as Verif ran over to try and contain me. She placed her hands on my arm and tried to pull me up, and I rolled away to shake her off.

"Master? Do you want Murks to help?"

"No!" I shouted out into the winter air.

Verif backed off for a moment, I could see the thoughts spinning in her head. She wasn't sure what to do. Looking over her shoulder for a moment, she checked to see if anyone was watching her then she shifted her body so her hands were hidden from the on looking hunters some hundred feet away. Whispering in a language that I didn't understand, her hands began to glow with a faint red light.

"Master! She is a wizard!" Little Murks was suddenly flooded with fear.

Surprisingly, some part of me was happy to see her summon this power. Before the joy could cause any change in my plan, I felt a crushing force pressing down on me from all sides. A scream was loosed from me in surprise and alarm.

"Stop struggling and I will end the spell," Verif said with a cold calm. "I don't want to kill you, but you are giving me little choice."

Another chain was broken below, and a dark laugh bubbled to the surface from deep within me. "You can't kill me, little girl. Now let me go before you make me really angry." The voice was mine but the words were someone else. It was the darker me, the one who found glee in the murder of The Ghoul.

"What will you do?" There was a twinge of fear in her voice.

"What?"

"What will you do if I let you go?"

Desecrated

My eyes glared at her with malice. I didn't want to answer her question, but it seemed like the quickest way to resolve this situation. "They need my help down there. If you don't let me go, everyone will die."

Still holding her glowing palms facing me she took stock of what was happening behind her. My eyes followed her glance. Once more the air was filled with the crash of metal on metal. This sound was quickly followed by a deafening metallic roar and a cacophony of chains being cast violently upon the stone floor of the temple.

Everyone on the surface turned their attention back to the entrance and away from me. My need to be free was stilled for a moment, and I stared with eyes wide open at the entrance to the temple. All of us waited together in the silent calm of the falling snow. The sounds of battle came up the tunnel to meet us. The crashing sounds of metal on metal, the chorus of grunting and screaming, and the inhuman metallic echo of the Doomed's voice became the dialogue of an unseen play that kept us all hoping and wishing. A loud crash shook the earth and caused dust to come rolling out of the hole in the ground.

The sounds of battle became louder and more distinct. All the hunters on the surface began preparing for the fight to come to them. Even Varif became so distracted that she let go of her spell on me and ran over to support her fellows. Lying on my side in the snow, instinct took over and I resumed my frantic struggle against my bonds.

"Murks will help you, Master," the little hemodan shuffled out of his secret pocket in my robes and crawled over me to the ropes.

Chapter 9

I let myself relax while Murks began to work at the knots in the thin rope, and I turned my attention to the entrance of the temple. The assembled crowd made it hard for me to clearly see the hole, but the sounds of the battle were drawing closer. "Hurry up! Hurry up!"

"Murks is working as fast as Murks can, Master! These ropes have been been magicked, Master!"

"Quit your whining and loose me!"

Like a jolt, disappointment from my little friend hit me like a splash of cold water. More and more of the old evil me was returning, and he knew it. "Yes, Master," he said, dejectedly.

Surrendering to my own sense of failure I let my head fall into the cold snow that had been building up on the ground around me. "I'm sorry, Murks. I don't know what came over me."

"It is ok Master. Murks-" Then there was a tiny pop from behind me and I felt pain fill me from my link with Murks.

"Murks? Murks, are you alright?" I wobbled back and forth so that I could roll over and see what had happened behind me, trying to avoid the possible accident of just rolling back over him.

He didn't respond.

"Murks!" My slower technique paid off. I had rolled over. Behind me was a smoking lump of dark red clay laying in snow that melted at the touch of it, a lump that had been Murks. "NO! Murks!" Realizing that I had been screaming out loud, I looked over my shoulder to see if anyone was paying attention to me.

The fight had moved to the surface, and most of the hunters were engaged in the frenzied dance of battle. Just before I turned back to Murks, I noticed Verif looking over at me. Her eyes

Desecrated

narrowed and she looked as if she were going to come towards me. If she came over here and saw Murks, I knew I was done. I had to escape

Clamor and commotion rang out from the battle as even the metallic Doomed had now reached the surface. Dancing pools of blue light darted around the graveyard, and I knew they were the manifested glimmering joy of Ukumog. It wouldn't be long before Verif reached me. Mustering all my strength I pressed and pressed against the ropes that bound me. The flesh on my wrists burned and tore under the strain of my desire. I felt the bones in my hands stress and pop.

Down in the hole, evil laughter floated down to me. I couldn't move, I couldn't breathe. The pain of a heavy iron rod was driven through me from side to side, just under my arms. The rod was then impaled into the ground. My hands and feet were bound together with thin black cord. There was a similar cord that linked my feet and hands and found its way around my neck as well. Exhaustion and disgust were all I could feel; it was so great that it even drown out the pain of the rod.

"Had enough?" The Baron's horrible voice called out to me.

In my tired state, I couldn't even form a response. My eyes opened, and I saw the black dirt of the hole like curtains surrounding me. The evening sky was red with rage and full of clouds. Even the Silver Lady could not watch what they were doing to me.

The Baron's dripping skull nodded at a soldier standing at the edge of my shallow grave. He was gaunt, with shadows of death around his eyes and mouth, like me, but wearing the livery of

Chapter 9

The King. At the Baron's command he twisted the rod that passed through my ribcage. A rush of agony pushed away all exhaustion and changed my disgust to pure hatred.

"Andoleth," a hollow whisper of a voice floated through my ears, "the boy is done. The blade is what we want. Your lust for his pain is . . . entertaining. But the longer we delay, the further the blade will get from us."

"Yes, my King." The utter disdain in The Baron's voice could not be hidden, even by a magician. "Then I will put this poor wracked soul to bed."

I felt the earth tremble as he approached me and then I saw the dripping blood mix with the dirt. The taint of his vitae caused tiny plumes of smoke to rise when contact with the ground was made. I could feel the life of that ground being extinguished like a candle smothered by wet horrible fingers.

"I have something for you, friend." He knelt next to me, his ichor occasionally dripping onto my robes or my flesh. Each time the burning ravaged that which it fell upon, causing me more pain, but nothing compared to the rod. "Do you see this?" His one gloved hand cradled my head and turned it towards a sword in his other. "I have saved this blade all these years. Sometimes I think I can still smell the last few moments of the old man's life here on this steel."

Rage took over my body. I struggled against the rod and my bonds. Trying to push past the pain did no good; I could not move and my body was broken. Eyes wide with hatred, I wanted nothing more than to take the miserable life of this monster before me. I wanted to devour his black terrible soul.

"Fitting that you should both die to the same blade." If there had been any flesh upon his face, it would have born a condescending gloating smirk. "Good night, you miserable fool."

Desecrated

Even as the blade sliced my throat I tried to get at him. My fingers pulled at his cloak and surcoat, trying to pull him down closer to me. My lips silently cursed him in every way my frantic mind could imagine. To both our surprise, I did not die.

Annoyed by the delay of my expiration, he came in close again. Weakly I tried to grasp at him, but I just did not have the strength.

"What is it with you? Hrm? You cannot win this little game. Give up, it is over. You lost." He laughed, "You don't have anything else for me to take away from you. Indeed, you do such a wonderful job of destroying all that you care about anyway. Makes it easy for me. Perhaps if it weren't, I would not be so annoyed by you. Surrender. It is over for you."

Burning reserves of energy that I did not even know were in me, I grappled with the front of his blood soaked surcoat and pulled his ooze-covered skull in close to my face. He reeked of death and blood, but I wanted him to hear what I had to say. Gurgling through the mortal wound in my throat, I mouthed the words, "This is not over."

His ferocity returned and he brushed off my weak hands. Letting loose a roar of rage, he drove the sword in his hand through my chest. I felt the tip of his sword shatter my heart, just like it had on the day when he drove it through my grandfather. In that one moment, we were joined, my grandfather and I. My vision dimmed as the sleep of death came to claim me, but as I looked up I thought I saw the old man standing behind our twisted murderer. His warm welcoming smile washed away the pain, and it made me grin.

"Why are you smiling? Who are you?" The Baron screamed with undead rage.

Behind him, my grandfather winked at me, just as he had in the forest all those years ago, and all became dark.

Chapter 9

After the flash of my vision had faded, I found myself still lying in the snow. The commotion of the battle behind me was raging stronger than before and the smoking lump that was my hemodan still lay motionless in front of me. There was no sign that Verif had come over to where I was. I looked around and did not see her even in the crowd behind me. Flexing my fingers I felt strength in me that was not there before. Just as before, I pulled at the bonds on my limbs trying to either slip them free or break the fibers.

A flash surged through me. The surprising feeling of being in two places at once tumbled through my soul, and it made me gasp for air. The dark strength in me chilled my spine and bit into my flesh with icy fire. Again I pushed against my bonds. My entire body flexed with dark power, and a roar escaped my lungs with such force that it caused me to shake uncontrollably. Then, with a simple crack, I was free.

For a moment I stared at the thin cords that had been my prison here in the snow. Memories of that shallow grave and the bonds that held me while The Baron tortured me filled my head with evil thoughts of a life I didn't fully remember. Pulling myself out of the darkness, I cast the ropes away from me and they vanished in the quickly accumulating snow. Immediately my focus became the hemodan that lay under a thin layer of snow. Brushing him off, I lifted the tough ball of scabby blood clay that was his body from the ground and searched for any signs of life. Whispering from within my soul, the monster within me spoke, "I know how to fix him. Let me come out and I will." My desire to repair this damage was greater than my reason, and I let the monster within me come to the surface.

Desecrated

True to his word, he quickly searched me for a blade and finding none, used the sharp corner of the black iron key that I still wore around my neck to tear the flesh of my hand. Collecting enough blood before the wound healed, he painted a circle with eight wavy rays escaping the center onto the lump that was Murks.

"Murks, my blood, my servant, my life, I call you to return and do my bidding," he whispered gently into the lump of blood clay. If I had not been right there, I would not have heard his words for the curtains of silencing snow.

The symbol glowed with a dark purple light for a moment, the color flaring intensely and then fading away. Murk's body shuttered, and creaked awake. "Murks is happy to return to Master!" the little hemodan croaked with the voice of person just waking from a long sleep.

"You have done what I asked, now back to the depths with you," I said to my evil self.

It laughed, "One day you will call on us again. Until then. . ." And it was gone. The ease at which it left surprised me, for I could not know with any greater certainty that it longed to be free.

Murks was soon collected and hidden away. I turned to discover what was happening in the battle just as a body came flying through the air and crashed into a headstone near me with such force that the stone was as broken, as was the man. The sheer curtain of snow concealed most of the battle from my eyes, but my instinct told me that it was not going well. Hoping to help, I rushed over to the broken man who lay at the stone. When I was able to roll him over, I was met with the bloody and broken face of Commander Garrett. Before I could even do anything to save his life he labored through a crushed chest to whisper, "Avar. Made me proud. Tell…" And he was gone.

Chapter 9

Unsure of what to do, I stood and started walking towards the fight. I was in shock and I wanted to enact revenge. While at first I thought these murderous thoughts were new and inspired by the death of my friend's father, the depth of that river became known to me. My hunger to devour the souls of the Doomed woke within me, and I was determined to feed.

The swarm of hunters that surrounded the Empty Armor swarmed around him, and reacted to his every move. With no weapons other than his giant form and metal hands he held them all at bay. The black steel and glowing arc of Ukumog clanged against the metal skin of the monster leaving only tiny dents in the tarnished surface. Gently, I pushed my way through the crowd, trying to get to the eye of this storm of metal and men.

The hunters in the back let me through without thinking, but the ones in the middle ranks were too busy to even notice that I was among them. Their training allowed them to know that I was an ally and not to crush me in their movements to attack and defend, but they did not acknowledge that I wanted to get through. Many of them were shouting single words out to communicate maneuvers, but their words were just noise to me. I was transfixed on the armor that stood three feet above the men he fought.

Something about this armor was familiar, but I could not place it. I just swayed with the movement of the army and let myself be hypnotized by him. "Not all of us have the advantage of being a brutish giant," I suddenly whispered. My eyes grew wide, and my heart sank. Deep within me, my evil self laughed.

With a swift and brutal move, The Empty Armor grabbed Ukumog by the blade and lifted both it and Brin off the ground. Immediately the hunters surrounding them backed up. Brin's eyes were glowing brightly with the ferocious lightening of Ukumog, and a feral sneer curled her face into a monstrous mask. The Armor

Desecrated

seemed to inspect her for a moment while she kicked and growled at him with unbridled hatred. No one else made a sound as they waiting impotently for their champion to wrestle free of the enemy.

Suddenly a voice called out from the crowd, "Wrack! He's free!" and all eyes shifted to me.

I scowled at the crowd and suddenly there was a circle of soldiers surrounding me. One of the hunters said calmly, "Just surrender, Wrack."

"No."

Several of them moved in to try and subdue me. As I had done once before I lifted my arms to protect myself, and a shimmering bubble of smoke and shadow surrounded me. It then burst and pushed outward, knocking all the hunters around me backwards. The cascading movement of the men created a hole in their ranks between the Armor and me. I took two steps toward him, and his gaze shifted back and forth from me to Brin's frothing face.

"Your move," I said.

Without saying a word he reared back and threw Brin at me as hard as he could. Time seemed to slow as I saw her hurdling through the open space at me, Ukumog first. Deftly, I evaded the blade and grabbed hold of her, shielding her from whatever impact we might encounter as we together found ourselves in flight. The scent of her hair and her warm soft body intoxicated me. The euphoria was enhanced by the seductive lust and rage of Ukumog flowing through her. Those few quiet moments where we spun through the air together were closer to heaven than I had ever been. We crashed into the ground and stones in the yard battered me, but somehow I knew that I had lessened the power of The Armor's throw. With dark cold power and the evil hunger flowing through me, my bones knitted in seconds and I stood up.

Chapter 9

Seeing his attack had not stopped me, The Armor tore the crescent moon from the limbs of the stone statue and used it as a weapon to bash hunters out of his way, then he fled into the cold snowy night. It did not take long for the layers of white curtains to cover his escape. With his departure, the power flowing through me ceased and instantly I collapsed to the ground.

Dazed, I was soon surrounded by hunters who did not know what to do with me. It was not long before the sound I dreaded most reached me, the pained wails of Avar clutching his dead father's body. Crushing remorse filled my heart, and as I clutched the limp hand of an unconscious Brin, I wept grey tears.

Desecrated

Chapter 10

Captured as I was, I did not even argue with Bridain when he ordered me taken prisoner again. The assembled hunters all saw him as the next commander, and he took the burden of leadership without breaking stride. Just as before, Verif was placed in charge of my incarceration. Doing her duty, she bound my hands in front of me with a thin cord like the one that Murks had found to be dangerously magicked.

"Do you always carry this much rope?" I asked, trying to break the tension.

She gave me a flirty smile. "Yes, but not all of it's for enemies."

Avar's wailing brought back whatever tension had been lifted away by her comment, and then some. Bridain did not know what to do with Avar, as every time someone tried to approach him, he would scream at them to leave him alone. Ferrin lingered nearby him, however, and waited until he wanted help. A few of the hunters picked up Brin's limp body, and started to gently carry her out of the falling snow. One of those who came to help picked up Ukumog from the snow. Within seconds there was a hissing sound like that of cooking meat, and smoke started to rise from the her hand. The malicious glow of Ukumog's runes flared nearly blinding on onlookers. With a blood-curdling scream, the hunter threw

Desecrated

Ukumog away reflexively. Tip over pommel, the blade twisted through the air a short distance before landing in the ground tip down with the handle pointed at me. I suddenly felt as if Ukumog wanted me to reach out my bonded hands, a desire that I refused to comply with.

"Where are you going to put me?"

"The same place that our previous evil creature was kept." Verif pointed at the entrance to the underground temple. "Only place with a single exit, and we can seal you in there."

Avar's cries of mourning followed me all the way into the temple below as Verif, and many armed guards, escorted me to the entrance. I looked over my shoulder to see Ferrin trying, unsuccessfully, to wrestle the hysterical Avar away from the corpse of Garrett. Having no choice but to keep following Verif, the hole in my heart pushed the bitter taste of helpless regret into my throat. When we reached the entrance, the other hunters remained on the surface while Verif took me alone into the temple itself.

There were others down inside collecting the wounded hunters and broken equipment from the first part of the battle. More than one lifeless hunter was carried past me as we walked down the hallway towards the silver altar. Once inside I saw the aftermath of the battle. The broken chains were scattered in different directions, but their ends still attached to the floor. One of the support pillars in the room looked broken, but delayed its collapse to the floor by standing crookedly amongst its brothers.

The altar shined even in this low light, its silver finish marred by the years of pressure from the plates of the Armor's skin. One chain, the one that was wrapped around the center of the Doomed, lay across the top of it as if to hold it down. Tiny pools of blood lay close to the walls of the room here and there. My eyes even found bloody handprints and footprint or two along the floor and

Chapter 10

walls. Small pieces of shattered swords lay strewn and discarded. Verif took note of these potential weapons and signaled for those cleaning to collect them. When I shrugged in indifference to their taking the shards of metal, Verif shrugged in seeming solidarity. As if to say, "I know it doesn't matter, but I am just doing my job."

Eventually the room was situated to Verif's satisfaction, and when the last of her fellows departed she turned to me. "Not all of us are afraid of you, but we have to make a show if it for the others who are. The opinions of passionate people can be very complex, even sometimes black and white, but some of us prefer the grey." Again she gave me a raised eyebrow and a smile. She came to collect her cord saying, "No sense in tying you up down in here." Her hands brushed mine, and she stood closer than she ever had before. Her catlike eyes danced between her work and my storm grey windows to the world. In her face I saw something I recognized. Lust.

Passively I stood while she removed the bonds from me, but I inhaled her scent and drank in her warmth. It was not as delicious as Brin's, but that tiny bit I was able to steal without her noticing would have to sustain me for my time alone in the depths of the temple.

When she finished untying me, she brought her face so close to mine, I thought she might kiss me but instead she whispered, "Be a good boy now." With a mischievous smile she turned and walked out, tossing one lusty glance back at me before she disappeared into the dark tunnel. Moments later, I heard the sound of grinding stone which could only mean one thing. They were sealing me in.

Left alone in the dark, dusty temple wasn't as bad for me as it would have been for any of the humans above me. For me, the passage of hours or days could flow by with almost no notice,

Desecrated

and I had no need for torches or food. Much time passed where I examined the room in great detail. My primary concern was the pillar that I thought might give way at any moment. I certainly did not want the ceiling to come crashing down upon my head. I did what work I could to sure up the stones in that made up the damaged support, and the rest was just hope.

The disc in the center of the room was something that I avoided. Standing on it sent shivers up my spine, and I dared not to touch either the altar or the chains that had once been the bonds of the Doomed. Each time my curiosity tried to pull me over to those artifacts, I forced myself to change my focus to something else, like counting how many stones were in a particular section of the circular outside wall.

After some time I found a place in the back of the room, and sat against the wall facing the circular dais. We were like two men challenged to a staring contest, and I was trying my hardest not to blink. I tried to lose this game of wills by forcing my thoughts up to the surface, and mindlessly watching Murks explore the chamber as I attempted to lose myself in my own mind.

My thoughts always drifted back to Brin and Avar. I was worried that she had been severely wounded by her exchange with The Armor, and that he was lost in his exposed regrets. There had been no time for me to even tell Avar about his father's last words, and it ate away at me. Occasionally, I thought about the barbarian brothers and Bridain's group. I hoped that Bridain in particular was acclimating to his position as commander of the hunters well, and that his heart would someday soften to let me out of this holy prison.

In one of my heavier sessions of thought, I found myself thinking about the Doomed and my visions. I was trying to piece things together and making no headway. Suddenly, I realized that I was sitting with my back against the altar while I was turning a

Chapter 10

broken link of the black chain over and over in my hand. Startled, I dropped the link and watched it as it clinked and clattered its way across the stone floor. The sound it made forced me to reflect on the vision of that smith's hammer pounding metal. A light grew in my mind, and with horror I backed away from the altar.

"Did I? Was I? I was here. I was here when he was locked away in this prison," I spoke aloud to no one. The thoughts that flashed through my mind like searing fire made my head throb with terrible pain, and left no real knowledge behind. I just knew that I had held the hammer that finished the chains that had locked that armor in place, lifetimes ago. Trapped in my solitude, the puzzle of my origin suddenly became of prime importance.

"Master was powerful, but Murks does not know everything. Murks was made after the Master had done something so great and so terrible that he would never be the same," the hemodan tried to comfort me.

My frustration made me laugh at Murks' comment. "Afraid to tell me too much?"

He climbed from my robe and looked up at me. Speaking aloud he said, "Murks doesn't know much more about the time before. Murks knows that Master is troubled, and Murks wants to help, but Murks doesn't know how Murks can help." The sad little hemodan remained with me, his tiny hand resting on my finger, and together we sat silently in the dark.

With no way to make any gauge of time, I remained trapped with my thoughts for what seemed like both ages and no time at all. I grew to know every crack of every stone in that forgotten temple. The dust that had been kicked up by the commotion of the past few days was given time to settle, and I sat for long enough that cobwebs began to form on me.

Desecrated

Something tugged me out of my trance. A slight breeze seemed to gently push against my skin. It was soft enough that I couldn't hear it at all as it drifted by my ears, but I could certainly feel it rustling the hairs on my body as it rushed over me. Confused, I looked around for the source of the draft. Never before had I been so thankful for my ability to see in the complete darkness of the room, yet there seemed to be no discernible answer to the breeze. As I moved around the room trying to find the source, the flow of air would stop and then start again from a completely different direction.

Quickly the thought occurred to me that perhaps something was toying with me. "Very funny," I said into the empty air with hopes that someone would step out of the shadows.

A man's little laugh lightly floated through the air. "Ever the smart one, Wrack. There is no fooling you." The Shadow's voice was followed by his blurry form stepping out from behind a pillar.

Try as I might, my vision could not pierce through the mist that surrounded him to see his face. He was but a dark smudge in the shape of a man. "How did you get in here? Isn't the entrance sealed?"

He laughed, "My dear boy, there is no seal that can keep the darkness out. You, above all others, should know this." His movement to the altar was less like stepping and more like gliding. Once there he bent over and touched the broken chains that lay at its base. "Tsk tsk. Nasty bit of work, this. One of them was trapped here, yes?"

While I did not respond, the look on my face told him everything he wanted to know.

"I see, yes. Hrm. All very interesting, interesting indeed."

The stun of my confusion wore off and left me with a tiny hint of anger. "So, what are you doing here exactly?"

Chapter 10

"Me? Oh, nothing." He sauntered away from the altar. "Just checking up on you. You left Yellow Liver in a bit of a shambles, didn't you? I suppose that Brin's quest will not be solved without a little blood being shed along the way, hrm?"

Without me thinking about it, my arms crossed themselves. "We didn't cause the destruction on the surface, if that is what you are implying."

"Oh no? I think your presence there had more of an effect than you know, dear boy." I could feel his sinister smile poking at me through the mist of his person.

"I fail to see why you are down here, unless it is to torture me."

"Torture you? I think I might be offended! No no, dear boy. I have not come here to torture you. Far from it, in fact. I came to help you. You see, we have something in common..."

The hair on my neck stood up, "Oh yeah? What might that be?"

A soft laugh escaped his vaporous form. "Let's just say we have a common enemy, and until you and your friends came to help me, I couldn't leave that hut I was entombed within. So, thank you for that. Now, shall we discuss how I can help?"

My gut told me that he was up to no good, and that there was no way for me to wriggle out from under his gaze now. Something was connecting the two of us, and only he knew what that was. Defeated, I slid down the wall and sat with my hands folded in front of my bent legs. With a note of sarcasm I said, "How exactly can you help?"

"Well, firstly I can tell you what is happening above you, and secondly I can help you resolve some of this." He motioned toward the altar and chains.

"Why do I feel like there is a catch?"

Desecrated

He laughed, "Because nothing comes without cost, dear boy. Nothing. Not even love or hope. Everything has a catch. The cost of my aid in this particular case, however, is very small. All I desire is a fragment of black cloth from an underground chamber north of here."

I knew that asking him more questions to glean the nature of his desire for this cloth would be a fruitless endeavor, so I opted to ask other questions. "Before I agree to anything, what exactly do you have to offer?"

"Bravo, friend. Personally, I wouldn't want to make a deal without knowing what my elusive shadowy friend had to offer. I tell you what, perhaps I will give you the first part for free, and tell you what I can do after. Sound good?"

His offer made me worry a bit. It seemed that he was offering a lot for free, which meant that his price was a lot more than just a shred of cloth. "Fine. Tell me what is going on topside."

"You have been in here for two months, friend. Ashy grey snow covers the ground up top and the world is rather silent and dead at the moment. Your friend Brin has fully recovered from her wounds, and is locked in a constant verbal battle with Bridain, who is the leader of the hunters if I am not mistaken, over something to do with you and this chamber." He floated across the floor and sat upon the edge of the round dais closest to me. "Your other companion, Avar, is still struggling with the death of someone close to him. I haven't seen him often, his time is mostly spent where it would be unfortunate should the hunters discover my presence."

"Wouldn't that really be anywhere? They are Shadow Hunters and you are The Shadow, correct? Seems to me like they might be looking for you."

Chapter 10

He dismissed my comment with a chuckle. "From the talk around the town, it seems that they have three problems. The one that worries them the most is someone they call The Mistress. They all seem rather worried that she is going to bring an army to wipe out the amassed soldiers here. The second concern is that of the Doomed that escaped this chamber. Seems that he has been rather unfriendly to the people who live in the area around Sanctuary. The last problem is you, dear boy. They seem convinced that you are a shill for one of the Doomed and that you might be compelled against your own will to work against them."

"Sounds fantastic. How do you plan to help exactly?"

"I have something, my dear boy." The greed and malice in his voice made my skin crawl. "Something that you can use to bring the Doomed that escaped this chamber back here. After that, you and your friends can destroy it."

I couldn't help but laugh, "You make it sound so easy. When we fought The Ghoul, he nearly killed all three of us."

"Yes, but this time you will have my help."

The idea of agreeing to his terms made me feel slightly ill, and I knew I shouldn't do it without talking to Brin first, but after our last encounter with The Armor, I knew we needed the help. Taking a few deep breaths I calmed my racing mind and made a decision. "Fine. I'll help you, if you help us."

"Excellent," he said happily. His voice felt like poison being poured into my ears. "Come over here so I can show you the place."

I was skeptical of what he was going to do, but I went over to him anyway. As soon as I was in arm's reach he lunged out towards me, and his incorporeal hand passed into my chest. A flash of light went off in my mind, and I saw a small abandoned village

Desecrated

with an overgrown well in the center. I felt drawn to the well so strongly that when the vision of the place faded, I still knew where the well was.

"There. Now you can find it. Once you have the piece of cloth, make camp away from the village, and I will come find you in the dead of night. Oh, and careful while you are down there, Wrack. Terrible things lurk in the dark under the town of Hollow."

"What a lovely name for a town." My words dripped with sarcasm, a skill I learned from Brin.

"Have faith in yourself, my boy. I know that I believe in you."

The mist of his person blew away like a cloud of dust, down the hallway to the sealed entrance. My solitary waiting in the dark had begun once more.

The Shadow's visit had done more to worry me than it had brought me hope. Being cut off, as I was, from my friends had become a horrible weight. I wanted nothing more than to talk with Brin and Avar, to discover with them what was happening with the forces against us and find a way to solve it. After my display of power in the battle, it was a fool's hope that they would treat me the same as they had previously. Never before, in all the times that the dark power that lived within me manifested, had they seen me do anything unusual. For good or ill, their attention had always been averted from my displays of power, and like a fool I never told them. Brin might surprise me, as she did when I introduced her to Murks, with a lack of concern, but Avar would not be that easily satisfied.

My mind played through terrible scenarios, the least horrible of which was Avar's disappointment being so great that he refused to speak to me again. The rest involved Avar's various

Chapter 10

attempts at revenge or imprisonment of an enemy which had not only lied to him, but had betrayed him in ways that made the fight between us personal. The hatred he bore for the Doomed was nothing in comparison to the rage he harbored in my imagination.

I wondered how long they would keep me sealed down in the temple and if The Shadow spoke true when he said I had been down there for months already. Occasionally, I would hear sounds from above and dust would sprinkle down from the ceiling. There was no telling if it were more attempts of The Mistress trying to get within the temple, or if it were simply work being done on the frozen ground of the graveyard above me. Inevitably, thinking about the graveyard made me think of all the lives that had been lost in this conflict. The ones that stood out to me were, of course, John and Garrett.

My thoughts sometimes dwelled on the other men and women who had been lost, standing there next to their fellows in each battle that I witnessed, and I could not help but feel the sadness of their passing. Indeed, some part of me even felt guilty for their deaths, as if somehow it had been on my orders that The Mistress sent in her waves of soldiers, or as if I had been the one to command the Doomed who lay secretly trapped within this dark chamber to attack and kill his captors.

I did not need this prison of stone; my prison was already made out of memories that I could not remember and emotions that I could not understand. The solitude that my physical incarceration provided, however, amplified the doubts within my mind until they were all encompassing.

After countless ages of self-induced torture, I heard the stone at the entrance move. The first grinding sound that came down the tunnel I thought was just my imagination, but the second was longer and louder. Uncertain as to whom or what was trying

Desecrated

to get in, I did not run to the entrance to greet them with the glee that I felt at the prospect of my release. Instead I remained in the chamber, calmly, and tried to prepare myself for whatever encounter the opening of the door should bring.

The sounds of the stone stopped sooner than I remembered from the closing, and almost no light came down the hallway from above. I heard the clacking of a single pair of boots against the stone, and a solitary glow of a torch flickered from the entrance. Step after step the boots drew closer to me, and my heart began to race. "What if this was The Mistress, come to work her magic within the temple after slaughtering the hunters above? Should I prepare for a fight?" I asked myself.

My small blades had been taken from me before I was imprisoned in this hole, so I looked for something else I could use to defend myself. Near the altar I found a small string of loose black chain. It was thick and unwieldy, but it was better than nothing. As my fingers grasped the black steel a biting cold shot up my arm making me jump. It was a familiar chill, the same one I felt every time the dark power within me awoke. Sadness flooded my face with tension and tears; I didn't want to fight. I was afraid of the power being unleashed without the temper of my desire to keep Brin and Avar safe. The stone in my gut pushed acid into my throat, and like a child, I hid behind the altar.

The boots came ever closer. Their *clackity-clack* against the stone echoed through the chamber preceding the oncoming glow of the torch. Murks was as anxious as I and when he could take it no longer, he scrambled out of my robe and peeked around the corner of the altar. Above me, I saw the glow of the torchlight up the stone ceiling. The intensity of it forced me to switch from my dark sight to my normal, human, vision, lest the brightness of the reflection off the stone surfaces blind me.

Chapter 10

I heard the clack of the boots enter the room and stop. There was a moment where only the licks of flames could be heard lapping up the life of the torch upon which they sat. Murks' anxiousness became comfort and I knew who the bearer of the torch had to be.

"Wrack?" Her voice called out to the room. I had not known such happiness before that moment. Brin had returned to me.

Suddenly wary that this might be some trick played upon me by either The Mistress or The Shadow, I hesitated in my response. Sensing her impatience even from across the room, I lifted my head to look across the altar at her. There she stood, my dark guardian, with torch in one hand and Ukumog silently dangling from her belt. "I am here, Brin," I said cautiously, fighting the urge to run to her embrace.

A smile appeared on her face, which made some of the fear in my throat fade away. "Wrack. It's uzkin' good to see you." Her smile widened and I saw the special twinkle in her eye. "I hate that they've kept you locked in this tomb."

I shrugged. "They did what they thought was best." My eyes glimpsed a scar on her neck that disappeared into the collar of her mail shirt.

"Doesn't mean it is right." Her eyes drifted to the ceiling and then to the crooked pillar.

"Looks pretty bad, huh? I did what I could to fix it." I came out from around the altar. She looked over at me and her eyes got wide at the sight of the chain in my hands, a chain that I had forgotten that I was still carrying. Awkwardly, I tossed the chain to the back of the chamber and remained focused on her. "So, what has been happening up there?" I wanted to ask about the scar, but I thought better of it.

Desecrated

A heavy sigh escaped her. "Too much. Too much, yet not enough." The frustration in her face was readily apparent.

"What?"

"I want to fill you in on everything, I really do, but we don't have much time. Talking about the fight that ended with you in here or Avar's problems would take too long," she blurted out as quickly as she could. She took a breath and slowed down a bit. "We have to find a way to bring The Armor back here."

I was more than a little confused. "What do you want me to do?"

A hint of defeat dashed through her eyes. "I am not sure. It's The Mistress. She is beating the ever-living gaak out of us. We can't keep on fighting her this way. Bridain found some more letters to Garrett from her. Basically they told us that Garrett knew she wanted into this chamber and that she needs The Armor for something horrible."

"Why would you want to help her do something that Garrett tried to keep secret from the hunters?"

Her smile became mischievous. "I don't. I want her to think that we are helpless and forced to help her, then we uzkin' murder the serpent-covered whore."

I felt my eyebrows lift so far on my forehead they nearly leapt off my face. "Wait. What? You want to trick her into thinking we are helpless and then kill her while she is doing whatever horrible thing she is trying to do?"

Pride gleamed from her eyes. "Brilliant plan eh? She will be most vulnerable when she is doing whatever it is she has to do, right? I mean, I am not stupid enough to think it will be easy, but Wrack, even with the two hundred re-enforcements we have received, she is kicking the gaak out of us."

"So, what do you need me for?"

Chapter 10

Knowing she already had my support, her smile welcomed me into her secret plan. "Two things. First, we need to figure out how we can bring The Armor back into this room. Apparently, she needs him in here to do her nasty business. Second, if I can't get good ol' Ukumog here to sing for me so I can kill her, you'll have to do it."

"Me?"

"Yeah! Don't think I haven't noticed how you look at him," she said playfully and tapped her fingers against the pommel of Ukumog. "There is definitely something going on between you two. And the way you handled that fight with The Ghoul…"

My eyes were drawn to the silent blade at her side. The sword's glistening edge of black metal and its bone handle starred back into my soul. A sick mixture of fear and desire bloomed inside me, and I knew I could not refuse. Before I could even try to come up with a solution to our problem, words started coming out of my mouth. "I think I know how to get The Armor back here."

This time Brin's eyebrows did the leaping. "Oh really? How?"

"There is a forgotten chamber, under a well to the north. I just need something from inside," I lied.

Her eyes became slits as she sized me up.

"I saw it in one of my visions," I lied again, trying to set her at ease, and after getting no response I continued. "What other choice do we have?"

The tension in her face faded. "Fair enough." Purpose filled her voice. "I will make the arrangements for us to go do this thing. It's going to take some smooth talking to get you out of here, but I will make it happen." She turned to walk away and took two steps away from me. With each step I felt the loneliness of the empty temple creeping back into me, but then to my surprise

Desecrated

she turned back around and came at me quickly. Before I knew what was happening, her warm arms were wrapped around my cold body, and she pressed herself against me. "I've missed you, Wrack," she whispered.

I never wanted that moment to end.

I was left alone in the dark for another eternity. The sound of the stone being moved back over the entrance haunted my thoughts; my desire to be with Brin and Avar had never been stronger. The monster in my soul wanted to find a way to crack the stone and make my own exit, scooping up my two friends and leaving the rest of these fools to their fate. These thoughts were tempered by my desire to do what was best for my friends, and abandoning the hunters to be slaughtered by The Mistress was not right. I had promised to help them, and that promise was the only thing giving my life a purpose.

The circling thoughts in my head spun faster and faster as the moments stretched themselves into ages. There was no comfort in my usual spots in the lightless temple, and instead I found myself pacing or sitting with my right leg bouncing on the ball of my foot. The rare moments of calm only came when I thought I heard something move the stone at the entrance. In those moments, my body would stop moving, but my mind would spin even faster as I tried to focus all my energy into my senses, nearly trying to will the stone away from the hole.

Just as before, it was impossible for me to tell how much time was passing, but it was even more infuriating. Anger started to take hold of me and the will with which I kept my monster at bay was worn away.

Chapter 10

Starting with just an inspection of the stone that kept me prisoner, eventually I started to try and wipe away the dirt and dust that lay at the edges of the stone. "This will just make it easier for them to open," I rationalized my actions. In short time, however, I was actively trying to shift the stone from its resting place. When my light attempts failed to have any effect, I pushed harder and harder. With panic and anger pulsing through my veins, I began to scratch and dig at the stone and the walls that held it up. I had become the caged monster that all the hunters feared I was from the beginning. Getting out was all that mattered anymore. I needed to escape and smell the air of on the outside. Thoughts of freedom gave way to my dark lust for the warmth that enveloped Brin. When I realized what I was thinking, a battle resurged in my soul.

Casting myself to the ground and against the walls, I beat away the monster within me, and crawled back into the chamber of the temple. In the pitch black of the timeless prison, I felt guilty for my thoughts and actions in my moment of weakness. My eyes were focused on my wounded hands and broken fingernails. They were a badge of my feral nature, and as surely as the monster retreated back into the depths of my soul, so too did the signs of his presence fade from my fingers. This extraordinary healing was both a blessing and a curse, for it made it very easy for me to hide the truth from everyone, even those closest to me.

Curling into a ball in the middle of the temple floor, I tried to fight through my desires, worries, and concerns, and I just waited for my dark champion to return. Eventually, she did just that.

At the height of my self-imposed hibernation, I heard the unmistakable sound of the stone grinding away from the entrance, yet I remained where I lay on the temple floor. The sounds of many boots clattered down the stone stairs and into the tunnel, yet I did

Desecrated

not move. The warmth of many people surrounded me and I saw the light of their torches flickering through my eyelids. Then one boot came forward and kicked my feet.

"C'mon, lazy bones. We have to go." Brin said with playful sternness.

I stretched, as many humans do when awaking from a slumber, and my joints screeched in protest. When I opened my eyes I found myself surrounded by hunters with their weapons at the ready. The look on their faces was one of complete mistrust. I started to say something and Brin shushed me, which surprised me. Silently and quickly I was escorted at the center of the hunters to the entrance of the temple, and then out.

On the surface the air was not as cold as before, but it was night, so I was not completely blinded by the change in lighting. There was evidence that the snowfall had been piled a few feet high during part of the time I was inside, and that it had already begun to melt. Bridain and his normal squad were there, along with Avar, whose sour expression said that he was not happy to see me. Quietly, I let the hunters continue to escort me away from the town of Sanctuary until we reached the edge of the magical protection.

The hunters surrounding me marched us further away from Bridain, Avar, and Brin, who began quietly speaking to one another as soon as the distance between us was deemed wide enough. I could not make out their conversation through the rattling armor and shifting weapons of my guards. All of this behavior saddened me a little. I had thought that their fear of me had begun to wane before the fight with The Armor, but now it seemed that I was the enemy. In my heart, I did not want to be their enemy.

Chapter 10

Brin and Avar said heartfelt goodbyes to Bridain, Verif, and Tarissa then walked over to me and my wall of hunters. A large coil of thick rope was handed to me as Brin said, "We are going down a well, right?"

I nodded in return and put my arm and head through the coil allowing me to carry it across my chest.

Then she nodded at the guards who then left me in the keeping of my two friends and the three of us started our journey. I looked over my shoulder once hoping that I would see one face sad to see me leave, and I found three. Nikolai, Piotyr, and Tikras were in one of the trees above us, and when they saw me looking, they gave me a small wave. It made me feel good that my actions had not severed my confusing and mysterious tie to them.

"What was that all about?" I asked quietly.

"Shut up, dark one," Avar commanded and then quickened his pace to get ahead of me. My heart sunk.

When he was far enough away Brin came and walked with me. "Don't mind Avar, he will come around. It will just take time. The others… They filled his head with the lie that you killed Garrett."

None of the desperate sadness of my time in the dark prison could be compared to the utter despair that I felt at that moment. Avar had always believed in me and somehow I had lost him.

Desecrated

Chapter 11

Traveling in the company of someone who hates you is never a good experience. Avar would barely speak to me as we made our way north of Sanctuary. Occasionally, we skirted patrols of freth who were circling the wounded village. Brin stayed with me while we travelled, and each time I looked over at her there was a strange look in her eyes. It made me feel like somehow she pitied me for the time I was forced to spend alone in that prison of a temple, or perhaps she felt helpless to try and fix my relationship with Avar. Whatever the reason for her concern, it did not feel good when she looked at me that way. In fact, it made me feel completely empty inside.

The miserable silence was filled with unspoken words that hung like bricks in the air. All of these unexpected changes completely confused me, but there didn't seem to be a good solution to resolve this painful tension. Every word I tried to form into sentences in my mind seemed so petty or pointless that I could not bring myself to utter them aloud. Luckily for me, I didn't have to sleep and therefore risk uttering secrets while my eyes were closed. Avar, on the other hand, seemed unlike his usual self when we camped.

Desecrated

The first night he tried to stay awake and keep watch on my activity. Then the next he allowed himself to sleep sitting up with his weapon in his lap, and strapped to his hand. I knew it had been several months since we had been around one another, but the difference to me was like closing your eyes when it was night and opening them a few moments later to be blinded by the sun.

After about two days of making almost no actual progress towards our goal due to avoiding freth patrols, and laying false trails to make ourselves hard to track, Brin finally nudged me. "You are going to have to talk to him, ya know. Avar is uzkin' stubborn, just like his dad. Sure, he was excited about being around you at first, so you didn't see the stubbornness, but to survive with my constant uzkin' belittling he would have to be strong willed."

We walked for a long time before I could even bring myself to respond, "I wouldn't even know where to begin."

Side by side Brin, and I stepped forward in silence through the grey needle covered trees of the forest. My mind continued spinning with the troubles ahead: Avar, The Shadow, whatever lay in the pit waiting for us, The Armor, and The Mistress and her army. I wanted so badly to have a simple way to fix everything, but there was no easy answer. This quiet continued until after the sun fell below the horizon.

That night Brin whispered in my ear, "Talk to him," then curled up under her blankets to sleep, leaving Avar and me alone.

The crackling of our tiny fire was the only sound in the camp. Avar continued to give me stone-faced glares from across those flickering flames. Uncertain as how to deal with it I tried to avoid his gaze, instead I focused on the changes in the landscape as we headed north. The trees here were a mix of leafless branches reaching in all directions and many of those grey-needled trees with wide branches at the bottom and a point at their top. The

Chapter 11

more of those needle trees that were around, the fresher the air seemed to be. This persistence of life from those trees was a little unexpected for me. It seemed that in nearly all the places I had been prior to these woods almost all living things had given up, letting themselves sink into a state of prolonged decay. The people in Yellow Liver were mostly hopeless shells who lived in constant fear, and the desolate land around it seem to reflect their misery with yellow dust and pools of sulphur smelling water. This place was altogether different.

"Why does this place seem so different from Yellow Liver or the Spikelands?" I asked without thinking.

Avar just glared at me, and then turned his gaze back to the fire.

Realizing that I had forgotten for that moment that he was upset at me, I felt stupid. I searched for something else to say, hoping that if I continued to talk eventually he would have to respond. "The trees just seem to make the air feel very different, ya know?"

"We are getting closer to Flay, The King's city. All this land used to be part of the kingdom of Ravenshroud thousands of years ago, before the names of places became unimportant and twisted," he said in his most condescending voice, which was not very condescending as far as voices go. It came across more as more know-it-all or arrogant than condescending.

I had missed Avar's compelling desire to share information. He really just couldn't help but answer my questions, no matter how mad he was with me. "Does that mean we are getting closer to Marrowdale?" I tried to pick a reference to a place I had seen before, both to collect my bearings and to keep the conversation moving.

Desecrated

"Sort of. Marrowdale is west of here. If we had been heading in that direction, we might have gotten there already, actually. Marrowdale is kind of in the space between Flay and Skullspill, which is probably why The King and The Baron used to fight over it so much. It was a good staging area for armies and all that." I could see some of the tension lift away from him as he talked.

Avar gave me a slightly incredulous look. "You really have no idea how far away we really are from the other places, do you?"

"What do you mean?"

He sighed, "The fact that you never get tired, and don't sleep, probably blurs the experience of some of our travels. For example, we have been traveling for four days away from Sanctuary, which is no small distance, and we aren't at this mystery location you are taking us to." Instantly his anger with me returned. "If there actually is a mystery place. It astounds me that Brin still believes your lies after everything you have done. I wouldn't be here if Commander Bridain hadn't ordered me to come along."

My sudden disappointment killed my flow of words. I felt like there was nothing I could say that wouldn't cause further friction between us. Silence became my only option, so I sat there looking at him, but said nothing.

Another sigh, more dramatic than the first, was forced from his lungs. "I just hope you don't murder us both and go off to do your dark work elsewhere." He crossed his arms tightly, and glared at me one more time before ending our conversation by staring at the fire.

The next morning neither of us said a word about that night, and Brin never asked any questions. I had a lingering suspicion that she had been awake the whole time. After we packed up and traveled on, Brin started taking direction from me on where

Chapter 11

we were supposed to go. I only knew which way we had to go, and a vague sense if we were far or near. On that day we crossed the threshold from far to near.

Two more awkwardly silent nights went by and I was too confused and afraid to say anything to Avar. At this point we were far enough away from Sanctuary that we no longer had the freth to worry about. Now we were avoiding contacts with the locals, so as not to stir up a nest of King's guard.

By the third day, we were out in the open, following an overgrown road through some more of those needle covered trees. While it was still cold, the ground was crunchier in the mornings and much softer by midday. By afternoon I realized that we had been going downhill for quite some time, and so I tried to get a sense of the greater terrain. From the look of the hills around us, we were headed into the heart of a small valley.

Brin also seemed to be investigating our route and eventually broke our collective silence, "Isn't this the old road to Hollow?"

Avar thought for a moment, "It could be. Seems like that might be right." He searched for something on his person, but then said, "Gods, I hate not having my journal! I hope that Sergeant Valence or The Vampire are having a good laugh at all my notes."

"With that terrible hand writing of yours, they probably threw it away," Brin laughed.

Avar was not so amused, "Let's hope so."

Before the sun went down, the ground leveled out and the trees began to thin. Through the gaps I could make out an abandoned town in the clearing beyond. There were only about six buildings that were still standing, and even then most of the roofs had caved

Desecrated

in. Apart from those standing six buildings, about the same number of other structures lay in piles of rubble, or were nothing but the stone foundation that a building once stood upon.

Brin's sense of danger must have flared, because she started walking with great caution as if she were stalking prey. Naturally, Avar and I followed suit and gave our leader space to scout. The closer we got to the center of the abandoned village, the stronger my sense of location became. As soon as I could see the center of this forgotten place and saw the stone well in the middle, I knew we were in the right spot.

The well itself was blackened, but not uniformly, and the buildings around the center of the town seemed singed and smashed. There was also a wooden wagon, stained with a deep red color, which was lined with armored plates in the bed. Built into the center was a twisted scrap of broken metal that looked like it might have been a very large silo to hold something. I whistled at Brin and motioned towards the well.

She nodded and quickly scouted around the middle of the town, only briefly looking at the ruined wagon. After a few moments she came back with a shrug. "Looks like we are alone. Whoever left this wagon here, they are long gone."

"Amazing. I think this is the first time we have ever gone anywhere for a mission and not had to fight anything," Avar said, half kidding.

Brin smiled, "I hope you aren't speaking too soon, Avar. We still have to go down into the well, right Wrack?"

"Yes."

Avar rolled his eyes. "Of course."

"Hand over the rope, Wrack. Let's get this over with."

Chapter 11

I gladly removed the heavy coil from my person and gave it to Brin. She tied the rope to one side of the wagon and yanked very hard on it. The wagon shook a tiny bit from the action, but it did not seem to stress the structure at all. The three of us looked down into the well, after twenty or so feet it was too dark to make out any details at all. Even looking deeply with my dark sight, I couldn't see the walls of the well itself.

"Well, this is spooky," said Avar. "Are you sure we need to do this? There has to be some other way of fixing this situation."

"Ok, then. I am listening." Brin feigned patience and Avar closed his mouth. "Right. That is what I thought. Listen, I don't like it either, but this is the only possible working solution that anyone has offered. And, like it or not, Wrack's visions have proved useful before."

"Yeah." Avar's slow speech displayed his disbelief without him having to say it outright.

Brin tossed the rope down into the well and there was no sound of a splash to come back up. "I suppose I will go first," she said with a slight bit of excitement.

"Then Wrack goes second. I am not going to let him trap us down there."

His distrust was still upsetting. "Sure. I will go after Brin," I conceded, as to prevent more discomfort between us. Suddenly, horrible thoughts traveled the ring around my mind. There was a tiny hint of worry that Avar may have been ordered to leave me behind or something worse. I really hoped it wouldn't come to something as drastic as that.

"We will probably need some light down there," Brin said as she began crafting a torch out of a stick, some lantern oil she had in her pack, and a few torn scraps of cloth.

Desecrated

Avar continued to observe me with judging eyes while we all waited for the torch to soak up enough oil. I tried to break the tension a little. "I don't think that the thing we are looking for is right at the entrance. We might have to look around a bit down there."

"Ok, I will make a second torch in case we need to split up," Brin said as she went off to collect more supplies for torch making.

As soon as she was out of earshot I turned to Avar, "Look. I don't know what happened during the months that I was locked away in that pit, but I want you to know that I didn't kill your father. He crashed into one of the headstones, and there was nothing I could do for him by the time I got there." I paused, hoping to give Avar a chance to say something. When he didn't, I continued, "He did have time to utter something to me before he passed. He wanted me to tell you how proud he was of you, and the man you have become. In those last moments, his only thoughts were of you."

Avar's face tightened. With an outburst of frustration, he stood up and turned away from me. I didn't know what to do or say; saying more or trying to comfort him might drive him further into a rage, and I did not want to even think about what the outcome might be. The silence was painful.

Brin came back with a few sticks in hand along with some scavenged cloth, presumably from one of the buildings. She stopped dead in her tracks when she saw Avar standing off to the side facing away from both of us. "Everything ok?" she asked with a surprised look on her face.

"No. Everything is not ok," Avar said without turning to face us. He then quickly moved over to his things and grabbed them without giving either of us a chance to say anything. From my

Chapter 11

vantage point behind him, I could see tears falling to the pack as he lifted it from the ground. Without another word, he quickly strode off into the woods.

Brin threw down the sticks and started to walk after him, but I stopped her by saying, "Don't. He needs time alone." The look on my face told her the rest.

She nodded, with a defeated look on her face, and went back to managing the torches.

A few quiet hours went by as the thirsty torches soaked up their oil. "You think he will come back?" Brin asked me.

"Honestly, I don't know."

Her eyebrows went up in surprise. "You guys must have had one hell of a talk in the few moments I was gone. Care to enlighten me?"

"We talked about Garrett, how I wasn't the one who killed him." I asked myself if I should tell Brin more and decided not to.

"About time," was all she said about that. Without missing a beat, "So, I think the torches are ready. While I would love to have Avar here, I think we should get this over with."

After a quick scan of the wood line for any sign of Avar, I nodded in agreement.

Brin lit the two torches and then let one of them fall into the well. It seemed to fall for a long time before crashing into the floor below. While we could see the flickering flame of the torch, we could not make out any details about the chamber it was trying to illuminate. "I suppose we could leave this other torch up here, so we can see the hole after the sun goes down."

She was right, the sun was already nearing the horizon. "I will go down first," I said and without waiting for a response I grabbed the rope, and started to shuffle down the small hole of the well.

Desecrated

There wasn't much room in that tight space. I was forced to slowly slide down the stones while constantly shifting my grip on the rope, for I could not properly bend my legs without pressing against the opposite side of the well. Once I had gotten a good distance down into the well, I could see the bottom open up to a large space below, and the rope freely dangling beneath me. "It looks like the well bottoms into a huge open chamber," I shouted up to Brin.

"How far are you from the torch?"

"Hard to tell," I shouted back. "Maybe twice more the distance of the well? Impossible to say."

I heard Brin laugh a bit. "I hope the rope is long enough!"

"Me too," I whispered to myself.

"What?" She shouted.

"Nothing!" Continuing my descent, I started focusing more on climbing down the rope. My struggle to try and find the best way to navigate the tight space became more work than the climb itself. Eventually I had to clear my head. "Enough. You can do this. It is just an uzkin' rope," I encouraged myself. Trying to heed my own advice, I took a deep breath, and then continued to crawl down the rope into the darkness below.

After I passed the bottom threshold of the well, I found myself in a very large chamber. With the light of the fading sun a good distance away; I could actually see more of the room itself. The first thing I noticed was that the room itself was massive. At least three or four of the medium sized two story buildings from Yellow Liver could fit easily into this space, and there would still be plenty of space for an army to move about within. The ceiling itself was domed, and the hole that I entered through was off to one side of the circular room.

Chapter 11

Letting myself down a few more feet, I had the distinct feeling that I had been here before. I looked up at the ceiling and found a circular mural had once been painted there. It was partially missing due to the erosion of the decorative layer that once rode the surface of these ancient stones, but I knew that it had been there. The distant hazy feeling of a vision started to cloud my mind, and I felt my hands begin to release their grasp on the rope. My instinct to survive gave me the strength to push away the mist in my mind and tighten my grip. I hoped that the vision would return once I was in a safer place.

My movement on the line caused it to sway. This unintended motion grew as I got closer to the end of the rope, an end that did not quite reach the ground. I shouted up, "The rope is too short!"

I heard Brin's voice echo something back, which sounded like, "Ok!"

Without thinking much about how I was going to get back out, I let myself slowly slide down to the end of the rope and then fall the distance to the stone floor below. The fall was further than it looked, and it hurt when I landed, but I wasn't damaged by the impact.

The air seemed thin and had the same wet chill that one might find deep in a cave. My eyes danced on every flickering surface that reflected the light of the torch. From the floor, all detail of the ceiling was hidden in the shadows. The well opening glowed like a portal into the heavens with the dark cable hanging limply from above. With a twitch the rope seemed to come alive and I knew that Brin was making her way down.

Waiting for her to join me, I continued to glean what I could from the space around me. The first thing I noticed was that there seemed to be a few tunnels which led off from this main chamber

Desecrated

many of which were collapsed. The shards of broken columns also lay strewn about the room. This caused me a bit of concern, for I began to wonder what was holding the roof over my head, since the columns were mostly broken.

Rattling around in my heart was the strong feeling that I had been here before. I had flashes of great curtains that could be loosened to encircle the centermost part of the chamber. There was a fading touch of the sacred here too. It was as if the neglect not only tore at the decorative walls, but also at the very spirit of this place. The questions in my mind were quickly answered from within my own spirit. I should not have come back here. Something terrifying lingered on the fringes of my thoughts, and it wanted to get in.

Panic growing in my heart, I shouted up to her, "Brin! Brin something isn't right!"

"No need to shout, Wrack. I am right above you," and so she was. I was distracted for a moment as I watched her glide down the rope with ease, her feet wrapped skillfully in the line to help her control her descent. Smoothly she worked, hand over hand and within moments she dropped from the end of the rope and was standing next to me. "So, what are you screaming about?"

I tried to focus, but my mind was starting to fill with smoke, "Uh. Something isn't right here. We should leave."

"Well, we just need to collect something, right?"

I nodded.

"Then let's finish that quickly, and we will get the uzk out of here, ok?"

Unable to form an argument against her idea, I just nodded again and began following her. She scooped up the torch that was lying on the ground and started off towards one of the tunnels.

Chapter 11

"How are we going to get up the rope?" I asked, suddenly concerned with the fact that it was too short.

"We'll figure something out," she said confidently, and that would have to be enough for me.

The first tunnel we went down was caved in shortly beyond the threshold. The next went a little further and even had some old bones that were too small to be a human strewn about, but this tunnel also ended in a pile of rocks. At the third tunnel we discovered a hallway that still stood and even had some flowing designs etched into the walls that followed us as we proceeded deeper into the underground ruin.

To my nose there was an echo of long forgotten incense. My ears heard ghostly voices from the tunnel ahead, and my eyes began to see things as they were, before they fell into ruin. I could even feel a lovely warm breeze flow over my skin. Having two experiences flirting with my senses simultaneously made it nearly impossible for me to tell what was real. Brin was my constant. My mind followed the dark curls of her hair as they flickered in the torchlight. A panic was gripping me. There was a presence here that was greater than that of the Doomed. Even the hairs on my neck were too scared to rise because of the thing with lurked at the edge of my thoughts. I was afraid of losing myself in a vision and coming face to face with whatever it was. I had to stay with Brin.

We found the end of the tunnel that came to a door of metal bound wood, and I knew that what we sought was on the other side. "We are here," I said weakly, still trying to hold onto what was real.

"This door looks ancient. I bet I could kick it down," she said, brushing some of the dust away with her free hand.

Twinges of fear hit me. "Careful. We don't want to alert anything that is down here."

Desecrated

She gave me a disappointed look. "I think the hinges are uzk'd though. Breaking it down might be our only option."

To me the door looked pristine. It was polished dark wood with gleaming metal bands all etched with flights of black birds and the crowned crest of Ravenshroud proudly set into the middle. My eyelids fluttered as I fought to keep them open. In my stupor I muttered, "But the King... The King..."

Everything went black but, I heard a thundering bang before my mind was pulled away.

"Yes yes," said a voice. "Come in boy. They are expecting you."

When my eyes opened, I was standing in front of the door with the Ravenshroud crest, but it was now open and a servant wearing the green stripe of the Kingdom was holding it. His other hand motioned for me to enter.

"Um. Yes, thank you," a voice that was mine said. It was a younger voice. A voice filled with the insecurities of youth and the cautiousness of a boy out of place.

Incense filled the air with a hypnotizing musk. The tension in my mind faded away and I felt a calm flow through my whole body. My heart did not know either pain or joy, but I was content. Without the noise of my worries, I could simply focus on the sound my shoes made as their soles scuffed the stone floor with each step. I tried to change the noise with each footfall, trying to achieve an impossibly silent walk while keeping up with the servant in front of me.

Chapter 11

A huge velvet curtain blocked the end of the hallway, which the servant gently pushed aside to allow me entrance. The walls of the chamber I entered were completely obscured by enormous fine tapestries depicting the heroic exploits of a handsome square-jawed hero. In their stories he was a leader of vast armies and the conqueror of all manner of villains. All darkness was banished at the skilled edge of the hero's sword or wit. His story was more valuable than the thousands of gold and silver threads that were woven into them. Every object in the room was a treasure in its own right. Nothing was simple or plain; everything spoke to the glory of the men within the room. I was proud to be in their presence.

"Ah!" exclaimed the man who would become The Baron, Commander Andoleth. "Here is your boy now, Se'Naat."

Se'Naat glided across the rugged floor towards me, his feet making no sound as he did so. "Indeed he has, brother. Perhaps he and I will leave you and His Majesty alone to do more strategy for your war," he smirked.

"Your brother has no mind for war, Andoleth. It is a wonder how he ever clawed his way to the top of the church," said the brown haired hero depicted in the many tapestries who sat in the room upon a chair of gold.

"It is a mystery to me as well, your Majesty," Commander Andoleth growled.

Se'Naat gave a dark chuckle. "War does not begin or end with the edge of a blade."

"Spoken truly like a priest," Commander Andoleth condescended. "Off with you and your apprentice. Make yourself useful and convince your dark goddess to favor us."

"She already favors us, brother. Have faith," Se'Naat smiled.

Desecrated

Commander Andoleth muttered under his breath and waved us off while the King gave us a huge amused grin.

As Se'Naat and I walked back down the hallway together he whispered, "Never you mind my brother. His faith in the Shadow Queen is as great as mine." His face became consumed in thought for a moment and he stopped in his tracks. Quickly descending upon me as if he had some urgent secret to tell, "How is your faith, boy?"

Before I could answer the scene shifted. In the space between visions, I could feel the outside force creeping into the cracks between my memories like black moldy ooze. Panic set in as I grew painfully aware of the infection within my thoughts. My lungs filled with air and prepared to give birth to a scream, but the scream never came.

"Listen to me and try again," Se'Naat said with his particular form of smug encouragement. "You must feel the words more than say them."

Again I was in the chamber where I had met the King except this time the room was mostly bare. The tapestries still hung in all their glory, but the treasures of regal comfort were nowhere to be found, nor was their kingly master.

"I'm sorry master, but I am just not sure what you mean." My voice was filled with aimless frustration and in my heart I felt lost.

Se'Naat sighed. "Do you know that feeling in your body when you run so very hard and so very fast that you can taste the very essence of your life being consumed by your actions? That is what you must feel, but you must learn to master it. Using the darker powers of this world without a mastery of this skill will only lead you to consume your own soul while trying to clean the floor."

Chapter 11

I wasn't entirely certain what he meant, but I nodded anyway. Taking a deep incense-laced breath, I focused on the burning candle at my feet and the small circle of salt that surrounded it. I knelt down so that I was not crossing the circle, but yet my face was as close as possible to the flame atop the candle. With the softest whisper I could summon, "I call upon the father of all things and his herald, Tarendar, to grant me audience." The light of the candle shifted, becoming hot flickering gold. Joy filled my heart, but I suppressed my emotions and continued to whisper, "I call upon the mother of the world and her seneschal, Idriani, to grant me audience." Again the flame shifted. The edges became dark and tiny flecks of black danced in the air above the candle.

"Now do the binding, before you lose it," Se'Naat commanded.

"Um," I stuttered, trying to remember the words. "Father and mother. King and Queen. I bind this power, from worlds unseen."

The light of the candle began to grow. Brighter and brighter it grew, its size only contained by the circle on the floor, but its intensity was limitless. Se'Naat waited for me to act, but I sat dumbfounded until I had to shield my eyes from the brightness of the light. The cracking sound of a consuming fire bloomed into the room, and soon it sounded as if we were standing inside a raging inferno.

"Vanquish it!" Se'Naat yelled.

My hands were shaking, and my thoughts drifted to a time when I ran from the expanding light of a candle. The memory of that old moment was slippery in my mind, for I saw only the outline of a bearded man on the other side of the candle. He too called out to me, but instead of doing what he said, I ran. Who was that man? I could not remember him.

Desecrated

"Uzk! Vanquish the magic, else it will eventually break through!"

My master's shouting forced me to put away the old memories and assert myself. I shook away the dreams and reached forward my hand passing through the circle, and into the swirling mass of black and gold fire beyond.

"What are you doing, boy? Just vanquish the spell!"

"I am." My fingers outstretched toward the center of the light I could feel the blistering heat of the torrent inside. Swirling trails of gold and black mist began escaping the circle and spiraling through the air around me. I opened a door in my mind and invited the power within. Violently, the light funneled through the tiny holes I had created in the circle and rushed under my skin. My soul was immolated instantly with unseen flames, but the doorway in my mind allowed for the fire to escape to a hidden place, and then all was quiet.

"Stay with me, Wrack. Stay with me," Brin's voice brought me back.

The sickly feeling of the black mold in my mind remained as I came to my senses. "Wha–What happened?"

Brin sighed with relief. "You collapsed as soon as I kicked the door down." Her eyes darted up towards the tunnel that led back to the main chamber. "I think you were right though. Something is down here with us."

Scrambling to my feet, I took a quick look around the room we were in. The door was only slightly open and the wood that had once held the handle on the door was scattered about in splinters. The rest of the room was filled with decayed debris. Old collapsed

Chapter 11

shelves, armoires, and even what I believed to be a disintegrated desk and chair. Part of the ceiling had also fallen in, and under the broken spot was a pile of stone that reached all the way up to the hole, filling it. Due to the crushed side, the room was a lot smaller than the one from my visions, but the placement of the furniture seemed to be the same as it was when I was training with Se'Naat.

A memory of Se'Naat placing his flowing black robes in one of the wardrobes flashed through my mind. That particular wardrobe would have been right under the place where the ceiling collapsed. I refused to make a connection as to why The Shadow would want fabric from Se'Naat's robes, but that is where I was being pulled. Quickly, I examined the pile of rocks. Silently I debated how I would get to the treasures I believed lay underneath. Pressure from my own fear of the thing that was around us, unseen, caused me to just start tossing rocks away from the pile.

"What are you –Uzk. What we need is in there, isn't it?" Brin asked and did not wait for an answer. She just starting helping me dig.

There was an infection in my mind and a gloom in my soul, and it weighed on me. No amount of work had ever made me sweat before, and it wasn't the moving of these heavy rocks that was doing it, yet there were tiny beads of grey sweat appearing on my skin. I could feel the cool drops running down the groove in my back. My sweat was not like human sweat. Not only was it an odd color, but it made me stink of wet earth. The stench of it was reminiscent of the shallow grave I had escaped from. Brin was also sweating, and I found it incredibly distracting.

The scent of her kept breezing past me each time she turned her head. The sweet smell of life pushed away the earthy stink of my own body, and each time it sang to me like that incense in the dream. The hungry darkness in me awakened and I tried to

Desecrated

fight it back, but I was weakened from the unseen force attacking me. My breathing became labored and I was forced to step away from Brin. Feigning exhaustion, I stumbled away and sat with my back against the wall.

Not willing to remain here any longer than necessary, Murks leapt from my robes and ran over to the pile of stones, lifting debris that was more than twice his size. I was impressed, but too preoccupied to express it.

"Talk to me, Wrack," Brin's voice was harried. "What I am I looking for in here?"

Caught in the haze of my internal struggle, I couldn't respond right away. The part of me that enjoyed brutalizing The Ghoul was clawing his way to the surface, and it was all I could do to hold him back. I strained to have control long enough to tell her what we needed. Eyelids fluttering, I was able to squeeze out a few words, "Black... Cloth..."

Brin and Murks worked with renewed vigor at the pile, while my struggle became so intense that my whole body started to shake.

"That can't be good," Brin said without stopping.

"No Brin lady. It's bad. Very bad," Murks sounded more frightened than I had ever heard him.

Whispering filled my mind and the confusion the sounds brought along with it allowed my darker self to push me aside and take over. At once my body surged with strength and I picked myself up off the floor.

"Run Brin lady," I felt Murks whisper to her. While the hunger in me was paralyzing to the part of me who was now along for the ride, the darker me was less hindered by it. The glare that I shot over at Murks, however, could have killed a small house pet.

Chapter 11

Brin turned and looked up at me, but I moved so quickly over beside her that it threw off her balance. She nearly fell over backwards but even in her unbalanced state there was a Clink! that echoed in the room. Ukumog was now unchained.

"Yes," I said with a calm quiet voice. "Use it." Unblinking, I waited for her to strike at me. I was completely confident that I would overpower this weak human child.

Brin held the blade out in front of her defensively, and neither of us moved. Then the runes began to glow brighter and brighter. A presence became known to me down the tunnel and I moved away from Brin to look through the open door. The clattering of Murks moving rocks infuriated me. "Hush yourself, hemodan," I sternly commanded. With it now quiet, I could hear commotion coming from the main chamber. I stepped through the opening and focused my concentration.

Faintly, ever so faintly I heard a voice. "Guys? Hey guys?" It was Avar.

I turned to look back into the room to find Brin still holding the bright blade of Ukumog at me, ready to strike. "Your Shadow Hunter friend is out there. Perhaps you should tend to him." My voice was cold and distant.

She moved to the side so that I could step back into the room and circled around me to go out the open door without ever turning her back to me. Once she had left the room, I heard her call out, "I am in here, Avar!"

Murks returned to digging in the pile of rocks, and I swiftly moved over to help him. The echoing shouts from the other room did not have an alarming tone, so I ignored them while I tried to unearth the treasure I knew was inside. It wasn't long before I was rewarded.

Desecrated

The rocks above us shifted slightly, but I had no fear, so it did not slow my pace. The fear that was coming from my hemodan, I found annoying, and I cast mountains of determination through my part of the connection. Eventually his fears were drowned in my confidence. With just a few more rocks pushed out of the way, we found it, the broken shards of the wardrobe. With cautious, yet eager, fingers I slowly picked out the pieces of ancient wood. Underneath there was a large piece of black cloth. I did not have the patience or desire to try and unearth the whole robe. "We only need a small shred," I said to both Murks and myself. I easily ripped a fistful of fabric from the mass. Something fell out of the fabric as I pulled it away from the rest. It was a small grey metal box, with a clasp made of gold. The original shape of the box had been lost in the cave-in, resulting in no way to keep it shut. Even with my darkness in control, our curious nature got the best of me and I had to know what was inside the box, so I reached out to claim it.

"Master! No. Se'Naat is tricksy! Master should not play with the box."

The glare I gave Murks forced him to step back and cower in fear. Once he had retreated, I followed through with my intended action, to claim the box and discover the secret inside. It was lighter than I expected and the decorative markings were almost invisible until the box was right near my face. This box was not meant to survive any form of attack to get at its hidden contents, but it was a treasure in its own right, even though it was smashed. Flipping it over I forced the deformed golden latch and cracked open the lid. The only thing inside was a slightly smashed candle exactly like the one from the vision. My darker self thought that finding this was funny, and so he gave a sinister laugh, a laugh that was nothing

Chapter 11

like the one I knew as my own. From inside my unseen prison deep within my body I wondered how he and I could be the same if even our expression of joy was so different.

There was hesitation as I tried to decide if I should take the candle or not. I could feel the darker me wrestle with the decision. Ultimately he decided that holding onto sentimental objects was a pointless sign of weakness, and he threw the box so hard against the ground that it broke into pieces. Further he found the brittle candle and crushed it under his boot and smiled. His destructive urges frightened me, for I knew that they were also mine.

Each of our steps out into the main chamber of the ruin exploded with raw confidence, and our shoulders leaned forward with a sense of purpose. Again, I marveled at the differences between us.

Avar was still hanging from the rope, and it looked like he and Brin were trying to extend the length of it by tying strips of fabric to the end, and that things were not going well. "This isn't working. I am going to have to climb back up and weave it together correctly. I can't do this while hanging from it," Avar blurted out.

"Fine, but be quick. There is something down here with us," Brin snapped at him.

He huffed in frustration and then started to climb back up the rope with the scraps of cloth pulled through his belt.

"How is it coming?" I asked.

"I really wish you had told me that the rope was too short before I came down here." She had obviously forgotten about Murks' warning from before, or maybe she thought that I was myself again.

Desecrated

My hand held the salvaged cloth, and my fingers slightly rubbed the old fibers together to sate my impatience with the situation. "I did call up to you. I suppose you didn't hear what I said, and you were the one who decided to drop off the rope once you saw that it was too short."

Her jaw flexed as she clenched her teeth. "I thought you were in uzkin' trouble. Next time I won't try and rush to save you."

"I don't need saving."

Rage lit up her eyes, but it was suddenly replaced with a little fear. Avar was already starting to reel in the rope from the top of the well. She quickly looked at the rope, and then her eyes darted back to Murks, who was only now walking into the light cast by her torch. "Oh, you are still…"

"Still what?" I asked aggressively. "Still weak and useless? Lost in your desperate quest for pointless revenge? Still stuck following the whims of fools?" Cold pain rushed to my fingertips, and I knew that the purple steam of my dark power was flowing into the air around them.

Her eyes grew wide and she brought Ukumog in between us, but her face spoke nothing except confused sorrow. "Why are you doing this?" she whined.

I loosed a quiet evil chuckle. "Doing what?"

Brin's long struggle with her own darkness made it much easier for her to control her emotions, for the sadness only lasted for a few more seconds before she pushed it out with a single tear. The very moment I saw the glistening embodiment of her sorrow leave her lashes, her face changed to the controlled fury of the warrior that I knew her to be. "You aren't yourself."

Chapter 11

"Am I not?" I casually mocked her. "Or perhaps I wasn't me before. The truth is, girl, you have no idea. And it frightens you, doesn't it? All that honey filled hope I poured into your heart, only now to find your trust torn apart by questioning who it is your faith has been put in."

Her face remained steeled and ready for conflict, but her chest was moving from heavy breaths and I could hear her heart pounding. She shifted her feet, preparing herself for the fight that might still come. "Avar!" She screamed up without taking her eyes off me. "How's that rope coming?!"

Thoughts of pure malice began flowing through me. I didn't know exactly what my dark self was planning, but I knew what his goal was. He wanted to steal the life of the woman I had grown to care most about, and take her sword. I was not about to let that happen. I reached out with my mind, my emotions, with every ounce of power that I could summon to try and wrestle control of my own body away from the dark foe that was me. Everything I did seemed futile, but then I felt the little voice of Murks in me. "Yes Master. I will help you, good kind Master."

Brin's face bore a sudden look of shock right before pain shot up through my leg. Lightning danced out past my feet and across the damp floor of the ruin. I saw Brin back away slightly before my attention was changed to the little hemodan that had hurt me. "You little gaak! I will teach you never to hurt your master."

"You are not my Master, Master." Another bolt of energy struck my leg, singeing my robe and causing me excruciating pain.

A guttural roar burst forth from my chest and I leapt at the little hemodan, who skittered away from me. "Come back here, you little monster! I will reclaim you, and take back the power I gave you."

Desecrated

He couldn't escape for long, but I chased him behind one of the fallen pillars. Back there, he had accidentally trapped himself in a corner. Again he shot lightning at me, hitting me in the chest this time. The energy of the bolt washed through me like a wave of fire. My dark self screamed in agony, and I enjoyed his suffering. His grasp on my mind was weakening, and the infection in my thoughts was also receding from the attacks from my little hemodan.

With hands glowing from dark energy, I lunged forward and caught Murks in my grasp. I grinned evilly at him and gave a gravelly laugh, a laugh that sounded much like that of The Baron. Suddenly I felt the iron rod through my torso, and I could smell the dirt of my grave. *Was this dark usurper really me, or is this something that The Baron placed in me?* The struggle within me began again, but this time something was different; I did not consider the usurper part of me.

The outside world vanished and I found myself in an empty landscape facing another me. The flesh of the other me burned, blistered, and bubbled before my eyes. When the smoke cleared, he was marked with the red skull of The Baron superimposed on his face.

He touched the hole where his nose should have been and laughed. "You know nothing. My master has seen to that. When the time comes, you will kneel before him and call him your lord, for he was there when your life began, and he will be there at the end of it."

"Are you done?" I asked, masking my insecurity and confusion.

His answer was nothing but a red toothy grin.

Chapter 11

My legs surged with power and I pounced on him, a blade appearing in my hand as I flew through the air. When I landed he too had a blade and the two came together with a shattering *clang!* The empty plane of our conflict suddenly came to life with dizzying images of my past. Every vision I had yet experienced blended together into a giant ethereal collage of mystery, and in the middle of that cloud of confusion, we collided.

He mimicked me so perfectly that no matter the spontaneity of my attacks, he easily parried again and again and again. My inability to overwhelm this simulacrum in my mind frustrated me. I let my attacks consume more and more of my energy. He was weakening me by using my own emotions against me.

"Give up, it's over. You lost." He laughed with The Baron's voice as the vision of my murder at his hands floated past my eyes.

Rage erupted in me again, and my furious assault was easily turned aside by his blade. All the while, the stupid red-toothed grin remained on his sinister face, mocking me. After countless futile attacks, exhaustion began to set in and my strikes slowed. As my rage turned to weakness, he began his attacks. I used what energy I had left to defend myself against him. It worked at first, but then his sword reached beyond mine, and he found my flesh. A few more parries then another hit was scored, and another, and another. My robe was being sliced to tatters by his barrage, as was my body beneath it.

A normal man trapped in this conflict with a bewitched part of his own spirit might have given up, but I refused. Even after I lost the use of my left arm and leg, I continued to defy him. Blood was flooding my mouth and I spit it back into his face, hoping to blind him, but his eyes were just empty sockets. Instead he kicked me, knocking me onto my back. I scooted away from him, trying to

Desecrated

get enough space so that I could safely sit up, leaving a wide trail of red behind me. He kept pace on the carpet of my blood, and savored every moment of my misery.

"Wrack! Wrack!" Brin's frightened voice called to me from a fragmented memory floating by. I wanted to give up, but I knew that I could not surrender. She needed me... She needed me.

This quiet moment of emboldened hope must have called out to my broken memories for help, for behind my attacker I saw the image of a candle bursting with golden light and I heard the voice of my grandfather, "Vanquish it."

His voice and those two words instantly calmed my fears. Without thinking, without pondering, without questioning I just let my instincts take over. "I will," I whispered. Dropping my sword on the ground I sat up, holding my hands up with their palms facing my enemy.

A triumphant chuckle added to the sinister grin on his skull like mask as he raised the blade over his head. I closed my eyes and breathed in, deeply, so deeply that I felt a tingling in my fingertips and then my whole hands, then it moved up my arms and to my chest. The tingling from either side joined in my heart and then shot up into my head. Unable to keep them shut anymore, my eyelids shot open.

My hands were surrounded in golden light and the light was causing the flesh of the usurper to flake away in to ashes. When the ashes floated away from the body, their substance and energy funneled through the light into me. He was powerless against this unknown force at my command, and the power itself glowed with a fury that was not only mine.

In seconds his body was reduced to nothing but a red skeleton, oozing with a thick river of blood. The light faded from my hands, and he collapsed to the ground in front of me. Weakly, I

Chapter 11

stood on the one leg that could support me. Defeated, he looked up at me and screamed with undead rage of The Baron, "Why are you smiling? Who are you?"

The wind of my tumbling memories blew by him and reduced him to a disappearing pile of ash. Triumphant but battered, I closed my eyes for one silent moment of peace before I was forced back into the world where I would one day have to face the real Baron. For the first time since I returned to this world of hopeless oppression and ancient evils I felt that I too had the strength to make a difference, even if it was only to help others. My mind took control of my body, and I opened my eyes.

Desecrated

Chapter 12

Murks was sitting upon my chest crying. When I lifted my head his entire world changed from one of sorrow to joy, and he lunged forward to hug my face. "Oh Master! You came back to us!"

I gently lifted him away from my eyes so I could see. "Yes, yes, Murks. What happened?" I asked him as I stood up.

"No time for explaining Master, Brin lady and hunter Avar are leaving you behind!" His quiet words contained only a fragment of the excitement and worry that flowed through his little body.

I sprung to my feet and ran around the fallen pillar. Each step splashed with dark water as I moved into the center of the room. Quickly I glanced around, trying to get a view of my current situation. Both Avar and Brin were climbing the rope, and in one corner of the room, water was flowing into the chamber.

"What happened?" I yelled up at Brin.

She stopped climbing and looked down at me. "Avar! Avar, Wrack is still down there."

I ran over to the rope and noticed that the extended end was tied around Avar's waist and was therefore already looping back up to the surface with him. I shouted up, "Avar, drop me the rope!" But he ignored my call and just kept climbing.

Desecrated

The freezing cold water began to flow into the room harder, and it quickly rushed past my ankles. "Avar! Throw Wrack the rope!" Brin shouted from above Avar.

"He won't be able to reach it unless I go down there too," he lied with no belief behind it.

The water was now halfway up my shin. "I will be able to swim up to it in a moment!"

"Then maybe you can swim all the way out," he kept climbing.

Brin had stopped above him. "Avar! Drop the uzkin' rope!"

"No! I won't drop the uzkin' rope, Brin. Bridain wants him gone, and so do I, alright?" Avar shouted.

Even from where I was standing, I could see the shock in Brin's eyes. "You uzkin' what now? You want to abandon the man who saved all our uzkin' lives back in Yellow Liver?"

Avar was dumbfounded. "He what? No. You were the one who–"

Calmly, Brin shook her head. "Nope. Wrack is the one that really killed The Ghoul. Now drop him the uzking rope!"

A tremor shook the entire chamber. Rocks and other debris fell from the ceiling. One of the remaining pillars collapsed from the vibration. The place where the water was flowing in from shook and rocks cascaded out of the of the water's path.

The cold wet cling of the dark water had reached my knees. "Toss me down the uzkin' rope!"

An unearthly screech that was so loud it could not have been made by anything small echoed through the chamber.

"Uzk!" We all said in unison, even little Murks.

The water was now up to my waist and seemed to be flowing faster than before.

Chapter 12

"AVAR! Silver Lady help me if you don't drop the rope right uzkin' now!" Brin screamed at him from above.

With one hand, Avar started fumbling with the knot at his waist, "I'm trying! I'm trying!"

The flow of the water was slightly entrancing. I had no idea if I could drown, and I knew that my body was mostly impervious to the effects of the cold, but the thought of being trapped in this watery tomb terrified me, to say nothing of whatever massive thing was the source of that screech.

There was another localized rumbling and the pile of rocks from where the flowing water was coming trembled, and trembled some more. "Um. I think something is trying to get in here!" I shouted up to my friends.

"I am working as fast as I can!" screamed Avar, still trying to untie the knotted rope.

From above, Brin hung helplessly from the rope and shouted back, "It will be ok, Wrack! We will get you out of here!"

The frozen embrace of the water had reached my chest, and I started fighting with the current in the water. It wasn't terribly strong, but it certainly was moving me around a bit. The rocks on the other side of the room fell away in a storm of rumbling and splashing, leaving a hole which was half filled with a river of black water. "We may have scored a break. I don't think that the entire place is going to fill up," I shouted.

Then the screech came again. This time there were no rocks to muffle the sound and it was so loud that I could feel my mind being shaken by the force of it. I took a few deep breaths and focused on the hole, waiting for this new threat to show itself. Each lung full of air carried with it a mix of stagnant water, mold, and death. This certain combination of scents in this particular make up made me feel exactly the same as I did when I noticed the infection

Desecrated

that was in my mind. This thing that was screeching at all of us had been here all along, probing our psyches for some unknown purpose, and now it wanted to meet us, face to face.

"How is the rope coming, Avar?" I impatiently shouted.

Finally making some headway on the knot, Avar shouted back, "It's coming. This is hard to do with only one hand!"

Unable to do anything but wait, both Brin and I just paused with eyes fixed on the opening in the wall. With my dark sight, I couldn't see anything beyond the threshold of the opening. I strained to pierce the shadows on the other side to no avail. The sickly feeling of something invading my body suddenly began to manifest. My breathing became more labored, and my wide eyes could not look away from the gushing opening across the room. The water swirled up a few more inches, making me struggle to stay anchored under the well opening above. Then they appeared.

Writhing tentacles, each easily as thick as a man and longer than I could have even imagined. They moved and felt around the hole in the wall. I could not see the true color of them, for my dark sight showed me images in strange hues, but they were dark and slightly translucent, much like the thing that I had wrestled with in the Captain's office in Yellow Liver. On the tips of each there were finger-like digits made out of the same rubbery mass as the tentacle itself, giving the each a hand-like grasper at the end of its many arms. If there were a body at the center of this thing, I had not seen it yet. Undoubtedly it remained in the tunnel beyond and was perhaps too big to enter the room through the hole. Perhaps I should say that I hoped the hole was too small.

While in my mind I knew that my friends were above me, and that they were doing all they could to save me from my situation, I also understood that they could not see this horror that currently had my full attention. Indeed, my conscious self was so

Chapter 12

focused on the terror that I was feeling, I nearly forgot that I had any friends at all. I was almost consumed by the utter madness that must have given birth to such a monster as this. All my petty self-reflection and insecurities were non-existent in my panicked brain. My thoughts were awash with my own destruction.

Several of the numerous tentacles felt around the walls, ceiling, and floor whilst others reached forward and opened their flower-like hands to reveal floating black eyes in the center of their palms. Like the quick fluid motions of a bird, the eyes of this terrible thing scanned the room, and all too quickly it found me.

The very moment that one of the eyes discovered me, struggling in the flowing water, the others all snapped to look in my direction. Another soul-tearing screech echoed through the chamber, and I nearly lost my mind to fear.

Above me, Avar and Brin made some noise that might have been words, but I couldn't understand them if that were the case. The paralyzing fear that controlled my actions shifted, and suddenly my desire to be away from this unknowable creature seized my thoughts. The level of the water had now removed my ability to keep my feet on the ground without submerging my head, so I opted to swim away from this thing, but I dared not look away from it while I did so.

Each of the many arms of the creature tensed and I felt the water ripple as it was pulling the mass of its body further into the room. Even more tentacles, these with frightening jagged hooks at their ends, squeezed through the very full opening. The flow of water grew calmer, for the thing had blocked the entrance with its gelatinous bulk.

Hooks splashed into the water next to me, making the choppy surface toss me about like a toy in a bath. Each moment suddenly became like a lifetime as the threat of my destruction

Desecrated

became instantly very real. Still flooded with panic, I tried to swim backwards towards the wall of the chamber, but made very little headway with the undulation of the water around me. Screams came from above as more tentacles found their way into the water around me, and I very quickly found myself grasped into their coils.

With unnerving ease, I was lifted from the water and brought close to several of the black eyes. The reflection of my complete fear was plainly visible in their shiny unfeeling orbs. I struggled and fought against the might of the slimly sinuous thing holding me, but it was futile. Even the dark power lay dormant within me. I was alone, and soon I would be ended. To further break my will to live, another screech echoed through the chamber. Many of the tentacles seemed to add to this chorus of fear, but the true maw of this monster called out from the hole from which all this madness originated. The mouth was made of many folds each with their own row of small pointy teeth. It was as if this thing had a multitude of mouths, all nesting within each other.

Something unseen attacked my mind, tearing at my memories. I grasped my head in pain and wept as I helplessly submitted to this thing's hunger for my thoughts. It didn't want to eat my flesh; it wanted to devour my very mind and soul, and I was ready to let it.

Unexpectedly, anger rose within me. A pure and burning hatred for something unknown seethed within my soul and it would not surrender to this thing. Strength from my dark power surged through my limbs and I renewed my vicious battle on both fronts. In my mind, I built walls and counterattacked the thing pressing me, devouring some of its thoughts, and my physical body pushed outward against the tremendous power of the coils surrounding me. I felt pulses of power, strength, and pleasure as my anger devoured more and more of the creature's energy. Suddenly I was falling.

Chapter 12

Still wrapped in the hungry embrace of the creature, I felt my lungs fill with fluid. Finding my eyes closed, I opened them to find my body in the murky blackness under the surface of the water. Above me I could see a white glow shining through the water. It swirled and arced through the air and each time it swung around, I heard screeches ripple through the water. Each screech brought me so much pleasure that my entire body tingled with insatiable delight.

The light came very close to me and then came straight down. I felt it collide with the body of the tentacle wrapped around me, and its grip on me loosened. The water suddenly filled with the acrid taste of poisoned earth, and even in my pleasure-filled state I flailed in every direction, trying to reach the surface. A hand reached into the murk, found purchase on my robe, and pulled me to the air above.

When I broke the top of the water, I came face to face with Brin, who grappled my struggling body and swam us both to the dangling rope. In her other hand she had a sword I barely recognized. The leather wrapped bone handle was still there, as were the runes on either side of it, but the angular rectangle shape was changed into a thin sharp blade with a tip that curved slightly backwards. The edges of the weapon still were still bright against the stark black of the flat sides if its blade, and the blue glow that I had become accustom to had changed to brilliant white. Ukumog had changed, just as it had when I wielded it, yet the form and color of it was very different.

Behind us, the massive tentacles flailed, bashing the ceiling and walls, and creating giant waves in the lake that filled the room. The wall that blocked its path was receiving most of the punishment from the creature, and it looked as if it were trying to force the mass of its body through that tiny hole. "We have to get out of here," I said between mouthfuls of water.

Desecrated

"That is exactly what we are trying to do! Here, grab this rope and climb." She yelled over the warring sounds of monster, cracking stones, and tumultuous water.

I reached out to grab the rope and stumbled a few times to grab it, but eventually I had hold of it. From within my robes, I heard Murks scream, "Master wait!" Before I could respond he leapt from my robes into the water. My eyes followed the direction of his motion and saw the fragment of cloth we had come to take from this place floating in the water a small distance away.

"We have to get that fabric!" I screamed at Brin.

She gave me an angry look, "Fabric? We came down in this gods forsaken gaak hole for a scrap of fabric!?"

I didn't know what to say, so instead I coughed out some of the water that still resided in my chest.

She gave a disgusted sigh, and even through the water I heard a clink! Ukumog had returned to her belt, and the white glow of the blade dimmed slightly. "Fine, get your fabric. I'm not waiting around for that thing to come after us again," and she pulled herself out of the water and onto the rope.

Across my connection to Murks, I felt his joy when he collected the scrap of cloth. Reaching out with my mind, I grasped my little hemodan and pulled him through the air into my waiting hand. With one swift motion I tucked him into my robe and began my ascent up the rope.

All my muscles were screaming in pain, and fear still existed in my mind, but for the first time since I placed my feet on the ground in this old ruin, I did not feel the lurking predator on the edge of my thoughts. I took one last look at the swirling frenzy of terror that was trying to press through the wall before I entered the stone tube of the well, and just after I was completely

Chapter 12

inside it I heard the crash of massive stones colliding with a body of water. I let my healthy fear of that creature spur me through the tight confines of the well into the moonlight above.

Gibberish floated down to me from the surface as I moved through the final lifts to the top. I thought the sounds were just my friends, who were already up top, talking. Just before I reached the mouth of the well, I realized that it wasn't them at all. Instead it was the same gibbering that I had heard from the freth in our previous encounters with them. As soon as my head crested the top of the well and saw what was awaiting me, I felt as if I had left one bad situation behind just to find myself in another one.

Avar and Brin were kneeling on the ground right next to the well with their hands behind their head. There were freth everywhere. I tried to slink back down into the well a bit to gain some time before I was spotted. I just needed to think, so I could come up with a way for us to escape. This did not go as I would have liked. As soon as I tried to hide again I heard a freth shout something incomprehensible in my direction, and I knew that I had been seen. Sure enough, a group of them peered over the well at me, their molten eyes glowing in the darkness of the night. One of them motioned for me to climb back up the rope and grumbled gibberish at me. I gave thought to going back into the well, but I could still hear the monster below and thought better of it.

Once I climbed out, I was forced to the ground and my knives were taken from me. "Fat lot of good they have done me so far," I thought to Murks, who chuckled in response.

The freth grumbled and gibbered at one another confiding in their darakka leader with occasional motions in our direction. Brin was right next to me and kept trying to look at me, but each attempt was noticed by our diligent captors, and so her focus kept switching back to the space in front of her. Trapped in our silence, we watched as the freth started pulling apart one of the ruined buildings and constructed a mounted beam in front of the well. Then they forcibly tied each of us to the beam using our rope from the well, with our feet dangling inches from the ground beneath us. The beam had to be high because of Avar's tall frame, and I being the shortest member of our little band was the furthest from the ground. The pressure of hanging from my arms was not anything close to pleasant, but it did not start out painful.

After hanging there for an hour or more, the pain was in full effect. My shoulders burned and felt as if they were going to pop loose. My wrists felt as if they were being slowly crushed in a vice made of ice. Even my breathing became labored, as I could not completely collapse my lungs with my exhalation. Both Avar and Brin seemed to be having a worse time of it, however. Avar would occasionally make little whining noises like some of the dogs I had seen in the back alleys of Yellow Liver, and Brin kept shifting her head back and forth trying to find a position of comfort, as if she could find the perfect spot that would make all the rest of the discomfort fade away.

I kept thinking about Ukumog sitting lifelessly on the lip of the well with the rest of our weapons. I wanted to pull it to me as I had done before and hand it to Brin so she could get us out of this mess, but try as I might, I couldn't make it happen. "We will get out of this," I said, trying to comfort my friends.

Brin just gave a pained grunt in return.

Our conversation attracted the attention of the freth, who in turn made their darakka commander aware of our activity. Soon thereafter, he was talking to us so closely that I could smell his rancid reptile breath. "Humans, you hunters of the Sanctuary. Yes?"

None of us responded.

Chapter 12

The darakka laughed. "We Zulinx. Commanders freth army. You humans prisoned. Mistress wants knowing of Armor. You understand?"

Again, none of us responded to his questions. Our silence seemed to anger him, and after a few moments of silence he reared back and roared directly in Avar's face. Green spittle splattered on Avar's pale skin, and apart from a disgusted look on Avar's face, there was no response. Zulnix walked away from us, gibbering at the freth who then began to build a fire.

"This can't be good," Avar said, sourly.

Large logs were built into the pyramid over the fire and the flames spread quickly to the old, neglected wood. Very quickly, the smaller fire became a much larger bonfire. Then some of the freth started putting the tips of metal objects into the flames.

I chuckled a bit, "How is it that we escape that monster below just to end up here? Seems like we can't win."

"Looks like the torture is about to start any minute," Brin noted darkly. "Just remember, the pain they can inflict is nothing compared to the pain of losing everything you love."

Avar began whispering prayers, and I started thinking about Brin's words. Silently I noted, "Everything I love is here."

Zulnix marched over to us as we saw some of the freth reaching into the fire to see if their implements were hot enough yet. When glowing tips came out of the fire, I knew things were really about to get bad. "Answer now. Yes?" Zulnix commanded.

"No. I don't think we will," Avar boldly responded. "You should just let us go and we will forget that this happened."

Desecrated

Unable to believe what he just heard, Zulnix blinked a few times, then when he realized that Avar was bring serious he laughed. This laugh cascaded to the freth that were all around us, until the entire clearing was filled with the joyous chorus of our enemies. It was not very encouraging.

Brin kicked her feet spinning her body slightly, so she could look at Avar more directly. "Don't give them anything, Avar. That uzkin' Mistress of theirs can eat gaak for all I care."

At that, Zulnix stopped laughing. "Mercy yours if questions, yes? No questions. Pain," he said gesturing to the glowing points of metal in the night.

"Perhaps my friend is being too hasty," Avar said with a fake sweetness. "What is it that you want to know?"

Zulnix focused his attention on Avar and stopped trying to menace Brin, while the freth holding the glowing prods seemed unhappy. "Armor. You speak."

Avar cleared his throat, "Armor is something that creatures of all types wear to protect them from injuries. Some armor protects only against certain kinds of attacks, while others can give protection against many forms of damage." His speech was interrupted by a loud hiss from Zulnix.

"No! Armor! Magic trapped! Speak!" Zulnix screeched.

"Yes! Some armor has magic trapped within it. This allows for–" There was a loud crack as the back of Zulnix's heavy reptilian claw pounded Avar across the jaw. The jovial nature of Avar's taunting had come to an end for all of us. Now everything seemed more real, more frighteningly real.

"Questions or burning fire," said Zulnix, again indicating the glowing metal tips that the freth bore.

Avar spit out some blood. "I don't have any answers for you. If you are going to torture me, might as well get to it."

Chapter 12

"Avar!" Brin screamed in disapproval.

A berserker like roar erupted from Avar. At first it was directed at Brin, then he turned it on Zulnix. "Torture me you unwanted slave of the ancient gods! Do your worst! I have nothing to lose, you festering mound of filth! What could you possibly do to me?!"

One of the freth handed Zulnix a hot poker and after admiring it for a moment he said, "This." With skilled precision he seared through the fabric at Avar's side and smoke rose from the sizzling sound underneath.

Avar struggled not to scream. He just closed his eyes and gnashed his teeth to hold back the terrible noise growing inside him. Zulnix removed the implement of pain just long enough for the agony in Avar's face to recede and then he struck him again. More smoke. The dam that held Avar's scream at bay was already starting to weaken.

"Hold on, Avar!" Brin shouted and swung her body around to try and kick Zulnix and missed. The darakka's reflexes allowed for him to bring down his smoldering implement on her leg as it passed by, however. Brin groaned in surprised pain from the touch of the glowing metal.

"HEY!" I shouted. "Leave the boy alone. He doesn't know anything. It is me that you want to hurt, not him."

Cold lizard eyes stared at me, but with his other hand Zulnix drove the hot end of the poker through the fabric of Avar's shirt again. This strike landed near his heart and finally drove the scream out of Avar's chest. The horrific scream seemed to go on forever and even after Avar was finished surrendering it to the world; the sound of it echoed off the trees and hills around us. The many

Desecrated

surfaces of valley created a ghastly choir of pain, reverberating that scream into my memory forever. My spine tingled and my body shook from the emotion the sound carried with it.

Satisfied at his receipt of Avar's pain, Zulnix ceased his torture and began talking again to Brin. "Armor. Now."

There was venom in Brin's eyes, but in her voice there was no malice. "We don't have anything to tell you. Your Mistress knows more about where The Armor is than we do."

I struggled against my bonds, but all I succeeded in doing was tearing the skin under the rope. As it kept healing almost instantly, I kept futilely working at it. Avar just hung there, with his head down, his chest moving with heavy breaths. I could not help but wonder what was going on in his head.

"Armor. Now," Zulnix said to Brin and me while making menacing gestures at Avar with his hot poker, the tip of which was beginning to dim. One of the freth promptly replaced the cooling prod with one that was fresh from the fire. He waited for a moment for Brin to say something, and when she didn't he jabbed Avar in the abdomen fiercely with the hot end of the fresh poker.

More of the same skin-chilling screams burst from Avar as Zulnix stabbed him repeatedly with quick lunges of smoldering pain. This did not succeed in the goal that the darakka desired. Instead of giving information, Brin flew into a rage. She started swinging, shouting, and kicking. The makeshift frame that we were all tied upon was quickly beginning to fall apart, so gibbering freth ran over to give it some support.

One of Brin's kicks came very close to Zulnix, and he deflected her attack with his free hand. This changed her momentum from back and forth to more of a loop. Her backswing made her crash into me, and with her legs flailing she tried to change her motion back towards Zulnix. Unfortunately, one of her boots

Chapter 12

accidentally kicked the handle of Ukumog which lay upon the lip of the well behind us. The force of her kick was enough to send the blade tumbling back into the well.

"UZK!" She screamed, now more frustrated and angry than before. "Now look what you made me do, you uzkin' gaak eater. I am going to murder you, and when I do, I will enjoy watching the light leave your eyes. Do you understand me? Huh? Do you, you uzkin' darakka imbecile!"

An unearthly screech erupted from the well. It was the same terrible roar of the creature we had just barely escaped. I imagined the sword falling through the well and hungrily digging into the flesh of the beast that had somehow broken through the doorway that had previously trapped it. The thought of Ukumog impaled into the body of that thing brought me so much joy that I almost became lost in the pleasure of it. I could still hear Brin screaming in the background of my mind, but I didn't care. My thoughts were aglow with pure joy.

Suddenly, I felt something tap my strength, as if something had begun draining away my thoughts. Opening my eyes, I found the freth to be preparing for battle, and Zulnix staring with unadulterated hatred at the three of us. I could see the thoughts spinning in his head. He was trying to decide if we were worth staying and fighting for, or if he should just kill us now. I was glad his decision was taking time, but time has a way of taking away our ability to choose if we wait too long.

The very earth began to shake as more screeching pierced our eardrums from below. Zulnix gibbered to his freth and they quickly moved to leave us to our fate. As they formed into squads, the darakka looked over at us with regret in his eyes. No doubt he wanted to finish what he had started.

Desecrated

With the freth no longer supporting the frame, Brin began swinging wildly from her wrists, the ropes holding the joints of the frame together creaked and moaned. "Don't just hang there! Help me!" she shouted at me.

I, too, began swinging and the frame continued to creak. Each pass made it seem like the frame was going to give, but the ropes were still holding it together through the flexing of the beams. Shouts started coming from the direction that the freth had started to depart in, and the sounds of battle rustled through the barren trees. "What is going on now?"

"Maybe the King's men have found us too," Brin joked.

"We have so many friends!" I responded in kind.

Avar remained hanging limply from the beam over his head. The stillness of his body was eerie. If I couldn't have seen him breathing heavily, I would have assumed that he was dead.

"Avar, are you ok?" Brin asked between breaths, as she continued her agenda to tear down the frame with movement. He didn't respond.

The bulk of the freth began retreating back into the clearing. They were still fighting an unseen force on the other side. Above us, the cloud cover parted and the light of the moon flooded the forgotten town. With one final swing, the frame finally came tumbling apart, casting the three of us to the ground. The wind knocked out of me for a moment, I wished that somehow I could have also come untied in the fall.

There was another screech from below, and a tremor rocked the ground beneath us. "I am really not looking forward to meeting that thing again," I said.

"Uzkin' thing better have my sword." There was no humor in her statement.

Chapter 12

A small squad of freth ran over near us with weapons pointed in our direction. While the freth were gibbering at us, I couldn't even understand their body language, for a mist started seeping into my thoughts. Pleasure and pain akin to what I felt when Brin was fighting the beast below was coming from an unknown source, and derailed my grip on the reality around me. A force was still sapping my energy, so as soon as the unknown pleasure entered my body it was swept away into the leech on my soul. I was helpless.

The beam I was tied to began to move sporadically, like something at the other end was jerking it around. There was a loud creaking sound followed by a pop, and the beam stopped moving. Instead, Avar stood up and growled with a feral anger that I had never seen him summon before. He charged into the freth standing over us and began tossing them around like dolls. They wounded him over and over, but he ignored their attacks and just brought a ceaseless assault of bare handed attacks to their glowing bodies. It was much like watching Ferrin fight when he was changed into the shape of a wolf man.

Brin, frustrated by Avar's freedom, railed against her own bindings and screamed in anger at them. The flow of burning power through me left me unable to even issue a passionate complaint about my situation. Sensing my state, Murks crawled out from my robes and moved to untie me, but was interrupted by a shout from Brin, "Unite me first!" I couldn't even form an objection.

Obeying her command, Murks used his deft little fingers to pry apart the knots that held Brin captive. Within just a few moments, Brin was free enough that she was able to wrestle her bloody wrists free. Immediately, she got to her feet and looked at the well. Without a word, she climbed up on the edge and looked down into the pit we had only hours ago escaped. "I can see it.

Desecrated

There is no way I am losing Ukumog now," she said mostly to herself. I looked on helplessly as she gave me one of her secret little smiles and dove into the well.

"NO! BRIN!" I was finally able to summon my voice for two short exclamations, but then I was lost in the whirlpool of power draining from my spirit.

Murks dutifully untied my wrists and brought my arms closer to my body while I watched the battle around me. Avar was holding his own against the freth with no weapon in his hands, and on the other side of the squad of enemies I saw the familiar forms of the Eisenwyr brothers and Tikras. Even in my weakened state I felt a little comfort that they were here.

More pleasure mixed with pain shuddered through me, causing my body to shake and my arms to involuntarily pull themselves into my chest. My eyes and ears, however, were unaffected by whatever was leeching my strength.

Around me the fight raged on. Each time I saw the freth score a hit against Avar, I thought he would fall over with a fatal wound, but he continued to fight on beyond all reason. Nikolai and Piotyr were doing significant damage to the freth near them, and I saw Tikras behind them with arms moving as if he were directing an unseen force. As the three of them came closer into the clearing, I saw something shimmer in the moonlight. What looked like gaseous translucent outlines of men were running and swirling around the freth, and causing them to fall.

I remembered that Tikras was a priest of the god of death. "Valik, I think he once called him," I thought to myself. Studying the forms he was commanding, I saw faces in their misty forms. The faces made me think that these were spirits of some kind. Perhaps they were men and women who died here in this village, or ancient allies of our barbarian friends raised to fight by their

Chapter 12

side once more, or even the very souls of the freth that were being slaughtered. What they were didn't matter at that moment, for without this half-real army we would all certainly be dead.

More waves of power flowed through me, stronger than before. Light flashed before my eyes and with each bout of pain came such pleasure and joy that I almost became lost. The parasite that was attacking me helped keep me from surrendering entirely to the pleasure, but at the same time it was feeding on me. The more it was able to feed, the more it wanted.

A few feet from me, the well started to emit a white light, and the sense of the infection in my mind crept back in. I wanted to crawl away. I wanted to get as far away from the well and the formless beast that lay below as possible, but I couldn't move.

The intense feeling of power grew in me as if struck with a hammer forging more and more power into my soul, and the appetite of the leech sucked it away harder and harder. Fear and pain built up in me until I had to let it loose. A cry left my lungs and with it a shockwave of dark energy burst forth from my body and knocked everyone in the area to the ground. The force of my scream cracked the well. Inside me, all that remained was pleasure and despair.

The ground beneath us trembled again, this time with more violent fervor than previously. I heard the sounds of cracking stone and splashing water from the well. My desire to get away from the well was so great that even through the noise of pleasure, pain, and despair, Murks was able to hear my need and came to my aid. He placed a hand on my chest and I felt a shot of pain from his hand as a spike formed and punctured its way into my flesh. "Kanderia hemograndata!" he shouted and I could feel him pull away some of the blood and power in my body. I lay helpless as his form swelled in size but then suddenly he looked at me with wide

Desecrated

eyes. He had felt the parasite that was attacking me. Before his spell had completely finished, he broke the connection by pulling away his hand. Quickly, he checked around to see if anyone had spotted him, and then he started to drag me away from the well.

The top stones of the well began crumbling away from it. Some fell to the ground outside, yet others disappeared into the well itself. As I was being dragged away, I saw the ground around the well lift slightly as the earth quaked again under me. This quake was so powerful that everyone ceased fighting and turned to look at the well. Another tremor shook the ground and the well collapsed into itself. The mind numbing screeching of the creature below filled the night. It was coming after us.

Fear was not something that the freth understood and none of them turned to run. Avar was so consumed by his feral rage that he continued his violent assault against them, and this caused the rest of them to spring back into the dance of battle. The ground heaved upwards all around us and a deafening crack of breaking stone emanated from the well. Soon afterwards, the earth began to crumble into the hole beneath. In the eye of the violent storm all around me, my only thoughts were of Brin.

With another terrible screech, the first tentacles of the beast emerged from the pit below. One of them was cast high into the air and riding upon it was my dark avenger. She clung to the brightly glowing blade Ukumog, which was sunk deep into the flesh of the rubbery limb that was trying to cast her off. Brin looked battered, but even from the distance between us, I could see her eyes glowing with the same brilliant white energy that made Ukumog hard to look directly at. She seemed to almost float in the air as time slowed, and the waves of her hair flowed haphazardly into the sky as she began

Chapter 12

her reckless descent back to the beast below her. As she did so, she removed Ukumog with one fluid motion from the wound in which it was lodged, severing that limb from the rest of the body.

Another screech came from the monster, but this time it was filled with more pain than rage. Much to its surprise, Brin turned the blade downward as she fell, allowing her to plunge the tip of the hungry sword deep into the central mass of the creature below. Instantly there was a blinding flash of white light that burst forth, lighting up the area as if it were day. My body surged with power, pleasure, and pain that was quickly slurped up by the parasite latched onto my soul.

"Master! Murks will save you!" he screamed as he leapt upon me. With a frenzied speed he began searching through my robes for something. A few moments later, he held the black scrap of fabric that we had collected from below over his head. It seemed alive as it writhed in his hand. Then I saw the dim gloom of shadow that clung to it, and I instantly knew that it was feeding on me. Murks cast it away from me, and within a heartbeat I no longer felt the parasite drinking from my soul. Still weak from the ordeal, I barely had the strength to sit up, but I did so with Murks' help.

A quick glance around the battle revealed that the freth were losing badly to the four men and unknowable number of spirits set against them. Zulnix still stood, commanding his forces with shouted gibberish. Light flashed through the clearing with every swing of Ukumog as Brin clashed with the twisting mass of tentacles trying to snuff out her life. She seemed driven by the light in the blade, and I was close enough to feel the explosion of energy each time the edge drank in the pain from the monster.

Avar eventually finished off the freth around him. In that moment of stillness, he looked over at me, the feral look still dominating his face. Glowing blood was smeared and splattered all over his body, mixing with dark fluid that I knew to be his own. As our eyes met, I saw a little smile appear in his eyes as if to say "Look what I did!" It was the first hint of the old Avar that I had seen since my departure from the underground temple. This simple moment was cut short by a spear that came bursting through his right shoulder, breaking the sacred armor that he wore. He roared with anger, and the simple smile in his eyes disappeared in a sea of feral rage. With his left hand he grasped the head of the spear and pulled the entirety of the shaft through his flesh, leaving a gushing wound behind.

With complete malice, he turned and looked at Zulnix who was just standing there dumbfounded. Avar took three steps towards the darakka commander and returned the spear with prejudice. The head of the spear found purchase in the reptilian hide of its target, near the same place where Zulnix had first planted the hot poker when torturing Avar. The commander howled with pain and clutched the spear, but could not remove it before Avar caught up with him and removed the spear himself. With his foot he kicked the large lizard to the ground. Avar broke the wooden shaft of the spear and then drove the sharp end of the spear over and over into the scaly hide of Zulnix. Each strike mirrored the locations of Avar's torture.

I felt a rush of joy and energy as a wriggling tentacle landed near me with a loud thump. It quickly became dull and lifeless as the movements of the thing slowed. Looking up, I saw a spewing stump where the tentacle had once been attached. The alien eyes of this disgusting aberration suddenly displayed fear, for the first time. The limbs of the beast started flailing in a defensive manner, trying to knock Brin out of range. Ukumog streaked the night sky, scoring wound after wound and spraying stinking, moldy

Chapter 12

black blood everywhere. One of the tentacles tore at the buildings around the area and found a large rock with which it began to try and beat Brin away.

The screams and howls of the freth and their darakka master dwindled to silence and all attention turned to this horrible seed of darkness that Brin valiantly battled. "Holy uzk! Vhat is that thing!?" I heard Tikras ask.

"Vhatever it is, ve need it gone," Nikolai answered.

The three barbarians and Avar rushed in to help Brin vanquish this unknown horror, but the thing was too quick. It lashed out with its many arms and kept them at bay. Finally, finding more strength within myself, I stood up. "No Master! Do not go near that horrible thing!" Murks screamed in my mind.

"I have to, Murks." And so I did. With the words of both Se'Naat and my grandfather spinning in my head I stepped forward slowly with my hand outstretched. "Vanquish it," I whispered.

Suddenly all eyes of the beast turned to me with unnerving speed. The beast started shimmying back down the tight hole that it had violently created, but the space was too tight for it to just drop into the depths.

Brin lifted Ukumog over her head and turned the tip of it towards the body of the thing, then brought the gleaming metal down into its flesh with as much force as her light-infused body could muster. The creature gave a frightening screech and doubled its efforts to escape, while energy visibly leapt as a parcel of light into my chest. Confused for a moment, but still determined to slay her foe, Brin started twisting the handle of the blade and pulled it back at an angle causing more black blood reeking of mold to spew from the wound.

Desecrated

Instead of reaching forward to touch the disgusting creature, I stretched my hand towards Brin. She looked at me for a moment through those glowing eyes and I could see her emerald irises gleaming in the center. She gave me one of our secret smiles and let her sword arm fall to her side and with her other hand, reached out for me. Our hands wrapped themselves together and I gently pulled her from the belly of the monster. As her foot left the surface of the thing, it fell into the darkness below leaving behind a few of its severed limbs, and a whole lot of stinking black blood. None of that mattered. Beyond all odds, we had survived.

"Thank you," Brin said softly.

I just smiled.

Chapter 13

As quickly as possible, we gathered ourselves and fled the old abandoned town of Hollow. I was pretty certain that the creature from below was still alive, and might try to attack us again if we stayed too long. Avar was in no condition to walk, so, just as I had done with David, I carried him out of the valley. Carrying Avar was different in two major ways. For one, Avar was much taller and lankier than I, so carrying him was a little awkward. Secondly, Avar was more aware than David had been, yet he refused to engage in any kind of conversation.

Our travel during the day was slowed by the general tiredness of our group, save for my seemingly endless endurance. We were all aware, however, that it was best to get distance between that location and us. There was no way for us to know if the freth had any other patrols who might happen in to check on Zulnix's group, and we were not in any condition to fight them.

Before nightfall, we were forced by exhaustion to make camp. After food was eaten, and Piotyr, Tikras, and Avar fell asleep there was time for answers to questions.

"So, Nikolai, how exactly did you end up finding us?" Brin asked with amused curiosity.

Desecrated

Nikolai gave his usual joyful belly laugh, "Less than a day after you left, ve decided to follow. Piotyr vas none too happy about the vay that Bridain vas running things, so ve picked up on your trail and followed."

Brin frowned. "I don't leave a trail."

"Of course not," Nikolai smiled, "but you have friends who do."

"Uzk. Wrack, remind me to teach you how to mask your tracks while you move," Brin joked. "But if you were a day behind us, how did you even find us in Hollow?"

"That vas tricky. Once ve got to vhere the ground vas rockier, ve had trouble tracking you. Lucky for us, ve heard someone shouting and it turned out to be Avar."

"Shouting?" I asked.

Nikolai nodded, "Ja, he vas shouting at nothing, and then he vent off towards the village vhere ve found you. Once ve saw the little town ve decided to rest. The freth must have snuck in vhile ve vere resting. I think Piotyr fell asleep on his vatch."

"Why didn't you just come down and join us in the village?" Brin asked.

"To be honest, ve did not know exactly vhat you vere doing out here. Uzk, I still don't. My brother said that ve should not interfere if it vas supposed to be secret."

"Probably a good decision, actually. If you had been down there with us when the freth showed up, we would all be dead now, I think," I said.

"Ja. Maybe so."

While Brin and Nikolai continued to talk, I let my mind wander into an empty place. I just stared at the small fire we had, and tried to meditate. It was surprising that no one had mentioned Murks. I half expected to be confronted by Avar or our Barbarian

Chapter 13

companions about the presence of my little hemodan during the fight. The only assumption I could make is that they were all too preoccupied during the fight to notice. I was glad for that, actually. More reasons for Avar to hold onto his anger for me would not be good.

"Wrack?" Brin's voice called my thoughts back to the camp.

"Hrm?" I found my fingers mindlessly caressing the piece of shadow fabric. Unnerved by the nature of my fidgeting, I put it aside.

"So, what is the next step here? This is your plan, remember?"

I sighed. There seemed to be no good answer to her question. The last time we dealt with The Shadow, Brin got very angry. I had no reason to believe that this time would be any different. "The next part I have to do on my own, and I am not looking forward to it."

Brin's face suddenly turned angry. "What? Uzk that, I am going to help you do whatever it is you have to do."

"I don't think you are going to like it."

Nikolai's back straightened, "Do I need to be vorried?"

I shook my head. "Right now, I am the only one in danger. From this anyway." While I didn't exactly see anything move in the area around us, I felt the presence of The Shadow, and I knew it was time to pay my debt. "I will be back in a little bit."

"Don't go farther than you can scream for help," Nikolai cautioned.

When I stood up Brin collected Ukumog and started to come with me. "You should stay here, Brin."

Desecrated

"Uzk that. I am coming with you." After a moment of silence she further attempted to convince me. "Who will protect you, if not me? Now lead on."

There was no way to make her stay, so I just turned around and walked into the dark woods with her following. I let the impulse of the shadow fabric lead me, and after a short walk I heard The Shadow's voice whisper to me from the darkness. "I see you brought a friend."

"Yes," I cleared my throat. "I think you know each other."

"Ah yes. The young girl bent on revenge for her charming father's murder. A pleasure as always." I saw him bow slightly in the darkness.

"Ah uzk." Anger and disappointment filled Brin's voice. "You did a deal with The Shadow? Really?"

Her words hit me harder than she probably intended, but I resisted the sinking feeling in my heart. Instead, I calmly replied, "I didn't have much choice."

"So all that stuff in the well was for this uzker? I hope you are getting something good for all that." She looked over at the Shadow. "We almost got eaten by that thing down there, whatever it was."

"Ah, the seed still lives, does it? Unfortunate."

"The seed?" I couldn't help but ask.

The shadow nodded, "Indeed. That monstrosity you encountered in the depths of that old temple is a seed of the secret brood, the twisting chaos which has infected this world with entropy and disease of the spirit." He paused, but not long enough for either of us to ask any more questions. "Did you secure the object, dear boy?"

"I did, but you know that." It occurred to me just then that the fabric had not been siphoning away my power; it had been him.

Chapter 13

The Shadow chuckled, "Now, why would you say that? And in such an accusatory tone. Tsk tsk."

My glare said all the words I couldn't think to form into sentences.

"Have you changed your mind about all of this? If you have, I can just take my little trinket back to the forest."

Wise to his coy game, I chose to say, "No. I still want it. I just don't approve of your attachment to me."

He laughed. "Dear boy, we are far more attached than you realize."

"Enough with the uzkin' games already. How is this thing going to help us?" Brin shouted.

The Shadow was silent for a moment. "Are we finished screaming, my dear?" When Brin responded only with a hateful glare, he continued, "Wrack agreed to collect something ancient of mine, and I promised to give him this." He reached within his own shadowy form and produced a tiny fragment of bone.

"What is it?" Brin asked.

"Ah. This, my dear girl, is the answer to your more immediate of problems. If placed upon the altar under Sanctuary, it will summon the absent Armor back to its prison."

"I don't understand," she said.

The Shadow sighed. "All people, living and undead, seek the things which they have lost. Myself, I seek the fragments of my former glory, perhaps in a vain attempt to breathe some small amount of life back into this formless shape. And even you, my dear, seek to restore some of your father to this world by reclaiming his things and ending the life of those who ended him."

Brin scoffed at the mention of her own goals. "Your information was not all that useful, by the way."

Desecrated

"Then allow me to give you one further puzzle, free of charge. You are very close to discovering who brought death to your father. Much closer than you realize. The question is, are you brave enough to see it?"

Growing tired of his taunting riddles, I intercepted the conversation's course. "Here. Take your accursed cloth and give me the bone." I held the black fabric out in my open hand. His shadowy appendage flowed over my hand like a cold thick morning mist, removing the cloth and leaving behind a tiny bone in my palm.

"Fingers are one of the hardest things for a person to lose," The Shadow said and then with a slight bow he drifted backwards into the night.

We took a few steps toward the light of the campfire, but Brin could not remain silent. "So what do we do now?"

"We use the bone to summon The Armor, and then we either imprison it or kill it," I said, turning the ancient bone over and over in my fingers. I explored every smooth surface and rough edge with my touch. "Whatever we do, we have to make sure that The Mistress doesn't interfere."

"If we imprison him, the hunters will have to guard that temple forever," Brin added.

"And if we kill him, they will lose some of their magical protections," I continued. "Either way, a battle is coming and I am not convinced we are ready."

She sighed heavily. "Maybe Bridain will have some idea of which course to take. Of course, if we do have to kill him, maybe I can just toss you Ukumog and let you handle it."

"No." My answer was quick and firm.

"Easy. I was kidding."

Chapter 13

I grabbed her arm and looked deep into her eyes. "I don't want to touch that blade ever again, if I can help it. It does something to me."

Her hand gently found the side of my face. "It's ok, Wrack. I think it is about time I did some of my own damage to the Doomed." She smiled.

Fire burned inside me. I wanted to lean forward and kiss her, but fear kept me at bay, fear that I might somehow unknowingly drink of her life. Images of her lifeless corpse in my arms after I had stolen her essence haunted my mind.

There must have been some desire in her heart as well, for my hesitation changed the look in her eyes to disappointment, and quickly she pulled away from me. "Come on, slow poke. Let's get back to camp," she said after she had turned away.

"Murks knows it's hard, Master, but it's for the best."

I tried to ignore the wisdom of my little hemodan, and instead silently followed her to the warmth of the campfire.

The few hours of the night that remained found me alone. Enough trust had been built between me and our barbarian friends that even they didn't stay awake the whole night. Even so, I found my thoughts drifting as I continued to fidget with the bone that the shadow had given me. The stillness of the night helped my thoughts drift off to another time, and another place.

"Boy!" The gruff voice of the Baron drifted through my mind. "Aren't you supposed to be with my brother right now?"

I was in the courtyard of massive ornate castle. Images of ravens and glorious heroes covered every surface, and the off-white and green stripe of the King's army rode on every man at

Desecrated

arms. Peasants mulled about their tasks, and one corner of the yard had been converted to a training ground for soldiers. The creaking of wagon wheels and the clash of steel made oddly comforting companions in this muddy open space.

"Yes sir," I meekly answered the commander of the King's army. His baleful stare seemed to bring a familiar sting, yet I knew not from where the pain came. Commander Andoleth had always been stern, but not unkind to me in our brief exchanges. Why then did I feel this hatred for him?

Quickly, I gathered up the books that lay strewn about the place where I sat studying and watching the brave soldiers of the King. I was proud to be in His Majesty's court, even if I was just the High Priest's apprentice. I deftly dodged through the meandering crowds of the castle, making my way to the Temple of Redress where my master awaited me.

The temple itself was both behind and beneath the castle proper, but it was still within the fortifications that protected it. I chose to take the more scenic route to the temple, rather than snaking my way through the castle and climbing down endless steps. Walking through the streets between the towers of the castle allowed me glimpses of the sprawling city on the many sides of the castle, and serene views of the glorious snow capped mountains to the north. As I came around to the backside of the fantastic castle, I could smell the fresh, clean air of spring, and it let me escape the duties of the day even for just a few breaths.

The cobblestone path led directly into the black and gold gates of the temple, and gigantic banners with images of the delicate crown of our divine queen floated above the rampant form of a stylistic multi-colored serpentine dragon. The booming voice

Chapter 13

of our King could be heard drifting down to the quiet pathway behind the castle, for his glory was great and the temple was not often visited in the afternoon.

Life was good.

Multiple layers of great velvet curtains separated the outside from the entry chamber into the temple, as the blasting rays of the sun should never touch this holy place. Entering the temple I was greeted immediately by the thick and entrancing incense that always filled the temple's large chapel. I went directly to the back of the great hall, which was lit only by hundreds of black candles and the glowing coals under the altar at the back of the chapel.

I made my way past the empty cushions on the floor, and the few petitioners who were silently praying. Beyond the lush dark curtains behind the altar and a massive door was the chamber of hidden mysteries and my master. As I opened the thick wooden door I saw his shadow on the wall, and heard his voice as he instructed the other apprentices.

It was unusual for an older boy to be taken into the temple as an apprentice, and I was much older than the other boys. Most of them had not even seen ten summers, and I had seen more than double that. I didn't remember many of those passing years due to the accident that I suffered as a young man. High Priest Se'Naat had seen something special in me. I was proud to be his primary student and I wanted him to be proud of me.

"You summoned me, Master?" I called out.

"Ah yes." He turned back to the collection of eight boys he was giving lessons to. "That will be all for today, children."

Desecrated

There was a hushed chaos as the boys removed their apprentice robes, and shuffled out of the chamber. I waited patiently as Se'Naat said his goodbyes to each of the boys and when we were finally alone he showed me the proud smile that he always carried for me.

"Do you know what day it is, boy?" He asked while he started making some tea.

I paused to think for a moment. "Twenty days before the festival of secrets?"

He chuckled. "Today is the day that you become a priest here within the temple." He waited for a response that I was too overwhelmed to give. "You would like that, wouldn't you?"

"Oh, Master. I am not worthy to be one of the priests. My training is not nearly complete."

Again he laughed. "You can abandon the act of humility. We both know that your knowledge of the unseen arts is far beyond even what some of the current priests can perform."

I fought to hide my pride. Often I was the subject of scornful glares at the temple for my natural skill with the unseen powers. It was the one thing that I truly knew was mine. With no family, no past, and no property since the accident, my pride and skill were the only things I had to cling to. Eventually a tiny grin gave my secret pride away.

"Ah ha! I see it there, on your face," he said with a smile. "So it is settled then. You will be elevated to priest at tonight's service. I will advise His Majesty."

"What? His Majesty will be here?" I could not hide the surprise in my voice.

"Indeed. His Majesty has taken great interest in you. He will want to be present for your elevation."

Chapter 13

Pride swelled in my soul. It seemed that my future was already set on a path of power, and that was nothing to be sad about. "Is there anything else, Master?"

"No no. I will make all the arrangements. Enjoy the rest of your day, apprentice, for tomorrow the real work begins." He smiled and then turned his attention to an unfurled parchment at his desk.

As I passed back through the curtains I was filled with a happiness unlike any I had ever known. I felt as if the world were my playground, and I could make up the rules as I went along. For a moment I closed my eyes and imagined myself as the High Priest of the Temple of Redress as my master currently was, standing before the altar and offering the secrets of our people to our Divine Queen, so that she might fuel the engine of our vengeance against those who would stand against us. I would be a terrifying vessel for the power of her revenge.

Then, through the cracks of my joyful pride I heard a tiny whisper. "Run."

I looked around to find the source of this hidden taunt, but found no one. Again I heard the same voice, "Vanquish it," followed with a hearty laugh full of love and joy. I knew as Se'Naat's apprentice that love was a lie, an illusion for the masses to be controlled by the mighty and the powerful. Yet, there was something in this ghostly laugh that weakened my resolve. The voice whispered again, "Run." And so I did.

I ran out of the temple into the sunshine and crisp air. I squinted at the searing light and filled my lungs with the joy of those marvelous mountains. Suddenly, I knew something was wrong, but I didn't know what.

Desecrated

There was a flash and the dream changed. It was night, and inside the temple the evening's service had begun, but I was not inside. Instead I was pacing on the street outside. It was quiet out on the street, as the service had already started. Se'Naat had told me that it was customary for new priests to drink in the darkness of the night sky. He suggested that I try and dwell on the immenseness of the secret that had given birth to the world, and to try and see beyond the great curtain of the heavens to commune with the gods who lived beyond. I was trying, but my thoughts kept wandering.

I had not been able to shake the whispers that invaded my pride earlier that day. As I walked through the streets of the city while trying to clear my head, I kept seeing three men who seemed to be following me everywhere. They all looked very familiar, but I could not place them in my memory, much like the whisper that had so easily shattered my happiness. I kept asking myself how real my happiness could be if a few whispers could so easily destroy it.

Caught in my internal strife, I barely heard the footsteps that came up behind me. The voice that spoke softly to me, however, I could not miss. "Alexander. You don't have to do this." The voice was strong and very familiar, and the name–the name was my name. This startling revelation made my eyes snap to the source of the voice.

His face looked rugged and handsome, and his head was topped with salt and pepper hair. I felt lost looking at him though, as I knew that somehow I had known him forever, yet I could not remember his name. I stared, trying to figure out the puzzle that faced me and when the answer did not come. "Don't have to do what?"

Chapter 13

"Fall into Se'Naat's web. We've come to take you home, Alex. Come with us," he asked so softly that he could not be from here. No one spoke that way in the city, and certainly not in the temple.

"Who are you? What do you want?"

His half smile was filled with worry. "My name is Marec. Many years ago your grandfather gave me the task of being your guardian, and only once have I failed. I am here today to try and repent for my mistake. Come back with me. Back to Sanctuary. Back to your home and your friends."

A breeze blew through my mind, lifting some of the smoke put there by the incense. I remembered the old man and his jovial laugh. I remembered his wink when it shot light into my soul. I remember the blade of Andoleth being driven into his chest, and my rage burned away what smoke remained. Suddenly, I was free of Se'Naat's control. I felt the tide of my guilt rise, but my rage mixed with it and the steam that remained was just a cloud of sorrow. Confused and hurt I struggled to say, "Marec?"

Tears appeared in his eyes. "Yes, Alex?"

"Let's go home."

The scrape and clatter of metal against stone came from the top of the wall right next to us. Atop were the familiar forms of two men: Valarian, the tall bald priest of the Silver Lady who had also been my guardian since I was young, and Lucien, the giant lion of The Brotherhood. They threw a rope down to the two of us and we climbed the twenty feet to the top. I stood at the peak of the wall and listened to the murmuring that escaped through the heavy curtains of the temple, and my heart hardened. My memory returned, and the knowledge that my enemy had kept me in thrall

Desecrated

for many years filled my soul again with a cold rage. Yet, the proud smiles of Se'Naat conflicted me. Would I ever truly be free of his influence? Had the darkness taken a deep root in my soul?

"We need to go before they find us," Marec urged.

While my body left that dark temple behind, some part of me remained. A part, that I felt, I might never be able reclaim.

When I escaped my dream it was nearly dawn. The sky had already become that dark purple color that it did before the heavens lit up. There was no more life in the campfire, and the snores of Nikolai would have chased away any beast that might have been stalking us. We were safe and alone.

Time seemed to fly by as I watched the dark smudges in the sky drift along their unseen currents, and the color of their ocean becoming brighter and brighter. Like all things, this peace could not last forever.

"I am not mad at you anymore. I think," softly Avar's voice called out from his bedding. "I have been angry and confused, and I am sorry I took it out on you." He turned over and peeled back his blanket and looked directly at me. "I'm sorry."

Not really sure how I was expected to react, I nodded in response. Then, feeling a little awkward, I broke my silence. "It's ok. You have been through a lot. First Matthew, and then your father. I can't even imagine what that is like. You and Brin are the only family I know."

Chapter 13

Avar gave me a pitying smile and nodded. We sat in silence for a long time, each of us keeping our thoughts to ourselves. Eventually Brin rolled over under her blanket and said loud enough for us all to hear it, "About time you two made up." That made Avar and me smile at each other.

"I didn't really know my father, but it's hard to for me to believe that his last words were what you told me before. I guess the fact that I will never really know who he was is starting to sink in." As Avar's words trailed off he drifted into quiet contemplation. I thought it best not to disturb him by engaging in more conversation.

More time flew by and the sky started to show the first real glow of morning. As was normal, Avar started getting ready to cook for everyone, and Brin woke up with a brisk energy and left quickly to hunt, taking Nikolai and Piotyr with her. The three of us who remained gathered some wood and guarded the camp awaiting their return. And return they did. Just as the bright sun finished its climb over the horizon and was fully in the sky, they returned with enough small furry and feathered creatures to fill our bellies for the oncoming day.

The transformation in the sky was wonderful. Darkness changed to light, and the bodies that floated in the ocean of the sky changed with it. They began as charcoal smudges and became azure smears, and then slowly became golden plumes and finally the brilliant white pillowy clouds. I thought a great deal about the visions I had seen, and the people I had met while watching that transformation. I wondered if I too might one-day change into something brilliant and colorful.

"So, tell them about what's next, Wrack." Brin caught me off guard while she waited for her breakfast.

Desecrated

Confused about how much to say, I tried to be as simple and vague as possible. "Well. We have to take this bone to the altar in Sanctuary." I held up the bone for everyone to see. "Then we have to… deal with The Armor. One way or another."

"That sounds ominous," Piotyr commented.

After a deep sigh, I felt the need to continue talking about the situation. "My understanding is that we have two options. The first is to re-imprison The Armor. This will allow for his power to keep the defenses of Sanctuary intact, but will leave one of the doomed under the feet of the hunters."

Piotyr interjected, "Vait. That prison of chains on that altar vas making the magic of Sanctuary vork? How do ve know this is true?"

"Garrett told us, Brother. Vhere vere you?" Nikolai answered. "Continue, Vrack."

I nodded, nervously. "The other option is to kill the thing, and I am not sure exactly how to do it. We know that Brin's sword was used to kill one of the Doomed in Yellow Liver, but I don't know if it can end the life of an empty suit of armor."

Avar seemed to get lost in thought after I mentioned Ukumog. Nikolai nodded and stroked his beard. Finally Tikras spoke up, "Do ve know vhat The Mistress vants vith it?"

"All we can assume is that she wants to increase her power, and somehow The Armor is connected to that," I replied.

Brin tossed in, "Maybe she just wants to tap into the power of the Doomed, and The Armor is the weakest one."

Nikolai laughed, "I don't know if I vould call him veak. He certainly gave us all a good tossing about."

Chapter 13

"No, I mean he might be too weak to resist whatever it is she wants to do to him." Brin's voice rose with excitement. "Think about it. He has been under Sanctuary, having his power used for something else. Maybe she wants to use that somehow."

Tikras smiled and wagged his finger at Brin. "You are much more than a pretty face! I think she might be right, Nikolai."

"In any case, we cannot let her do whatever it is she is planning," I added.

"So, vhich one are ve going to do?" Piotyr asked.

"Well," I paused for a moment, "really it's Bridain's call. Garrett wanted to kill it, so I imagine that is still the plan." Thoughts of the fight in the graveyard flashed through my mind. "Though, after the last attempt, he might change his mind."

Everyone except Avar nodded in agreement. We sat there silently thinking while they ate their food.

Avar finally spoke up, "Where did you get the bone from?"

I hesitated. When we met The Shadow before, the idea of working with him caused Avar to have a dilemma about what was right. I had no desire for that to happen again, especially with everything that has happened since. However, I just couldn't lie to him. "The Shadow gave it to me."

Avar stood up and shouted, "I knew it! I knew you got it from some dark thing out here. I am so stupid."

Brin tried to calm him down. "Avar, it wasn't like that."

"You knew?" His face told me how foolish he felt. "You knew this whole time and you went with it anyway? Don't you remember when we dealt with that thing last time? The whole idea of working with that…that creepy thing bothers me. I mean, for all we know it is one of the Doomed." As soon as the word left his

Desecrated

mouth, he stopped speaking, and his eyes got very big. There was some powerful idea spinning in his head, and it looked like he was just trying to get his thoughts around it.

"What?" Brin asked impatiently. "What is it Avar?"

"I think I have just figured something out." A huge grin appeared on his face. "Where did your father's sword come from again?"

Brin smiled, "I like the story about the betrayer making it-"

"Exactly! The betrayer was one of the Doomed whose name has been stricken from history. He turned against the rest of the Doomed and for that they imprisoned him. After he escaped, they killed him or imprisoned him again, or something. Anyway, I think I just figured out who our shadowy friend is."

Brin's brow furrowed. "You think that The Shadow is actually the betrayer?"

"It makes sense! And something else makes it even better! You know how I have been trying to figure out which one of the Doomed Wrack is tied to?" Avar made motions with his hands asking for Brin to finish his thought.

I answered instead, "You think I am tied to the betrayer?"

Avar's smile became bigger than I had ever seen it. "It makes sense! He seemed to know you from the first time we were there, for one."

Brin's eyes were huge. "And it would explain your weird connection to Ukumog!" When I gave a look of protest she said, "Don't think I haven't noticed how you look at my sword."

"Would also explain why The Shadow showed up just in time to help us kill this other Doomed. I am telling you, I feel good about this." Avar was filled with excitement.

"Does this change our plans at all?" Nikolai asked.

Chapter 13

"Only that now I think we might be able to trust The Shadow. For now at least. He wants the Doomed dead just as much as we do." Avar smiled. "It feels good to have someone on our side for once.

I felt uneasy that Avar was jumping so quickly to conclusions, but I kept those thoughts to myself and just smiled.

Avar was not satisfied with my lack of response. "What do you think, Wrack?"

I smiled politely. "Certainly is an interesting theory."

"Aw c'mon. It's the best guess any of us has."

"And a fine guess it is, but I don't know anymore about my connection to the Doomed than you do," I lied. With the collection of fragmented memories I had seen, but not shared, I had a little more insight. However, I don't think it gave me more answers. Just more questions. "Let's just take each encounter with The Shadow as they come. If he decides to turn on us, I would be much happier if we weren't completely caught off guard. If he really did betray the Doomed, what makes you think he wouldn't do it to us too?"

Avar rubbed his chin. "You're right. Still, takes some of the weight off us to know that we might have help."

The sorrow in his eyes spoke of the loss of his family. He was searching for something to fill their holes, something that he could count on. I wished that I could give him some kind of assurance that things would be ok, but I was being hurtled through the darkness just as he was. Perhaps there would be some solace that we shared this suffering.

My hand patted him on the shoulder, and I smiled at him. "Shall we go back to Sanctuary?"

He nodded and smiled back.

Desecrated

Travel back to Sanctuary was uneventful, but that didn't mean that we weren't extra cautious about potential freth scouts. Brin and Piotyr were constantly looking for tracks or other kinds of signs that we might not be alone out in the wilderness. As the trees cleared, we quickened our pace trying to close the distance to the town before anything could spot us. The closer we got, the quicker we traveled. When we neared the town itself, sheer excitement mixed with a twist of fear chased us into the failing protections of the town.

No one stopped us when we came back. Instead, they pointed us in the direction of the commander's house. It seems we were expected. By the look of the buildings, it seems that the hunters here had spent all their time fortifying and repairing, making preparations for the great conflict that was to come, no doubt. There were new faces in the crowd as well; those reinforcements must have arrived. All in all, it looked like The Mistress had ceased her harassing attacks. It was most curious.

With haste, we were ushered into the commander's house by the back entrance that led to his meeting room. As we walked behind the house, I glanced at the graveyard to the statue that marked the hidden temple where I knew this conflict would come to its final climax. While my desire to have the struggles of my friends come to an end, I was not looking forward to what was to come. The guards posted near the entrance to the temple paid me no mind as I glared in their direction. It was comforting to at least know that Bridain had not given up on the temple's protection.

Once inside the room we were greeted by Bridain, Ferrin, Verif, and Tarissa. Bridain motioned for us to sit in the chairs assembled for the endless stream of briefings the room looked like

Chapter 13

it had been host to. "Welcome back," Bridain said casually. His face gave the signs of days with no sleep. "Tell me, how did the mission go?"

"Well," Brin immediately responded. "We found the place where Wrack was leading us, encountered some strange unseen force that eventually came out into the open, but we managed to collect and escape with our objective."

"Unseen force?" Varif curiously asked.

No one spoke right away. "It seemed to reach out into our minds and change things it found there. Later, it burst through a wall and tried to physically devour us. It was an unknowable tentacly thing. If we were honest about the conflict, it almost killed at least one of us," I offered up.

Bridain looked at me with a questioning concern, "Thank the Silver Lady you escaped." Turning back to Brin he continued, "So, you obtained whatever it was you needed? I'm sorry, you were never quite clear on exactly what it was you were looking for."

"This bone is what we needed," I held it up in my open palm. "This bone will force The Armor to return to the temple below us. Once it is there, we can do whatever you like with it. However, I do not think that this method will make it compliant. We should be prepared to apply force, if necessary."

Bridain nodded. "Verif and I have been searching through the old hunter documents, and have found almost nothing about how the thing was trapped down there or why. Garrett's notes do support what he said about the protections of Sanctuary falling without The Armor as the source." He paused, struggling with his own thoughts. "With us facing this unknown enemy, The Mistress, I almost think it would be better to chain the thing up again. Killing it will leave us vulnerable."

Desecrated

This was a complete change from before, and it was surprising. With the way that Bridain had previously acted towards me, I was certain that his fervor would drive him to choose destruction over imprisonment.

"Can we even rebuild that prison?" asked Avar.

Bridain opened his mouth to respond but Verif spoke before he could, "I believe we can. There was one set of notes that we found that had images carved into the leather pages. Images of chains and the altar. I think that I can decipher the text with Wrack's help." She looked at me with those cat-like eyes and raised an eyebrow. I could feel the desire in her, and it was not wholesome.

"Perhaps," was all I could say.

Nikolai boomed from the back of the room, "Vhat about The Mistress? Vhat if she comes in to disturb us in the middle of this…thing you vant us to do?"

"We might need to be flexible," said Tarissa. "If she attacks, our plans may change to destruction. Better it be destroyed than we allow her to do whatever it is she is planning."

All three of the barbarians murmured and nodded in agreement.

"We will plan for both situations. The only difference really will be the actions we perform once the thing is in the chamber," Bridain tried to assure everyone.

My heart grew restless, and while everyone else in the room began talking in more detail about strategy and resource placement I found myself staring at the bone turning over and over in my fingertips. Unlike what happened in Yellow Liver, I could feel this storm coming and I knew that we were not ready.

When I looked around the room I was met by happy smiles. Seeing the light of hope in their eyes, I couldn't bring myself to express my doubts. Instead I tried to feel the hope that lifted them

Chapter 13

up, but it didn't work. I hid my worry, and with a smile I tried to be a part of this moment where it didn't seem like we were hounded by the relentless entropy of the world. And after just a few moments, I believed the lie.

Desecrated

Chapter 14

The morning following our return to Sanctuary found Verif and me pouring over the short stack of notes she had on the magical chains that had kept The Armor imprisoned. The keystone to the puzzle was a fragile piece of leather which had images tooled into the surface. Each time she handed me that particular fragment, my stomach ached with a sickening tickle.

"The language is odd, no?" she asked me for the third time.

Pushing the leather at her, and looking away from it I answered, "Yeah. What do you think it says?"

"Seems like some kind of rite to me. If it works like the magic I am familiar with, there is probably chants along with a physical element, but those things really only exist to harness the unseen power." She paused and smiled knowingly at me. "They say that the most powerful of the ancient wizards could weave the unseen without words or even motion."

I scowled at her. "You have a misconception about me."

She smiled and her head tilted back, "Oh yeah? What's that?"

"I'm no wizard."

Desecrated

Her face lit up with giggles. "Right. You, the mysterious tainted with a hemodan, are no wizard." She pulled me close and whispered in my ear, "Your secret is safe with me." Her hands found their way around my torso, and the warmth of her body invaded me.

Electricity shot up my spine, and my extremities tingled. A haze drifted into my mind as I began to surrender to the intoxication of her scent. My arms involuntarily lifted and began to wrap around her, but I wrestled control of my hunger instead placing my hands on her shoulders. With a slight push, I separated our bodies.

With a face full of disappointment she said, "If you don't want my body, what do you want?"

Embarrassed and a little ashamed, I turned away. "Nothing. I don't want anything from you."

"How else am I going to learn more about the unseen power?" she pouted.

My patience was at an end. "Listen Verif, we are here trying to figure out this rite so that we can follow Bridain's wishes. I know you have this unexplainable desire to know the secrets that I have, but you have to know–I don't remember anything from my life before Brin found me. If I have some connection with this magic you are interested in, I am afraid that I cannot teach you anything."

Then there was silence. She sat on the table of the room where we were working, kicking her legs as she collected her thoughts. Eventually I found my way to the corner, and scorning all other surfaces, sat upon the floor and cast my eyes into the shadow that crossed the opposite corner of the room. The table creaked with each rotation of her swinging legs. At first I found the repetition of the sounds annoying, but then I just accepted their presence and they nearly vanished into my thoughts.

Breaking the silence she asked me, "How did it come to you?"

Chapter 14

"What?" I answered, trying to focus my wandering thoughts.

"The magic. How did it come to you?"

My jaw flexed at her question. A resentful anger rose within me, but it broke as quickly as it had come. I found a little humor in the fact that I seemed to be picking up Brin's mannerisms. "I don't know how it came to me. I don't remember anything about my life before."

She stared at me with incredulous cat-like eyes. They probed me for signs of treachery. When she found no deceit, her look softened. "They say that every wizard is marked somehow. That this strangeness is a warning to all other people that inside that person there lies something dangerous. Some hidden power." Even from across the room I could see her eyes fill with the distance of memories. "My parents abandoned me because of my... strangeness." She motioned at her eyes.

Nodding was the only way I could express my understanding that we did share a connection. People feared us because of the secrets that lay just beneath the surface of our skin. The fear I could taste in her breaths told me that we shared more than just that. We both had been left alone to discover just how frightening those secrets could be.

Finally she gave a deep sigh. "Well, this isn't going to work. We should just tell Bridain that we cannot solve this puzzle and that we have to kill the thing."

A flash of the smith's hammer and my arms covered in blood passed through my mind. I heard the distinct clash of metal on metal echo through my memories, and in the background I heard chanting. "Wait," I climbed up off the floor. "Let me see that skin again."

Desecrated

Surprised, Verif complied and again as my fingers touched the leather they tingled. Fighting through the discomfort I stared at the squiggles on the sheet and eventually they made sense.

'With punishing hands of steel
Cold iron your heart must feel
Pound through flesh ancient cold
To seal away this evil old

Chains of icy black
In, around, down, and back
Swaddled in sin
The accursed suffering begin

Unholy righteous and wrong
May this prison prolong
Sealed with glory, song, and doom
Until his living corpse exhume'

"Well," said Verif, "seems like we may have found the words. From the images around that part, it seems that you have to seal the chains around him just using a hammer and no actual forge to heat the metal."

"How will that work, exactly?"

"I dunno. Maybe it is lit with another kind of fire, from the unseen. From the other parts it sounds a little like hatred or rage."

Cold ran up my spine as she said the words, and images of Ukumog flashed through my mind. Not the saber-like form of Ukumog as it was now, but as it was before, a sharp dark rectangle of anger. Could these chains have been forged in the same way? "Sounds like it will be hard. Who has enough rage to summon an unseen fire hot enough to heat those links?"

Chapter 14

"I dunno. I am just glad we don't have to make all the chains. We can probably just forge back the ones that are broken."

Pondering how the whole rite would work, I continued to glean what I could from the delicate leather page. Below the rhyming chant there was another part written at the end in a different handwriting.

> 'I am the warden,
> the way-maker,
> and the lighthouse.
> Ever shall I be the beacon
> of your redemption.'

"That is the seal on the rite, Master." I had almost forgotten that Murks was in my pocket until his words floated through my mind. With my thoughts I thanked him and then repeated his direction to Verif.

"Hrm. That seems to seal the rite to a particular person. That means that even if the chains are broken, whoever does this will still be linked to the rite," she said.

"What about the first person who did it?"

She shrugged. "If they did this part, I suppose that they are still connected." Then her brow furrowed with worry. "The rite for the protections of the town is not on here. I think that the two rites are connected by way of the person who did it the first time, which means they are still alive."

I was confused, "I don't understand. The person who did the rite to grant protections over Sanctuary is still alive? How is that possible?"

She looked at me with an incredulous look.

"Oh. They must be one of the Doomed or something."

Desecrated

"Yeah."

"That can't be good."

She shook her head.

After some more study of the leather fragment, Verif and I went down into the temple below the graveyard to inspect the chains and altar. Even though I had spent months sealed in that chamber, I now looked with different eyes upon the pitted black metal of those chains. The seal on the rite made some part of me believe that perhaps this prison was penance for the things that The Armor had done. That perhaps being chained up is where he wanted to be.

While I examined the silver altar, my thoughts drifted to the monster that I knew lived inside me. Back in the chamber under the well, with that beast The Shadow called a seed, I had fought against it and won, but there was still evil living inside my skin. The sins of an unknowable past haunted me from behind the velvet curtain of forgetfulness, but they still lingered. Standing there, in that prison of torturous atonement, I felt alone and afraid.

"What do you think?" Verif asked after the prolonged silence of our study.

I gave a little shrug. "I think we can try it. Honestly, I don't know if it will even work, but I feel we need to give it a go." My thoughts turned to The Armor as my hand rested on the smooth surface of the altar. Just how long was he here? How much longer would he have had to remain for his sins to be forgiven, and who is it that would give him absolution?

"Well then, I suppose we should find a hammer."

My drifting mind had been jolted back to the matter at hand by Verif's voice. "A hammer. Right."

Chapter 14

A smithing hammer was easy enough to find. There were several to choose from, and after feeling their weights and giving them each a few test swings I picked out the one that felt right. It was old and worn; the handle stained with the grime and sweat of many years of service, and the metal head of it was scarred and scorched. The smiths tried to convince me to take one of the newer ones, but the old one felt right. It was ancient and punished, just like The Armor.

After finding the hammer we would use, Verif and I met with Bridain. The three of us talked over the rite and explained what we did and didn't know. The whole time he sat listening to us with a look of deep concern on his face, but in the end he said, "We will just have to give it our best shot. If it doesn't work, Brin will be there to help kill the thing."

I nodded, and we shook hands. After just one day of planning we were about to risk the lives of everyone in Sanctuary, and he didn't want to wait. We were given one night to rest and ready ourselves, but the next day would be it. The anticipation of your tomorrow possibly being not only your last day, but also the last day of everyone you cared about does funny things to the very air of the evening before. Each moment seemed to have more meaning, and every wrinkle in everyone's face became lodged in my memory.

Brin eventually found me in the corner of the mess hall, sitting apart from the rest of the hunters yet watching them laugh through the hours on what might be their last night. She pulled over a chair and sat next to me, Ukumog glowing dimly on her hip. "You ok?"

"Yeah. Just seems so very strange."

She picked at the untouched plate of food which had been placed before me. I wasn't actually eating it. "What do you mean?"

Desecrated

"Everyone here knows that tomorrow we might all die, yet they aren't worried. In Yellow Liver the people lived with this horrible cloud of fear over their heads. The hunters are just very…"

"Different?"

"Yeah."

She smiled and touched me gently on the arm. "People are different wherever you go. These people," she motioned towards the hunters gathered, "are soldiers, and so they are used to facing death. You might say they kinda expect to be challenged with it. Especially here."

"Why?"

She chuckled. "Because, Wrack, these aren't just regular soldiers. They are people who have made the boldest of statements to the Doomed. Their very existence means that the campaign of terror that the Doomed have waged against the humans of this world was not entirely successful. As long as they are around, there will always be an itch that the Baron and his companions can't quite scratch."

"You sound like you admire them a little bit," I joked.

"Ya know, I think I might."

We sat there watching the young and old soldiers of the Shadow Hunters enjoy each other's company. Brin kept picking at the food off my plate without even asking, and I kept the plate near me so that she would have to keep leaning close. It felt good, just being there with her. There was no lust within me to consume her warmth, nor desire to take Ukumog from her. I had no dark questions circling in my mind. I never wanted that night to end.

Later, most of the hunters had gone off to their bunks, and Brin stayed with me in the mess hall. Eventually she fell asleep with her face buried in her arms upon the table, and I silently remained as her guardian. Through the open doorway I could see the light

Chapter 14

outside change and just as I had done many times before, I sat next to Brin as the sun came up. Somehow, this day was different. I wasn't worried about the rite or The Mistress anymore. I knew what needed to be done, and like the hunters around me, I was ready to face death and come out victorious.

It was just past midday when everyone was gathered and prepared for the rite to begin. The first step of which was to place the bone on the altar as The Shadow had instructed. Once everyone was ready, the few hunters I had grown to know as well as my friends were all gathered in the temple beneath the graveyard. Everyone dressed in their best armor or clothes. It really looked like we were doing something important and official.

In the town above us there were specific patrols to watch for both the approach of The Armor, and to be mindful of a possible attack from The Mistress. The chamber, hallway, steps, and even the graveyard were heavily guarded by rows of hunters. All of them were ready to fight and die for the hope that this rite had given them. It was a little overwhelming because I had doubts that this rite would even work, and further doubts that The Shadow had been forthright with the information about the bone. Only time could tell, however, so I tried to maintain a facade of hope and excitement.

When the time came, a scout whispered into Bridain's ear and he gave me a solemn nod. With exaggerated gestures so that all who wanted to see what I was doing could watch, I placed the bone slowly onto the altar while Verif and I stood behind it. To my left was Brin, ready to strike down anything that should try and interfere, and on Verif's right was Avar. Even the tiny tap of the bone to the silver surface of the altar seemed to echo through the chamber in an unusual way. But then, nothing else happened.

Desecrated

Hours went by, and yet we all maintained our positions. Silently and diligently, our force of will was steeled by the hope that we were doing the right thing for not only ourselves, but all those who need the help of the hunters. Food and water was delivered to each of the hunters waiting on their feet for news that The Armor was approaching, but none came.

My own thoughts turned against me. Had I allowed The Shadow's lies to bring additional danger to the hunters of Sanctuary? I felt stupid for believing his lies. After all, he had gained much more by my collection of the cloth than I had by obtaining the bone. That ancient fabric had stolen some of my power, and he had sent me and my friends into extreme danger to collect it. I believed myself a fool for having trusted The Shadow, The Betrayer.

When I could wrestle my attention away from my own thoughts, my eyes would occasionally meet those of one of the many young hunters in the chamber with me. Hope remained in their faces, and they looked to me for reassurance. I could not let my guard down, to show my doubt would cause this entire thing to crumble. The chaos that would follow was just what the enemies of the Hunters needed. I had to find the hope within me that this bone would bring The Armor to us, and that we could triumph over the array of evils that hounded us.

As the light dwindled, so, too, could I feel the hope departing. I could not give up. My resolve was steeled. Something had to give. Just as the sun went behind the horizon, a scout came running into the temple and whispered to Bridain. His face exploded with excitement, "The Armor has been spotted. It's on the way!"

My heart leapt. Deep breaths soothed my joy for I needed to remain calm for the rite that was to come. I felt a rumbling from somewhere distantly above me. It came again and again, like the footsteps of a giant. When I looked to Brin, I didn't have to

Chapter 14

even ask if she could hear them. The look on her face was one of uneasy resolve. She was ready to fight, but unsure. It was then that I realized that the rumbling was a feeling and not a sound traveling to my ears. I could feel him coming.

Closer and closer the drums of giant's footfalls came. Closing my eyes, I imagined him as a silhouette against the trees, and walking slowly across the field into the town of Sanctuary. Like small children playing at soldiers, the hunters gathered around his massive form and became a cloud around him as they escorted him to the graveyard. The tremors grew closer still as I could feel his hesitation among the ancient headstones. His compulsion to return to his prison did not prevent his anxiety. I wondered how much of his return seemed like his own choice or if he felt driven by an outside power to return.

The faint creaking of plates of armor started to float down into the temple chamber through the entrance. Slowly, I felt a rumbling for each of the steps as he descended into the well-guarded depths. More clanking and rumbling, then his crouching form breached the shadows of the hallway and came into the light of the chamber.

He seemed taller than I remembered, standing with most of the hunters coming just higher than his waist, he truly was a giant. The Armor that made up his body was no longer gleaming with bright metal, but instead showed the wear of the wilderness. After surveying the room, causing some of the hunters to flinch or raise their weapon in self-defense, he started walking towards the altar.

Each rumbling step seemed to shake the fabric of my mind, yet they disturbed no dust that lay hidden between the ancient stones of the pillars in the room. He stepped up onto the dais were the altar resided, and looked down at the black chains which were

Desecrated

lain about the disk ritually. The rumbling stopped when he reached the altar itself, and he did not even look at the four of us standing behind it. He was completely focused on the tiny bone that lay on the altar. With an unseen, but metal clad, hand he reached out to collect the small fragment. After a short and simple examination, he brought up his other hand and seemed to place the bone where his pinky finger should have been.

A wind swirled the air in the chamber, and before my eyes I saw the tiny bone change into the finger of a man where his hand should have been. Then it became translucent, fading away to the place where the rest of his body was hidden. The horrible sound of screeching metal burst from his hand and plates of armor appeared to form over the invisible finger. As far as any of us could tell, he was finally whole.

Everyone in the room was on edge. My personal fear was that now that he was repaired, he would unleash his power upon us and any chance we had of actually completing the rite would be gone. The hunters in the room tightened their ranks, ready to attack if required. Much to our surprise, however, our tension was unnecessary. His empty visor looked down at the chains carefully placed in preparation, and the altar shining brilliantly in the torchlight. After that silent moment, he seemed to nod at no one in particular and without even the smallest struggle, he laid his metal form down on the altar. It was as if he wanted us to seal him back within those torturous chains.

Moving as quickly and correctly as we could, Verif and I wrapped the first chain around his waist and anchored it to the floor, then the chanting began.

There had been a second part to the rite that we found, words that we deciphered, but did not know the meaning of. It was the place of those attending the rite, but not actually participating

Chapter 14

to say the words slowly and in unison. "Vitriana Karandosa Forim Chun," the host of hunters whispered slowly as we did our work. Each time they reached the end they would take two deep breaths and begin again. The constant repetition helped me focus my mind and seemed to almost let my body do the work of the rite with no need for thought.

Once all the chains were wrapped around The Armor and placed in position, it was time for the forging to begin. I picked up the hammer and walked over to the first chain, the one around his waist. The broken link was away from the altar, near the ring on the floor that held the chain down. The hammer felt heavy in my hand and I could feel power rushing down my arm into it. Verif stood on the other side of the chain and nodded to me when I arrived at it. I nodded back.

The broken part of the chain in my other hand, I raised the hammer over my head and began to say the words of the rite. "With punishing hands of steel," my voice boomed through the chamber and dust from the stones above our heads drifted down through the air around us.

"Cold iron in your heart must feel." A grinding sound erupted from the chain. I saw spikes shoot from the black links around the Armor's body, sending their points into his unseen flesh. The Armor gave a blood-chilling scream of pain, but did not struggle against his bonds.

"Pound through flesh ancient cold." The hammer became a radiant beacon of purple light. I saw Verif avert her eyes from it due to the sheer intensity of the light. Without having to think about it, my hand brought the brilliant hammer down upon the link that waited to be forged. The glow of the hammer was transferred to the black steel, and the light began to forge the chain anew.

Desecrated

"To seal away this evil old." The roar of breaking metal rang backwards through our ears as I pounded the link two more times. The light faded from the link and the hammer to reveal that the chain had been made whole. It was time to do this part of the rite again.

Next I moved to the chains around his legs. These had broken links much closer to his body. As I approached I could hear the pained breaths of our captive, yet he did not struggle to escape. I held the next link in my hand and proceed with the rite again. When the spikes punctured his unseen flesh this time, I was sprayed with black blood from the wounds, but I did not let it interrupt me. Again we were bathed in the intense purple light and again the link was remade.

The second leg worked in much the same manner, and again blood sprayed all over me. The sticky fluid was all over my hands and wrists, but I did not let it bother me. Just as before, my voice shook the room and at the end the chain was reforged.

I moved to the chain around his left arm. The broken link here was right around his wrist, and so I had to get very close to him. As I approached, I could hear quiet sobbing echoing through the metal visor, yet he did not struggle against his bonds. I could not help but respect his discipline and resolve. If our situations were reversed, I doubted that I would have had the strength to endure this torment. It made me doubt that all of the Doomed were as evil as we really believed, but that doubt was not strong enough to change my current course of action.

Again the words of the rite filled the chamber and the spikes tore at his flesh, covering my forearms in the black blood of my victim. His screams not only echoed through the room, but also my memories. Flashes of a worn hammer and blood-covered hands distracted me temporarily, but I pushed them aside. This was

Chapter 14

no time for the past to haunt me. With crashing metal, bright as the sun with purple light, I repaired the broken link of chain. Only one chain remained.

This link was actually broken atop his wrist. I would have to reforge it by beating down upon him, which I thought might cause him further pain. With deep breaths focused on the task at hand, I pulled the broken chain into its correct place. "Vitriana Karandosa Forim Chun." The whispering chant urged me on. It soothed away my compassion for the man under my hammer and silenced my doubt. There was no choice but to finish the prison. It was the only answer.

"Well, well, well," the voice of The Mistress came down the hall. At hearing her voice, the chant ended and the hunters took their places to defend the room. Without the chant, I was brought crashing back to my senses for the trance it had kept me in had ended.

Without the cushion of the trance, I now heard the sounds of battle ringing down the entrance towards me. How long had the hunters above been keeping the enemy at bay? It didn't matter, for now she was here, and the rite was not yet complete.

The Armor also seemed to come out of his trance and began to struggle against his newly formed bonds. He grabbed me with his one free arm, and before I even realized what was happening he had thrown me against the back wall. I heard bones in my body shatter and the rock wall behind me cracked. My bones pulsed with pain that faded as they mended. The wall was not so lucky.

With the wind knocked from my lungs I crawled back towards the altar and the struggling Armor. A conflict had already erupted around me; the sheer amount of different sounds was overwhelming. I picked myself up off the floor just in time to see Brin bring down the faintly glowing Ukumog on The Mistress who deflected its edge with her empty hand. The snake beads in her hair writhed and snapped at everyone around her, and she counterattacked Brin with her claw-like nails, driving Brin into a defensive posture. Avar came up from the flank and tried to smite The Mistress with his mace, but the snake beads kept him at bay. I heard the distinct laugh of The Mistress as she pulled both of her hands to her chest.

Circling winds of fire rippled out from The Mistress' body, driving everyone back from her. Seeing the oncoming wave, I ducked behind the altar and it passed over my head. Suddenly, I was trapped within the eye of a firestorm. Through the flames, I could see the battle still raging between the Mistress's army and the hunters. The disk upon which the altar sat seemed to mirror the ring of spinning flames that separated me from my friends. Only The Mistress, The Armor, and I were inside. Unsure what to do, I remained hidden behind the altar while I tried to think of a plan.

I heard the hard soles of The Mistress' boots clatter against the smooth stone of the dais as she walked towards the altar. She raised her voice above the rushing fire and sounds of clashing weapons on the other side of the barrier. "Poor little humans! You just don't realize when you are outmatched. Now, I will finish what I have come for. Once I am finished in here, I will allow all of you to be the first to feel my new power." She laughed with such overwhelming confidence that I envied her.

The chains holding The Armor rattled as he tried to escape. Sounds came from his hidden mouth that sounded like panic echoing through a metal tube.

"Now, now," The Mistress condescend to him. "Struggling will not help matters. The time has come for you to give up the power that you never wanted in the first place."

More metallic grunts of protest came from The Armor.

Chapter 14

"Shhhh," she said like a mother calming her baby. "It will all be over soon." A wave of heat came from the other side of the altar, and I saw flickering red light, more powerful and intense than the luminance of the wall of fire. The Mistress began whispering words that I could barely even hear.

There was a feeling of rage that began to well up inside me, but it wasn't my rage. This rage came to me in the same way that I might share Murks' feelings, but they weren't coming from him. The source of said rage was completely unknown, and it starting coming in such strong waves that I had to concentrate to not get washed away by it. Closing both my fists I tried to force the anger from my mind. I remembered the fight with myself in the ruin under the well, and tried to visualize my opponent. When I opened up the floodgates to get an image, a searing white light entered my head. Quickly the pain of the light passed, and at its center I saw something dark. Determined to see what was there I pushed through the powerful raging light, and as I pushed the object got slightly clearer. It was a dark rectangle hanging in mid air. I drew closer yet, still unable to see what it was for the bright light trying to swallow the form of it whole. Then, very suddenly, I could see it. The image of Ukumog as it had looked when we first found it hung in the air, the runes on its blade glowing brightly. The rage was coming from it.

With shock, I shook my head and opened my eyes. My own confusion overwhelmed the rage and started to pushed it away. Metallic screams from just above me suddenly brought me out of my own head.

"I can feel it! Oh, my glorious parents! I can feel the power surging into me! It is working!" The elated voice of The Mistress sung out to the very heavens.

Desecrated

Like a head snapping to look quickly in another direction, I felt a change in Ukumog. It was suddenly focused on The Mistress. There was a horrible crack that sounded like the breaking of metal and bone. My curiosity would not allow me to sit back any longer, and so I stood up behind the altar.

Instantly our eyes met, and smile appeared on The Mistress' face. "What do we have here? A lost and lonely Hunter without his precious friends?" She stared at me, both her hands around the wrist of The Armor. "Wait a moment. There aren't any tainted in the Shadow Hunters. Somehow I'd think that was rather against their ideals," she said smiling.

I stood there motionless. My hands flexed, wishing that they had not left the hammer next to the back wall. Scanning the burning ring of fire, I could only make out the simplest of forms on the other side.

"Do you see what I am doing here?" She asked me as if I were some kind of student. "I am going to take his power. You see, little tainted one, the Doomed possess something akin to a spark that, in the right hands, could ignite a fire hot enough to reforge the entire world." There was a madness in her grin, a madness that I remembered seeing in the face of The Ghoul when he thought he would kill me. A madness that told me that she believed herself to be invincible.

"HEAR ME O' GOD OF DEATH!" Tikras' voice echoed through the chamber.

The Mistress raised an eyebrow and turned her head slightly towards the source of the voice, but then refocused herself on the task at hand. "Now it is time, Doomed one. Time for me to leech away what life remains in you." With this sinister taunt she pulled on the wrist of The Armor and he screamed so loud as to shake the very stones of the chamber. She pulled again, and again

Chapter 14

he screamed and dirt fell from the cracks in the ceiling. One more mighty yank upon his wrist and his scream shook loose the pillar that I once had tried to repair. Though it was outside the wall of fire, I saw the ceiling crack and collapse behind The Mistress, which was followed by screams and shouting.

In her hands The Mistress cradled the forearm plate and gauntlet from The Armor. Her face was lit by exalted joy. Without further hesitation, she gave me one look as if to share her victory and then placed the mail upon her own arm. A stone filled the pit of my stomach as I saw her close the straps and finally flex the metal fingers of the gauntlet. A disturbance rushed through the air, like heat rising from a stone in the desert. It began at the severed arm of The Armor and flowed into the arm of The Mistress herself. With eyes wide, the overwhelming, strange joy she was feeling was magnified through her face and her lack of condescending dialogue.

"OH VALIK! OBSIDIAN LORD OF DECAY!" Tikras continued to call out to his god, yet The Mistress seemed unconcerned.

The Mistress flexed her fingers and stared at the arm, looking at things that I could not see. The connection persisted in the space between her and The Armor, who remained chained to the altar. The pain of whatever she was doing to him rendered him unable to do anything but weakly struggle against his bonds and weep quietly. I had to do something.

Without really thinking, I stepped around the altar and tried to block the flow from The Armor to The Mistress with my body. The Mistress was alert, however, and intercepted my attempt to foil her plans. "Just what do you think you are doing, little tainted one? Hrm?"

Desecrated

Aggressively, she came towards me, making me backpedal away from my goal, but she was too quick. Before I knew what was happening, her metal hand was wrapped around my neck. Lifting me off the floor she scolded me with a few chiding noises, as if I were a child. She opened up her mouth as if to scold me further.

"BLESS YOUR SERVANT VITH THE SECRETS KNOWN ONLY TO YOU, OH MASTER OF HER MAJESTY'S VAULT OF VHISPERS!" Tikras interrupted. With amazing speed, the wall of fire suddenly collapsed into the space of one man. Inside the now column of flame, the form of Tikras could be seen through the veil of fire. His flesh began tearing from the whirling sear of the fire, yet he seemed to be fighting the pain with a frenzied concentration.

As soon as the wall collapsed, I turned my gaze towards the fight that had been hidden from me. Quickly, my eyes settled on the glow of Ukumog. I could feel a sliver of rage from it still, and now I knew why. The hand that clutched the handle of the blade was not Brin's. It was one of the darakka. Fighting furiously against that darakka was Brin, wielding her other sword, and from the looks of it they had been engaged in this fight for some time. Each of them would occasionally turn to fend off some other opponent, but it never distracted them for long enough to let the other get away. No surface was safe from Brin either, using it to absorb the blows from the Darakka, or even from her launching herself at her enemy. The two seemed locked in a dance which might never have an end.

Avar was amidst the fray as well, or at least what I thought was Avar. Instead of seeing one wolf-man fighting with the Hunters, I saw two. One was short and dark haired, while the other was tall and skinny, with light hair and blue eyes. The taller one was even still wearing the mantle which Avar was never without. Suddenly, his quick recovery from various wounds along our journey made

Chapter 14

more sense. Trapped in The Mistress' choking grip, however, I could not do more than watch him and Ferrin toss and claw their way through the freth that kept trying to break the hunter's defense of the entryway.

"Now I have you, Nozskaza!" Nikolai yelled as he charged out of the crowd onto the dais.

With the simple wave of her hand, The Mistress threw the large barbarian backwards. He landed not too far away and began choking on black plumes of smoke that seemed to be coming from his nose and mouth. She gave a mockingly triumphant laugh. "Each time we meet, Nikolai, your pathetic bravery gets you killed. I should have never summoned you or your friends back from the realm of death to begin with. Pathetic 'heroes'," she scoffed. Then she turned back to me, "Now, where were we?"

Over her shoulder, I watched the seemingly endless struggle between Brin and the darakka. The tight grip of The Mistress' armored hand began squeezing my throat harder. I felt the burning pain that comes with being unable to really breathe. While I wasn't sure if she could kill me by choking me that way, it was definitely painful. My eyesight began to dim, and I felt the cold sting of deathly sleep begin to drape me in the first of its many blankets.

Struggling to say anything, I finally pushed out one whispered word. "No."

The runes on Ukumog flared, and the darakka who possessed it was distracted for the briefest of moments. His hard-fought opponent was not going to let this tiny advantage slip by, and so Brin lunged with all her strength at the draconic beast. Her sword found purchase in the center of the creature's body and while it protested in high-pitched screams, she quickly withdrew

Desecrated

the blade to strike again and again. After a series of unanswered attacks, the darakka looked down at its riddled body and fell to his knees, then slumped over dead.

Before the blanket of cold slumber could take me over completely, I watched the charming green-eyed man from my many visions pick up Ukumog from the darakka's hand. Then I watched as he danced and moved as Brin always did through the freth that had moved to protect their Mistress from further attacks. I blinked, and the dark haired woman I had come to know replaced him. One more time before the sleep took me, I blinked and saw him again in her place. Then, my eyes closed.

The tall grass was yellow with autumn colors. The giggles of a small girl were carried softly by the whispering wind that made the grass dance. Making paths through the overgrown field there was a tiny dark haired girl. She ran, skipped, and laughed filling the world with the sounds of her joy.

"I'm gunna get you!" The playful voice of a man followed her and she gave an excited shriek.

Quickly darting through the grass the charming green-eyed man came rushing after her. From somewhere above, I watched them run and skip and play. She would hide in the grass and he would pretend to not know where she was. Each time he drew near she had to hold both hands over her mouth so that she didn't loose a shriek and give herself away. Eventually he reached down into the grass and scooped her up into the air with a playful shout. She screamed in joyful surprise that quickly changed into

Chapter 14

laughter. He threw her tiny body up into the air, sending the dark trails of her hair sprawling in every direction just before she would fall back into his waiting hands. I was overwhelmed with their joy.

Later, they picked up sticks and pretended to fight with swords. While they played he taught her in the sneaky way that charming parents do. He showed her how to stand and how to hold her stick. Over and over they would play at attacking and defending. This was her favorite part of time with her father.

"Teague!" a familiar voice echoed over the field and the charming man looked up.

"Daddy, no!" the little girl said.

He smiled at her and scooped her up into his arms, "Daddy has to go, but you keep practicing with your stick. When I come back I want see how much better you are, and it will make me even more proud than I already am!"

"But you always say that you are proud of me!" she laughed.

"That is because I am! You are the best daughter I could have ever hoped for." He kissed her on the cheek and set her down.

"Teague!" The voice came again, and I felt like it was me shouting for him.

"Coming!" He shouted back then turned to the little girl. "Take care of your mother for me ok?"

The little girl nodded in the exaggerated way that only children do.

"Bye bye, Brinny bear," he said with a pat to her head, and then he reached into the grass beside him and lifted the saber-like form of Ukumog from its hidden place beside him. The runes on its side dimly glowed in the early evening light, and with a *clink!* it rested on the ring upon his belt. With one more smile and a wave to the little girl he climbed the hill of grass towards the voice that

Desecrated

had been calling him. Three figures in black robes much like mine awaited him at the crest of the hill and they turned to walk away as he reached them. With one last wave to the little girl, he, too, disappeared over the hill, and she ran through the grasses towards a tiny cottage with a small pillar of smoke rising from the chimney.

Heat from a distant fire warmed my flesh, and my mind traveled back to the time and place where my body was, but I didn't want to leave the simple joy of the little girl's laughter.

"No," the thought echoed in the empty space between awake and asleep.

Heat from a nearby inferno flashed over me, leaving me cold at its departure. Groggily, my eyes open and I found my body still limply hanging in the powerful grip of the armored fist of The Mistress. In front of me, the snake beads hissed inches away from my face. The tumultuous mass of hair before me made it extremely difficult to see what was happening on the other side of her, but her attention was definitely not focused on me.

Fire had broken loose in the room and was consuming anything it could. Off to the side, the shadow of Tikras could still be seen to silently scream in his private tornado of flames. Most of the remaining freth and darakka in the room were still trying to protect The Mistress. At the entrance to the chamber, Avar and Ferrin still held off the push of the enemy from outside like beastly sentinels. Bits of torn freth lay strewn haphazardly around the entryway and there was a growing pile of bodies in the tunnel. The sheer ferocity of Avar's hidden savage talent was both frightening and comforting. It meant that I wasn't the only monster traveling with us anymore.

Chapter 14

On the floor some distance from me, Nikolai still lay struggling with the black smoke in his nose and mouth. I felt a shift change my vision slightly and after I blinked and looked again at the smoke I saw the most curious thing. As each plume rose, it seemed to have taut threads reaching down into Nikolai. Their other ends seemed to fade away inches above where the smoke would vanish. Without thinking I reached out with one of my hands and imagined that I was plucking the strings from his nose and mouth. Much to my surprise, the threads twitched in response to my tugging, so, I tugged harder. With one swift pull, I loosed the smoke from his passages and both it and the strings faded away like smoke taken by a brisk wind.

With a startling quickness, The Mistress snapped her head around to look at me. Her eyes glowing with hidden divine fire and smoke, she snarled at me. Before she could loose the arrogant remark that was brewing in her mind, Nikolai, Brin, and Piotyr pushed through the ranks of her guard and forced her to protect herself.

Each time a blade came near her, she moved her free hand in the way, and before her flesh could feel their sting there would be a flash of light, and the blade would simply be turned away. The three continued to press her, but she was too quick with whatever magic it was that she used to protect herself, only occasionally having to give some ground to step out of the way of a blow rather than blocking it. As she shifted her feet, her grip on my neck tightened again. I had to get free. My hands wrapped around her metal covered wrist, and tried to influence her to let me go. With the distraction of the blades being whirled in her direction I felt her grip loosen and for a moment I thought I would be able to slip away, but I was wrong.

Desecrated

Her body tensed and her grip became crushing on my throat. I knew something bad was about to happen, but I could not choke out a warning to my friends. She growled with an unearthly rumble and whipped her writhing locks of hair at her three attackers. Nikolai and Brin jumped out of the way, but Piotyr was not as lucky, for he was the first person in the sweep of the angry snake beads. As the tendrils of red and silver were pulled back from their sweep, The Mistress stepped back again.

There was a pause as everyone checked for fang marks on their exposed flesh. Piotyr's arms and chest had several tiny wounds that almost instantly started turning black. Before any words could be said, Nikolai stepped in to catch his brother before Piotyr weakly fell to the stone floor. Even from where I was, I could see the tempest growing in Nikolai, but then The Mistress laughed.

It was as if everyone in the chamber could feel the violent anger growing within the brother of the fallen barbarian. Piotyr still lived, but he weakly clung to what tenuous life remained within him as the black of his wounds spread. Nikolai's brief sobs quickly changed to a low growl, which quickly shifted to a rumbling roar as he climbed back to his feet. The Mistress continued to laugh, harshly mocking the imminent death of Nikolai's cherished brother. Nikolai's roar shook his entire body as he raised the sword in his hands over his head. It gleamed in the flickering reflection of the many fires around the chamber, and The Mistress stopped laughing.

In one smooth motion, Nikolai brought down his massive glimmering sword and The Mistress let go of my throat. The edge of Nikolai's blade crashed mightily into the plates of armor that The Mistress now wore upon her forearm, and she pushed the blade to the side hissing like a snake at Nikolai.

"Girl!" I heard a familiar voice call out from near the altar. "Bring your sword over here!"

Chapter 14

When my throat was freed unexpectedly from the grasp of The Mistress, I had fallen quite suddenly to the floor. From my spot on there on the ground, I tried to find the source of the familiar voice and my eyes found themselves resting on the gesturing stump of The Armor. He seemed to be waving for Brin to come close to him. Fear, regret, and panic flooded my heart, and I did not know why.

From his berserk rage, Nikolai was able to grunt out something that sounded like, "I have this, go do vhat you need to," to Brin. With only a small hesitation, Brin left Nikolai locked in conflict with The Mistress.

Scrambling to my feet, I wanted to rush over to the altar with Brin but there was a sudden flash of fire from around The Mistress blocking my way. Nikolai patted out the flames on his beard and continued trying to batter his way through the physical and magical defenses of his ancient opponent. Watching the two of them, they looked like two figures on a tapestry, locked forever in a struggle that would statically be trapped in a stalemate.

When I looked back to the altar, Brin had climbed atop it and straddled The Armor. I took a few steps closer and heard the metallic familiar voice speak again, "Do it girl! End my torment!" Brin lifted herself up on her knees and raised Ukumog into the air with its curved point downward towards The Armor.

Another flash of heat exploded from nearby, and as the heat rolled over me, I felt the grasp of The Mistress again close around my neck, this time with exposed clawed hand. "Ah ah ah, girl," she said to Brin. "Think of what you do. You might kill him, but would it happen before I turn your tainted friend to ashes?"

My eyes drifted to the cyclone of fire that was slowly disintegrating Tikras nearby. The fact that I could not share in his pain by bearing the burden of hearing his screams seemed to

Desecrated

make his ordeal even worse. Nikolai lay on the ground with his brother, half his beard seared off and replaced with grey smoke, and a black snakebite on his left wrist. He cradled it in terrible pain. The snakes that writhed around The Mistress' head taunted me with threatening displays of their shining fangs. The temple was devoid of any other allies who could pay attention to what was happening with us, those who were still on their feet were being pressed at the door by the countless forces trying to surge through and aid their Mistress.

The Armor craned its head around to look over at The Mistress and began to stare at the two of us. Ever so faintly I could see eyes within the visor sparkling in the firelight that filled the room. A heavy stone pressed on my chest and tears stung my eyes. The hollow space in my throat persisted through the vice grip of The Mistress' claws. I could not explain the sorrow I felt, and I was powerless to stop it.

"You," The Armor whispered. "It is you, isn't it?" There was a certain serenity to his voice, a strange calm in this storm of violence and death.

"What?" The Mistress looked at me with surprise and shock. "That isn't possible!"

The Armor turned back to Brin. "Kill me."

Brin paused. She looked over at me and The Mistress, who was shaken by the Armor's familiarity with me. Brin looked over Nikolai, Piotyr, and Tikras all struggling with the pain and strife that The Mistress had caused. Brin watched for a brief moment as Ferrin and Avar fought at the entrance of the chamber and then she calmly replied, "I will end you, but answer me this first. Did you have anything to do with my father's death, Doomed One?"

Chapter 14

He gave a slight laugh that sent my memories spiraling back to a patient giant of a man that had been my guardian, my mentor, my friend. Lucien. With a voice I knew to be that of my long lost friend he replied, "I have been trapped in a prison of hatred and anger for so long, I cannot remember anything. It was never supposed to be this way. I have only myself to blame. End me."

Satisfied, Brin raised Ukumog again to strike at the heart of The Armor. The Mistress flexed her grip and I felt the bones in my neck strain under the pressure. "NO! You will regret your actions, girl! I swear to it!"

"Die, you ancient bitch!" Nikolai screamed from behind us, swinging his sword directly at The Mistress' head. The whirl of his blade was followed by the clattering of five or six silver serpentine heads bouncing on the stone floor, the only heads he was to claim, but The Mistress' ire had been raised.

There was a loud bang as The Armor finally broke his left hand free of its bond and he grabbed Brin's arm. "Do it, girl! End me, then turn the weapon against her!" He screamed. "Kill me now!"

The runes on Ukumog's blade suddenly came to life, glowing brightly with white and purple flames. In the light it cast, I saw Lucien as I had remembered him from my visions lying upon the altar, his right hand severed and spilling blood liberally upon the floor. The same calm he used to so long ago to gain my trust lived in the eyes that looked up at Brin, begging for release. In my head I heard my own voice say the words, "I am the warden, the way-maker, and the lighthouse. Ever shall I be the beacon of your redemption." I felt something unlock and my soul screamed with remorse.

Desecrated

"NO!" The cold pain of my dark power ignited within me. I felt it wash outward through my limbs and my hands pulsed with its frozen heat. "Lucien! No!" Two forces collided in my heart. The pure love that a student has for his mentor crashed into the complete hatred that I had felt when I faced The Ghoul. Love and hate. Rage and sorrow. "Don't kill him!" I did not want him to die, unless it was me that could drink of his life as it drained away into the void.

Fear and confusion was reflected back at me through Brin's eyes. Waves of power pushed outward from my body, breaking the grip that The Mistress had upon my neck and forcing her away from me. The strobing cold power forced Nikolai to shield his eyes, but Brin could not look away from the terror that was me.

"KILL ME NOW!" Lucien screamed. "KILL ME BEFORE HE STOPS YOU!"

Broken from her trance, Brin lifted the blade to the apex of her arm's reach and brought it down without further hesitation. As if it were sliding into a crafted hole, Ukumog cut through the breastplate that covered Lucien's chest. His body seized with the pain of his heart being cleaved by the unforgiving bite of Ukumog's edge. The runes upon its side became as bright as the sun on a clear day, and one rune in particular grew significantly more intense. Power and light pulsed outward. The greater of two streams came from the glowing rune into the twisting cold that surrounded me, the other followed the connection from Lucien's severed arm to The Mistress' armor clad hand. This storm of power was so blinding and great that everyone in the room was helpless to do anything but watch.

I struggled against the power, trying to pull the blade from Lucien's chest with my mind and force the energy back into his body. Giant scores from an invisible whip raked across the stone walls of the chamber, and tore at the altar and the chains around

Chapter 14

it. My power was out of control, and I could not put it back. By the time the sorrow caused me to give up, the chains were all broken, Lucien's body was nearly severed in many places, the altar had been knocked off of its stone seat, and the two pillars in the back of the chamber looked as if they were about to collapse.

As suddenly as it had appeared, the energy ceased its forceful flow, and I fell to my knees weakened by the ordeal. I lifted my head as I heard a weak laugh of joy come from Lucien. He turned his head to me and with blood streaking away from every opening on his face that I could see he said, "She did what you could not. Farewell, my boy. You must finish what you have begun." With one final smile the rune that glowed the brightest upon the side of Ukumog burst like a soap bubble of light, and he was gone.

I screamed with agonizing sorrow for a man that I once knew. My rage and frustration burned not only for the loss of someone I had once loved, but also for the memories of our past that had been robbed from me, and the twisted form that we both had become trapped in. Tears fell freely from my eyes and mixed with the streams of dirty blood that streaked the floor.

Brin wasted no time and stepped over to Lucien's lifeless body and forcefully reclaimed Ukumog, who still shone brilliantly in the darkness of the temple. She looked over at The Mistress, who suddenly looked lost and found herself surrounded by enemies.

Ever so faintly I could still see a thread of power, connecting me to the bracer on the Mistress's arm. The same hatred I had felt many times awoke within my heart for her, a hatred that I only felt in the presence of the Doomed. Howling with all my frustration, I forced dark power into the connection to waken it. A black and purple band appeared between us. With haste, I wrapped it around my arm and began to pull.

Desecrated

Feeling her newly found power being stolen from her, The Mistress pulled away from me, but my hunger for her life was greater. Her boots slid on the bloody stone floor as I pulled her closer and closer to me. Waves of purple light flowing from me, frost began to appear on my hands, and steam rose from my eyes. For the first time, The Mistress knew real fear as I began to pull away her very soul.

Panic filled her inhuman eyes as I dragged her closer and closer to my hungry hands. I could feel the lust for her life pulsing through my spine. My jaw popped and I began to issue forth a sickening hiss. For a moment, I felt as if I might unhinge my jaw and try to swallow her whole.

A streak of white light came down between us as Ukumog severed the tendril of energy that connected us. Like a noodle, her end of the power was slurped up into her eager soul. Mine turned to a cold fog and joined the other power swirling around me. My hunger for her still urged me on, but before I could leap upon her like a wild predator, Brin stepped between us and lifted the shining saber of Ukumog above her head.

The same flashing light deflected Brin's flurry of attacks, but with each use the light of The Mistress' magic grew dimmer. When she knew that her tricks would not continue to save her, The Mistress extended both of her arms and called the cyclone that surrounded Tikras back into her, leaving him to fall to the floor. Within the nova of fire and smoke she transformed into a winged beast made of a blazing inferno. The wall of heat that burst forth from her change pushed Brin back just long enough for The Mistress to take flight and streak out the door. Her passage set the fur on both Ferrin and Avar's flesh aflame, and we were all helpless to see her streak out into the night sky above.

Chapter 14

From outside, a horn sounded and the freth began their retreat. None of the hunters seemed willing to give them any quarter and so it was that the battle followed their retreat all the way to the border of the burning ruins of what was Sanctuary. Many freth were killed as they escaped, but before the sun rose all that remained of The Mistress and her army were piles of dead.

I, however, did not follow my friends out of the temple chamber to kill the fleeing servants of the ancient gods. Instead, I found myself staring at the withered corpse of a man I had only met in dreams and visions. A man who I knew had been there for me at every turning point in my life before. A man that I would never know again. "Farewell, Lion of The Brotherhood," I whispered to the corpse on the altar.

Nikolai, Piotyr, and Tikras were too wounded to follow as well, and could only stare in apprehension as I changed from the monster who might have swallowed The Mistress whole to the undead man they had met in the Spikelands. Nikolai checked on his barbarian friends while I wallowed in lost memories.

Shuttering with pain and shock, Tikras said, "Ve almost had her that time," and smiled at Nikolai.

Knowing his friend would not survive with huge portions of his body turned to ash, Nikolai swallowed back his sadness, "Ja, Tikras. Ve almost had her."

Tikras shivered and twitched for a moment longer then stopped. In silence, Nikolai closed the half melted lids of Tikras' eyes and kissed him on the forehead. "Sleep in the arms of your master tonight, old friend."

Much silence passed through the room before any of us spoke.

"I know you," Nikolai said, breaking the quiet. "At least, I have memories of you, Alex."

Desecrated

The hair on my neck stood up at the mention of that name. "I don't know who that is."

"Shame," Nikolai said. "From vhat I remember, Alex vas a great man."

"Whoever he was, he is dead now," I said with bitter coldness.

Piotyr's head finally slumped and Nikolai began screaming at him. I couldn't just sit there and watch him lose his brother, so, I walked over to where they both sat, and took one of Piotyr's daggers.

"No," Nikolai grabbed my hand.

I smiled, "Let me repay your kindness and faith." I drove the point of the blade into my wrist and poured a little of my thick blood into each of the black wounds on Piotyr's body. We did not have to wait long for the black to recede and his wounds to begin healing. This time something unforeseen happened, however. As his wounds faded, I felt my own flesh bruise and burn, something I hid from Nikolai. "They mustn't know," I motioned upwards.

Nikolai nodded. "It is a long way to the Rise, Vrack. My brother and I should leave."

I was confused by his haste. "So soon? The battle hasn't even ended."

"In fact, my friend, the battle has only just begun." With a jovial smile from his half bearded face, he lifted his brother and started for the entrance. Just before he left, he looked back, "Send Tikras to his god through the flames please, friend?"

I nodded and they were gone.

It was about dawn when the host of hunters returned from their hunt. Brin pushed through the crowd who would not come near me. "Wrack, are you ok? What the uzk happened during the fight?"

Chapter 14

"I dunno, Brin. That power you saw is part of me, somehow, and The Armor–Well, I think I knew him, in another life."

Avar came in, his clothes torn to shreds, making him look like a man of the wilds. "I think I was wrong, Wrack. I have no idea who the uzk you are."

"Did you see–"

"I saw enough," he interrupted me.

The hunters hugged and celebrated their survival quietly. Above us their homes were burning and around us lay many of their friends who gave their lives for them. Bridain still stood among the survivors, but his thoughts were elsewhere. I saw Tarissa secretly steal glances at Avar from the back of the crowd. My eyes met Verif's hungry gaze as she lifted an eyebrow at me. Brin looked around quickly as if something was missing. "Where are Nik and Piotyr?"

"They left," I said.

"Left? They just up and uzkin' left?"

I frowned. "They said that their battle was just beginning and asked us to burn Tikras' body."

Brin's frustration could not be hidden, but she seemed to understand.

After the other hunters left, Avar pulled me aside with Brin and asked, "Tell me this, Wrack. How did the Doomed seem to know you? I heard him call you his boy. What is going on? Who are you really?"

"I dunno Avar," I said shaking my head. "I really don't know."

Brin could only whisper in frustration, "Uzk."

Made in the USA
Charleston, SC
07 January 2014